The Institut

A Novel By

John Warmus

Published By
Barclay Books, LLC

St. Petersburg, Florida

PUBLISHED BY BARCLAY BOOKS, LLC
6161 51st Street South
St. Petersburg, Florida 33715
www.barclaybooks.com

Cover Design by Barclay Books, LLC
Printed and bound in the United States of America

ISBN: 1-931402-09-4

This novel is dedicated to my wife, Kathryn Warmus
and to Becki and Brantley McNeel who believed in me.

In 1854, Pope Pius IX proclaimed the dogma of the Immaculate Conception.

PROLOGUE

February 1938

A thousand miles from the North Pole within the desolate boundaries of the Arctic Circle, the Royal Norwegian Meteorological Society's weather station on Svalbard Island tracked a major weather disturbance. Franz Josef Land, a frozen mass of glacier ice, was constantly monitored for the children it produced. Unusually heavy snows during the winter months were a sure sign of increased iceberg activity in the coming spring. Shipping lanes, safe as tiny dotted lines on weatherproof maps, became notoriously dangerous as captains and their vessels swept north to meet the midnight sun.

Hundred and fifty miles an hour winds gusted from the frozen wasteland. Weather warnings were issued in Copenhagen, Amsterdam, London and Paris. People stockpiled food and boarded their windows against a killer they could not fight, but could only hope to evade.

At the last moment, a front over the North Sea tightened, forcing the storm away from the British Isles towards France. On the last day of February, the full force of the Great Storm of 1938 smashed into the city of LaRochelle, and flung itself into the Atlantic Ocean.

For days, only icy winds screamed in the dark, the midnight toll lost in the ear-crashing winds that howled through the province. Power plants that had nonchalantly supplied electricity failed. It would be days before the city could once again lay claim to its title, *"Petite City of Lights."*

Young and old alike stayed home. Locked tightly inside, children slept under heavy blankets and dreamed of sleds and snow forts, unaware of the dark shadows that sometimes slid in under the cover of winter. Their mothers and fathers made the sign of the cross, mumbled the prayers of their religion, and chanted pagan incantations, trusting not only in God, but in their ancient superstitions as well. They sat before the fire for warmth and light and listened for the soothing cadence of the church bells, yet heard only the awful sounds of the slamming and *hammering* on the cathedral's doors as if something very large and very powerful wanted in out of the cold.

CHAPTER ONE

An explosion of earthbound noise interrupted Father David Proust's repose. *Slam!* The constant crashing and banging of an open door invaded his privacy. On the second floor of the rectory, his room faced the rear of the cathedral. The thumping sound came from the street—from the front of the church. Mentally, he ran through the list of precautions he had taken to secure St. Margaret from the onslaught of the storm. Had he forgotten to bolt the church doors? Only the cathedral's massive doors could create such chaos.

Carried by the wind, the beat echoed through his room and head. He closed his eyes and prayed it would go away.

Slam! The window rattled with a surge of wind, the curtains fluttering in the invading breeze like ghosts in the shadows. David looked at the clock. He had been listening to the cacophony for over an hour. It was no use. He would have to investigate the source of the noise himself.

Slipping into his robe, he grabbed his overcoat and walked down the hall. The old wooden floor creaked as he made his way to the top of the stairs. Except for the sounds of his escape, the building was silent.

He hurried through the kitchen and out the back door. Soaked from constant snows and rain, the gardens had turned into vicious black mud that sucked hungrily at his slippers. Shrubs and low hanging branches that bloomed in summer with fragrant flowers snatched at him with sharp icy twigs. The wind whirled and whispered—*stay!*

At the wrought iron gate that allowed him access to the Plaza Urian, David struggled with the frozen latch. It surrendered with a protesting screech. Pulling his overcoat tighter, he walked quickly towards the church. The power was out, he saw with no surprise. The electric street lamps were dark, and the streets empty. The Dutch Elms that lined the Plaza slashed the skies as they sought to escape a wicked wind.

As David's eyes adjusted to the dark, he could see the church doors swinging wildly, and the dark opening laughing at some joke he could not understand. *I could have sworn I'd bolted those doors.*

Carefully, he started up the ice-slicked stairs unaware, even now, that as he approached the doors, they had ceased their constant motion. The storm seemed to wait for his approach, blessedly still.

Father David paid no attention. It would not have mattered if he had. He latched the left door with efficient movements. His hands, thin and white against a dark background of polished wood, clasped the sculpted iron handle of the right portal. The wind shrieked. The portals slammed wide. Like a skater with no balance, David slid across the icy stoop and was thrown from the sanctuary of his church into the snow and frozen world outside. The door slammed shut.

Tenderly, he picked himself up. Friend or foe, he wondered as he stared at the church. In areas, the outside of the door was covered with strange ice angels where the wind had chiseled mysterious apparitions. Other parts had been swept clean by the shifting air currents. He noticed all of this as he grasped the heavy doorknob between his sleeves, twisted, and pulled.

For a moment, St. Margaret's refused him entry. Then, quite suddenly, he was relieved to find himself back inside the church, although he could not remember slipping past the heavy door. As the cathedral's silent bells should have been striking the midnight hour, Father David Proust started to make his way across the vestibule towards the church proper. It was March 1, and he had just turned thirty-five.

It started as a sudden, frightening surge of energy soared through his tired legs and arms. His eyes suddenly became clear, the remnants of exhaustion wiped away. For a fleeting moment, he felt more alive than he had at any other time in his life. He looked around the dark, shadowless cathedral. The blackness sparkled and illuminated everything around him—making it all come alive. The wooden pews pulsed—living entities stripped from their natural environment—they refused to succumb to the axe and saw that had once fashioned them.

Fascinated, David stared as he watched individual molecules dance with life. From deep within him, a surge of warmth caused his wet clothes to steam with vapors that rose and danced before his eyes. Mesmerized, he watched the microscopic ballet reveal the earth's secrets. He was a living creature, privileged to see the wonders of a world locked away from mortal discernment, trying to touch the visions that appeared before him. Before he could make contact, the slick, cold, floor rose swiftly beneath him like a swelling sea. His feet slipped and, with a sickening thud, his head cracked on the marble floor. The sea engulfed him in a wave of unconsciousness.

Suddenly, shed of his skin, his body lay helpless. A dark shadow hidden in still darker shadows, it was no longer him on the floor. He was soaring out of the church, and into the night, amidst an incomprehensible world that existed around him. Searching—searching for something. *Someone.* Searching like a vulture high above the plains of Africa for a taste of carrion. His senses—hearing, smell, and sight—were alive beyond his conception. He was flying, yet he knew he lay senseless in the vestibule of the church. Even with his eyes closed, he could see his prone body held captive to the ground while he soared over the city: a creature of the night, immune to the wind and the cold.

He had not needed his clothes for warmth. They remained with the body that lay in the church—a chrysalis left behind. Naked, alive, a hunter of the night filled with sensations he had never experienced before, David became engulfed in a dream. *Her dream.*

The room she slept in was clear and cold. He saw it with a sharpness his eyes had never conceived possible. It was a small room with a narrow bed against the wall, a dresser, a chest of drawers, and a chair that held her properly stacked clothes. Awaiting the morning sun, the heavy dark curtains were held open by a red sash.

She was naked. Dreaming. Gently breathing in and out, curls and tentacles of miasma sweeping from her delicate nostrils, searching the night sky. *(He became the hunted.)*

"No!" he cried. "No!" But too late. The wisps that were his spirit, *his soul*, touched and mingled sensuously with hers. *(He became the hunter.)* She was glazed and filled with rivulets of sweet nectars too tempting to resist. The tiny buds of her breasts beckoned his mouth to taste their honey.

"No! No!" He tried again to resist. This was not what he wanted in life.

For a few brief moments of time, Father David Proust was ripped apart. Stretched beyond his wildest imagination, he had been cast into the world around him to perform an act he had desperately fought to avoid all of his life.

Hungrily, his tongue licked her young taunt skin. Soft hairs tickled his legs, rising and falling with every movement of his body. She twisted beneath him, flesh meeting passion.

Her bed was soft and filled with her desire. If she wept from pain, from pleasure, from the basic instincts that drove her to seek him out and demand that he fulfill his duty, David did not know. He did not care. He only knew he must. "Yes," he whispered, "yes."

His mouth found the tiny seashell of her ear and licked the salty tears from its inner tracings. *"I am the messenger . . ."* The words became garbled and meaningless. He might have understood them had he tried, but their message was awe-inspiring and past his awareness. *"You have been chosen to bear the child . . ."*

His tongue was on fire, rendering speech impossible, and his explosion, uncontrollable. A thousand years of denial erupted in a burst of pleasure he had never known. The grainy image of her face was hidden behind a veil even his tears could not wash clean.

A gust of wind carried him away. As quickly as his dream, *his nightmare* had begun, it was over. He was lying on the vestibule floor shivering from the cold. His wet clothes were filled with the dying embers of a night sky that now lay dormant outside the cathedral of St. Margaret. The pain in his head would not allow him to open his eyes. He struggled desperately to stand, but his strength was gone. Like leaden extensions of a man cast as some bizarre figurine, his legs were useless. His arms refused to push him off the cold, damp, marble floor. All he could do was remain locked behind the doors of St. Margaret's Cathedral praying silently that someone would find him before his life ebbed away.

***

It was four in the morning. George Marcil awoke as he had every day for the last forty years. Outside his window, he could hear the storm crying in the darkness. *There won't be many people at mass this morning,* he thought, wondering if anyone would show. Still, he had to go to the old church and feed the boilers the rich coal that would warm the parishioners for the early mass. It was more a habit than a chore.

Fighting the wind and snow, he struggled to reach the church—to be in a place where no wind howled. He was sure no one would show for six o'clock mass today, but the boilers would be going full blast, if only to warm the priests. Grabbing his shovel, he began to feed the furnace. An hour later he could feel the warmth oozing from the vents. Taking off his heavy coat, he made his way to the front of the church to unlock the cathedral doors.

In the vestibule, he flicked the light switch. Nothing. Digging in his pockets for a match, he began to light the candles that lined the entrance to the church. Only two flickered with flame before he noticed the dark form curled on the floor. Unsure what the storm may have abandoned, he approached cautiously.

The match burned his fingers and fell to the floor. "Father David!"

In a flash, George Marcil was running across the Plaza to the hospital of St. Margaret, oblivious to the wind and ice that tried to freeze his mission of mercy.

Summoned from his sleep, Dr. Antoine Curvise, the director of the hospital, hurried to the infirmary, arriving in time to be a doctor, he hoped, and not a priest.

So slender he would have been hard to track through mud, Curvise moved quickly down the corridor, his long legs making it easy to hurry without appearing to panic. Worry darkened his olive-hued skin, but only those who knew him well could have recognized the turmoil within. Antoine Curvise was known for his competent, soft-spoken nature. Although his dark hair was already thinning in the front, no one thought of him as old. His gentle ways and serene countenance made him ageless, but it had not always been so.

Curvise wore two collars within the church. He had been a physician during the Great War. He had seen the effects of man's cruelty inflicted on his fellow man—the blown away limbs, the cut off hands, and feet filled with gangrene—and he had healed the body when he could. At that time, he had not thought of the soul. After the war, he had joined the seminary and had studied to become a priest.

A man of great intelligence, and respected by both the medical profession and the religious community, had he possessed a richer personality, he might have risen further in the church. The Great War had left him with a weary outlook on life. Pleasant, easy to converse with, there was something in his dark brown eyes that forbade strangers and friends alike from getting too close.

At the emergency room door, he was met by Mother Superior Monique. Her chubby face had been haphazardly stuffed into her wimple and cowl. Wringing her hands, she let out a sigh as Curvise walked through the door. Without a word, she led him quickly to the room where Father David rested.

Like everyone else who had come into contact with David Proust, she had fallen under his spell. The young priest had a child's sense of wonder and mischievous humor. His regular features—a slender nose and a generous smile—would have beckoned the ladies had he chosen another way of life. Always on the go, always involved, his many duties kept him fit and trim, yet he found time to stop and chat with everyone. In need of a haircut, his blond hair was fashionably unkempt and his flashing blue eyes gently pierced a dishonest veil as well as those who were only shy. His parishioners adored and accepted him as one of their own. The sisters loved him.

Hovering behind the doctor, ready to carry out his smallest command, Monique filled him in on Proust's condition. "Temperature's 102. Blood pressure's low. And he's having a difficult time breathing."

Pneumonia, Curvise thought. His examination was brief, but thorough. Oxygen was ordered and sulfa was injected into the cold skin. The struggle to keep David Proust alive had begun.

***

For three days, David Proust clung precariously to life, struggling to overcome the forces that tempted him into eternal sleep. Part of him wanted to expire without ever opening his eyes, without ever seeing the faces that worried and fretted over him each day and each night. Another part of him refused to allow the pleasure of such an easy escape from his sin. He had to live to atone for the awful nightmare he had suffered in his moment of weakness. And, something else. *The task was incomplete.* He felt that as much as he felt the fever draining his body, and as much as the sharp pains that ricocheted through his head.

What urgency tugged at his sleeve? What command—what powerful *longing*—kept him bound to life? It would be so easy just to let go, but the siren's song, the confusing temptation of learning *(forbidden knowledge),* would not let him surrender.

***

On the fourth day, David Proust regained consciousness. Usually bright, the color in his cheeks was ashen. His brilliant blue eyes had lost their sparkle, but they were open and gazing at his friends.

Antoine Curvise peered into his patient's face, pleased with what he saw.

"Antoine?" David questioned. He had no idea what had happened.

"Don't try and talk just yet, David," Curvise silenced his patient and re-examined the bruise on Proust's head. It was starting to go down he noted with relief.

"What happened?" David glanced around the room. "Where am I?"

"You're in the hospital," Curvise said matter-of-factly, checking David's ears for swelling. Satisfied there was none, he straightened. "I'm going to give you an injection. Something to help you rest more peacefully."

David closed his eyes and briefly wondered why Curvise would think he needed help to sleep. Simply waking up had been an effort that had sapped all of his strength.

***

The grounds outside the rectory were still saturated from heavy rains, and the morning air still heavy with cold. Wiping his shoes on the small rug outside Monsignor Meric's residence, Antoine Curvise came to report, as he had every day of David's illness, on Father Proust's progress. Today, he smiled.

"He will be fine, given more time to recuperate," he told Meric.

They sat in the dining room sipping coffee.

Meric was relieved his young protégée was out of danger. Not a man given to expression, his large face and heavy jowls turned foolish when pressed into a smile. Still, he allowed himself a slight grin. Like everyone else, he held a great deal of affection for Father David Proust.

Just as Curvise had made daily reports, Meric had called David's father in Bordeaux each morning to report on his son's status. Today he would sound more confident than he had the past three days.

"Have you examined his heart?" Meric's question had been asked with regularity since his very first conversation with David's father.

"No, Jean-Paul. He is still weak and suffering the effects of pneumonia. When he is better, I will ask François to give him a thorough examination."

At the sound of Dr. Martine's name, Meric cringed. His aversion to the doctor was unnatural for a priest—a man who should express only charity towards his fellow man. "I had thought you would examine David, Antoine." He tried to hide his whine of displeasure, but not very hard.

"Dr. Martine is a heart specialist, Jean-Paul." Antoine Curvise was one of the few people in LaRochelle who actually got along with François Martine. "We would be doing David a great disservice by not allowing him to be examined by the best physician available.

"I have examined David and found nothing irregular with his heart, but you have a right to be concerned. The fact Monsieur Proust mentioned David's uncle passed away from a heart attack early in life makes it necessary for us to take all available precautions. A thorough examination by Dr. Martine will help us all rest easier at night."

Much to his chagrin, Meric found himself agreeing. Still, he said nothing, filling his mouth with half a sausage instead of words.

Assessing Meric's silence as criticism, Curvise gently defended his friend. "François Martine is a patron of our hospital. His contributions in money and time are needed and appreciated."

Meric swallowed. "I'm well aware of Dr. Martine's contributions, Antoine." The other half of the sausage disappeared. He reached for another. "When will Father David be able to return to his duties?"

Curvise sighed. "A month at least. He's lost weight and will need time to regain his strength. He does so much."

And he did, Curvise thought. From the moment he had joined St.

Margaret, Father David Proust had exhibited nothing but boundless energy. The young priest's days lasted from sunrise to midnight. He taught catechism to the seventh and eighth graders at St. Margaret's parochial school, had a soccer team that practiced every second evening (except Sundays), and came to the hospital every day to visit with the elderly and anyone else who needed a friend. The youngest priest at St. Margaret, he said the early mass every morning and was responsible for overseeing the upkeep of the old cathedral. How he found time to fit all of his activities into each day was a mystery to Curvise. A last rights call in the middle of the night? Call Father Proust. Monsignor Meric needed something done? Call Father Proust.

David's colleagues at St. Margaret were all well into their sixties. All of the five priests, including Monsignor Meric, had distinguished themselves with long and resolute service. They were priests cut from a different fabric than David Proust. From a different time. Theirs was an era when a handshake and a visit from the parish priest were considered an honor *(or a curse, if the news a priest brought was grief-stricken)* and not a social visit. Their past was etched in hard stone and rough timbers. Affable priests like Father Proust were a new breed—men who mingled equally well with older parishioners and children alike. Relaxed standards brought on by His Holiness were softening the firm rod of the church. In a short time, some feared, the priests would be looked upon as just men.

For many, the transformation would be impossible. For others, like Antoine Curvise, it came as a pleasant relief. The church needed men like David just as it needed to remember that men were men and not slaves. Now at least, Antoine thought, David could rest. Something he well deserved.

Meric nodded. "He'll have all the time he needs," he mumbled, spewing out bits of his breakfast. "When would it be appropriate for me to visit?"

"Another three or four days. He's still under sedation."

Meric's concern resurfaced. "I thought you said he was out of danger?"

"For the most part, he is, Jean-Paul. He just needs rest. He's young and his resistance is strong." Curvise tried to reassure the Monsignor.

"I'll be sure to convey your positive attitude to his family." There was one sausage left. Meric reached, thought better of it, and pulled back his pudgy hand. "Now, if he needs anything, let me know."

Curvise finished his coffee. "I will, Your Grace. Thank you." He stood to leave. "If you'll excuse me, I have other patients who require medical attention."

Meric nodded his goodbye. Waiting only until Curvise had left the dining room, he snatched the last sausage from the plate.

CHAPTER TWO

Three days later, Antoine Curvise's entrance into the hospital was greeted from behind the reception desk by a smiling Sister Grace. Immediately, he knew David was completely out of danger.

Since the moment Father David Proust had been carried into St. Margaret's Hospital, the staff had fallen into a melancholy mood, colored by the swings in David's recovery. A grin, and he was feeling better. A scowl, and he had suffered a worrisome night. Sister Grace's smile was the first Curvise had seen in eight days. It was contagious.

"Good morning, Doctor," she chimed. It was a song Antoine Curvise had missed.

"Good morning, Sister."

Each of the nuns he passed on his way to his office greeted him with the same exuberance. He had not realized how much he had missed their cheerful salutations.

Hurrying through the morning mail and the admittances of last night, he hastily scanned the charts of his patients, then made his way to David's room. When he had left the hospital last night, David had been conscious, although terribly weak and still feeling the effects of his illness. He had assumed it would be at least a few more days before his patient would be able to really begin his recuperation. He was surprised to find David sitting up in bed with a tray on his lap.

"That smells good." Curvise picked up the chart and quickly checked his patient's vital signs. They were almost normal. "You seem to be making a remarkable recovery."

"I feel much better," David agreed between sips of hot broth. "And hungry."

Curvise sat down in the straight-backed chair. It was still warm from the nun who had occupied it during the night's vigil. "What's that?" The odor was tantalizingly familiar, but the doctor could not place it.

David was quick to share. "Beet soup. Would you care for some, Antoine? I have more than enough."

"Beet soup! How did you manage . . .? I don't recall that being on the menu."

David shrugged. "I happened to mention to Mother Superior I liked it . . . and, well . . ."

Curvise laughed lightly.

David held out his bowl. "Really, Antoine, I have enough for the both of us."

"No, no, you eat it. I'm sure the chef will appreciate knowing you enjoyed her soup. Especially since it was made for you." Curvise hesitated. It was obvious his patient was strong enough for conversation. "What were you doing in the church that night, David?"

Proust looked at Curvise. Their eyes met and quickly separated. "I went to close the doors," he began, wavering. "They were banging and I couldn't sleep. I guess the wind knocked me down. I'm afraid I don't remember after that. When I woke up, I was here and you were standing over me."

There was more David knew, but he could not remember. The dream—or the nightmare—had faded. Possibly, it had never occurred.

"Well, no matter. Your health is returning now."

The two men's brief conversation was interrupted by a new arrival.

"Is that borscht I smell?" Dr. François Martine walked into the room.

Meticulously dressed as was his habit, today he was attired in a dark blue suit with tiny slivers of silvery pin stripes. Even in winter, a fresh flower graced his lapel. New shoes (he had them made in Italy) shone with mirror perfection. His hair was combed back into a well-oiled shimmering silhouette, and the tiny moustache he sported was neatly trimmed. Always surrounded by a pleasant scent, François' finely-boned, exquisitely attired physique was a stark contrast to the darkness of the church, both in manners and dress. Curvise envied his friend—not harshly, but with enjoyment. Knowing Martine had brought a pleasant balance into his life.

"If there's anything Russian around here, *you* would smell it, François."

Martine ignored the remark and walked to David's side. "Are you going to eat all that soup yourself, young man?"

David smiled. "You're more than welcome to some, Dr. Martine."

"Don't do it," Curvise warned. "There's an old saying. If you feed a communist, you'll never get rid of him. It's like feeding a puppy."

Martine already had the bowl in hand. "Don't listen to him, David. His pride would not let him eat your soup. Fortunately, I have no pride, so I am free to share this." He sniffed the savory liquid and sighed. "Delicious! You don't know what you're missing, Antoine."

François Martine and Antoine Curvise's friendship was old and weathered. They had served and survived together in a medical unit during the war. Afterwards, Martine had come back to LaRochelle and opened his own practice. It was during this course of time that he joined the Communist Party. Envisioning war as an extension of religious hatred, he had decided the only way to end the terrible slaughter of man was to eliminate the cause—God. Then he'd discovered Marx's and Engles' doctrines calling for the redistribution of wealth. Having a tidy sum of money from his family, his loyalty to the Party cooled, but not to the extent that he had returned to the flock. François Martine was anything but another pious lamb. He enjoyed living well, and would not give it up for Marx or God.

Curvise offered up his chair. "Here. Sit down, François. Enjoy your meal. It's the only payment you'll receive for your services today."

David looked up at once, curious. Uneasy.

Sensing David's anxiety, Curvise was quick to explain. "I've asked Dr. Martine to give you a thorough examination. I did not expect him to be here today, but as long as he is, we might as well take advantage of him."

Martine nodded. "As long as you're feeding me, you might as well get the best service possible." He winked at David and tasted the soup. "How did you manage the borscht? It certainly wasn't your personality. What power do you have over the nuns, eh? I think you should tell me. I seem to remember hearing confession is good for the soul." Martine waited for a reaction. He liked to dig into people and find out what made them angry. Not to harm, but to tickle. His sense of humor was as well known as his quick temper.

"Sincerity, Doctor."

"Sincerity. Now there's something to work on, Antoine. You could use a little sincerity. As for me, sincerity is my middle name."

David laughed.

Curvise shook his head. "Sincerity. Yes, that's the quality I most admire in you, François. Your ability to act sincere."

"It's a gift," Martine acknowledged before his rich laughter joined David's.

Mother Superior's words preceded her into the room. "What's going on in here? This is a hospital! Not a place of comedy." She pushed open the door, immediately silencing the laughter. "Oh, I should have known you'd be at the bottom of this, Dr. Martine. And you," she chided Father David gently, "should be resting quietly. Shall I take your tray? Or would you like more soup?" Spying the bowl in Martine's hand, she quickly retrieved it, returning it to the tray with an air of practiced disdain.

"No thank you, Mother Superior. I've had quite enough."

16

"I certainly wouldn't mind sampling some," Martine said regretfully.

"Certainly, Dr. Martine," Monique replied without pause. "When they wheel you in here with a nasty bump on your head after the next great storm, I'll personally make you whatever you'd like."

Martine feigned hurt. "What has happened to your Christian spirit, Sister?"

"It's still in my heart, and not wasted on godless communists like you."

Martine hung his head and sighed. "It appears I am an outcast, Antoine." He brightened. "Perhaps, at least I may have your pity?"

"You'll get no pity here until you return as the young man I taught many years ago," Monique answered for herself and Antoine. "And I'd say Dr. Curvise would agree with me."

"One hundred percent, Mother Superior."

Once again righteous, she left the room mumbling, "Communists. What's the world coming to?"

The three men heard her, and burst out laughing. Martine quieted them. "Please, gentlemen, she'll come back with her pointer and my poor knuckles simply cannot stand another whack." He rubbed the back of his hand.

"She was your teacher?" David asked.

"Oh yes. Sister Monique was my teacher. Without her and that pointer, I would not be as articulate today—or as bruised."

"You're her lost lamb, François. She won't be happy until you come back to the fold."

"Bless her heart, Antoine. I wish I could." Martine reached for the chart at the end of the bed.

Respecting the professionalism and the limited amount of free time Dr. Martine had, Curvise bade his friends good day and left the room.

***

Finished with his rounds, Antoine Curvise retreated to his office to catch up on the mounting pile of paper work feeling somehow more like a bookkeeper than a physician.

Two hours passed before François Martine knocked on his door. Looking none the worse for wear, Martine sat down carefully so as not to destroy the sharp crease in his pants. "You'll be happy to know David Proust is in excellent health," François said. "All things taken into consideration, of course."

Curvise relaxed. He'd had no reason to be anxious, but that did not change the fact that he had been. "His heart?"

"His heart is fine," Martine said, removing a speck of lint from his pants leg. "In another week or so he should be back to his old self." Martine sought out Curvise's eyes. "Why this concern over his heart?"

"Monsignor Meric has had several conversations with David's father. Monsieur Proust's brother passed away when he was about David's age."

"Heart attack?" Martine asked, instantly reviewing his examination of David. Content he had not missed any signs of a defective heart, the frown on his face disappeared. "It happens. Even young people are not immune." He shrugged and reiterated his previous statement. "I found nothing wrong with David's heart."

"Thank you, François. I had come to the same conclusion after my examination, but it never hurts to be careful." Curvise hesitated, tapping his finger against the desktop. He was almost hesitant to ask his next question, but . . . he noticed things. Even little things did not usually escape him. Something was not right with David Proust beyond his recent illness. Something with his eyes. Since the first day Curvise had met him, David Proust's eyes had been bright, blue, and flashing. Since the young priest's admittance into the hospital, the fire was gone. David's eyes had become reptilian flat. "Did you notice anything different about him?" he finally asked.

"Different? In what way?" The nagging suspicion he had missed something agitated Martine. His personality would not allow him to be incompetent—or wrong. "Explain yourself."

"His eyes, François. Did you notice David's eyes?"

"I'm not an ophthalmologist, Antoine! What's wrong with his eyes? You asked me to examine his heart."

"Yes, I did. I just thought you might have noticed. The warmth—the sparkle David's eyes always carried. It's gone."

Martine took a deep breath and relaxed. "What are you trying to do to me, Antoine? Making me think I had missed something of importance. Of course David's eyes are dull. I noticed. It's expected after the ordeal he's been through." Martine adjusted his suit coat more comfortably. "Did you expect him to be exactly as he was before he got sick? What you are worrying over is nothing more than the aftereffects of the medication and the fever. You know that as well as I do."

Curvise shook his head. "I thought that also, Francois—at first. No, there is something missing. One just does not lose a part of their persona even when they fall ill."

"I've known you too long to disagree with your observations, Antoine, but this time I simply must. You are wrong. David is merely weak and tired.

In time, the glow you so ardently speak of will return. Mark my words, Antoine. In a week, David will be back to normal."

Martine's prophecy was on the money. Exactly one week after François had examined Father Proust, Curvise released the young priest from the hospital. It was a pleasure accompanying him on his short walk to the rectory. Cautiously, Curvise repeated his directive that David should not return to his full work schedule immediately.

"It will be at least another three weeks before you're back to normal," Antoine said in a firm but fatherly tone. "You have only to look at your suit to know how sick you were."

Having lost twenty pounds, David's clothes hung on his emaciated frame. The tiredness in his eyes had consumed his entire being. The only feature that remained intact was his smile.

"I understand completely, Antoine." Even this short walk made catching his breath difficult. His legs ached, and his arms felt burdened as if he had carried a heavy load. "Believe me. I don't wish to suffer through that again."

Jean-Paul Meric greeted them at the door of the rectory. In a most unusual show of affection for the dour Monsignor, he gave him a hug. "How are you feeling, David?"

"I feel fine, Monsignor," Proust said with a smile. "Please don't worry. If Dr. Curvise had his way, I would languish in the hospital for another three weeks. I'm fine. Just a little tired. If you don't mind, I think I'll just go to my room and lie down for a while." David walked quickly to the stairs, embarrassed by the attention being showered on him.

Meric and Curvise watched him struggle up the steps. Reaching the top, he felt like a mountain climber having ascended the peaks of Mont Blanc. He would have waved his hand in a victorious salute, but he had no energy to expend. Still, he knew he must alleviate his friends' worry. "Monsignor Meric, have you added some steps while I was gone?" he asked with a grin.

At the bottom of the stairs, both men smiled.

"I'll be by tomorrow morning to check on you," Curvise called.

David waved. "Thank you for everything, Antoine." He walked down the corridor to his room at the end of the hall.

Once David was out of earshot, Meric turned on Curvise. "Are you sure he's all right? He looks awful."

"Yes, Jean-Paul, he's fine. Just very weak. He was quite ill, whether he wants to believe it or not."

"And his heart?"

"There is nothing wrong with his heart. He just needs to rest and enjoy Mrs. Odettes' cooking for a while."

"That's not a problem," Meric said with all the authority of his position. "He'll stay in his room for as long as you prescribe, Antoine,"

"That's not necessary, Jean-Paul. He needs to move a little. Possibly you could assign him some duties that would allow him to get outside and walk a bit each day. In a month, we won't be able to tell he'd ever been sick." Curvise tried to reassure Jean-Paul Meric. Even more he tried to reassure himself. It bothered him that David's eyes were blank and . . . well . . . that they were no longer David's eyes. That the young priest had lost so much weight so quickly. And that during their last conversation about the night he had fallen ill, David seemed to have forgotten most of the details. One did not readily forget a night such as David Proust had suffered.

Curvise had wanted to keep his patient in the hospital longer. He feared the crack his friend had received to his skull might have caused more damage than either he or François Martine had diagnosed. A mild case of amnesia? Possibly. When he had asked David if he had written his family—his father, his brother—David had looked bewildered as if he had not known to whom Curvise referred.

Things like that worried Curvise, but in the past François had accused him of being a mother hen. He had dismissed David from the hospital, hoping the return to a regular lifestyle would return his friend to normalcy.

Yes, Antoine Curvise tried to reassure Monsignor Meric just as he tried to reassure himself. He fervently hoped his words comforted Jean-Paul. They did nothing to console him.

***

David had not realized how weak he had become. After climbing the stairs and gasping for breath, the walk down the hall, not long by any stretch of the imagination, had seemed endless. It was all he could do to open his door and struggle to lie down. He was not sick, but he was not the same. He knew it. His memory seemed to work in spurts. At times, everything was clear and recognizable. At other times, it was all he could do to remember who he was and where he had come from—to remember his father, his brother, Andre, Andre's wife, and children. He was like a light bulb about to burn out, surging with power one second, dimming into the darkness the next—a darkness that, strangely enough, did not frighten him.

He just needed to rest. He needed to eat Mrs. . . . He struggled to remember who cooked for the rectory. To visualize Mrs. Odette's . . . Now he could remember her name, but it was impossible to bring her visage to mind. Closing his eyes, David drifted off to sleep.

***

Jean-Paul Meric stringently followed Dr. Curvise's prescription for David's recovery. He adamantly refused to allow the young priest to perform any of his previous chores, insisting that David sit in the rectory office and act as secretary.

The remedy was working. Slowly, David regained the lost weight. His face began to fill out and, once again, his clothes began to fit properly. Physically, he began to resemble his old self. Mentally, he struggled to retain some connection between his past and present.

Dr. Antoine Curvise's visits had lessened from daily to once a week. Outwardly, Curvise seemed satisfied with his patient's progress, yet the doctor refused to proclaim him healed. To allow him to resume his full duties. David's feeble arguments fell on deaf ears.

Only Monsignor Meric, it seemed, was satisfied with his recovery. So much so that he lifted his ban on David's evening walks. It was, Proust suspected, a part of Antoine's cure, but he graciously accepted Meric's encouragement to move about the city and, as Meric said patting his large stomach, build up an appetite for supper.

His office duties finished for the day, David grabbed his hat. He could no longer stand the thought of being confined to his room. He knew it was his imagination, but he had felt like a prisoner these past two months. Today he would walk—walk and prove to himself that he was fit.

LaRochelle was flat and colorless. The storm's damage, still only partially repaired, left small areas of the city without electricity. Walking the cobblestone streets, peering in the windows of the small shops, many of which were closed, entire neighborhoods seemed strangely out of place. This was where David had lived for the last ten years. A place where people greeted him warmly. Now as he walked the partially deserted streets, the people he passed were strangers. When tragedies like the storm and his sudden illness transpired, people kept their distance, unsure of just who or where the wrath of God would strike next. A nod of the head as they hurried on was David's only sign of acknowledgment. What bothered him more was that he did the same. Before the storm, he would have had several conversations with the people he met on the street. Why were they passing him in silence? Why was he hurrying away?

He walked aimlessly and was surprised to find himself at the docks standing between what was left of the towers of St. Nicolas and de la Chaine, staring out at the obscure blackness of the ocean. In the distance, he could hear the bells of St. Margaret toll the eight o'clock hour. The city should have been alive. The restaurants packed with diners, the boutiques filled with shoppers, the docks reverberating with the colorful language of fishermen and the laughter of young couples as they strolled hand in hand to the ends of the earth. What had the storm done to LaRochelle? His insides twisted. What had the storm done to him?

It was June before LaRochelle returned to normal. Once again, neighbor greeted neighbor with smiles instead of suspicions. In the countryside, the fields began to bloom in the early summer. Soft rains fell. There were warm days and cool nights and the Great Storm was forgotten. The parishioners of St. Margaret filled the pews for Father David's first mass since his illness.

The fact it had taken David almost three months to fully recover surprised Dr. Curvise. Antoine could not understand what had caused the young priest's recurring bouts with weight loss and insomnia. Just as now, he could not fathom his young friend's return to perfect health. As always, he acknowledged, it was in God's hands. He offered his own small prayer of thanks now that everything in LaRochelle, including Father David Proust, seemed to be back in its rightful place.

CHAPTER THREE

The hour was dark, not yet heading towards light. It was past the time of witchcraft and rising moons, but not dreams. Deep inside his slumber, Father David Proust entered the world of nightmares.

The darkness was numbing, so black his ears hurt from trying to hear away his blindness. The loss so great he had been split in two and stretched to an impossible size. There was no end. Only traveling, running ... running forever (beneath the sheets David's legs kicked as if searching for a support that was no longer there), *the stabbing shortness of breath,* (his breath caught and held, refusing to be expired gently), *and the awful knowledge that this nothingness was eternity. He had been let in on a terrible secret (**forbidden knowledge**) and there was no one left to share the prize—or the agony. He struggled to find his voice. "Hello," he screamed, deep in his mind. The words never reached his lips. "Hello," he shrieked into the abyss. And then he saw her coming toward him. Floating in the air like a tiny sun. There were lights in her hair. Unfelt winds whipped the clothes from her body and she came for him. Naked. Hungry. And he ran.*

David woke up screaming, sucking in great lungfuls of air as if he had not breathed for a long time. His head pounded wildly, occasionally blinding his left eye—each unseeing moment sending him back into his dark dream. The pain was so intense, unbidden tears rolled down his cheeks. It was 3:45 in the morning.

Once fully awake, he knew better than to try and sleep. Although exhausted, he found the pain in his head slightly better if he sat up. Moving the chair to the window, he stared out into the night, waiting for dawn. The stars shimmered and winked. David was surprised to find so much solace in their beauty when the night had been so wicked. Unmoving, he sat and waited for the pain to end.

***

"Gently." Inspector Edmund Defont ordered the body to be cut down.

Those who did not know him would suspect he feared he might hurt the dead girl—or wake her. The two policemen who worked silently under his command knew his sole intent was to preserve the crime scene. This was not a homicide. After all, the girl had hung herself. But, was not suicide a crime? So young. So lovely. Defont watched as his officers lay the girl on the bed and covered her naked body with a blanket.

The family had dispersed to other parts of the house. Camille Robéson's mother was resting in her bedroom down the hall. She had fainted at the sight of her daughter's twisted face staring sightlessly from the rafters. Mr. Robéson sat on the top step of the stairs just outside the small bedroom, stunned into silence. Downstairs in the living room, an older brother and two younger sisters huddled together for consolation. Their whispers of *why* were not actually heard, but felt by everyone in the house.

"Who found her?" Defont asked the oldest officer, George Rorke.

"Her father. He works at the market and gets up early. He stopped in to . . . ," he stuttered for a moment, not quite sure why the girl's father would look in on his teenage daughter at four in the morning, "to see if she was sleeping," he finished weakly.

Defont eyed the officer suspiciously. "Is that what he told you?"

"No, he was too upset. I just assumed . . ."

"How old was she? And don't assume!"

"Fourteen," Rorke said flatly.

"Why would a fourteen year old girl take her life?" Defont mumbled to himself. Then, sharply, "Why?"

Having no answer, his subordinates remained silent.

"Untie the sash." He pointed to the rafters. The image of Camille as she should have been—the blush of life in her cheeks, her long hair brushed back, and the smile on her face mirrored in her eyes—had disappeared. The vision of death was before his eyes, yet his manner did not change. "Where does it belong?"

"Here," the younger officer pointed to the window. A matching red sash held the left curtain open.

Defont glanced around. Except for the overturned chair in the middle of the room, everything appeared in order. Camille was a very tidy fourteen year old, he thought. Stacked neatly on the cedar chest were the clothes she had worn the last full day of her life. Curious, Defont moved to examine them. It was strange that someone so fastidious would have put their shoes on top of the pile, soles down. Small bits of dirt from the loafers clung to the outside fold of the young girl's underpants. Underneath her plain white panties, Defont discovered her stockings, brassiere, and the blue skirt and crisp white blouse that made up the uniform of the female students at St. Margaret's Catholic School. Carefully, he replaced the clothes as he had found them.

Officer Rorke handed him the piece of sash from the rafters before wiping the sweat from his forehead. The knot had been very tightly pulled.

"Was there a note?"

"We haven't found one, sir."

"You looked?"

The officer shrugged his shoulders. "Where?" He, too, looked around the small room. Defont followed his gaze. The cedar chest, a bed, and the chair the girl had used to hang herself from were the only fixtures of Camille's bedroom. There was no other place to hide a note.

"Have you called the ambulance?"

"Yes sir."

"Have her taken to St. Margaret's Hospital. I want an autopsy done."

Rorke nodded.

Defont stepped into the dimly lit hall. Instinctively, he put his hand on the shoulder of the dead girl's father. "Mr. Robéson, please come downstairs with me." His voice was gentle as he gave the order. He had found early in his career that those in mourning responded much better to commands than options that presented them with the problem of choosing. Simplifying life for a moment was the least he could do. He had no words to console the grieving father.

Defont led Mr. Robéson into the living room and watched as the weary man slumped into an arm chair. He could see Camille's brother and sisters. The girls had been crying; the brother fighting back tears, too proud to cry.

Defont had questions that needed to be asked, but not now. Still, there were some things that could not be avoided. "I'm having Camille's body sent to the morgue at St. Margaret's Hospital," he said.

Mr. Robéson jumped from his chair. "The morgue! Why the morgue?" The word sounded more frightening than it was.

"I'm sorry, Monsieur. It is the law. We must have an autopsy done."

Mr. Robéson closed his eyes tightly. Defont knew he was picturing his daughter being dissected under the cold lights and hands of a coroner. Twice, he looked at Defont as if he wanted to argue, but could find no words of protest.

"I'm sorry. It's obvious to me how she died, but French law requires we do a post mortem on anyone who has not died a natural death. You'll be notified when we've completed our inquiries." His speech over, Defont walked back upstairs and left the family to their sorrow.

It was a shame, he thought. Camille Robéson's suicide had ended not only her life, but the life of her family. The Catholic cemetery would refuse her remains. She would be buried in unconsecrated ground. No mass could be said for her soul. No priest would be present when she was lowered into the ground.

Condolences would come, as would the gossip—vicious and dangerous. *Her father was too strict. He had eyes for her. He beat her. Her mother was jealous. The brother too old to be under the same roof with a girl so vibrant.* The wagging tongues would begin almost before the grief.

Officer Rorke and his partner came to a particular attention as Defont reached the landing. At the far end of the hallway a door opened, casting a dim glow of light on the three policemen. François Martine, the family doctor, emerged from Mrs. Robéson's room, and quietly shut the door behind him. Defont moved down the hall towards the intruder. His officers pushed themselves against the wall to allow his passage. Dr. Martine moved to meet him.

"I've given her a sedative, Inspector. She's had quite a shock." Called by the family, François Martine had been the first outsider at the scene. He had called the police.

"What time was she found?"

"Just before 4:00 this morning. Her father leaves for work around then. She hadn't been dead long. Ten, maybe fifteen minutes."

"Why would she do it, Martine?" Defont asked in quiet desperation. "You are their family doctor. Why would Camille want to take her life?"

Martine hung his head, whether in sorrow or shame at having no answer, Defont could not tell. "I can think of no reason on this earth why she would want to hang herself. It is a terrible way to die."

Was there a good way to die, Defont wondered, but he said, "Everything now is as it was when you arrived?"

"Of course," François replied sharply. "If you'll excuse me, I must go downstairs and console the rest of the family." He squeezed past the much larger policeman.

Defont let him go, but he refused to move aside.

For reasons unknown to the vast majority of inhabitants of LaRochelle, Inspector Edmund Defont and Dr. François Martine did not like each other. Speculation as to why, ran a large gauntlet. The simple truth was that the two men were physical and mental opposites. Defont was a large man who bullied his way through life. Martine, small and delicate, could not, although he tried. Defont had been decorated with the Legion of Honor for killing in the Great War. François Martine, a doctor who had labored to save lives in the same war, had received no such recognition. Defont viewed life simply—right and wrong, black and white. There were no in-betweens. Martine sought underlying reasons for men's actions, and was quick to blame society on the whole for the crimes men committed. The last straw, so minor as to be almost unnoticeable was Martine's communistic beliefs which countered Defont's staunch Catholicism. They were simply men who disagreed and, as such, were disagreeable with each other.

But, for all of their differences, one common thread ran through both men. Life was sacred. No one should die without cause, without an explanation, be it murder or suicide.

Defont waited until Martine was downstairs before turning to his officers and the immediate problem on hand. "Did either of you know Camille?"

"No sir."

"I didn't know her personally, Inspector, but my daughter went to school with her. They were in the same class."

Defont thought for a moment, and then came to a decision. "Thank you, Officer Rorke. Within the next day or two, I want you to make discreet inquiries about Camille to her classmates and friends. I want to find out *why*. Do you understand?"

Rorke snapped to attention. It was an honor to be selected by the Inspector to work a case. "Yes sir!"

"What is today? Oh yes, Thursday. One week, Rorke. By next Thursday I'll expect your report on my desk."

"Yes sir."

Defont opened the door to Camille's room and shut it behind him. Outlining the shape, the peaks and valleys of a young teenager, the blanket was a shroud which should have moved evenly with the rise and fall of Camille's sweet breaths. Nothing. Edmund sat down on the edge of the bed and pulled the blanket from the dead girl's face. Strands of long black hair twisted like cryptic spider webs across her nose and mouth. Gently he pushed them away. Looking into her horror-filled eyes he asked, "Why? Why would you take your life?" then waited as though expecting her to answer. He did not understand, and it drove him crazy that there was no logic behind her death. There was always a reason!

He shuddered. Downstairs, Camille's family was helpless to comprehend just as they had been helpless to prevent her death. What had driven her to take her life? What thoughts could have been so horrible?

"You were only fourteen years old. Why would you do this, Camille? What worries could you have had?"

He covered her face for the last time and left the room.

***

With a bounce in his step, Dr. Antoine Curvise walked across the plaza. It was a beautiful spring morning. Wispy clouds floated easily over an azure sky. Even though his quarters were in the hospital wing, on mornings like this he preferred to exit through the emergency entrance at the rear of the building and travel the sidewalk to the main entrance of the hospital.

"Good morning, Sister Grace," he smiled at the nun behind the reception desk.

She nodded curtly. It was the first sign that the day was not as lovely as Curvise might have imagined.

Continuing down the hall towards his office, he was stopped by Mother Superior Monique.

"Good morning," he tried again, still reeling from the beauty of the day. Her sour expression changed his smile to a frown. "What's the matter, Mother Superior?"

"A young woman, Camille Robéson committed . . ." she struggled to get the word out, ". . . suicide."

The lovely spring day was over before it had a chance to bloom.

"She's been brought here for an autopsy."

The old city morgue that had served LaRochelle for too many years had been torn down, and a new high rise was being built in its place. In the meantime, the morgue had been moved to St. Margaret's Hospital.

No official coroner presided in LaRochelle. Instead, the doctors whose offices were in or near the vicinity of the hospital served on a rotating basis. Death was an infrequent visitor to the city. People lived long and presumably happy lives. When it did occur, death was usually the result of old age, such as a father or mother passing away in their sleep. Prolonged illness was not yet in vogue. Cancer and TB took a terrible toll on life, but the death, though not painless, was swift and certain. Occasionally an auto accident would claim a life. A newborn child would expire hours or days after birth. It was God's way of sparing the innocent the cruelties of life. The last violent murder had occurred four years ago when a farmer had gone berserk and butchered his wife. Gossip had it that she had nagged him into his act. Both were now together in death.

Curvise walked to his office, the weight of the young woman's suicide weighing heavily on his shoulders. The worst of sins. Damnation forever. To take one's own life in LaRochelle was an unheard of act. It had never happened in the fifteen-odd years Curvise had lived here.

Checking the roster, he found it was his turn to perform the autopsy.

Curvise was surprised to find his hands shook as he slipped on his gloves and entered the operating room.

28

Three hours later he removed the bloodied gloves and smock and dropped them into the laundry basket outside the operating room. Grabbing a clean towel, he wiped the perspiration from his face, and walked into the scrub room. He washed his hands vigorously. Twice.

Returning to his office, he filled out the required forms pronouncing death. On the line for cause of death, he hesitated before writing: *Strangulation. Self-imposed.*

He had done as the law required. Samples of the young girl's organs had been labeled and forwarded to the laboratory for later examination. His gross examination had revealed nothing. Aware of the rumors that would fly, he had even checked to see if Camille was pregnant. He was not surprised to find her purity had not been violated—her hymen intact. Camille Robéson had been a fourteen year old with life stretching before her like an adventure. What had gone wrong?

Antoine Curvise put the report in his desk to await the final results of the lab tests. The desk phone jangled loudly, startling him.

"Hello," he answered, then listened quietly as instructions for the disposal of the body filtered over the lines. Camille Robéson's family had decided to forego the embarrassment of burying their loved one in the citizens' cemetery. She would be cremated. It seemed to Curvise that Camille had been doomed, and the family felt it only right that the eternal fires of Hell should begin on earth. He sighed as he thought of their sorrow. At least it would not be sensationalized. The evening newspaper would carry headlines of news other than her demise. The obituaries would devote just enough space for a grainy photograph to accompany her death announcement. Eventually her act would fade, leaving behind only the nagging question, *why?*

***

Unable to see the sunrise from his window, David felt the dawn as the pain in his head diminished. Early morning birdcalls confirmed the new day. By 5:30, he knew he felt well enough to say the six o'clock mass. By breakfast, he was hungry and the fears of the night were fast becoming intangible. By 7:30, he was planning the day's tasks. Today was Thursday, he suddenly remembered—the day he visited the sick.

His morning chores occupied him until early afternoon. It was after lunch before he made his way to the hospital. Usually greeted warmly, he was surprised by the somber mood of the nuns. Today the snippets of pleasant conversation had been replaced by brief and shaded "hellos." Father Proust made his way to Antoine's office to pay his respects.

"Hello David," Curvise said, sitting behind his desk. His face was a montage of emotions.

"Father Curvise," David acknowledged as he took a seat. "You don't look well, Antoine. Are you ill?"

"No, no, I am fine. A bit upset, that's all. I just finished an autopsy on a young woman who died last night."

"I'm sorry. Who . . .?"

"Camille Robéson. Did you know her?" Curvise was anxious for any information he could gather.

"The name sounds familiar, but I can't quite place it. Wait a minute! Did she have a brother? Felix?"

Curvise pulled out the forms he had put away earlier and scanned one of the pages. "Yes, here it is. Felix Robéson. An older brother."

I know Felix. He is a member of our soccer club. A fine young man with a host of talents for football. How devastating for him. For his family." David looked up suddenly as he realized he was intruding on his friend's solitude. "I didn't mean to barge in, Antoine. Perhaps now would be a good time for me to visit with Felix and the family?" He stood to leave.

"No, no," Curvise interrupted his own thoughts. "Please sit down. You're not intruding. It's just that I am still in shock over this matter. Actually, I'd feel better if I can talk."

David returned to his chair. "How did it happen?"

"She killed herself."

"May God have mercy on her soul," Proust uttered automatically as he made the sign of the cross. But somewhere deep within himself he felt afraid — as if he had known the answer to his question before it had been asked. *(Forbidden knowledge.)* Unconsciously, he refused to acknowledge his thoughts.

"She was only fourteen." Curvise suddenly shifted gears. "Have you ever thought of suicide, David?"

"Of course not!"

"I have," Curvise said softly. "Several times." He smiled at the shocked expression on David's face. "It was during the Great War. The sight of men torn limb from limb at times made me contemplate ending my own life. The thought was most persistent just after I had lost a young man on the operating table—too badly mauled to even be put partially back together." Antoine battled his memories. "The nights were a living hell, then."

"Under those circumstances, Antoine, even the Lord might have forgiven you. I know I would."

Curvise smiled. "Yes, you would, but I wonder if He would, David? Even under those horrible conditions."

"Surely the answer must be yes," David almost pleaded.

Curvise smiled. "I suppose He might. His capacity for forgiveness is much greater than ours."

"Fortunately you are here. War is a terrible thing."

"The next time you are talking to Dr. Martine, you may wish to mention those sentiments. He seems to think we're on the verge of another world war and I think he's looking forward to it."

David shook his head. "I like François, but sometimes I don't understand him. You would think after seeing the destruction the war brought on everyone, he would never wish to see another.

"You and he served together if I remember correctly."

"Yes. We were both assigned to the Medical Corps. He's a brilliant physician, but like you, sometimes I don't understand him. I have tried to figure him out—what made him turn from the church and embrace communism. He can be quite an enigma."

"Have you ever asked him?"

"Many times." Curvise relaxed back in his chair. "He just says it's an alternative to the church that's worth his time. Of course, his fire for it has cooled somewhat lately."

"Maybe we should tell that to Mother Superior," David said with easy humor. "She's still under the impression he's a devout Bolshevik."

"Don't you dare! One of life's pleasures is watching her take him to task for his 'heathen' activities." Curvise laughed.

"She spares him no mercy," David agreed.

This felt good, David thought, laughing and talking as if his past illness had not occurred. For weeks he had felt as if people were watching him from the corner of their eyes, waiting for him to collapse or explode. Curvise had been one of the biggest offenders, but today, in his sorrow, he had turned to David for help. In doing so, he had given the young priest back his strength. Suddenly David was glad he had not gone to Monsignor Meric and confessed his sinful dream. Even the terror of this morning's headache had faded to distant and buried thunder. He turned his attention back to what Curvise was saying.

"If you think Mother Superior and Dr. Martine do not get along, you should be present when Inspector Defont and François are in the same room. That, in itself, could start another world war." Curvise was enjoying himself. It felt good to laugh and forget about Camille's death for a while.

"I had no idea."

"Oh yes. You see, David, we all went to the same school. Edmund was a star football player. A most imposing individual, even as a young man. François, well, he's rather delicately built, wouldn't you say? He tried to make the team. Unfortunately, he ran against Edmund one day and . . . Poor François, he was never the same after that.

"We were worried at the time, but it's funny now. He was so—crumpled. It was a bit like the story of David and Goliath, only that time Goliath won. They carried an unconscious François off the field of battle but, instead of treating him as a fallen hero . . . Well, you know children can be hard. I'm afraid we teased him rather badly.

"Since that day, Inspector Edmund Defont and Dr. François Martine have never indulged in a cordial word to one another. Oh, as professionals they are always civil, but socially—never!"

"That surprises me. Dr. Martine has always treated me most graciously."

"I am sure he has. He's a fine man, but rather bourgeois. Edmund's family made their living in the fish markets. Socially, François believes himself above the Inspector. Actually," Curvise leaned closer into conspiracy, "François believes himself above us all." He laughed. "A most endearing trait, wouldn't you say?"

"As I said, I have never seen that. It's amusing to think that, in this day and age, class is still considered an important gauge for men."

"I'm not sure I'd choose that particular word. There are a lot of men who simply have no idea what it's like to suffer from day to day. And too many men forced to struggle to stay alive. Equality is a fine attribute, but it isn't evenly distributed."

"Maybe someday that will all change, Antoine."

"Maybe, but the inherent qualities of man, I'm afraid, leave no room to allow everyone to succeed. We'll always have those individuals who can't care for themselves, just as we occasionally have those individuals who rise above the rest of mankind. I'm sure you have your own favorites, David ... but people like Mozart who created a lifetime of music before his untimely death, Alexander Bell and his telephone, and Edison and his light bulb .... There are people like the Gautiers down the street whose little boy will never be able to walk or speak or care for himself for the rest of his short life. These people can't be equal, David. Life is not equal. That is a burden we must bear with grace. Only *after* life are we measured with the same criteria. Death is the great equalizer in which God loves us all totally, equally, and without reservation." He noticed the clock on the wall. "My goodness, look at the time. It's already three o'clock. I have to prepare for my afternoon rounds."

David swung around. "It's that late already! I should be going. I won't have time to visit all of the wards now." His disappointment was evident.

Curvise immediately became a physician again. David's bewildering illness had worried him so that now, even after spending a normal and relaxed afternoon in conversation, he prescribed: "There's always tomorrow. Don't push it. By the way, how are you feeling?"

"Fine. I had a slight headache this morning, but it went away. Other than that, no problems." With that lie, David walked out the door.

CHAPTER FOUR

"Mrs. Odettes, the chicken was excellent." David wiped his mouth with a clean napkin. Monsignor Meric echoed David's sentiments as did the other three priests sitting around the table.

"Thank you," she beamed. "Are you ready for dessert?"

They all nodded. David poured coffee for the priests.

"Thank you, David." The formalities of the meal over, Meric reached for the evening newspaper and began reading. The back page carried the tiny print and grainy photos of the obituary column.

David's head began to reel. There, staring at him from an out-of-focus newspaper print, was the woman he had raped. His eyes widened and glassed, but his vision remained clear. He could almost count each gray shaded pixel that made up her picture. With a gasp, he reached for the back of the chair to steady himself, but it did no good. He collapsed to the floor, pulling the chair down on top of him.

Immediately, all four priests were at his side, anxious to help, but custom dictated the Monsignor delegate their positions. Jean-Paul Meric did not fail them.

"Mrs. Odettes," he called. "Get Dr. Curvise immediately. Father Mosie! Father Brussand! Take David to his room."

***

Monsignor Meric paced the hall, back and forth, back and forth, waiting for Antoine Curvise to arrive. Hearing the front door of the rectory slam shut, he hurried to the top of the stairs. "Come quickly, Doctor," he said softly, not wanting to break the spell of silence.

Curvise climbed the stairs two at a time, an easy task for his long legs. Breathing a little harder upon reaching the top, he did not bother to catch his breath. "What happened, Your Grace?"

"I'm not really sure." The Monsignor's gray eyes reflected his concern. "We were at supper. David had just poured the coffee. He gasped and fell to

34

the floor. I don't know whether he was unconscious when he collapsed, or if the chair hit him. He knocked it over when he fell," Meric said by way of explanation. "We carried him up here to his room. Father Mosie is sitting with him."

Opening the door to his patient's room, Curvise was pleased to see David struggling to sit up in the bed. He let out a mute sigh of relief. "Stay in bed, David," he ordered.

"I feel fine. I was just dizzy for a moment." David's voice carried a hint of mild protest.

"Let me be the judge of your health." Curvise ushered Father Mosie and Monsignor Meric out of the room. Just before he closed the door, Meric mouthed the words, "His heart."

"Okay David, you know the drill. We've been through this before. Open your mouth." Curvise fed Proust the thermometer, and then took his pulse as the silver mercury registered 98.6°. The young priest sat quietly while the doctor listened to his heart and took his blood pressure.

At last, Curvise put away his instruments. "I can't find anything wrong with you, David. Why don't you tell me what happened?"

"I felt a little dizzy and the next thing I knew, I was in bed. Father Mosie told me Monsignor Meric had called and you were on your way." David looked away. "I'm sorry to have caused so much trouble."

Curvise ignored the humility. "Look at me, David." He studied the young priest's eyes carefully. They were tired and bloodshot, but there was no trace of pain. Still, the glint that Curvise had been so familiar with before the storm had not returned. "You complained of a headache this morning. Is it still bothering you?"

"No, I feel fine. Maybe I ate too much."

Flustered at not finding any reason for the sudden fainting spell, Curvise sat down in the arm chair. "Quite frankly David, I don't know what I'm going to do with you. You're not sick, so I can't prescribe any medicines. Perhaps it's exhaustion. I'm going to ask Monsignor Meric to relieve you of your duties for a few days."

"But there's nothing wrong with me," David protested. The thought of being confined to his room was frightening.

"A few days in the rectory won't hurt you. I must insist upon your obedience." *Maybe I ate too much.* The thought flashed through Curvise's mind. Perhaps his friend was not eating properly. Could he be anemic? Hypoglycemic? "I want to take a blood sample and have the lab run some tests."

Startled, David sat up on the edge of the bed. "Why? Is there really something wrong with me?"

"I just want to make sure there isn't," Curvise reassured him. "It's a simple test to count your blood cells. Do you have a history of diabetes in your family? Anemia?"

"No."

"That's good news. Stay in bed and rest tonight. I'll be back in the morning for the blood sample. Don't eat or drink anything else until after I see you tomorrow." Curvise picked up his bag and started to leave, but instinct caused him to hesitate. "There's nothing bothering you? Nothing on your mind you'd like to talk to me about, David? I'm not asking as a confessor or even your physician. I'm asking as a friend."

"No, Antoine. I feel fine."

"I'll be back in the morning. Until tomorrow, David." Curvise walked back to the hospital in the cool night air.

***

Tormented by the grainy image of Camille Robéson, David prowled his room, finally perching on the chair. He could not get her newspaper photograph out of his mind! He did not know how, but he knew her! She was the girl in his dream.

He began to pace the room again. It had only been a dream—a dream. His nightmare. Until now, he had never really believed he had dreamed of a real person. A stranger! Surely it was nothing but coincidence. It could be nothing else. He tried to reassure himself once more that it had been a nightmare. But, if it had only been his nightmare then why had she killed herself? *She was not the right one.* The thought was there and gone, but one thing David knew for certain—Camille Robéson had killed herself because of him.

The bells tolled midnight. Exhausted, he climbed into bed and fell into a deep sleep filled with strange and unbelievable visions.

She undressed slowly, stacking her clothes neatly on the chair. She was not yet grown, but she had breasts. Full, lovely breasts with tiny perfect nipples. Not wanting to scare her, he waited until she held out her arms. If he could have seen her face clearly, he would have known if she were happy, sad, or frightened, but her image was filtered and grainy. Occasionally she turned her head slightly and he thought he recognized her, but the marred image made identification questionable. Yet he must! Or she knew him. If not, why was she accepting him? Why were her legs spread apart so invitingly?

He heard voices coming from somewhere in the house, but they did not matter. What mattered was her willingness to have his child.

Ecstasy drove him to new heights. His eyes watered and tears ran down his cheeks. His mouth was full of hers and she tasted like sugar. Smelled like flowers. He wanted to stay in her forever. Nothing could match this moment . . .

A silent scream drove him from his bed. "What have I done?" In the darkness, David felt for the girl, but could not find her. Wrapped in panic, he searched his closet and looked under the bed. She had to be here! No dream could have been so real. So terrible. So sinful.

"What have I done?" he moaned and knelt on the floor with prayers of forgiveness.

After a while, his knees began to hurt. He had no idea how long he had asked God to forgive him. He only knew he had prayed until he could no longer remember the words of contrition. Slowly, he climbed back into bed, too frightened to sleep, but too weak to fight. Surrender came in a black cloud of slumber that swept away the starlight and his own strong will.

The vision tore at his insides, strangling with cold iron hands the basic needs of life. His breath was coming in short gasps, whizzing through his nostrils, raking his throat with each gasp. An avalanche tumbled down the majestic Alps engulfing him in a sea of white snow. Trapped, he struggled and flayed about for something, anything to grasp. Something poked at his eyes. Fingers. Twigs from fallen trees. Insects, biting and gnawing at his face. A hand tried to push him away, off of what lay beneath him, which was . . . what?

It was not snow that engulfed him, but the white, strong arms and legs of a woman. A beautiful woman. He could not see her clearly and wondered if it were snowing still. Was it rain or tears? She was not a woman, but a young girl crying, pleading, trying to keep him off of her. Naked. Sensuous. Desirable. He could not stop. He wanted to, but like the avalanche that had started this odyssey, she had him trapped. The explosion erupted from deep inside. He was losing control and felt himself wanting to urinate. It was impossible while he lay on top of her. The moment of pleasure passed— ripping at his testicles, scratching at his brain. Hot shots jolted his eyes and ears. An electrical current flowed, sparking his hair. He was on fire, but it was a hell he justly deserved. It ended with a torrent of fluids that he hoped would never stop.

David struggled awake and slammed his head against the wall. The pain was instant reality. The girl had been different—the outcome of the dream, the same.

Shame, disgust, and hatred for his weakness filled and spilled over the sides of his bed. With a start, he sat up and covered his face with his hands.

"Our Father, who art in Heaven, hallowed be thy name." Once again he began to pray and plead for forgiveness of his human frailties. His human desires.

The pleasure had passed. Now his thoughts returned to his bed and the sticky mess he would have to clean up. The remains of his morality. The indigent reminder that he was but a human animal. No more, no less.

Climbing slowly out of bed, he flicked on the light and prepared to change the sheets. He could not let Mrs. Odettes see his offense. With surprise, he suddenly realized he was dry. No sign of his violation covered him or the bed. Confused, he sat down. Never had a dream been so real or horrific. So filled with pleasure and pain. Sin and desire. Why had he dreamed of a young girl? Was it not bad enough to dream of a woman? But a child! God, please forgive me, he whimpered. But she had not been a child. Nearly a woman. And her breasts had been tiny and perfect.

Violently he shook his head against the vision that threatened to arise.

Why was he being punished? But instantly he knew. He had sinned. He had lied to Antoine Curvise about his headache and too proud (*a sin*), too embarrassed, he had not confessed his first dream to Monsignor Meric. Tonight's nightmare had been a simple reminder that forces more powerful than Father David Proust were in command.

***

It had been four days since Antoine Curvise had posted David's blood slides to the lab. He was hesitant to release the young priest before the outcome of the tests were known and it would be an additional four days before the results were forwarded back to his office. He decided not to wait, but dropped in unexpectedly to see how his young friend was doing.

"I dreamed of Camille Robéson," David confessed to Curvise. "I dreamed I seduced her." He swallowed hard, fighting back the anger and shame that threatened to overwhelm him.

Stunned by David's revelation, Curvise looked around the room for a chair. His legs felt weak. His eyes sought David's, but David looked away. "Are you telling me this as a priest or as your friend?" His face was a mask of neutrality.

"As a doctor, Antoine."

"You had an erotic dream, David. That's all."

Deep inside, Curvise felt relief. David saw his problem as insurmountable. Antoine Curvise knew better. Now, with the problem defined, obstacles no longer stood in his way. "It's not unusual. We all suffer

38

through it."

For a brief moment, David was encouraged. "You, too?" He shook his head. "I think not, Antoine. This was not just a dream. I forced myself on her. I seduced her. That's why she killed herself. My sin is not only that of seduction, but of murder."

"No one knows why Camille killed herself, David, but I can assure you, it had nothing to do with your dream."

"You don't understand. I was in her room. I watched her undress and then . . ." He turned away from Curvise's stare. "I wanted her to bear my child," he blurted suddenly.

"David, my friend, don't torment yourself. I can assure you Camille was not violated by you or anyone else. I did the post mortem on her. She was not pregnant. What's more, she had never had sexual relations of any kind. She was a virgin. "You had an erotic dream," Curvise repeated firmly. "Nothing more."

David's voice dropped to a monotone. The entire scene was slowly being replayed in his memory. "She undressed, putting her clothes on the chair. The room was small. Curtains on the window held open by red sashes. A bed, a dresser, and a cedar chest." He looked up suddenly. "How do you explain that? I was in her room." When silence filled the room, he asked: "You don't believe me?"

Curvise glanced quickly about his surroundings. "Describe your room, David."

"A bed, a dresser, curtains . . ." He stopped. "It was a woman's room, Antoine."

"You're making too much of this matter. You had a dream. A dream all men suffer."

"I've never dreamed of a woman before. I've never had an erotic dream."

Curvise could not decide whether to believe his young friend or not. If David were in a state of denial, Curvise's support would only worsen his friend's condition. If he were not, and was just now, this late in life, dealing with latent feelings of sexuality, and Curvise ignored those feelings .... "Surely you've had these dreams before?"

"No. Never. The first time was with . . ." it was hard to say her name aloud, ". . . Camille Robéson."

"And you dreamed of her once. Correct?"

"Yes. No." David looked up, his eyes troubled. "I . . . I only dreamed of her one night, but I dreamed more than once."

"Okay," Curvise dismissed the confession with a wave. "You said 'the first time.' You've dreamed of another woman since Camille?"

"Yes. Last night."

"Can you describe her?"

"No. I can only visualize her through a haze, like she's in a cloud or something. I can't see her clearly."

"When you dreamed of Camille, was she in this haze?"

"Yes."

"So you can't describe her clearly either?"

David nodded.

Curvise plunged forward with logic. "Or the room?"

"Yes . . . No. I can describe the room, but not her."

David's confusion was obvious. More and more it looked like denial to Curvise. "You saw Camille's picture in the newspaper. The photograph was fuzzy, was it not? You thought you recognized her and passed out? Is that what happened to you earlier, David?"

"Yes."

"If I ask you to describe the woman from last night, you can't, is that right? And if I ask you to describe exactly what you did to her . . ." Curvise let the question trail.

"I . . . I seduced her."

"But exactly what did you do, David?"

"I don't know! I don't know exactly." His face flushed hot. "I was on top of her . . . She's fuzzy and out of focus . . . I can't see her clearly. It's all hazy." Except for the woman's face, David remembered every last detail of his dream, but he could not bring himself to speak of his sins.

Curvise did not know this. He could not. And so he developed his own theories—*incorrect theories*—of David's abnormal behavior. The doctor presumed avoidance. Denial. These were things everyone experienced in small doses. David had combined them into a great barrier that, for the moment, not even his friend could conquer.

It was painfully obvious David was suffering in his mind. To imagine seducing a young girl he had never met was bad enough, but to believe he was responsible for her death bordered on an illness of which Curvise knew little. He wondered if François Martine had a copy of Freud's Psychoanalysis and made a mental note to ask. David needed help, and he would help him if he could.

"You say you would know the woman you dreamed of last night if you saw her or her picture?"

"Yes," Proust said softly, and then adamantly, "Yes!"

"How can you be sure?"

David had no answer for his friend. How did one explain a moment of truth?

"I have no prescription for what ails you, David. Celibacy affects us all in different ways. Our obligation to Christ is to remain pure. It is a most difficult task, and one we all must face from time to time. You are only making it harder on yourself by ignoring a basic function of life. You would be better off if you accepted the fact that you're human. Pray for forgiveness, David. God will forgive you. That's the easy part. Then you must learn to forgive yourself."

Curvise walked around to perch on the outside edge of David's bed. "This is something you must learn to deal with. I can only reassure you that you are not responsible for Camille's death. We'll never know what drove that poor girl to take her own life, but it was not you."

David let out a sigh. He did not know why, but he had expected his friend to believe him. "It's not that easy, Antoine."

"I never said it would be. Talk to your confessor, David. Unburden yourself to Monsignor Meric. He is very fond of you. He will understand. Perhaps together you can find it in yourself to get rid of your guilt. Perhaps, then you can rid yourself of the dreams.

"I wish I could say it won't happen again, but I'm afraid it will." Curvise hesitated in his speech. They were not meant to be, but his words sounded harsh to his ear. "If you need to talk to a friend, you can always come to me."

"Thank you, Antoine. I appreciate your patience in this matter. If only I could visualize this girl of last night's dream more clearly, I could search her out. Warn her."

"Against what, David?"

"I don't know, Antoine. Me?"

"Talk to your confessor, David. When the results of the blood tests come back, I'll come and visit you again." Curvise extended a strong hand. The two men shook hands firmly. Friends.

***

Two days later, Monsignor Jean-Paul Meric sat with his eyes shut, his head resting in the crook of his hand, listening to Father Proust's confession. He thought of the suffering the young priest had been put through—not only physically, but mentally as well. The curse of a woman's scent was well known by Meric. Like his brothers, he had suffered through many a night filled with lustful dreams. Using his appetite to conquer the ungodly curse, he had fought his battle and won. He found a full stomach at bedtime kept him from the soft footsteps of haunting females.

So Meric listened with patience and understanding. The dreams were nothing. Men were men. The fact that Christ and the church demanded the very best of their followers only meant another battle to be fought and won. But David's adamant belief that the dreams were real and that he was responsible for Camille's death troubled Jean-Paul. He would caution David to set aside his guilt or keep it as penance, but above all, to stay silent. The church needed no hint of scandal.

CHAPTER FIVE

Edmund Defont read the report Officer George Rorke had compiled on Camille Robéson. Thorough and concise. He liked its brevity. It had been easy to find the one item that stood outside the norm. Camille had confided to Rorke's daughter that she thought she was pregnant.

The autopsy report received a few days earlier had stated she was a virgin. How could a fourteen-year-old girl in this day and age believe she was pregnant? Surely, Defont thought, the young adults of France were not that naive. Was it possible Dr. Curvise had erred? He doubted it. Antoine Curvise was a more than competent physician. Still . . . Camille had thought herself pregnant. It was a fact she had kept hidden from her immediate family. If she had confided in them, no one admitted it. They had not even volunteered information on a boyfriend. Camille's family had been strict. A protective older brother and a fearsome father had kept Camille pure. Defont decided to pay a visit to Dr. Curvise.

***

Mother Superior Monique knocked gently on Father Curvise's office door and, as always, waited a moment before opening it. "Inspector Defont is here to see you, Doctor."

"Show him in, please." Curvise looked up from his desk. He had been reading Freud's psychological treatise on the interpretation of dreams. Taking off his reading glasses, he rubbed his eyes and the bridge of his nose where red imprints told of long hours over tiny print.

"Good afternoon, Father Curvise." Edmund's presence instantly made the office seem small.

"And how are you today, Inspector?" Curvise indicated the chair in front of his desk. The two were old friends, but the presence of Mother Superior dictated that the formalities of titles be used. Curvise waited until she had shut the door behind her before continuing the conversation. "What brings you to the hospital? I hope you're not ill."

"Not ill. Just confused," Defont said with a smile.

"There seems to be an epidemic of that going around lately." Curvise returned Defont's smile. "How can I help?"

"I read your autopsy report on Camille Robéson. You stated she was a virgin."

Curvise nodded.

"I've just finished reading a report submitted by one of my officers. You know him, I believe. George Rorke. He interviewed Camille's closest friends, one of whom was his own daughter. In his report, he states Camille confided to a friend she believed she was pregnant."

The image of David Proust, the sound of the young priest's voice flashed through Curvise's mind. *I wanted her to bear my child.* Could it have been just over a week ago?

"Impossible. Well, not impossible that she might think herself pregnant, but physiologically there is no way she could have been," Curvise said.

Defont cleared his throat. "We've known each other almost all of our lives, Antoine. I would never question your ability as a physician, but is it possible . . .?" This was very hard, Defont thought. "That's all I'm asking. Is it *possible* you might have missed this fact?"

Curvise's temples began to pound with a disturbing thought. Had David been telling the truth? Had he . . .? No.

"In this world, anything is possible Edmund, but not this. Once I noted that the hymen was still intact, I saw no reason to run up the expense of unnecessary laboratory tests. She was intact. Do you understand what that means? There had been no penetration. There was absolutely no way for Camille Robéson to have been impregnated."

Defont hesitated before asking his next question. As a man of intelligence, it embarrassed him. As a digger for truth, it had to be asked. "Then you're saying it is impossible for a woman to be a virgin and pregnant at the same time?"

"Yes, that's exactly what I'm saying. Physiologically it's impossible. However, that doesn't mean that psychologically a woman cannot believe herself with child. It happens quite often in the animal world. It's a rare, though not unknown occurrence in humans." Curvise leaned forward emphatically. A teaching tone crept into his voice. Defont proved an avid listener. "Sometimes a woman wants a baby so badly that she can "will" herself into missing her menstrual cycle. Once her period has been missed, her mind takes it as proof of pregnancy. The brain then can go on to produce certain hormones which will cause that woman to have morning sickness or produce milk for a child who does not exist." Curvise leaned back in his chair. "But a woman would have to be sexually active to believe that. Camille was not sexually active."

"Her body has been released to the family, yes?"

"Yes. They had her cremated."

"I know. I signed the release myself. At the time I could find no reason to prolong their sorrow." Edmund stood to leave. "It was just a thought."

"Do you suspect foul play?"

Defont shook his head sadly. Crime was something that could be brought to justice. "No. I only want to know why a young girl about to become a woman would so suddenly take her own life. Do girls of Camille's age understand the process of birth, Antoine?"

"That's a question best asked of her mother."

"It is a question I cannot ask. The family is suffering enough as it is. To ask that question would only raise ugly speculation."

"The speculation has already arisen, Edmund. Perhaps you should talk to Camille's young friend. Maybe her friend's mother would speak to Mrs. Robéson for you."

"An excellent suggestion, Antoine. Thank you." Defont managed a smile. It was a relief to be able to do something. He would order Officer Rorke to make the inquiries. After all, it was Rorke's daughter who had acted as Camille's confessor.

***

Curvise found Edmund Defont's questions had only added to his confusion. He tried to get back into Freud's theories, but could not concentrate. David and his dream kept interfering. According to what he had read so far, if left unchecked, David's ailment could lead to violent outbursts. Curvise would never believe his young friend capable of murder. While he should have been able to take comfort in that fact, Freud had gone on to state that if no outlet were found for the sufferer, insanity could very likely occur.

A week ago he had been in David's room hearing the stricken priest confess to an intentional act of murder that was not a murder. Three days ago, David had visited him in his office and received the results of the blood test. They had been normal just as David had been normal. There was nothing physically wrong with Father Proust.

Curvise had stayed away from leading questions, but let David find the paths of conversation. The young priest had spoken freely of the dream in the past. Three days ago, he had acted as though nothing had happened. Was his power of suppression really that great?

***

Summer sifted away easily. September came and with it light rains and cold winds off the Atlantic Ocean. Schools opened and the parade of neatly dressed young men and women marched through the streets each morning, eager to learn. The suicide of Camille Robéson was lost with the green of summer. Her family had moved to Paris—the gossip too much to bear.

Father David Proust resumed his full duties and his soccer team began to practice each evening. He missed his star forward, Felix Robéson, but the team would continue. With the color back in his cheeks, and lost weight regained, Curvise pronounced David fully recovered. Freud's <u>Psychoanalysis of Dreams</u> was returned to François Martine. Once again, LaRochelle returned to its peaceful existence.

***

The waters of the Bay of Biscay were cold and rich. God had nourished the dark green ocean with an abundance of life-sustaining nutrients. Peter was a fishermen of souls. The inhabitants of LaRochelle were fishermen of the sea. The crops could fail, the orchards turn sour, but the sea was consistent. Its turbulent waters forever produced a bounty to feed those who respected its dangers.

David Proust was jolted from sleep, his scream echoing through the rectory. He clutched his head and tried desperately to hold his skull together. "No, no, no, no, no," he screamed over and over until rough hands grabbed him, and forced him back down on the bed.

Father Mosie's room was adjacent to David's. The old priest heard the screams and was the first to arrive. Very quickly he was joined by the other priests who resided in the rectory.

Monsignor Meric came in as David was finally calming down. Even in the dimly lit room he could see the terror in Proust's eyes. This was not the time to ask questions.

He hurried down the hall to his office where he growled curt orders into the receiver. He wanted Dr. Curvise at the rectory immediately. With satisfaction, he hung up the phone and retreated to David's room. He would wait for the doctor there, and this time he would refuse to leave until he had some answers. Unlike before, this time he would allow no door to be shut in his face.

***

"I've given him a sedative. He'll sleep the rest of the night," Curvise told Meric. David's incoherent mumbling had finally ceased with his drugged sleep.

"What was he saying, Antoine? Could you understand what he was trying to say?" Although his anxiety might have caused him to crowd the physician, Meric took a step back. He had discovered early in life that he appeared taller than he really was if he stayed away from anyone against whom he might be measured.

Curvise wiped the syringe with an alcohol swab and returned it to the case. With a snap, he placed the hypodermic safely in his bag. "Let's go down to your office, Jean-Paul."

Meric nodded and led the way.

"It was hard to understand him, but I thought I heard him mumble 'she's dead.'" Curvise sat in a chair. Meric perched in the chair next to him. "I believe that's what he said," Curvise repeated after a pause. "She's dead."

"But who can he mean? Who's dead?"

Who indeed? Curvise started to shake his head, but stopped as he looked at the Monsignor. In a flash, he recalled his conversations with David some months earlier. At that time, David had come to him as a doctor and not a priest. If he had only come as just a friend, Curvise thought. Then I could tell Monsignor Meric everything that had been said. But he came to me as his doctor. Any mention of those conversations would be a violation of his physician/patient morals.

"Who was he talking about, Antoine? If you know something that might help David, I order you to speak." Meric was angry and determined to get to the bottom of this. He had completely forgotten David's earlier confession and his belief that he had caused Camille Robéson's death. It had never been mentioned after their one conversation. David had slowly resumed all of his duties and remained in the best of health. It had been easy to forget his transgressions.

"It's not that simple, Your Grace. A few months ago David came to me— not in a confession, but as his doctor. He spoke to me of some problems he was having. He hasn't mentioned them since. I simply thought he and God had come to some understanding, and that he was no longer troubled."

Meric suddenly recalled David's confession. Gently, he put his hand on Curvise's arm. Within minutes of each other, they had both remembered David's dream of Camille and the other woman, but neither could speak of it openly without violating a sacred trust. Words were chosen carefully.

"It was only a dream," Meric said. "A dream to which all men are susceptible."

47

"Yes," Curvise said, acknowledging Meric's caution. "I did some research on this particular subject. It seems that men interpret these dreams in different ways. For some, they are pent up emotions. A couple of hundred years ago, they were visitations by demons. Some men cry after these dreams. Others get angry. Some go mad. The majority though, take their moment of pleasure without such large doses of guilt. They do not find it a sin."

Meric rubbed his hands through his hair. "That's all well and good," he shot Curvise a look, "but let's get back to David. He is obviously sick. Do something to cure him." The Monsignor was exasperated, but not nearly so much as Curvise.

"No, Your Grace. He's not obviously sick. I have run every test I know. Father David Proust is a normal, healthy individual who has nightmares. Other than to suggest he be returned to lighter duties and remain here to rest, frankly, I don't know what to prescribe." Curvise felt defeated. He hoped it did not show.

"I'll see to it that David gets the rest you prescribe," Meric said. Curvise had given him an intelligent explanation for David's behavior. Guilt was a powerful tool. Meric knew this. The church used it masterfully, but so much guilt that Father Proust should become mad, all over a dream of lust? How did one stop a man from dreaming? He, too, was at a loss.

"I'll stop by after my rounds at the hospital and look in on him, Your Grace."

"Thank you, Father." Meric's appreciation was obvious.

***

Antoine Curvise had come back to the rectory early. He had planned on visiting David after his morning rounds, but had decided to come before. He was worried about his friend, although he was positive there was nothing physically wrong with David.

Curvise had lain in bed last night trying to get back to sleep, and had come to a hard decision. He would recommend Monsignor Meric bring in a psychiatrist to examine David. It had not been an easy decision to make. To brand David Proust unstable could possibly ruin his career. The hierarchy of the church took a dim view of abnormalities in its ranks. But Curvise did not know what else to do. To delay could cause irreparable harm to David. He had held off long enough, hoping David would have forgotten his dreams. Hoping his world would remain rational.

"I'm possessed, Antoine," David said calmly, and without emotion. He sat on the edge of his bed, staring into Curvise's eyes. Curvise stared back. "Please don't look at me like I'm crazy. Well, perhaps you should." A smile played around Proust's lips. "I suppose I would think the same thing. If I am not possessed, insanity is my only other choice."

"You're not crazy, David. You're going through a stage of life that should have come earlier when you were more equipped to handle the emotional strains of these battles, but you're not crazy. These are feelings all of us have survived, only you find them impossible to live with. If I could just get you to understand that. Your suffering is normal."

"Is it normal to be in so much pain I pray to God that I might die? Is it normal to lust only after death? Is it normal to kill? What about the girl, Antoine? The one in my second dream. She's dead, you know. She died last night," he said sadly.

Curvise did not know whether to remain calm or throw a fit. Perhaps an outburst would show David just how foolish his words were. But that was not his way. Instead, he challenged the young priest. "What girl, David? Do you know her? What's her name?"

"I don't know. I don't know her, and I don't know her name. But she is dead, Antoine."

To continue in this vein would only give David's imaginings credence. Curvise became a physician. "How is your head feeling this morning? Any more pain?"

"No, it doesn't hurt any more," Proust lied, but his eyes told a different story. His head pounded as though an anvil was being struck by a heavy hammer.

"Are you hungry?"

"Yes." Another lie. The thought of food was disgusting. He wanted to sleep. Wanted it to be night so he could search out another woman. He no longer thought he was possessed. He *knew*. Slowly, he was succumbing to the evil that lived inside of him. *He would be fine after he found her.*

"Fine. I'll have Mrs. Odettes bring you breakfast. You are to stay in the rectory today. I'd prefer you stay in your room."

"As you wish, Doctor." David forced a grin on his face, but it faded quickly. "Am I going crazy, Antoine?"

"No. I don't really know if what you're going through is what one might call normal, but we'll find out. Together," he added to reassure David once more that he would not be allowed to suffer alone.

Father David Proust looked out the window. The sun was only beginning to rise. It would be a cold day in LaRochelle.

49

CHAPTER SIX

Edmund Defont stood with his hands behind his back. The waves crashing on the sandy beach were the only sounds he heard. The wind had disheveled his fine brown hair. In his haste to arrive, he had forgotten his overcoat, but it was not necessary. He did not feel the cold. Behind him, Officer Rorke and his partner huddled inside their heavy top coats, hands pushed deeply into their pockets.

Louisa Markey had been reported missing at 3:00 that morning. Her distraught mother had come into the police station in a state bordering hysteria. Her daughter had threatened to kill herself, she cried. Find her! Save her! The officer on duty had calmed the woman and taken a description of the missing girl. After the form had been partially completed, the woman had presented him with a photograph and additional information. Her husband, Pierre Markey, was out looking for his daughter.

Thank God, Defont thought, he had not found her.

Louisa Markey had once been pretty. Slim. Willowy. Defont looked down at the photograph. Without it, he would have been unable to note that she once had very dark eyes and a captivating smile.

She had not been in the cold waters long—perhaps five or six hours, maybe more. That was all it had taken to destroy her budding beauty, dull her eyes, and replace her smile with a grimace of horror. Her skin had been the beginning of a feast for the fish of the bay. Her body had washed ashore on the sandy beach just south of the city. It was a popular beach that, in summer, filled with children and happy parents on holiday. A young man trying his luck at surf fishing had found the body.

Defont wished he could turn away from the remains of Louisa Markey. He desperately wanted to look up at the heavens, at the horizon. *Anywhere.* Instead, he watched as she was covered with a canvas tarp and loaded onto a stretcher. Another suicide? The question burned in his thoughts. If what her mother had told the police officer at the station were true, it would mean two suicides in less than a year. Two deaths too many. In a town where death came walking with old age, it was cause to wonder.

"Who's working as coroner this month?" Defont addressed his question to the ambulance driver.

"Dr. Martine."

"I want an autopsy done immediately. If you must, wake Dr. Martine. I want his report today. Understand?"

The driver blinked. He did not understand. What the Inspector wanted was not a smart thing to do. He decided to be sure. "You want me to go to Dr. Martine's house and wake him up? Dr. Martine's not exactly a man you issue orders to."

Defont was not a man to be defied. "You heard me."

Stuck in the middle, which was always the way with the working class, the driver walked to the ambulance, mumbling to himself. "Tell him this . . . Wake him . . . Do it!" Normally, Dr. François Martine would jump down his throat if he only looked at him crossways. That was bad enough. Now he had to knock on the man's front door and wake him up. And it was just barely after dawn!

Defont turned his attention to the young man who had found Louisa Markey. The boy was standing by the water's edge, fishing rod still in hand. Defont signaled for Officer Rorke. "What did he tell you?" He indicated their unofficial bystander.

"He came here early to fish. About four o'clock. He lives just down the way and comes here about twice a week. Says his father works for the fish-packing company on Rue de la République. It was dark when he arrived. When the sun started to come up, he noticed something floating near the shore. At first he paid no attention, but as it got lighter he noticed it looked unusual, so he came over and had a look. When it got close enough for him to realize it was a body, he ran home and called us."

"Did he know her?"

"No sir."

"How old is he?"

"Twelve, sir."

Defont waved the young man over. He placed a gentle hand on the boy's shoulder. "Have you ever seen her before?"

"No sir," the boy replied clearly.

"Thank you, son. You've given your name to the officer, eh? Yes, good. And your address? Fine. Good. The Police Department of LaRochelle thanks you for your courage. Please, you may go home." He patted the boy on the back with one hand and waved Rorke over with the other.

"Is this Louisa Markey?" he asked.

"She fits the description."

"Where did she live?"

Rorke wrote the address on a slip of paper and handed it to the Inspector. Defont was surprised to find the Markeys lived only a few blocks from where he resided.

"Has the family been notified?" He knew the answer before the question was asked. "Never mind. I have the address. I'll tell them." He looked out over the ocean, imagining all the places he could be that might be happier than where he was. "I'll need one of them to make a positive identification."

"Have you found her clothes?"

"Not yet, sir."

Defont's gaze returned to the ocean. The tide was in. "Send one of your men to the naval station and find out which way the tides are running."

"May I ask why, sir?"

"Yes, you may, Officer Rorke." Defont was impressed by the police officer's curiosity. "As you may or may not know, the tides come from different directions at different times of the year. If we establish which way the tides are running now, we may be able to find where Louisa Markey entered the water."

Rorke was impressed, not only by Defont's knowledge, but by the fact that he had not been ridiculed for his own stupidity. He snapped a sharp salute. "Yes sir. I'll get right on it."

"When you find her clothes, don't touch them. Just call me immediately."

"Yes sir," Rorke said quickly, then asked: "You don't suspect anything other than suicide, do you, Inspector?"

"I don't suspect anything at the moment," Defont growled. "A citizen of our country is dead. Until we find out how and why, we'll investigate this matter with all of our resources. Understand?"

"Yes sir."

"I'll be at St. Margaret's Hospital later if you need me."

***

The apartment Louisa Markey had shared with her family was clean and orderly, on a quiet street not far from Defont's apartment. It turned out Mr. Markey was a tailor. Mrs. Markey worked as a seamstress in their shop. Two younger sisters shared Louisa's home.

As expected, the news that the police had found a body they believed to be Louisa was unsettling. For everyone. Mrs. Markey broke down and cried hysterically. Her two living daughters took their cue from their mother and burst into tears. Mr. Markey set his jaw and asked Defont what needed to be done.

Defont took him outside, away from the wailing women. It was always hard, he thought. "I need you to accompany me to the morgue. I'm very sorry Monsieur, but I must have positive identification."

Pierre Markey did not speak, but nodded his head twice while he was with Defont. The first time was when he acquiesced to be driven to the morgue. The second time was when he identified the remains of his daughter.

***

Dr. Martine and the orderly had waited for Defont and Mr. Markey to identify the girl. Once it had been established that the body was indeed Louisa Markey, Martine had the attendant push the gurney into the examination room. He glared at Defont. He was in a cross mood and did not care who knew it. He did not appreciate being out of bed before eight o'clock most mornings unless it was an absolute emergency. A corpse, any corpse was not an emergency. Even a physician as brilliant as François Martine could do absolutely nothing to change the condition of the body.

The ambulance driver's words still echoed through his brain. "Inspector Defont wants you . . . ." That was as far as he had let the poor man get. Under the frown he now wore, he was smiling at the helpless expression on the ambulance driver's face as he had lit into him. Peasants! All of them ordering aristocrats around. It was enough to drive a sane man to an asylum.

Martine waited until Louisa's father was outside the room before approaching Defont. "What is so important that this could not have waited until a decent hour, Inspector?"

"The law says that an autopsy should be performed as soon as possible. Now that the girl has been identified, I expect you to comply with the law, Doctor!" Defont walked away, leaving behind a sputtering Martine held fast under the unwavering eyes of the attendant and his tight grin.

"Idiot," Martine commented to himself. Pushing the doors to the examination room open, he stormed inside. "Peasants and idiots."

***

Defont drove Pierre Markey back to the apartment. "Can you tell me what could have driven your daughter to do such a thing?"

Trying to compose himself, Pierre said, "I don't know. We never treated her badly, but sometimes she got wild. She ran away last year, but came home after a few days." He shook his head sadly. "I don't know."

"But your wife said she threatened to kill herself. Why would she have said that?"

"She was upset lately. Moody. I don't know about what, but she couldn't sleep. At night sometimes I would hear her up, walking around her room. I tried to talk to her, but she told me nothing. She wouldn't speak even with her mother or sisters."

"Was she wearing her school uniform when she left the apartment early last night?"

"I think so, but I don't know for sure. I was still at my shop. It wasn't until I got home that my wife told me what Louisa said. That's when I sent her to the police. Then I went out to find Louisa."

Defont asked no more questions. The tears that had been concealed were finally rolling down Pierre Markey's face. More than satisfied by the report Rorke had done on the Camille Robéson case, he decided to have the officer question the family a bit later. After he dropped off Pierre Markey, he returned to the hospital to await Martine's completion of the autopsy. If rumors were to rise that Louisa Markey had been pregnant, he was going to be able to pronounce, without qualification, whether or not they were true.

***

Antoine Curvise was in his office, unaware that a corpse was being autopsied in the examination room. He had been on the phone with Bishop Vasai in Bordeaux trying to find out the procedure for having a priest examined by a psychiatrist. They were old friends.

"It would be catastrophic to bring in a psychiatrist," Vasai told him, not knowing the circumstances or for whom the analyst was intended.

Curvise did not wish, just quite yet, to reveal who the priest was. At the moment, he had presented it as a hypothetical question.

Vasai told him it might be possible to bring in another doctor to assist should the matter become more than hypothetical. But it would have to be done with the strictest of silences. "Reputation, Antoine. Reputations are valuable and not to be disregarded. Discretion must be maintained at all costs. Call me if you need any further advice." The connection had broken.

Curvise was relieved. It was possible to have David analyzed without bringing the matter into public domain. Of course, it would spread like wildfire through the ranks of the church.

Mother Superior Monique knocked, waited, and opened Curvise's office door. "Are you busy, Doctor?"

"Please, come in."

Monique entered, followed by another nun. "We have a new sister at St. Margaret. I just brought her to meet you, Doctor."

"It's always a pleasure to meet one of your nuns, Mother Superior." Curvise smiled at the newly consecrated bride of Christ.

"Sister Mary Franza, Father Antoine Curvise. Father Curvise is our physician at St. Margaret's," Monique said proudly.

"How do you do, sister?" Curvise came out from behind his desk and took her hand. His considerate mannerisms instantly put the new initiate at ease.

"Very well, Father." Her manner was shy. She kept her gaze focused on the floor.

"I'm sure you'll find working here at St. Margaret's a most pleasurable experience. You aren't," he began hopefully, "proficient in nursing, are you?" He was always on the lookout for a good nurse. Most of the nuns, like Mother Superior, had been teachers at parochial schools throughout France. Although all were anxious to help, few were medically skilled.

"Yes, Doctor."

"Excellent! We'll use your skills to their fullest."

Beaming and proud, Mother Superior showed Sister Mary Franza out. Before she left the office, she added, "A young woman died last night, Father. Dr. Martine is doing the post mortem on her now." Her face showed her pain.

"Thank you, Mother Superior." The thought saddened Curvise. "How old was she?"

"Fourteen. She was one of our girls," she said, meaning the dead woman was from the neighborhood. "Louisa Markey. It's said they found her washed up on the beach."

She closed the door quietly behind her leaving Curvise leaning on his desk for support. His head was reeling. His only rational thought was that he must get to the morgue and find out exactly what Martine's autopsy would reveal.

***

Defont peered through the porthole in the door and stared for a few minutes at the back of François Martine. As much as he disliked the cocky little rooster, he admired the man's professional abilities.

"He's a rough little bastard," the attendant commented. "Him and his fancy ways."

Defont looked down on the puny man who stood beside him. "I hope you're not referring to Dr. Martine."

Surprised the Inspector would defend a man who had spoken to him so harshly earlier in the day, the attendant stammered out a lie. "No, no sir. I was thinking of someone else." He turned away from Defont and busied himself with paperwork.

It was in the ensuing silence Antoine arrived.

"Inspector Defont," Curvise greeted him with surprise. He had not expected to find anyone in the attendant's room.

"Dr. Curvise, how are you today?" Defont echoed his friend's greeting.

The attendant jumped to his feet and left the room. Now that his visitor had company, he no longer felt duty bound to be at the desk. It was a relief to escape the Inspector's heavy gaze.

Curvise peeked through the small round window into the examination room. "I just heard," he said absently. "It was a young woman. What happened?"

"My understanding is that she killed herself. Just last night."

Curvise whirled to meet Defont's gaze. "No!" First came the denial. It was automatic. Then came the interminable question. "Why?"

"That's what I hope to find out, Antoine. If it's true, it will be the second suicide this year. You remember the other?"

"Yes, Camille Robéson." Curvise joined Defont, sitting down next to him.

"Do you suspect something other than suicide?"

"I don't know what to think. After the Robéson death, I checked our old files. The last suicide we had here was in 1913. Twenty-five years ago, Antoine. Now, two in less than a year and both of them were young women." Defont looked at the door. He had already been here over an hour. "How long does this usually take?"

"A good two or three hours," Curvise said.

The phone rang. Curvise excused himself and answered it. "Yes, he's here. One moment. It's for you, Inspector." As did Defont, Curvise automatically switched to the formalities of titles when in the presence of others, be they in the room or on the phone.

"Inspector Defont here. Yes, George. I'll be there as soon as possible." He hung up the phone, once again shutting out all outsiders. "Antoine, would you please ask Dr. Martine to wait here until I return? I shouldn't be gone more than an hour."

"Certainly, Edmund. Has something happened?"

"I don't know yet. I'll be back as soon as I can. Thank you."

Curvise waited until Defont was out the door before he buried his face in his hands. "It can't be. It just can't," he said to himself. "I refuse to believe it." But the truth would not be denied. He began to pray—not for himself but for David Proust, the young woman inside the examination room, and for her tormented soul that no longer had a path to heaven.

The realization that David had known the girl was dead had struck Antoine Curvise like a fast moving train. He had left the morgue just after Inspector Defont, his mind set. He would have to speak to Monsignor Meric.

Now, entering the rectory he could hear loud voices raised in argument. The Monsignor's office door was heavy, but Curvise thought he recognized one of the voices as David's. He knocked sharply—once, twice. Meric called for him to enter. Both David Proust and Jean-Paul Meric were seated. Both chairs faced the door. They have had trouble communicating, Curvise thought.

"Come in, Antoine," Meric said with relief. David had just told the Monsignor of his premonition of Louisa's death. That was Meric's explanation. Actually, David had stated he was possessed and had murdered a young girl. He now wanted to turn himself over to the authorities. "Please sit down. This matter we are discussing involves you as well."

Curvise wasted no time in getting involved. Ignoring Meric, he asked David: "Did you know Louisa Markey?"

"Was that her name?"

Meric was confused. Except through David's ranting, he had not yet heard of the morgue's new occupant. "Who is Louisa Markey?"

"A young woman who committed suicide last night," Curvise said impatiently.

Meric's round face became as red as the sun. He stared fixedly at David. "It's no longer a premonition then, but a fact? How could you have known?" he whispered.

"I felt her pain in my head. In my heart," David replied softly.

"What's going on here, Antoine?"

"You know as much as I do, Your Grace. David is the only one who really knows."

"David, tell us what's happening to you."

"I've told you everything I know, Your Grace. I dreamed I seduced Camille Robéson. I . . . I wanted her to have my child. Now she is dead and obviously useless to me. I sought out another woman. I didn't know who she was. I only know I found her in my dreams and seduced her while she cried." David paused, unsure whether it was really necessary to go on. "Now she's dead. I don't know how or why. I only know their deaths are my fault. I drove them to commit suicide as surely as if I had killed them with a knife."

"How long ago did you dream of Louisa, David?" Curvise asked his question as gently as he knew how.

Proust shut his eyes and tried to remember. "Two, three months. It was right after Camille died." He opened his eyes wide in sudden terror. "Help me, Antoine. Help me! I will dream again. I can't control it. It comes, and young girls die. I don't want that on my head. Please. I pray all the time. I ask to be taken from this life before I take another's. Don't you see, Antoine? I will dream again. I will kill. The evil is inside of me." He paused to look at the men who shared the room. "There is no other answer. I am possessed."

The words were no sooner out of his mouth than Meric was up and out of his chair. "Go to your room, David. Please. I must talk to Dr. Curvise alone. We'll continue this discussion later." His voice carried all the authority he had ever possessed in life.

David hesitated in the doorway. "I need your help, Antoine. I have tried to talk to him, but he does not believe me. You've got to help me convince the Monsignor. Help me drive this demon from my soul before I kill again." He left the two men in silence.

Meric began to pace the floor. "Demons. Possession. What is going on here, Antoine? We're not living in the Dark Ages. We know better than to label a quirk in someone's personality as a demon." He ran his hand through his hair. "My initial reaction is to tell him he's crazy, but I'm not sure which is worse. Demons or insanity!" He stopped his pacing in mid-stride. "He's not crazy, is he?"

Curvise made a difficult decision. For David's sake, he broke the trust the young priest had placed in him and told Meric everything he knew of the matter. As he had suspected, it did nothing to calm the Monsignor's nerves.

"A scandal! Can you imagine what the newspapers would say? A young woman driven to suicide by a priest. A priest who dreams of fornicating with young girls!" Too nervous to stand, Meric sat down behind his desk. "How could Camille Robéson believe she was pregnant? She wasn't, was she?" The Monsignor was no longer sure of anything.

"No, Your Grace. Camille Robéson was not pregnant. I did the post mortem on her myself. I've tried to convince David that she wasn't, but he insists."

"And Louisa Markey?"

"I don't know yet. Dr. Martine is performing the autopsy right now."

"Who else knows of this?"

"No one."

"It must remain that way, Antoine. For David's sake," Meric added. He was not thinking of David, but of the church. No matter what or who or why,

58

the church came first. "As his physician, what do you suggest we do?" He wanted to avoid making his own decision regarding this matter. At the moment, he had no idea what should be done.

"David must remain here. I have already spoken to Bishop Vasai."

Meric's eyes opened wide in fear. "You didn't mention . . .?"

Curvise cut him off. "No. I only spoke hypothetically to His Excellency about the matter." He reassured Meric their secret was still safe.

"Bishop Vasai is no fool. He'll put this all together."

"He will not have to. Eventually we'll have to tell him."

"Yes, yes. Of course. I didn't mean we could hide it," Meric stammered. His fear of authority escalated, especially when his career was in jeopardy. To be caught in a delicate web like this could very well ruin his chances of ascension through the church. His one true desire, even greater than food, was to wear the scarlet of Cardinal.

"May I make a suggestion, Your Grace?"

"Certainly, Antoine."

"I think you should inform Bishop Vasai of this. All of it. Let him decide what's to be done."

"Yes, of course. I was just thinking that. Thank you, Antoine." Meric started to reach for the phone and hesitated. "You never answered my question. Is David insane?"

"Insane, no. He's sick. His dream of Camille was the first of that kind for him. He doesn't understand it as we do," Curvise said kindly. "If you'll excuse me, I think I'll go sit with our friend for a while." He looked at his pocket watch. It would be almost another hour before Dr. Martine finished the autopsy.

Meric waited until Curvise closed the door before picking up the phone and dialing Bishop Vasai. Twenty minutes later, he hung up the phone. His ear was red and sore from pushing the receiver tightly against the side of his head. Now he closed his eyes and remembered the Bishop's last cryptic words. *"Do nothing. Keep David confined to the rectory. I will be in LaRochelle in a few days to interview Father Proust."*

The words circled Meric's thoughts. *Interview.* Was the Bishop talking excommunication? Surely not. David had done nothing wrong. If only he had not mentioned demonic possession. If only . . .

The finger of guilt Meric felt pointing at him was not justified. He had only done his duty. A priest who believed himself possessed was a threat to the sanctity of the church. Bishop Vasai would come to LaRochelle and straighten out this entire affair—one way or another. He looked down at his pudgy hands and laughed to find them shaking badly.

Edmund Defont stared down at the neat pile of clothes at his feet. Officer Rorke was in the middle of telling him how they had been found.

"I followed your advice Inspector, and went to the naval station. The officer on duty checked the tidal charts and told me the tides had been coming in since eleven o'clock last night. Anything dropped into the ocean from any of the docks would wash up on the beach south of the town. We checked the piers until we found those." He pointed to the clothes.

Defont heard, but paid little attention. His thoughts were on the unusual manner in which the clothes had been placed. A pair of polished, but worn loafers sat on top, their soles resting on top of a pair of panties. Underneath, in a startling familiar order, were Louisa's socks, bra, blue skirt and white school blouse. Why had she undressed so precisely? And why, after all outward attempts at neatness, had she placed her shoes on top of the pile? As in Camille's case, the soles were dirty and had left their mark. The coincidence was too much and yet, he had expected Louisa Markey's clothes would be found in exactly this position. That raised another question. Why was he not surprised?

Officer Rorke interrupted his thoughts. "We questioned a sailor on the StrenVerds." He nodded to the ship tied to the dock. "The night watchman claims he saw a girl walk down the pier around 2:30 in the morning. She was wearing the same type of clothes we found here."

"How could he tell?" Defont asked.

"She passed under the light which was near where he was standing. At first he paid attention because he thought she was a whore coming to see if she could make some money. But when he saw her clothes, he recognized the school uniform. Obviously he lost interest at that point, but I questioned him about it. He says he couldn't see her face, but he did remember she had long dark hair."

Louisa Markey had long dark hair, Defont thought.

"Inspector?" Rorke again vied for his attention. "He says she never walked back."

"What time was his watch over?"

"Three o'clock this morning." A single question burned in Rorke's mind. It had to be asked. "Was she murdered, Inspector?" Secretly, he hoped Defont would say yes.

"I don't think so, Officer Rorke." If it had not been for the way the clothes were piled, Defont would have been adamant in his denial. But it was possible, minutely possible that there was another party involved, although he did not see how. Yet, the parallels between Camille and Louisa were remarkable. It went beyond a pile of clothes. It encompassed their very stature. Both had been just barely 14. Both had dark hair and dark eyes, stood between 5'3" and 5'4" and weighed approximately 95 to 105 pounds. And, Defont was sure Dr. Martine would prove this assumption correct, they were both virgins.

"Officer Rorke, tomorrow I want you to question the Markey family. Then question Louisa's friends. I want your report on my desk as soon as possible. Understand?"

"Yes sir." George tried to hide his delight. He would be out of uniform soon at this rate. Perhaps a police inspector in his own right, behind his own desk.

***

"You've read the report, Inspector." Martine tried to remain calm. "I refuse to go back in there and desecrate the body of that poor child any further. She died by drowning *and* she died a virgin. I see no reason to slice her open to examine either the Fallopian tubes or her uterus. Good God, Defont! Leave the family with something."

Defont was exasperated—his patience wearing thin. He closed his eyes and counted to ten. Under the threat of arrest for impeding a criminal investigation he could order Martine to comply, but he could not. He had no solid evidence of foul play in Louisa's death. Besides that, to order Martine was to guaranty that the fool would only become more stubborn.

Difficult as it was, the attendant sat with a straight face. He wondered if the Inspector would defend the cocky aristocrat now.

Defont opened his eyes and stared into Martine's scowling face. "As a favor to me, François." His tone was soft, almost pleading. "Would you do as I request?"

Martine was taken by surprise. He blinked and relented, if only slightly. "What are we looking for, Edmund?" It had been a long time since he had addressed Defont by his first name.

"I have to know, positively, if she is pregnant or not." Defont felt foolish saying it out loud.

"There is no possible way," Martine started to protest, then thought better of it. "Am I supposed to be looking for a pregnancy in the first trimester? The second? Certainly you can see for yourself the child is not six months pregnant!"

"I don't know, François. That is why this is so important. Could you tell even if she had just become pregnant say, a week ago? Two weeks ago?"

"I'll have to send blood samples to the lab. It will be a few days before the results come back." Martine stood to resume his work, but hesitated. "Her blood will tell us everything, Inspector. I see no reason to cut further."

"Please."

François Martine shrugged and walked back into the examination room. "It will be a few days before the results are known. I'll telephone you when they arrive."

"That would be fine. Thank you, Doctor."

The attendant snickered. Both men had compromised.

"What is your name?" Defont demanded, glaring fiercely at the cowering attendant.

"Marcus Forbré," the orderly stuttered.

Defont poked the attendant in the forehead once, twice, and then again. "If word of what Dr. Martine and I were discussing gets out of this room, I will come back and wring your neck. Do you understand?"

Marcus Forbré's eyes bulged at their sockets. Edmund Defont was not a man to be trifled with and he knew it. All he could do was nod, which he did, very fast.

CHAPTER SEVEN

Curvise did not want to believe what David told him. To believe it was to admit to the dark past of the church—the existence of evil demons and spirits that roamed the night. Modern psychology had all but driven spiritual demons from men. If evil existed, and he was sure it did, then it no longer existed as ghostly apparitions, but in the minds of men. David would not, he rationed, *could not* have left the rectory to violate either Camille or Louisa. The words he spoke held no truth. Yet they did. Both girls had believed themselves with child. Had a spirit floated over the town seeking innocent victims? Taken residence in Father David Proust's body? Was it possible the mysterious ways of the dark past were not really dead? That there was truth to the ancient stories? Or that dreams were sometimes so strong, so powerful, that they actually met in some blank place and intermingled to become reality?

As far as Curvise was concerned, David's night would begin an eternal fight for his sanity. He had wanted to give his young friend a sedative, but David had resisted adamantly. "I can't sleep!" Curvise remembered how frightened David had sounded. He touched his arm where Proust's grip had made itself known. "If I sleep, I dream. If I dream, another innocent girl will die."

Curvise could not think of these words as those of a sane man, but they were not the words of a violent beast without conscience. David wished for no one's death. Did that make him crazy?

The autumn winds had picked up a little. Curvise hurried across the plaza to the hospital. He did not want to miss François Martine. He had to know. Had Louisa Markey been a virgin?

The attendant's room was empty when he entered. Curvise looked into the examination room. François Martine was still busy with the corpse. With a sigh, he sat down to wait for Martine to finish the autopsy.

***

"Antoine," Martine exclaimed, seeing him sitting alone at the attendant's desk.

"François, how are you?" But at that moment he did not care. He only thought of one thing. "Have you finished?" There! The question within a question was out. How could it have not been asked?

"Yes," said Martine with some exasperation. Caught up in his own web of petulance, François failed to notice Antoine's anxiety. "Actually, I was finished an hour ago, but our dear friend Defont insisted I do both a gross and microscopic examination of her uterus. Can you believe it! After I told him Louisa Markey was a virgin, he still insisted I check to see if she was pregnant." He shook his head in disbelief.

The color drained from Curvise's cheeks. He wanted to ask if she had been, but he dared not. His heart would feel no lighter freed from its burden of doubt.

"Can you believe him? Sometimes I think he's a complete fool. A sexually active virgin! Can you believe such nonsense?"

Curvise's mouth went dry and he ignored Martine's rhetorical question. "What were the results of your work?" It was the most indirect way he could think to ask what he, as a physician, already knew.

Still caught up in Defont's idiocy, Martine answered his friend's question without thought and more as a continuation of his earlier speech. "Of course she's not pregnant! Oh, as I promised that idiot policeman, I'll wait for the results of the blood samples to come back from the lab, but we both know what we'll find, don't we?"

Martine motioned dramatically towards the examination room. "We have a fourteen year old virgin who doesn't stand a chance in Hell *(Curvise shivered. He wondered how appropriate Martine's choice of words really was.)* of being with child. Her demise, as I told Defont, was death by drowning. There are no signs of a struggle. No bumps, no bruises. She walked off the edge of a pier." Martine calmed down enough to discard his bloodied surgical gown in the clothes hamper.

Curvise realized he had been holding his breath. Slowly he exhaled. "Don't you find it strange that within the last six months two young women have committed suicide, François?" He followed Martine into the scrub room.

"With the state of affairs in the world today, I'm surprised there haven't been more people killing themselves," Martine commented. With the quick movements of a practiced surgeon, he turned on the hot water, lathered and thoroughly washed his hands. "We live in a sick world, Antoine. A world filled with imbeciles and parasites. I guess for some people, death's not as frightening as living. Maybe these two young ladies had a deeper insight of life than either you or me."

"But to kill themselves! They've condemned themselves to suffer the fires of Hell forever. Is that an acceptable alternative to living? At least alive, they might have tried to change the world for the better."

Martine shrugged. "Maybe they didn't believe in Hell. Maybe they saw death as a peaceful alternative." He dried his hands, combed his hair, and slipped on his suit coat, all with the same efficient air with which he attacked life. "Whatever reasons they may have had, we'll never be allowed in on their secret now, Antoine."

"No, we won't. And isn't it a pity?"

***

Curvise accompanied Martine to the main entrance of the hospital in time for afternoon rounds. In the lobby, the two doctors ran into Sister Mary Franza.

"Mother Superior has asked me to accompany you on your rounds today, Doctor," she said softly. "I hope you don't mind."

"Not at all, Sister. Have you met Dr. Martine?"

"No, I have not," she replied shyly.

"Then allow me. Sister Mary, Dr. François Martine." The two strangers smiled in greeting. "Dr. Martine is a volunteer on our staff and always ready to assist us when necessary."

"It is my pleasure to meet you, Sister Mary." Martine bowed gallantly.

"Thank you, Doctor."

Curvise dismissed the young nun. "I'll meet you at the nurses' station in a few minutes, Sister."

"Until we meet again, Sister Mary," Martine called with a smile.

Both men watched her walk away.

"My God, Antoine. She's stunning. Did you look into her eyes? I've never seen eyes so dark and mysterious." Martine's voice was filled with longing.

Curvise countered sharply. "She's a nun, François."

"I'm aware of that. But one doesn't stop looking at a flower just because it is in Christ's garden."

"No," Curvise said, "one doesn't. Especially if that one is you. You're incorrigible, François."

Martine laughed. "But likeable, yes?"

"Yes," Curvise agreed.

Walking alone to the nurses' station, Curvise experienced a little more bounce in his step. Louisa Markey was a virgin. David had not violated her. Given time, maybe everything would turn out for the best.

"Dr. Curvise," Sister Mary said as he reached for the charts of the patients he would visit this afternoon, "Father Proust left a message for you."

She handed him a folded slip of paper.

Curvise opened it and read it quickly. It was a request that he stop by David's room that evening.

"Thank you, Sister." What could possibly be wrong, Curvise wondered, but he said, "Shall we begin our rounds?"

***

Antoine Curvise knocked once on Father Proust's door, then waited until he heard David call, "Come in." The young priest was standing by the window looking out across the plaza towards the hospital.

"How are you feeling, David?"

"Fine. I feel fine." And then, "Monsignor Meric told me I'm to be interviewed by Bishop Vasai," he blurted.

"I've heard he's scheduled to arrive within the next day or two."

"Why would the Bishop want to interview me?"

"Because he's concerned. We all are."

"I have been acting strangely, haven't I?"

Curvise was at a loss for an answer. David's sincerity confused him. Earlier in the day, the young priest had been pleading for help. Now he acted as though nothing had happened. "Are you aware of our earlier conversation, David?"

"Yes, of course. Am I supposed to be losing my memory?"

"You told Monsignor Meric and me that you wanted to go to the police." Curvise searched for the right words. "You were upset about the two young women."

"Camille Robéson and Louisa Markey," David said quietly. "It's all right to call them by their names, Antoine. Even if they didn't get a chance to use them for very long."

"Do you still feel responsible for their deaths?" Whether David's eyes glazed in memory or pain, Curvise could not tell.

"I didn't want them to harm themselves, Antoine. You've got to believe me."

"I do."

"There was no reason for them to do what they did."

"Obviously they thought they had a reason, David. Do you know why?"

"I don't know. I'm so tired I don't know what to think anymore."

It was the opportunity for which Curvise had waited. "Then let me give you a sedative tonight. You can't stay awake forever. This will help you sleep through the night. In the morning you'll feel better. We can talk then."

David blinked and came back to reality. "Sleep. Yes, I need to sleep. Thank you."

Curvise began to prepare an injection of Phenobarbital. The sound of David's voice made him turn around.

"Am I to be excommunicated, Antoine?"

"Why would you think that? You've done nothing to warrant excommunication."

"Then why is Bishop Vasai coming here? I won't resign my vows. I'll never resign." David glared at Curvise. "They can't force me."

"No one is asking you to resign, David. Bishop Vasai is concerned about your health. That is the only reason he's coming to visit. Now let me give you this." Curvise pushed up the sleeve of David's robe and injected him. "There, that should give you a decent night's sleep."

"It wasn't my fault. It wasn't! I didn't want those girls to die, Antoine. You have got to believe me."

Curvise gently freed himself from David's grasp. "I believe you. Now get some rest. I'll be back in the morning."

By the time he had repacked the hypodermic syringe, his vials of medicine and made his way to the door, David was drowsy. His last words were sluggish, though coherent. "I won't resign. They can't make me."

Curvise would have reassured him, but his exhausted patient was already asleep.

***

It was raining in Bordeaux. Bishop Armand Vasai had just finished a late evening snack. Sitting in an overstuffed armchair in the library in his chateau outside the city, he put down his copy of "Extreme Spiritual Possessions and Analysis of Erotic Behavior" written four hundred years ago by Archbishop Monguia. The text of Monguia's thesis was still the basis to be followed in the awful business of excommunication. Several chapters were devoted to the erotic world of priests caught up in the web of sexual encounters through dreams and nightmares. It was a primer for the young men who vowed celibacy and the haunting dreams that accompanied this unnatural characteristic of man. Monguia's work had become as confusing to him as Jean-Paul Meric's telephone call.

67

A priest having erotic dreams was nothing over which to be alarmed. If Father David Proust were truly meant to be a member of the Catholic Church, he would find a way to overcome his weakness. It had happened to almost all of the members of the clergy since the inception of celibacy. Meric's ramblings over Father Proust's dreams of a young woman who had committed suicide were, of course, a bit unusual. Vasai had searched the index and found only one brief reference to this sort of behavior.

In 1603, a Jesuit in France claimed to have been responsible for the deaths of four young women. Young women who had committed suicide after what the priest claimed were mutual copulations during the darkest of night. The Jesuit, whose name was not mentioned, claimed he was the appointed Messenger of God whose sole purpose in impregnating the young women was to bring about the resurrection of the Savior. From what Vasai could recall of Meric's conversation, David had not made any such claims or expressed any such justification or excuse. It was just as well. This reasoning, according to Monguia, had not spared the unnamed Jesuit excommunication.

To excommunicate a member of the clergy was a most trying ordeal—one that could bring adverse publicity to the already weakened image of Catholicism. Vasai had no intentions of trying to force Father Proust into accepting this course of action. A transfer to another parish—one which did not possess a great number of young women who might tempt and tantalize a young priest's mind would be a better solution.

Resignation was always a most pleasant option that spared each of the parties any embarrassment. Yes, reassignment or voluntary resignation. Father Proust would be allowed to choose one of those options.

The last act Vasai wanted to evoke was excommunication. As more than the titular head of the Catholic Church in southern France, it was in his power to act in any of the above manners. Having read Father David Proust's résumé, he found this young man to be most suited to the clergy. His fine family background was rich in faith as well as money, and had contributed another member of their family to the service of Christ. Unfortunately, Monsignor Michael Proust had died at an early age.

No, Vasai decided. David Proust would not be subjected to the horrific act of excommunication. He deserved better. After all, dreams were not something any man could control with ease.

As soon as his schedule allowed, he would pay a visit to LaRochelle and speak to Father Proust. He would impress upon the young priest the importance of keeping this unfortunate incident buried inside the church. Coming from a man of his stature and importance, he was sure David Proust would do the proper thing. Tomorrow he would find a parish, or better still, a school somewhere in France that catered to young men. Father Proust was a teacher and as such, invaluable. Take away the temptation and, Vasai was sure, the sin would disappear.

The storm that washed over Bordeaux did not miss LaRochelle. Dark rolling thunderclouds, masses of up-rushing, down-rushing air shuddered and split against the cold illumination of electricity. Out of reach, the heavens echoed with a noise that refused to be contained. Beyond the beach line, the Atlantic Ocean rose and fell in great swells and choppy whitecaps. In an instant of lightning, the black waters looked as they must have in prehistoric times. Without light they were shadows within shadows, unseen. But not silent.

Dr. Curvise's sedative continued to work its magic. David Proust slept soundly despite the cold winds that swept away even the stars. It was not until much later, when the storm had blown to sea and left the land unaltered that David began to moan.

***

Monsignor Jean-Paul Meric had been worried enough to assign each of the three priests in the rectory a specific hour to rise and check on Father Proust. Even though Antoine Curvise had assured him the sedative would cause David to sleep through the night, Meric needed more than the doctor's reassurance the priest, *his friend,* would be safe.

Father Mosie awoke to the clanging of his alarm clock. This was the third time his sleep had been interrupted. He would be glad when the night was over. Slipping into his house slippers and robe, he wearily made his way to David's room. As he had twice before, he edged the door open just enough to allow the light from the hall to cast its thin beam on David's bed. Still groggy from sleep, Father Mosie peered in expecting, as always, to see the twisted sheets covering Father Proust's thin body.

The bed was empty. Father Mosie stepped into the room. His eyes were suddenly wide open.

My dear Lord, have mercy!" He grasped David's legs to his chest and lifted him, relieving the terrible pressure the rope had made on his colleague's neck. Only then did he scream for help.

***

The paint on the ceiling was chipped and peeling. Funny, David thought, you live somewhere ten years and never notice the ceiling. He avoided looking in Antoine Curvise's direction. His throat hurt. He should be dead. The bruises on his neck would disappear in a few days, Curvise had told him. His act would live burned in Father Mosie's mind forever.

"He saved your life, David."

Words. Just words. He had wanted to be dead. Not now, but right after the dream had occurred. In that one brief instant when he felt like he had remembered who he really was, he had wanted to be dead. It was not fair, he thought. Both of the women before him had had the strength to destroy the buttress between life and death. Why had they succeeded when he had failed?

"Am I so evil that even Hell rejects my soul?" The voice that echoed these words did not belong to him now. It belonged to another David Proust. The David Proust who had had the courage to stand in a chair and slip a noose around his neck. The David Proust who had kicked the pedestal from underneath his shaking legs.

Curvise had not heard his words—only the rough-edged sounds as David tried to communicate.

"Would you like some water?"

David shook his head and swallowed hard. "What time is it, Antoine?" Painful as it was, this time he made himself heard.

Antoine pulled out his pocket watch. "Almost seven o'clock. It will be light soon." He slipped the watch back into his pocket. "You dreamed again last night?" Already knowing the answer, he had the courtesy to pretend ignorance.

Mutely, David nodded.

Curvise no longer harbored any doubts as to David's illness. His young friend was mentally unstable. He was not, as David himself thought, possessed. Proust laid claim to a demon that had ridden the winds of the Great Storm earlier that year. Curvise knew better. Still, it was almost impossible to completely dismiss the notion. It would answer so many questions. "Who was she?"

"I don't know, but I know her. That sounds stupid, but I feel I've actually seen her somewhere other than in the dream."

Curvise wasted no time being gentle with his questions. If the pattern David had followed with his past encounters with dreams held true, by tomorrow his memory would start to fade, resurfacing only at the girl's death.

"Where did you meet her last night? In her room?"

David nodded.

"I know it hurts to talk David, but please try. Can you describe the room for me?"

Shutting his eyes tightly, David tried to remember what he had dreamed.

"It was a small room. One bed with a brown blanket. There was a crucifix over the door and a picture of the Virgin Mary holding the Christ child. The walls were white. There was a chair. Rafters in the ceiling."

"What did she look like? Was she young? A child?"

David shook his head and blinked back tears. Whether from frustration or pain Curvise no longer cared. "Try, David! For her sake and yours, you've got to remember what she looked like!"

"Like the others," David started slowly. "Her skin was dark and soft. Black hair and dark eyes that watched me . . ." He sat up in bed. "I can't remember anymore. Please don't ask me to, Antoine. I don't want to remember."

Curvise let him be. His description would fit a thousand—no, ten thousand women in LaRochelle. If only he could remember her more distinctly. And the room he had described. How many rooms in LaRochelle were small and decorated with the symbols of their occupant's religion? A hundred? A thousand? Maybe even every single bedroom in LaRochelle for all he knew.

Father Mosie knocked and poked his head around the door. "May I come in, Father?"

"Yes, please do."

"You're wanted downstairs, Father Curvise. I'll sit with Father Proust until you return."

"Thank you." Curvise turned to David. "I'll be back later. In the meantime, Father Mosie will stay with you. If you can think of anything definite, write it down. We'll talk about it when I get back. Okay?"

Curvise's entreaty fell on deaf ears. In his shame, David had already turned away from Father Mosie, shutting out his friend and the world.

***

At four in the morning, Bishop Vasai was roused by his secretary's sharp knock on his bedroom door. The news of Father Proust's attempted suicide jostled him awake. By four-thirty he was in his car, prodding his chauffeur to drive faster. On a good day, the drive from Bordeaux to LaRochelle usually took a little over three hours. His chauffeur would cut thirty minutes off that time today.

The matter of Father Proust could be ended with dignity now. David could not help but resign his vows under the circumstances. Suicide was a mortal sin of the greatest magnitude. The priest would resign and be excommunicated, closing the cover on this unfortunate incident. Even his family's position and wealth could not save him now.

The threat of exposure, not of the dreams, but the suicide attempt, would be the iron rod to drive Father Proust out of the church. There was no law against dreaming, but suicide was not only against the laws of God, but of France herself. Surely, his dignity and pride would not allow him to suffer this humiliation. At least that is how Bishop Vasai would have reacted. Thus, he expected the same from all others of the human race.

"Your Excellency." Curvise took Vasai's hand and kissed the ring of St. Peter. Monsignor Meric made the formal introductions, but they wereunnecessary.

"I know Father Curvise, Jean-Paul. How are you, Antoine?"

"I'm fine, Your Excellency."

Meric was surprised to find Curvise had friends in such high places. He began to look at him with new respect.

Mrs. Odettes joined the men in the living room. "Breakfast is ready, Your Grace." She gave a slight curtsey; all her humility exposed for the Bishop's pleasure.

"Come, join us, Antoine. We have much to discuss." Vasai led the way into the dining room. He had not yet had his breakfast and was famished.

Curvise tried to eat, but could only pick at his food. His thoughts were on David. He knew Vasai had come to convince David to resign. Yesterday that would have been an impossibility. Today he was not so sure.

After breakfast they retired to Meric's office where Vasai took Meric's seat behind the desk. It was a position of power.

Curvise could not help but notice the portly stature of the two men in the room with him. He wondered if obesity were a prerequisite for advancement in the church. Had they always been overweight or had they started their careers like him, thin and sallow, and grown in stature as they grew in status?

"How is Father Proust doing, Antoine?" Vasai asked. It was the first mention of David since his arrival.

"Physically there's nothing wrong with him."

"Good. As I'm sure you know this . . ." he chose his words carefully, "setback of Father Proust's has escalated the necessity for action. The church does not want to appear too hasty. If the Father had been ill, perhaps?" Vasai hesitated just enough to allow his audience to feel he was giving them a chance to speak. It was the mark of a true persuader. He was being considerate, drawing support for himself and the difficult decision he had reached. "Yes, I know, Antoine. You have always contended Father Proust was not suffering from any physical ailment." The Bishop sighed. "This is a delicate situation and one I am sure we never expected to occur. However, I see no alternative but to ask Father Proust to tender his resignation. Under the circumstances, I am sure he won't object."

Meric nodded in agreement.

Curvise, however, did not sway. "I'm not so sure, Your Excellency. I have spoken to David before on this subject. He is adamant in his resolve to maintain his vows."

Bishop Vasai was incredulous. Speechless, he took a deep breath and expelled it slowly, biding his time. When he spoke, his words were slow and measured. "You mean to tell me that the thought of being publicly humiliated and possibly facing criminal charges will not persuade him to change his mind?"

Curvise shrugged. What could he say? David would never be the man Bishop Vasai had imagined.

"But he must!" Meric exclaimed, coming to Vasai's aid. "He cannot bring his shame down on us."

At once, Vasai waved down Meric's outburst. "No, we can't force him to resign and yes, that means he can bring this shame upon the church. It will be up to us to convince him to resign his vows. We cannot excommunicate him unless he agrees to give up his position in the priesthood. We can, however, if we so choose, bring in the state authorities to prosecute him for attempted suicide. They would find him guilty and sentence him to prison. He would go there as a priest."

Meric's jaw fell open. He was aghast. Not sure now which side to choose, he fumbled for words to defend David.

Vasai was quick to put him at ease. "Of course we won't do that. Father Proust has harmed no one but himself. If he refuses to resign, he will face the punishment the Holy Father deems proper and just."

Meric breathed a sigh of relief. The thought of seeing David hauled off to prison was too objectionable to bear.

"And if he has murdered someone?" Curvise was curious. "What would we do then?"

Vasai looked up with a pained expression. "I hope Antoine, that this is another one of your hypothetical questions?"

"Yes, of course it is. I'm just curious."

"Frankly, I don't know. We are not immune to the justice of any country we serve. I am sure there have been many occasions over the centuries when one of our own has had to face the consequences of justice." Vasai hesitated. "These dreams of Father Proust's. Are they just that?"

Curvise avoided a simple "yes" or "no." Instead he answered what he hoped had been the Bishop's unasked question. "There is no possibility

David could have been physically involved with those women. He never even knew what they looked like until he saw their pictures in the newspaper." Curvise had decided not to mention David's latest dream. Instead he pressed forward with forbidden subjects. "David thinks he is possessed. Have you given that supposition any deliberation?"

Antoine's words were like bricks, Meric thought. Each one building a crypt in which to bury Father Proust, and themselves beside him. Why could he not remain silent? But, again, the Bishop surprised him.

"As much as I hate to admit it Antoine, I have thought about it and I'm ashamed of those thoughts. We are living in a new and modern age. We have new understandings of diseases and new medicines with which to cure them. Like yourself, I have read some of Freud's ideologies. I don't agree with him totally. Quite frankly, sometimes he is a perfect idiot, but quite a few things he writes make sense. We have come out of the Dark Ages. I am afraid asking for an exorcism would be fruitless. While the church has not completely ruled out the reality of possession, it moves quite carefully in treating any matter as such. Father Proust would pretty much have to be flying around in mid-air to convince the Holy Father that an exorcism was imperative.

"Actually," Vasai said, smiling for the first time since the three men had entered Meric's office, "that is about what it would take to convince me." The Bishop's eyes hardened. "Do you think he's possessed?"

"He can't be," Meric interceded. "I refuse to believe David's possessed by demons." He spoke as if saying it would make it so.

Vasai turned on his subordinate. "Then how do you explain what has been happening to Father Proust?"

Meric looked to Curvise for help. When none came, he decided to be blunt. "Women."

"That's probably as good an explanation as either of us could give," the Bishop agreed, "but I think there's more to it than just a desire to have sexual relations with a real woman. Unfortunately, I don't have the answers." He looked at Curvise. "Antoine, you still haven't answered my question."

"At this very moment I would say yes, I believe David Proust is possessed." Curvise regretted the words the moment they were out of his mouth. They sounded different, spoken aloud, than they had when he had rehearsed them in his mind.

Vasai leaned back in his chair and spread his hands expansively, including both men in his dilemma. "There we have it, gentlemen. Jean-Paul believes it is the pain of celibacy that has driven David to his present state of mind. Antoine believes it is a demon. I appreciate your honesty, gentlemen, but the question remains." Vasai closed his eyes for a moment. "What do we do now?"

He had expected no answer and received none.

"I'll talk to Father Proust and try and convince him to see our side of this matter. If he still refuses to do the honorable thing, then he'll be subjected to whatever his Holy Father decides." Vasai pushed himself up from behind the desk. "Please take me to Father Proust, Jean-Paul."

Meric was up and ready, feeling oddly as though he had done more to assist David's case than Curvise. "Immediately, Your Excellency."

Curvise stood, waiting to be dismissed.

"Please wait for me here, Antoine. I wish to see you after I've spoken with Father Proust."

"Yes, Your Excellency."

                                        ***

Curvise stood when the door opened. Armand Vasai told Meric he would like a few minutes of privacy and closed the door softly behind him, shutting the Monsignor outside of confidentialities.

"Sit down, Antoine." Vasai ignored the comfortable chair behind Meric's desk and chose to sit next to Curvise. "It didn't take me long to realize what you said was true. Our young man is exactly of the mind you had told me he would be. I was quite blunt. I outlined all of the options available to him—his resignation, which would be kept in the strictest silence, commitment to a mental hospital for an indefinite period of time, excommunication, and possibly even legal action taken against him by the state.

"He's quite intelligent as I am sure you know and very much aware of his situation, yet his desire to remain a priest stays strong. I found his faith quite admirable. In fact, after meeting him, I find it hard to believe you can really think he is possessed." Vasai studied the priest next to him. "It was a posture of defense, wasn't it, Antoine? I can see it in your eyes."

"David's ill. His mind is simply under too much pressure."

"Then you don't believe him possessed?"

Curvise sighed. "I wish I felt I could honestly answer that question with a no, Your Excellency. However, I really don't know what to make of this. Common sense tells me possession was a word frequently used by our ancestors to explain the unexplainable. Perhaps that is what I am doing now. Perhaps it became an explanation because it was the truth.

"David Proust has been here over ten years. I have known him since the day he first arrived. He has never shown any inclination to do or be anything other than what he is—a fine young man whose only wish is to serve Christ. And then," Curvise spread his hands in a hopeless gesture, "suddenly he changes overnight. Give him a day or two and he won't even remember any of this. Why?"

"Suppression of guilt?" Vasai put forth. "Certainly not possession. But I know how you feel, Antoine. I believe he's sick and I will say so in my report to the Holy Father."

Vasai could almost see Curvise sink under the weight of his words. "There's nothing else we can do for him. I offered to pay, out of my own pocket, for his confinement in a mental hospital of his choice if he would only resign. He refused. Of course I know his family is more than capable of any expenses he might incur, but he simply refuses to give up his vocation. It's sad that his convictions can do nothing but harm him."

Curvise looked up sharply. "What will happen to him now?"

"I don't know. Any further discussions about the future of Father Proust will be taken up at the Holy See. It's disheartening to see an obviously fine young priest get caught up in a mess like this, but it happens. At times, it happens with a frequency that's alarming. We can ill afford to lose men like Father Proust, but what else can we do?"

Curvise could not answer the question. Instead, he asked one of his own. "Would you do me a favor, Your Excellency?"

"If it is in my power, Antoine. Of course."

"In your report to the Vatican, would you suggest to the Holy Father that it would be in his best interest to send David to a psychiatric hospital. I believe he could be cured of this—this affliction, but it will take a physician better skilled than me to find the real cause of his illness."

Vasai took the matter under consideration. It was a while before he spoke. When he did, they were the words Curvise had hoped to hear.

"Yes Antoine, I'll make that recommendation to the Holy Father."

"Thank you, Your Excellency."

The discussion at an end, Bishop Vasai reverted to addressing his colleague more formally. "Now, Father Curvise, please ask Monsignor Meric to step into his office. I must speak with him directly." Automatically Vasai pushed himself up and extended his hand. Curvise kissed the ring.

"It was nice to see you again, Antoine," he said softly. "I hope the next time we meet will be under better circumstances."

"Me too, Your Excellency. And thank you for your understanding." Curvise bowed slightly and left the Bishop to prepare for his meeting with Monsignor Meric.

***

"Who else knows of this matter, Jean-Paul?" Armand Vasai gazed steadily across the room at Meric. He had let his subordinate regain his seat behind the desk. He wanted Meric to feel comfortable and confident enough to give him straight answers.

"Besides myself, only you and Father Curvise."

"The priests in the rectory. Do they know or suspect anything?"

"They know David's been sick, but beyond that—nothing. His attempt at suicide has been dismissed as a symptom of his illness." Meric rubbed his hands together nervously.

"It must stay that way. When the opportunity arises, you will remind Father Curvise that this matter is never to be spoken of again."

"Yes, Your Excellency."

"As soon as the Holy Father has made his decision, you'll be informed of how to handle Father Proust. I caution you, Jean-Paul. Whatever instructions come, they are to be followed to the letter. It is imperative that you understand this." Vasai's voice rose in volume, but dropped in timbre. He left no room for Meric to doubt the importance of his words.

"I will do as I am commanded, Your Excellency." Obedience was the law of the church. Had it not been, Meric might have run from the room. The hairs on the back of his neck rose in fear as if someone, *something* were watching to see how well he could carry out orders.

"Until you hear otherwise, Father Proust is to stay inside the rectory. He is not to leave under any circumstances and he is not to have any visitors."

"Yes, Your Excellency," Meric said. Again he felt the cold hand of fear grip his heart, and wondered if he would ever be free of its presence.

CHAPTER EIGHT

François Martine took the most comfortable seat in Curvise's office. "How is Father Proust doing? I haven't seen him for a while."

"He's still a little weak, but getting better each day." Curvise found he could say the words without guilt. His faith would forgive the white lie he had just told. After all, it was to protect his church that he did not tell François it had been five days since he had last seen his friend—that he was no longer allowed.

"I'm sorry, Antoine. No one is allowed to visit Father Proust."

"Not even his physician, Monsignor Meric?"

"He is fine. He is eating and resting well. He has accepted his confinement as he has his faith. He has put his future in the hands of the Pontiff. We must do the same."

"I understand, Your Grace, but David and I are old friends. Surely a few minutes with him could cause no harm. I only want to wish him luck . . . and to say goodbye."

"No, Antoine. I am sorry. It's out of the question." Meric refused to surrender his authority.

"Then please, tell him I wish him luck and I'll be praying for him." Curvise suddenly realized he would never see David again. It was a sad feeling.

"I will see that he gets your message."

"With you as his physician, I'm surprised he's still alive," Martine joked. When his comment refused to bring a grin to his friend's face he asked, "Are you feeling okay, Antoine? You look a little under the weather."

"Hmm? No, I'm fine, François. I was just lost in thought for a moment. What brings you out on a day like today?" It had been raining earlier, but now the sun shone brightly through his office windows.

"Well, for one thing, it's a fine day. For another, I have a patient here." He looked closely at Antoine. "Are you sure you're not ill?"

"Yes, yes, I'm fine. Just a little tired." Sleep had been hard to find this past week. Curvise could not get David Proust off his mind. What would

78

become of his young friend?

Martine changed the subject. "How is your new nurse working out?"

"She's doing wonderfully. For someone so young, she's quite skilled. A real credit to the Catholic university she attended." Curvise tried to sound enthusiastic. It was hard when the only thing he really wanted was to be left alone.

"I was talking to her before I came to see you. She's well versed," Martine agreed. "I have a tonsillectomy scheduled next week. I'd appreciate her assistance?" He made it a question. Even among friends, protocol had to be observed.

"I'm sure we can arrange that. Have you spoken to Mother Superior?"

Martine dusted imaginary lint from his pant's leg. "Well . . . If you must know, no I haven't. You know how she feels about me. I was hoping you might arrange this little favor."

"Of course, François. Just let me know the day and time."

"You know," Martine mused, "it never ceases to amaze me why a young woman like that would want to spend the rest of her life as a nun. She's most beautiful, you know. And those dark eyes. They remind me of a woman I knew many years ago. She was from the Middle East. Palestine, I believe. Where's Sister Mary's birthplace?"

"You're shameless, François." Curvise laughed in spite of himself. "Only you could think such a thing! I don't know, but . . ." He turned to his friend with a wicked smile. "Of course, you could ask Mother Superior. I'm sure she'd be able to answer your question."

Martine's face fell instantly from fantasy into reality. "Never mind. It's not really important. I was just trying to make conversation."

The short silence between the two men was comfortable, each occupied with his own thoughts.

"Have you talked to Inspector Defont lately?" Martine asked.

"I haven't seen him." Curvise was suddenly interested. "Why?"

"Nothing of any importance. I just believe the man is going senile. He's got this fantasy that Camille Robéson's and Louisa Markey's suicides are connected."

"Connected!" Curvise was alarmed. "How?"

"Their clothing. It seems both of these young women took their clothes off and stacked them neatly in exactly the same order. I don't remember exactly in what order, but I'm sure Defont has it in his notes somewhere." Martine tried not to smile. The whole idea seemed so ludicrous it was hard not to laugh out loud. "That, and the fact both girls believed themselves pregnant." He snorted. "Can you believe it! You know I've never liked

Defont, but I have always respected him. Now, I'm not even sure he deserves that. I mean, how idiotic can one man be? I told him Louisa was a virgin. I know you told him the same thing about the Robéson girl. How in God's name can he possibly think these two girls were pregnant? How can he believe they thought they were?"

"I had heard a rumor Camille believed she was, but I had not heard the same gossip about Louisa."

"Evidently, Louisa confided her secret to her younger sister." Martine shook his head. "What do they teach children in school nowadays? Surely she was old enough to know the requirements."

"It was definitely suicide in both cases?" Curvise was beginning to doubt what he knew to be true.

"I don't see how it could have been anything else. I was the Robéson's family physician. They called me the minute they found her body. I told them not to touch anything and was there within twenty minutes. It would have been impossible for someone to get into her room without waking the entire family. She lived in the attic.

"I suppose it is possible Louisa could have a different story, but she was seen walking toward the end of a pier, alone, and she never came back."

Curvise was careful to keep his sigh of relief unnoticed.

***

For five days and nights, Monsignor Meric fretted by his telephone. Each minute of each day he expected it to ring, and then, he did not know what he expected. He just wanted this business over with. On the seventh day, when God rested from his labors, Meric received the phone call he had anxiously awaited. Although no introductions were made, he recognized Bishop Vasai's voice.

"When you retire this evening, leave the door to the rectory unlocked. You will be in your room before midnight. Every priest shall be confined to their rooms before eleven. Lock your doors and stay inside. Regardless of what you hear, no one is to leave their rooms. Is that understood? No one!"

"It will be taken care of," Meric said, but the phone line was already dead.

Sweat poured down his face and under his arms. He thought of asking Curvise for some form of sedative, but he could not afford to appear weak under the circumstances. It would be a sleepless night, but sleeping was something he could always do tomorrow night. *Afterwards*. He would be glad when this ordeal was finished.

Monsignor Jean-Paul Meric struggled to find the right words to tell his subordinates what he had been told. He did not want them alarmed. After spending most of the evening on the problem, he decided to be blunt. At ten, the usual hour the rectory retired, Meric told his priests: "Tonight, under no circumstances are you to leave your rooms. Lock your doors." He tried not to sound sinister. Under the circumstances, he failed miserably. Surprisingly, no one questioned his edict. Each of the priests had suspected that sooner or later David would leave the rectory in the darkness of night.

Meric checked the front door twice before climbing the stairs to his room. With his hand on the doorknob, he stopped and looked down the hall towards David's room. A single hall light cast grim shadows over the walls.

The priests never locked their doors at night, and yet . . . Meric wondered if David's door were unlocked. Fearful that something might go wrong if he did not take it upon himself to verify the priest's accessibility, he hurried down the hall to David's room. Slowly, he tried the knob. It was unlocked. Relieved he let go and retreated to his room, feeling like a coward and a traitor. There, he found he was unable to sit still. David had been a fine young priest. A friend. And he had turned away from him in his last hour. Was that not Apostle Peter's reaction when asked if he knew Jesus? Had the church not learned to better itself through history? Meric hesitated only a moment. It was not yet twelve. He would not stay long. Just a brief moment to let David know he was not alone, and then back to his room and the safety of a locked door. He walked back to David's room and knocked once.

"Come in," the young priest called, his voice rusty from non-use.

"How are you tonight, David?"

Father Proust turned to face the Monsignor. "Is tonight my last?"

"Yes," Meric told him honestly. "I'm sorry to see you go." He walked over to stand by the window, to stand close to a man he had learned to care about over the last ten years.

"Where am I to go?"

"I don't know," Meric said sadly. It seemed to be a time for honesty. "But wherever it is, it will be with friends."

"That is not my concern, Your Grace. The church has been my life since the day I was born. I have no fear of my safety within her folds. After all, we are all brothers."

"It's not too late, David," Meric offered. "You can still walk away from here."

David moved to sit on the edge of his bed. "Christ could have easily walked away from his crucifixion, but he didn't. He suffered and died for us. My fate is not so drastic. Whatever is in store for me, I will gladly accept as the will of God."

A cloud erased the faint light of the moon casting the room into total darkness. The hall light went out and footsteps could be heard on the wooden floor. David looked towards the door expectantly. Trying desperately to disappear, Monsignor Meric squeezed himself into the shadows. Bishop Vasai had said for him to be in his room after midnight. Surely it was not that late yet! Surely God would know his disobedience had not been purposeful— only driven by the desire to help a fellow human being at his time of suffering. Frantically, he clutched the cross that had always given him strength. Surely, fate would not punish him. He whimpered, unheard. He crouched, unseen. "Please," he prayed with all the earnestness he had ever possessed, "let the moon stay hidden. Let the dark hide me from my enemies. Please."

"Father David Proust." A voice of gravel called roll.

Meric shut his eyes tightly. He did not want to see. He felt rather than saw David rise from the edge of his bed, waiting.

"Yes, I am Father Proust."

"I am Father Zigman Bronski," the voice of the dark angel countered. "I come in the name of our savior, Jesus Christ, with an invitation for you to join us. If you so choose, it is of your own free will."

And Meric heard David's reply: *"I accept your invitation."* There had been other sounds—the quick, sure footsteps of David as he crossed the room and opened the door, the creak of a floorboard bearing the weight of two, possibly three men where it normally had held one, the door to the outside opening and closing downstairs with only a whisper of movement. When he opened his eyes, he was surprised to find the hall light illuminating the passageway and the empty bed where Father David Proust had once slept.

On unstable legs, he made his way to his room and shut the door soundly behind him. His heart was beating so loudly he thought he would waken the entire rectory. His hands shook, and sweat stung his eyes. After a moment's hesitation, he turned the key in the lock.

The power of the church was immense. This same church that had taken him into its fold and had never made him feel fearful and alone, now, for a brief instant, was a frightening place to be.

***

Not too far from St. Margaret, Edmund Defont kept his small apartment. Tonight, as usual, he could be found sitting in his favorite chair under a dim reading light. Lonely. He missed his wife in quiet times like this. She had been dead for over three years, but he still found times when he looked up, hoping to see her soft profile.

The investigative reports submitted by Officer George Rorke rested in his lap. The brown manila folder they were used to hiding in, stood alongside his chair, balanced precariously between his shoes. He was a solider at ease. The suicides of Camille Robéson and Louisa Markey nagged at him. His supervisors were satisfied with the coroner's judgment. The families had accepted the verdicts. Everyone connected with the two cases seemed content to let them fade from memory. Everyone, that is, but Defont. If it had not been for the clothes. Those damn clothes! Folded so neatly, placed so precisely. If it had not been for the vicious rumors of babies having babies. These were the threads that refused to be cut, refusing to set Defont free of his duties.

He put the reports back in the folder. Maybe François Martine was right. Maybe he was going senile.

He crossed the room in quick strides, coming to rest by the window. In the distance, the soft sounds of bells struck the hour. He counted them . . . ten, eleven, twelve. It was midnight, and soon it would be a new day. The night could show him nothing.

Next year he would be able to retire. Thirty years as a policeman. Two of those years he had spent in the army, killing men. He had seen too much of death for it to affect his thoughts. Death came easily. It was life that was hard to fathom.

There was a hole in his sock. His wife would have darned it for him before he would have had the chance to notice. As it was, he would have to do it himself. He missed her terribly. They had both wanted children, yet had none. For twenty-three years, they had carried a guilt neither deserved. Was that why he persisted with this case? Was he seeing the daughter he never had in the dark eyes of Camille? In the long dark hair of Louisa? How would he have coped to find his own child, a girl on the verge of womanhood, hanging from a noose or being dragged from the cold cruel ocean?

With a sigh, Defont plodded back to his chair and once more picked up the case files on the two teenagers. Something or someone had driven them into death. He was determined it would not go unpunished.

***

The knock on the door was explosive, impatient. Once. Twice. Antoine Curvise sat up and turned on the lamp next to his bed. He glanced at the clock on the nightstand. It was just after 1:00 a.m. He was surprised to find Sister

Grace standing in the hallway.

"Come quickly, Doctor," she said. "Mother Superior is having an attack."

Grabbing his medical bag, Curvise hurried after the floating robes of the fast departing Sister.

***

"I'm sorry we had to disturb you, Father," Mother Superior Monique said with short intakes of breath. She suffered from asthma. Curvise had given her a stimulant and now, with an oxygen mask over her face that she refused to keep in place until she had offered her apologies, she was breathing much better.

"You have not interrupted me." He patted her hand in a fatherly fashion. "You just rest and breathe as deeply as you can. In a few minutes, we'll try it without the mask." He pulled a chair over to the side of the bed. This was not the first time this had happened, and he knew the pattern well. Once the medicine allowed Mother Superior to resume normal breathing, she would be exhausted and fall asleep almost at once. He would stay with her until then, to make sure there were no complications.

She tried to take the mask off again. He smiled at her persistence, but held her hand. "We'll talk in the morning, Mother Superior. It will be a lovely day, and lovelier still if you are awake enough to enjoy it."

She managed a small smile and began to relax. Curvise's attention wandered around the room. The first thing he noticed was a crucifix over the door, and then the picture of the Virgin Mother holding the Christ child. The walls were stark white. The small bed was covered with a coarse brown blanket.

He glanced at Monique. Her breathing was normal and steady. She appeared to be asleep.

"Are all of your rooms like this one?" Curvise asked Sister Grace.

"Yes, Doctor."

"I should have known," he muttered.

"Did you say something, Father?"

"Just a prayer of thanks for your quick feet and steady hands," Curvise said quickly. He looked from Mother Superior to Sister Grace. "She shouldn't wake tonight, but if she does, put the mask on her face and call me." He picked up his bag. "She'll be okay."

He hesitated at the doorway and looked once more around the small room. It was exactly the way David had described the room in his dream.

Curvise did not go back to his apartment. Instead, he hurried across the plaza towards the rectory. This time he would see David. No one would stop him.

Even behind a locked door, Meric found he could not sleep. The events of the night were too fresh in his mind. His clothes were wrinkled from when he had lain in bed and tried to rest, but it had been useless. At last he had given up, and retired to his office. There, he left the door unlocked, no longer afraid, but terribly, terribly distressed. As was his habit, he ran his fingers through the little hair he had left. Usually it gave the effect he had just finished his toilet. Now, he ran his hands backward and forward. Wisps of hair curled around his forehead and stood on end. He sat in the dark of his office, staring at the hall. He expected no guests.

"Antoine!" he called to his surprise visitor.

"Jean-Paul," Curvise replied, surprised himself at finding someone up at this hour.

"Come in, Antoine. Sit down."

Curvise stepped into Meric's office. He made no attempt to turn on the light. The darkness seemed to suit his mood. "Why are you here in the dark, Jean-Paul?"

"He's gone, Antoine."

"Who's gone? David?"

"Yes."

Then he was too late. "When? Where?"

"They took him away at midnight." Meric's voice was hushed. He glanced around the room. Although he knew he and Curvise were the only two people there, he had to be sure.

Dejectedly, Curvise sat down. "Who took him?"

"Our brothers. They came tonight." Meric's voice rose a notch. "He went voluntarily. He was . . . happy, I would have to say."

"Do you have any idea where they were going? It's most important that I talk to David now. Immediately!"

"I'm sorry, Antoine. I have no idea where they went. I didn't even see who came for him. I only heard the one voice, Antoine. It was an old voice. He said his name." Meric paused, forcing himself to remember through his terror. "Father Zigman Bronski."

CHAPTER NINE

LaRochelle seemed empty. Cold winds blew off the Atlantic Ocean, chilling bones to the marrow. All Saint's Day came and went. The trees that had bloomed with beauty and majesty now stood bare and exposed for any who wished to glance their way. The grass in the plaza turned brown and lost its softness. Shrubs withered and hibernated. Nature became harsh, ugly.

An epidemic of influenza struck the city. The wards of St. Margaret's Catholic Hospital filled. The soft leisurely days of summer became long, dreary nights of labor.

The reality that Antoine Curvise had discovered two months ago of grave robbers who stole living victims in the dark of night, slowly faded into a loose thought that occasionally filtered through his mind. And yet, he never associated it with David Proust. David was, in Curvise's thoughts, safe in a hospital somewhere in France. Psychiatrists were taking care of him. In time, he would be cured and return to his friends. But cured of what? Dreaming? Curvise could no more weed the persistent thought from his mind than he could cease to enjoy life.

A new priest came to St. Margaret—a young man fresh from the seminary—dour, quiet, and shy. In time, Curvise thought, he would learn to like the young man. As it was, David's friendly smile and warm personality were still too vivid to replace.

Life continued its course in LaRochelle. Children were born. The old died. The fleet of fishing boats hauled out of the water and put into dry dock. Men bundled against the cold and worked leisurely to repair their means of existence. Wives complained the men had too much time on their hands, spending too much time in bars laughing and flirting. Women complained during the long winter months.

***

"You look exhausted, Antoine," François Martine said, cheerfully. The influenza had been a boon for his practice. "You need a holiday. Why don't

86

you go to Algiers and spend some time in the sun?" He sat down, crossing his legs carefully so as not to wrinkle his pants.

Curvise gave him a weak smile. "Algiers. Have you been there, François?" At that moment the thought was very pleasant. The warm sun and waters of the Mediterranean were most alluring.

"Yes. A few times. It was most agreeable. I've been there, Palestine, and Egypt." Martine fancied himself an amateur archeologist. "Fascinating places." He smiled, remembering his travels.

"Maybe some day."

"Yes, yes, that's what the peasants say. Maybe someday," François said. "Let's go now." Excitedly, he leaned over in his chair. "I'll take care of your expenses, Antoine. We'll call it my contribution to your good health." The small smile that played around his lips had grown.

Curvise looked at him in disbelief. "You're serious?"

"Of course. What do you say? Shall we visit the Sphinx? Stand at the base of the great pyramids and look to the heavens in awe? I tell you, Antoine, it's almost enough to make me believe in God."

Curvise studied his friend. One of the many pleasures of knowing François Martine was that one never knew what or where he was going. The man had an adventurer's heart and soul. He not only spoke of great journeys, he took them, sometimes at the drop of a hat. Just like now. All Curvise had to do was say "yes." A little word, perhaps, but one, sadly, he could not bring himself to say.

"As tempting as your offer is François, I'm afraid I can't. I have too much to do here."

"Like what?"

"Well, for one thing, I have to give the good sisters their annual physical."

"Bah! I'll assist you. In two days, we can proclaim all of your nuns healthy and fit to serve the sick." Martine saw no obstacles. He was still excited at the prospect of a holiday.

Curvise laughed for the first time in a long while.

"Are you laughing at me?" Martine asked suspiciously.

"No, François, no. I was just picturing Mother Superior's expression when I tell her you are going to examine her nuns."

Martine pursed his lips and frowned. Almost instantly the image formed and he, too, began to laugh. At once he turned to Curvise and tried to appear serious. "This is not a pleasant picture, Antoine." He gave up his facade. "Oh well, maybe we can find the time next year." He started to rise. "Algiers. That is where women have the eyes of Sister Franza," he said happily.

Curvise looked at his friend with arched eyebrows. "What has Sister Mary Franza got to do with Algiers?"

"I would bet my life, that's where she's from. Believe me, Antoine, I know these things. She is Algerian," he said proudly.

Curvise shook his head. "I'm afraid I still don't understand."

"Remember a few months ago? We were discussing Sister Franza, or actually, we were discussing what her heritage might be."

Their earlier conversation came back to Curvise. "Oh yes. You and your fixation with Sister Mary Franza," he chided Martine.

"Well, I told you I had dated a woman from the Middle East, but I could not remember from where she hailed. It was Algeria. She was part French and part Jewish. A marvelous combination. The bad side of both nationalities removed." Martine smiled wickedly.

"But what has that to do with Sister Mary?" Curvise persisted.

"Actually nothing. She just reminded me of my Algerian woman. If I could only remember her name . . ."

Curvise laughed again. "You're a scoundrel, François. You love women, yet can't remember their names."

"Ah, no matter. The image is there." Martine smiled. "Well, I really must go. So maybe next year we'll take a holiday in Algiers or Egypt?"

"We'll see." Curvise evaded committing himself so far in advance. Instead, he walked Martine to the door. They were surprised to find Sister Franza walking down the hall towards Curvise's office.

"Sister Franza," Martine exclaimed.

"Good afternoon, Dr. Martine." She looked past his shoulder to Father Curvise.

"May I help you, Sister?"

"If you're not busy, Father Curvise, may I speak with you please?" Her voice was melodic. It immediately brought to mind a sense of grace, the softness of violet petals.

"Certainly. Please, come in."

Both men stepped aside as she walked past.

Instead of leaving, Martine turned and followed her back into the office. "Sister Franza, may I ask you a personal question?"

Curvise cleared his throat. "Dr. Martine was just leaving," he interjected.

Martine looked at the shy nun who now stood in the center of the room, looking lost in her fragility. There was also a warning look in Antoine's eye that he did not miss. As always, chivalry overcame curiosity.

"Yes, please excuse me. I'll see you later, Antoine." He bowed slightly, and left the office.

Curvise shut the door and positioned himself behind his desk. "Please, have a seat, Sister. Now, how may I be of service?"

Sister Mary looked at him for a brief moment, then back to her lap.

Curvise sensed there was more than simple shyness keeping her quiet. She was uneasy about whatever it was she had to say. He waited. Whatever battle she was waging, she must win with her own resources.

Once again she looked up. This time her eyes met his and stayed. "I'm going to have a child."

It was Curvise who broke their stare. He was not sure how long it was before the shock wore off. A minute? Five? Ten? The only sound in the room came from the clock that hung on his wall.

"Are you sure?" he finally asked, avoiding her eyes.

"As sure as I can be," she replied without emotion.

The image of the rooms in the convent—small, white, a crucifix, and a picture of the Madonna flashed into his mind. *(David.)* The urge to ask who the father was *(David)* struggled to get past his lips. It took all of his fortitude to keep from asking the question. It did not matter now, he told himself. Perhaps it did not matter at all.

"First of all, we will need to positively determine if you are in that condition," he said discreetly. "I will need to take a blood sample."

Pushing back the sleeve of her robe, she approached his desk. Her arm was small and delicate.

Curvise drew the blood and wiped the needle mark with alcohol. She had made no sounds when he stuck her. She had said nothing since her admission.

"I'll have the results back in a couple of days, Sister. Until then, may I suggest you make no mention of this to anyone else?"

"As you wish, Doctor." Now, at last, she rubbed her arm. "Is that all?"

"Yes. I'll get in touch with you when the results are back."

He thought she was already gone when he sensed her hesitate in the doorway.

"Yes?"

"May I ask you a question, Doctor?"

"By all means, Sister."

"What was Dr. Martine going to ask me?"

Curvise blushed slightly and hoped she did not notice. "He was curious. Where were you born?"

She laughed, not loudly, but rather happily. "You may inform Dr. Martine I was born in Algeria."

Curvise smiled. "It will make him very happy to find out he was right. Now, if only we could teach him humility to go with his ego."

No one had a reason to suspect the events to come unless they had remembered the clichés of their parents and grandparents before them. The platitudes that had become just that, because of their truths. Their ancestors would have bolted the doors and hung their talismans of protection early on. *Bad news travels in threes.*

Curvise sat in his office organizing his patients' notes for the morning rounds. He had just sent the blood sample of Sister Franza to the lab with a fictitious name on the tape—*Madame Dusit.* A rush order.

The knock on the door and the voice that called was familiar. "It's Mother Superior Monique."

"Come in."

"A gentleman to see you, Doctor—Monsieur Proust."

Startled, Curvise expected to see David walk though the door. His excitement waned as an unknown elderly gentleman entered his office. His disappointment was evident, even to the elder Proust.

"I'm sorry, Doctor. I am David's father, Alain. Or perhaps I should say I was."

Curvise was confused. "Has something happened to David?"

"He died last week."

Mother Superior Monique let out a gasp, crossed herself, and bowed her head.

Stunned, Curvise could only stand and stare at his visitor. It took a few seconds before he snapped out of his melancholy mood. "Please sir, I've forgotten my manners. Sit down. Mother Superior, would you please bring us some coffee?"

"Yes, Doctor."

"I'm so sorry to hear this. You have my profound respects, Monsieur. David was a very special person to us. To me."

"I know, Father Curvise. In David's letters you are mentioned more than once, and always with fondness. That is why I came personally to tell you."

"I appreciate that. Especially now in your hour of suffering."

Alain Proust struggled to retain his composure. David's loss was tearing at his insides. "I have another . . ."

Mother Superior returned with a tray and coffee. Alain Proust waited until she had served them both and left the room. Only when the two men were alone did he continue.

"As I was saying, I have another reason for coming to see you, Doctor. You were David's physician." He paused, trying to be tactful, not accusatory. "David trusted you. How did you miss the problem with his heart?"

Curvise had been ready to take a sip of coffee when Proust made his statement. His arm froze, the cup only inches from his mouth. Slowly, he put the cup down and looked into Alain Proust's eyes. "There was nothing wrong with David's heart, Monsieur Proust. Not only was David examined by me, but also by my colleague, Dr. Martine. I can assure you, when we examined him, his heart was sound."

The color drained from the elder Proust's face. He fumbled with his coat. Searching the inside pocket, he pulled out a piece of paper. It had been handled roughly, gently, and with great sorrow. It was with trepidation that he handed it to Curvise.

Antoine read the letter. It was short and cold. "It is with deep regret we inform you that your son, Reverend David Proust, S.J. passed away on this day of our Lord, November 5, 1938. He died in his sleep. Cardiac arrest. All efforts to revive him failed."

Curvise dropped the letter on his desk. "I don't know what to say, Monsieur Proust. David was under an intense strain here the last several months. The illness that came during the storm left him weak and disoriented, but I never suspected for one moment his heart was this weak." He slammed his hands down on the desk, surprising Alain Proust and himself. "No! No, Monsieur, it wasn't. I would stake my reputation on that statement."

"I'm not here to question your medical abilities, Dr. Curvise," Alain said pulling yet another letter from his inside pocket. "I'm looking for an explanation."

Curvise took the second letter. It was old and dog-eared, written on the same rich ivory, watermarked stationery as the notice before it. The contents were almost identical, cold and impersonal. "It is with deep regret we inform you that your son, Reverend Michael Proust, S.J. passed away on this day of our Lord, December 9, 1905. He died in his sleep from heart failure." The letter slipped from Curvise's hand and landed on top of David's death notice. He looked to Alain for answers.

"My father received that letter, Dr. Curvise. Michael was my older brother. A priest like David. Exactly like David."

Curvise struggled to keep his thoughts in order. He could not make any sense out of what he had read. How could two members of the same family, serving the church, pass away under the same circumstances thirty-three years apart? It did not make sense. A hereditary defect, he wondered, but without much conviction. "Do you recall the circumstances of your brother's death?"

"I've racked my brain for the last few days trying to remember. I do recall Michael had become quite ill while serving in LeHarve. He was transferred to another parish, possibly a hospital, but I'm not sure. I know my father was very distressed at the time. He never found out exactly where Michael had been taken. His letter, like mine, came from the Vatican."

"And Michael's remains. What became of them?"

Alain Proust shook his head. "I don't know."

"And David's? Where are . . . where is he?"

"Entombed at the Vatican. I called." Alain reached for the letter, and sought out the name of the priest who had written it. "Father Rovich. He told me David's last wish was to be with his brothers in the Holy City."

"Did you inquire about Michael?"

"Then, no. Now, yes. Father Rovich said David was buried next to Michael." Alain took a deep breath. "We now have two members of our family entombed in the Vatican. Too many, don't you think, Dr. Curvise?"

"I don't know what to say Monsieur Proust. David was a good friend. A fine priest. A credit to his family and his church. I wish I had an explanation that would ease your pain. And mine." Curvise slumped back in his chair.

"I'm sorry, Dr. Curvise. I didn't mean to put my burden on your shoulders. But, I am glad I came. I can see now why David thought so highly of you."

The words ricocheted through Curvise's brain. Alain Proust could not have known. His only concern had been to help David. Not destroy him. Yet he could not strike the image. *Judas.* It was unjustified. *Judas.* It was a guilt with which he had to live.

"Do you intend to pursue this matter further?" Curvise asked, ready to help in any way he could. A pall had been cast over his church. It was one he did not understand or like.

Alain shook his head. "I can't bring David back, but I certainly intend to keep my grandsons from entering the priesthood."

"Andre's sons," Curvise said. "David spoke many times of his brother and nephews. Under the circumstances, Monsieur Proust, you are more than justified. I know I certainly would do the same."

Those seemed to be the words of comfort for which Alain was searching. His demeanor lifted immediately. "Thank you, Dr. Curvise." He stood to leave. "I've taken up enough of your time. It has been a pleasure to meet you."

Curvise shook Alain Proust's hand. The words he had left to say were inadequate, but he said them anyway. "Again, I am deeply sorry for your loss."

***

As expected, word of Father Proust's death spread like wildfire through the hospital and convent. If Curvise had expected anger at the news of David Proust's death, he was disappointed. There were tears and silent prayers, but outrage failed to come. How could it? Man had no control over life or death. It was all God's will.

But that did not make it easier to bear. Curvise felt sad, and the need to talk to someone. He hurried through morning rounds, anxious to be outside—anywhere but in the confines of the church. He placed a call to François Martine and asked his friend to meet him in the plaza at lunch time.

"I don't believe it!" Martine exclaimed on hearing the news of David's death.

"We are all destined to die, François."

"Yes, of course. I'm not disputing that fact, but dammit, Antoine! David's heart was sound. Healthy. I refuse to believe he died of a heart attack." Martine's statement was adamant. His face flushed with righteous fury. He glanced at Curvise and saw the pain. It was the same pain he felt. David had been their friend. "I'm sorry, Antoine, but I'll never believe David expired from a defective heart. Never."

"Is that your pride speaking or your heart?" Curvise asked. Both he and Martine had examined David. Neither of them was infallible. Slowly, he was resigning himself to the fact that he had missed the physical problem David had suffered. Even more slowly, he was coming to terms with the fact that he was, in a way, particularly responsible for David's untimely death.

A fidgety Martine crossed his legs, forgetting about the crease in his pants. "I know my limitations as a physician as well as you, Antoine. We are in a profession that is not perfect by a lot of standards." He paused. The specter of his words slowly gained weight. "By the knowledge we have and the methods we used, until my dying day I will never believe David died from a defective heart."

Until that point of the conversation, Curvise had not brought up David's uncle, Michael. "Do you believe physical defects are hereditary, François?"

Martine pondered the point for a few minutes. "To a certain degree, yes, especially when you speak of such things as hair and eye color, facial features, height." He stopped and looked at Curvise, suspecting he was being led down a path that might make him look foolish. "What are you suggesting?" he asked warily.

"David's uncle, Michael Proust, was also a priest. He died at age thirty-five."

Martine looked hard into Curvise's eyes. Not trusting his memory of their earlier conversation, he verified his facts. "Of a heart attack?"

Curvise nodded.

It was a while before either man spoke.

"A genetic defect, passed from one generation to the next," Martine broke the silence.

"I was under the impression that genetic defects skipped a generation. Of course I know there are no set rules. Only theories. Are you familiar with that school of thought?"

"Yes, of course. For example, a mongoloid child born into a normal healthy family. If you trace his heritage back, in most cases you'll find, skipping a generation, or sometimes two, other mongoloids in the family tree. Are you suggesting that David's family suffers from a hereditary ailment? One that we could not see or hear?"

"It's quite possible," Curvise agreed, "but like you, I find it difficult to believe it was his heart."

Martine was not sure now what to believe. "Why do you do that to me, Antoine? You were just starting to sway me to your way of thinking. I was just beginning to believe David might have suffered from a destructive family trait. And now you tell me you believe as I originally professed." Martine was exasperated. He had no patience with fools. Occasionally, even his friend crossed this unmarked border. "What do you want to hear?"

Curvise wondered what Martine would say if he knew the entire story behind David's illness. The dreams and the suicides. He wondered what his friend would say if he were informed Sister Mary Franza believed herself pregnant. The test results would be back in a day or two. If only he had not been the one to examine David. He would have had no problem believing his friend had suffered heart failure had he not heard through his stethoscope the organ pumping strongly and steadily. That made it impossible to believe.

But it was as impossible to believe his church had murdered David. Alain Proust had said he would let the matter rest. Curvise had not spoken those words.

Martine had asked what he wanted. "Just the truth, François. Is that so hard?"

The death of their mutual friend receded quickly into the hidden recesses of both men. Lingering with death was inviting it into your home. Life had to continue.

For a brief moment, Curvise wished he had the pipe he had given up smoking many years ago. His thoughts had circled and landed. The prior conversation at a standstill, he changed the subject.

"By the way, François, Sister Mary is from Algeria."

"I knew it!" Martine exclaimed, immediately happy again. He liked nothing better than to be right. "I told you she was. There's just something about a woman from the Mediterranean that appeals to me."

Curvise tried not to laugh, but could not help himself. "What is it about the women from Algeria that brings out the rogue in you?"

"I really don't know how to explain it to you, Antoine. That makes me very sad." Martine did not look sad. In fact, his face reflected a gourmet's appetite for the opposite sex. "I am attracted to the soft shade of their skin. Almond. Yes, I think I would label it almond. A fine rich color, Antoine. And, of course, their eyes. Their large, dark, mysterious eyes." He sighed and stared out into the autumn sky.

"You seem to me to have described the women of France. Are they not as you have so vividly portrayed?"

Martine thought about Curvise's question for a moment. "In words, yes, but the real essence is . . . well, it's the mixture. Most North Africans aren't pure. The Negroes are of course, but over the years the Arabs and the French and Jews have mingled and blended into the most alluring combination. It's quite remarkable. At least from my point of view." He sighed again.

"You don't see the disintegration of the French race through this intermingling?" Curvise was a nationalist. It was all right if others wanted to dilute their heritage, but he believed in the sanctity of the French people.

"We are a dying race now," Martine said. "Someday we'll be attacked by the Germans and lose our identity completely. Our day has come and gone. Too much blood of the pure Frenchman was spilled in the Great War."

Curvise was surprised by the comment. "I was under the impression you were looking forward to another war, François. Have you changed your mind?"

"No. It will come. I am only saying that when it does, we will not win. We will falter, and so will France."

"Our future sounds dismal."

"That, my dear Antoine, is exactly why I live for today, although I could have done without the news today has brought." Martine stood and looked at his wrinkled pants. "I must go. I have an appointment at two, and I see by the grand clock of St. Margaret that it is nearing that time."

"Thank you for stopping by, François."

Martine waved off Curvise's thanks and goodbye at the same time. "That's what friends are for."

For the second time today, Curvise read a simple statement as an indictment of his loyalty. He had done what he thought best for David—or had it been for the church? The persistent notion that he had sold out David in order to protect the church from a scandal rose and pricked at his thoughts.

Suddenly, it occurred to him. Sister Mary Franza. He had to see her and tell her he knew of David's dreams. Had to tell her . . . No, he should wait until the test results were back. Then he would tell her what he knew. And try to comfort her.

It never occurred to him that she might commit suicide like the others. She was not a child caught up in a supernatural nightmare like Camille and Louisa. Sister Mary Franza was a grown woman. A woman who had spoken to him of her alleged pregnancy with confidence. Surely she would understand it had only been a dream.

***

Ten after four that afternoon found Antoine Curvise waiting restlessly at the nurses' station for Sister Franza. She was scheduled to accompany him on afternoon rounds. Never an impatient man, he was today, anxious to see this day come to an end.

The phone rang. Sister Margaret picked it up and spoke softly.

Curvise watched her. Watched her face change from soft serenity to hard terror. Watched and wondered in a brief instant of curiosity what news could cause such changes in a person who was constantly subjected to the blood and pain and sorrow of the hospital. He did not have time to ask.

"Mother Superior has fainted in the living room of the convent, Dr. Curvise. You're needed there immediately."

***

Curvise leaned over Mother Superior Monique. This was more than just a fainting spell. Her heartbeat was erratic and quick, her pulse was weak, and her eyes were dilated. He fumbled with the wimple and headdress, unable to unfasten it quickly enough to suit himself. "Sister Grace. Remove her clothing. Quickly!"

He hurried to the phone in the kitchen and spoke urgent words into the mouthpiece. "Send a stretcher to the convent immediately."

By the time he returned to the living room, Sister Grace had expertly removed all of Monique's clothing, and modestly covered her with a light sheet. With only a white slip as her protection against the outside world, Mother Superior looked frail and small.

"How long has she been like this?" Curvise demanded.

"A few minutes. She came into the kitchen for a cup of tea and a cake." Sister Grace looked upset. "Of course, after hearing of Father Proust's death, who could blame her?"

"This is more than just a fainting spell, Sister. Did she complain of any pains in her chest or upper stomach? Along her arm?"

"No, Doctor. She finished her cake and tea and said she was going to the chapel to pray for Father Proust. The next thing I knew I heard her scream. When I ran to her aid, I found her lying on the floor. That's when I called for you."

"Where's the chapel?"

"Behind those doors." Sister Grace pointed to the far wall.

Slowly Curvise opened the doors and looked towards heaven. The angel that had frightened Mother Superior still flew. Closing the doors behind him, he gripped their handles until his hands hurt. It was all he could do to keep from screaming. Unable to stand alone, he rested the weight of his head against the hard wood.

The hospital attendants arrived. With efficient motions they transferred Mother Superior to the gurney, covered her with the same sheet that had protected her earlier, and then hesitated, waiting for Dr. Curvise's next instructions.

It was an effort to speak. "Take her to the emergency room. Get Dr. Martine over there immediately."

The attendants wasted no time in wheeling the gurney past the small group of nuns who had gathered in the doorway. Sister Grace started to follow them, but stopped. Dr. Curvise had not moved from his position at the chapel doors. He did not look at all well.

"Are you coming, Doctor?" She could not keep the alarm from her voice.

"No."

"But Mother Superior Monique needs you." She fought back her tears. Something was terribly wrong. Mother Superior was ill and yet Dr. Curvise refused to move. It was almost as if he were scared to leave the chapel and follow his patient to the hospital.

"She'll be fine."

Antoine closed his eyes, then opened them quickly. "Sister Grace," he called to her before she reached the exit. "Telephone Inspector Defont and tell him to come here as quickly as possible. Don't mention that he's coming to the others."

Her voice trembled. "What's wrong, Doctor?" What she really wanted to do was scream. *Why? Why is your face drawn in terror? Why do you stand rigid against the chapel doors like you are the last soldier on duty? What terrible secret are you keeping out or keeping in?*

"Please, just do as I ask." It was too late to answer her question.

Whatever was wrong had been wrong for a long time. There was no way to stop it now. His insight had come too late. Perhaps God would see His way to spare Mother Superior, at least. He should, Curvise thought. He had certainly reclaimed enough of His children for one day.

***

Edmund Defont took one quick look at Sister Mary Franza and found he had to turn away to breathe. At last he felt strong enough to look again.

"Who found her?" he asked Curvise.

"Mother Superior Monique."

Without emotion, Curvise watched the two hospital attendants, the same two who had arrived to transfer Monique to the hospital, take Sister Franza's body down from the rafters on which she had hung herself. The Rope of Chastity she had worn about her waist had been her instrument of death. It would take them only a few minutes, Curvise thought, to take the nun from the heights of the chapel into the bowels of the morgue.

Defont waited until the body had been removed before he began walking slowly up and down each of the five aisles searching for her clothes. He found them on the first pew, stacked neatly. Her shoes were placed precisely on top as he knew they would be.

***

Antoine Curvise had failed. He had failed his friend David Proust and now, he had failed Sister Mary Franza. Sitting in his room that night, staring at the door, he waited for it to open. He was not sure who would enter, only that he expected someone would come to his room.

The knock came. He called out "come in" before it had a chance to be finished.

"Are you all right, Antoine?" Monsignor Jean-Paul Meric stood in the doorway.

"Yes, Your Grace." Curvise started to get out of his chair, but Meric waved him down.

"Sit. May I join you for a moment or two?"

"Yes, please." Curvise tried to sound any way but how he felt.

"Is this the end of it?" Meric asked. He avoided Curvise's eyes.

"Yes," Curvise finally said. "She told me she was pregnant. I didn't believe her and I still have my doubts. We'll know after Dr. Martine finishes the autopsy tomorrow."

"Like the other two?" Meric was cautious in his approach. He saw this as an ending. The last thing he wanted to do was entice this entire affair into a new beginning through an incantation of the wrong words.

Curvise spread his hands helplessly.

"Do you understand any of this, Antoine? I've tried to straighten it out in my mind, but I'm afraid I can't find any reasonable explanation. Was Father Proust possessed? Is there such a thing—a demon who rides the winds searching out the most faithful priests?" Meric was in a morbid mood. Frightened.

"If you had asked me that question this time last year Jean-Paul, I would have laughed and said no. Now, I no longer know what to say."

"Antoine! How can that be? We are grown men. How can we believe in spirits and demons? I have never believed in possessions. *(Until now, he thought.)* I've never been a frightened man. *(Until now.)* The church has been home for most of my life. I love Christ and His teachings. I know that evil exists in the world, but how can I believe in supernatural spirits?" *(Tell me that I can't, Meric prayed. Tell me it's not possible and I'll forget my imagination.)*

"Fortunately Jean-Paul, we are not supposed to believe in the supernatural. We are to believe only in Christ and His teachings. That is all very nice when the world goes forward in its natural rhythm. But, when the natural flow of life is upset, what is left to believe in except for something that is not natural?

"David was the first to mention demons. He told us both, he was possessed. That he had seduced two women, although we both *knew* he could not possibly have done such a thing. And yet . . . What force was at work those nights, Jean-Paul? Surely, not the merciful work of God.

"David never knew the women and, yet, at the time each of them died, he became ill, complaining of intense headaches and pain. I had no medicine at my disposal to ease his suffering. I thought he was battling a psychological disorder. *I* recommended he see a psychiatrist. I did not believe him. I refused to admit there's more in this world than we are willing to acknowledge. Now he's dead. Three women are dead." Curvise looked up and caught the Monsignor in his steady gaze. "All that remains of this matter is you and me."

"And Bishop Vasai," Meric added quickly, unwilling to be left out on a limb with only Curvise as protection. "We did what we thought was best. Who can blame us?"

"No one. We did what we thought best, but it wasn't enough. Now we must live with that as our penance."

Meric's fears brought him back to Sister Franza. "She couldn't possibly be pregnant, could she? I mean, unknown to us, David could have met her in the hospital. They might have arranged a rendezvous."

Curvise shook his head. "He couldn't remember her face, although he wanted to, very badly. He felt he could save her if he could just remember her face. But her room he described perfectly."

Meric shuddered.

"Where did they take David after he left?"

"I don't know."

"Do you think you could find out?"

Suddenly Meric regretted coming to Curvise's room. "I will not inquire, Antoine. As far as I'm concerned, this episode is closed."

"I am surprised at you, Jean-Paul. David was a friend. Don't you think that, as his friends, we should try to find out what happened here? What happened to him?"

This time it was Meric who shook his head. "The matter is closed, Antoine." He stepped out of the room and closed the door solidly behind him.

CHAPTER TEN

François Martine guided the scalpel with expert hands. It cut easily into the dead flesh. The news of Sister Franza's suicide had brought a cold, sinking feeling to his stomach. "What kind of madness has gripped us, Defont?" he had asked when the body was delivered. "Is there a disease in the air driving young women to this lunacy?"

He thought of those unanswered questions now as he made a long cut in Sister Franza's abdomen, exposing her organs: all healthy—stomach, liver, intestines, uterus. He had not been asked to verify if she were pregnant. Like the others, she had been a virgin. Martine would have been very much surprised to have found otherwise. Still, he cut just the same. He would find no sins here.

Deftly, he opened the uterus and separated the pliable organ. His touch was sure. His findings almost complete and then . . . Hidden behind the white gauze mask, his jaw grew slack. His eyes widened. He glanced up at the windows of the examination room's doors. They were empty.

The madness now had its cold hands on his thoughts—and he was alone. Mechanically, he stitched his prior incisions closed and cleaned up the examination room, erasing any evidence of what he had stolen from the body.

***

François Martine was not sure how long he had sat at the small desk outside the examination room massaging his temples. The coroner's report was complete except for one line. Twice he had started to write "virgin." Frozen between his fingers, the pen refused to move.

It was impossible, yet he had seen the fetus with his own eyes. Again he had glanced at the examination room doors, unsure if he was happy or frightened to find himself alone. Had she known it was inside her?

As he thought about it now, he remembered how he had forced himself to study it as he would any unusual condition found during an autopsy. The apparition had been human, yet incomplete. It had been alive. Yet, it had not.

Already, the fetus was being reabsorbed by its mother's body. It would never have been born. Still, a malignant life had somehow managed to invade the body of Sister Franza. How? Martine could not say. It was a question he wished had never been asked.

But there was no doubt. *It had been inside her.*

Even as he sat in the attendant's chair, Martine slammed his hand down upon the desk. The pain was real. What he had seen was real.

François Martine shuddered against the memory, and quickly scribbled the nun's true state—*virgin*. Then, as if it were the enemy, he dropped the pen and stood. He had to get out of this place. Out into the fresh air where there were no more reminders of what he had done.

Burned with that day's trash, the fetus was gone. Sister Mary Franza was innocent, and innocent she would stay to the world. François Martine carried no judgments. She was just a flower who had died in the winter cold.

***

"She was pregnant, Antoine. Why do I have to keep repeating this?" Martine's nerves were on edge. "I removed the fetus and had it burned."

"It was only a dream, François. What you say is impossible." Curvise repeated his words again. It seemed to Martine that was the only thing his friend could say.

"A dream. Whose dream? Yours? What nonsense is this? Listen to me, Antoine. She was pregnant *and* she was a virgin."

"Are you sure?"

"I've told you three times. Yes, dammit, yes! Yes, to both parts of your asked and answered question. I don't understand it either, but I do know enough to get past square one and ask the other, more intelligent questions this situation brings to mind."

Curvise had never imagined Sister Franza could be pregnant. The dream had become a nightmare. "David Proust," he said finally.

Full steam into his own thoughts, Curvise's comment brought Martine up short. "David? What has David got to do with all this?"

"Sit down, François. I'll tell you what I know."

***

Every December for the past fourteen years, François Martine took his holiday. This year he had been planning on revisiting Egypt. At the last minute, he changed his plans and decided to spend his holidays in London.

The dour English would fit his mood.

Had anyone other than Antoine Curvise told him the same tale, he would have undoubtedly recommended them for psychiatric care. Had he not seen the fetus with his own eyes, held it in his hands . . . The ghastly image still turned his stomach.

A man seducing a woman through her dreams—his dreams. Impossible! Although the idea intrigued him, dreams were not social gatherings. It might be a pleasurable experience, but even in the ancient religions of India where shaman's spells granted the wielder the power to rape a woman by incantation alone, this metaphysical union was certainly not capable of renewing life.

Camille Robéson and Louisa Markey. Was it guilt or fear that had driven them to lessen the value of their lives?

Antoine had mentioned possession. Possession was religious hogwash. A weak excuse for a man's inability to cope with the problems that surrounded him each day, Martine thought. Blame a demon. Point a finger at a ghost. At anything except one's self. Repressed anger. Repressed sexuality. Repressed this and repressed that. Excuses. Weaknesses men created to save their miserable egos. It hurt to think David Proust, his friend, had been caught up in this old wave of repression.

The more Martine thought about it, the less he believed David was capable of committing the acts Curvise had so vividly described. He had known David Proust for ten years. Known and liked him. He had understood why others respected and held affection for the young priest. It simply could not be helped. At times, nature endowed the world with such men. And, damn it, took them too soon away.

And the beloved church to which David had dedicated his life—what hypocrites they had turned out to be. Instead of following Curvise's advice, they had sent David to . . . God knew where. A dark asylum that had sucked the life out of him. Martine wondered—did the integrity of the Almighty have to be preserved at all costs? It seemed the Catholic Church, as noble and powerful as it acted, could not withstand the threat of scandal.

Frustrated and angry, François wanted to clear David's name, but he had no idea how to even begin such a task. It would be best to get away for a while and let his head clear. Yes, London would be appropriate for his holiday this year.

***

The week before Christmas, the Catholic Hospital was quiet. Good

Christians never died during the holidays. Sister Grace knocked and stuck her head inside Antoine Curvise's office.

"Inspector Defont to see you, Father." She had taken over Mother Superior's duties while Monique recuperated.

"Thank you, Sister. Please show him in." Curvise had known Defont would come eventually. His only surprise was that it had taken almost three weeks since Sister Franza's death.

"Father Curvise." Defont nodded. As usual, the policeman seemed to fill the office.

"Inspector Defont, Edmund, how are you?"

"I'm tired, Antoine," Defont said. "Tired and confused."

"How can I help?"

"Tell me the truth?" Defont was already resolved to hear nothing.

"The truth about what, Inspector?" But Curvise knew.

"We've known each other many years, Antoine. Since grammar school. I've never deceived you. I have always respected you as a priest and a man. I liked and respected Father Proust too, as did everyone in LaRochelle who knew him.

"I didn't know the three women: Camille, Louisa and Sister Franza. I am sure I would have liked them also."

Curvise looked down at the top of his desk. He was sure Defont could see the shame in his eyes.

"If nothing else, they were citizens of our country and, as such, deserve the same rights and considerations we all expect. None of them deserved to have their lives ended so early. I can't bring them back to life, Antoine, but I can and will find out why their lives ended. They are all connected, you know." It was not a question.

"I don't understand, Edmund. If they are connected in some way, it is that they are all dead. Nothing more."

"Of course. That does not seem to rouse your suspicions, but it has certainly raised mine. I keep asking myself why, Antoine. Why are they all dead? And I keep getting the same answer. Because somehow they were all connected." Defont's voice remained steady. He had fought this battle before. With his superiors. With himself.

Curvise appeared to consider the words he had just heard. He straightened an unkempt pile of papers on his desk and cleared his throat.

"Coincidence, Edmund. Similar situations that have caused terrific grief. Nothing more. The drastic endings of these lives makes it hard to view them impartially." Even as Curvise said them, he knew the words sounded weak.

"Coincidences!" Defont exploded. It was like watching a train wreck.

"Like the fact each of the young women undressed and placed their clothes in exactly the same manner? Each one was a virgin? That each chose to end their lives prematurely? Those cannot be brushed aside as simple coincidences, Antoine."

Curvise grew decidedly irritated at the tone Defont had taken with him. "Just what are you driving at, Edmund?"

"I've told you. These three women were driven to their untimely deaths. But wait. hhre are a couple of similarities I forgot to mention." Defont reached into his coat pocket, pulled out a note pad and began to read: "Sister Mary Franza. Born, June 1, 1908 in Algiers. Her father was French. Her mother, Jewish. Camille Robéson. Born May 5, 1924 in LaRochelle. Father and mother were both French but her grandmother was Jewish. Louisa Markey. Born January 10, 1924. Father and mother also both French, but once again her grandmother was Jewish."

Curvise shook his head in disbelief. How far had Edmund gone in search of a common thread?

"Is it a similarity, Antoine, that each of them believed they were with child?" Defont asked coldly.

Curvise started to protest, but Defont stopped him. "I could be wrong. Maybe it really was the blood of Madame Dusit you sent to the laboratory. Just because it was the same type as Sister Franza's does not necessarily mean it was her blood. You might even call that a coincidence." Defont was vicious. "What were the results of that test, Antoine?"

It no longer surprised Curvise to find Defont had dug so deeply into the nun's death. He supposed he would have been disappointed had the big policeman not. Defont was a meticulous man.

"The results were negative."

"That must have made Madame Dusit very happy," Defont commented sadly. All of his previous anger vanished. It was easy for Curvise to read the pain in his eyes.

"I've been told by my superiors to drop this investigation immediately, Antoine."

"I can't help you, Edmund. I'm sorry." And he was. "I wish I could."

"I believe you, Antoine. Like myself, you have to follow orders. I must drop this investigation as you must remain silent. Because of our devotion to duty three, possibly four lives have been taken away under circumstances that defy normalcy. We have lowered our standards a bit, wouldn't you say? As in the Great War, life has once again become cheap."

***

Defont's visit had an unsettling effect on Curvise. Life had indeed become cheap, yet its price had been raised. Like honor. It was easy to speak of life and duty and honor, but they were just terms to fit the circumstances of the moment. The Great War had shown him where life was valued. Somewhere between the dirt of a grave and the bloodstained sheets that hid the dead. Life wasn't cheap. It was worthless.

What of honor? Duty? Men cursing God for the pain He had inflicted on their pitiful bodies. Honor could be lost with a single bullet or a simplemisstep. It was unfair of Defont to accuse him of having no honor. His duty was to the church. He had to believe that. Without that, he had nothing.

So why was guilt pounding at his door each night? What would be served if the truth were known? It would not bring back the dead or make their dying more comfortable. It would serve no purpose.

"But it would," he said aloud. "It would prevent it from happening again." But exactly what "it" was, Curvise could not say. A demon riding in on storm currents? A priest being host to unholy spirits? It suddenly dawned on him that his life was unimportant. To speak out would seal his fate. Perhaps he, too, would have a heart attack—like David.

The church bells tolled the midnight hour. Again, Curvise sat and waited for the knock on his door. Another night passed. It appeared he was being given another day to live. Another day in which to fight the demon that waited outside his door.

***

"Your Grace," Curvise greeted Monsignor Meric in the dining room. He had come to have breakfast with Meric—to break bread and then break the silence that had grown between them.

Meric had become uneasy, fearing Curvise would not stay silent. Yet, when Curvise had mentioned the early morning get-together, Meric had been unable to find an excuse to avoid his friend.

"You don't look well, Antoine. Are you sleeping?"

"No, Jean-Paul, I'm not. I won't be able to sleep until I find out what has happened to David Proust."

"What do you mean?" Meric was exasperated at Curvise's insistence David's death was not a natural occurrence. He sighed heavily and took the opportunity to make sure no one else was within earshot. "Why do you insist on pursuing this matter, Antoine? Why can't you accept it as God's will?"

"Because it is not God's will," Curvise said. "God does not diminish life. Men do, Jean-Paul. Only men diminish life. I have to know what happened to

106

David. I will know." Curvise was determined to force the truth from Meric. Funny, he thought. Defont had been determined to force the truth from him and he had failed. Why did Curvise expect to succeed?

Meric was fearful of the subject. Like Curvise, he, too, wanted to know the truth. He was not an ogre, uncaring and heartless. The events of the past year were too fresh and real to be put aside with ease. Several times he had picked up the phone intending to call Bishop Vasai and demand some answers. Each time he had put the receiver down, his hands shaking. He looked down at his hands now. They rested on the tabletop, calm and steady.

"I'll try and find out something," he whispered. "It may be our ruination, Antoine."

"I would not mind entering the gates of heaven by your side, Jean-Paul."

"And the truth shall set us free," Meric added. "You're a bastard, Antoine."

Curvise smiled. "But an honorable one, Jean-Paul."

CHAPTER ELEVEN

"Your Excellency. It's Jean-Paul Meric." Monsignor Meric's voice wavered, but only for a moment.

"What can I do for you, Jean-Paul?" The Bishop was curt. He sensed Meric's call was not good news.

"I've been speaking to Father Curvise. He . . . *we* would like to know more of Father Proust's death."

"I was under the impression this matter was closed."

"It was, Your Excellency, until the unfortunate death of Sister Franza." Meric was hesitant to mention her name. He had written Vasai about the nun's death, sparing no detail, but he had not known of her pregnancy; only of her belief that she was.

"Just what is it you and Antoine want to know?" Vasai asked tersely.

"Father Curvise was wondering where David was taken. How he died."

"And you are of the same mind?"

Meric almost said no. "Yes, Your Excellency. I think we have the right to know what happened to our friend." The Monsignor was surprised to find once he had committed himself, it was almost a relief.

Vasai's voice turned to honey. "Let me get back to you, Jean-Paul. This may take a few days. A week at the most. Will that be satisfactory?"

"Yes, Your Excellency." Meric was almost happy. But *almost* is a powerful word he thought as he hung up the phone. He wiped his brow free of sweat. It was becoming second nature. He had been sweating a lot lately.

***

Vasai disconnected Meric with the touch of a finger. Dial tone buzzing in his ear, he rang for the long distance operator. "I wish to make a person to person call to Lord Cardinal Emanuel Gaston. He's at the Vatican. Rome, Italy."

Why? He examined his nails—their square cut corners and buffed surfaces. Why was there always someone who persisted?

Father Antoine Curvise, Vasai had known him for many years. Curvise was an honorable man. A physician without peers. Why, Antoine? Why did it have to be you?

There was not the rending of cloth or the moans of the bereaved. Just the same, Armand suffered a loss. At the moment of Meric's fateful call, Vasai's friendship with Antoine Curvise was terminated. The Bishop's duty to the church that nourished and kept him overrode any other loyalties he might harbor.

Meric could be easily handled, he knew. A promotion would ensure the Monsignor's silence and ease his conscience. *Bishop Jean-Paul Meric.* Yes, that would satisfy him. Vasai thought briefly of elevating Father Curvise to Monsignor, but the thought ended quickly. Antoine was not the type to be bought off—damn him!

Armand had been recently notified that he was to head the Department of Antiquities. This meant not only his elevation to Lord Cardinal Armand Vasai, but a permanent move to the Vatican on a full time basis. He had been led to believe it was a prestigious position and one from which he would spend his days among the wealth of the Catholic Church. He had been planning another to take over his position in Bordeaux, but now . . . Meric would do. And probably just as well.

The phone rang, interrupting his thoughts. In a bad accent, the long distance operator informed him his caller was on the line.

"I have need once again of your Brothers," Vasai said quietly into the receiver. He listened to the brief reply and supplied some additional information.

Antoine Curvise wanted to know what had happened to David Proust. Well, he would. Very soon. It was a shame, Vasai thought. Curvise had done a wonderful job at St. Margaret's Hospital. LaRochelle would miss him.

***

"A few days, a week at the most," Meric said excitedly. "His Excellency has assured me we will know." He faltered for a moment. "We still want to, don't we, Antoine?"

"Yes, if for no other reason than to sleep at night."

"You don't really suspect David was killed?" Meric shuddered at the thought, but it was a most delicious shudder. The intrigue of this whole affair was intoxicating.

"I don't know what to believe anymore," Curvise said. "We have not always been a church of kindness, Jean-Paul. One has only to read our dark history to understand that power can corrupt."

The Monsignor's face turned ashen.

Curvise was quick to apologize. "I didn't mean to alarm you and, no, I don't believe David was killed. But his death has left too many unanswered questions." He decided to take Meric into his confidence. "Sister Mary Franza was pregnant," he said.

Meric's face paled even more. When he managed to speak, his voice was almost a whine. "I don't understand! You told me the tests came back negative."

Curvise said nothing and the Monsignor regained some frantic control. "How, Antoine? How could she have been pregnant? She was a virgin." He stared at Curvise through the narrowed eyes of one who feels he has been duped. "Or was that a lie also?"

"No, Jean-Paul, she was a virgin. No matter. She would not have carried it to term. It would never have been born."

Meric closed his eyes, wishing desperately that when he opened them Curvise would be gone. It was not to be. "She knew?"

"Yes. Not of the circumstances surrounding the fetus, but she knew she was pregnant."

"Then why did she kill herself if she had already accepted the fact she was with child?"

"I'm afraid we'll never know."

"Then how will . . . Was it David?"

"Yes."

"Antoine, you knew this when you came in here, yet you neglected to make any mention of it until now." Meric thought about his phone call to Bishop Vasai. He was truly frightened now. "Father Proust is dead. How will knowing what happened to him answer any of these questions? We may have put our necks in a noose, and for what?"

"So we can enter the gates of heaven together?" Curvise said with a gentle smile. He was untouched by Meric's fear.

"That is not funny, Antoine. Not funny at all."

"You needn't worry, Jean-Paul. We'll get our answers. I believe Bishop Vasai knows them. We have only to wait."

Curvise had done a lot of thinking about the matter. The long sleepless nights had afforded him many opportunities to think clearly. The realization that what had happened to David had happened before, had taken shape slowly, but the proof had been supplied by the church itself, delivered by the hands of Alain Proust. Reverend Michael Proust had suffered David's fate before him. The church kept records on everything, Curvise knew.

Somewhere someone knew the answers. He was positive he would find out soon.

"There's more to this than you're telling me," Meric accused.

Curvise shrugged his shoulders. "We'll know soon enough, Jean-Paul."

***

A light snow dusted the cobblestones of LaRochelle's streets. Warm roofs kept it from accumulating on the tops of houses. The constant drip of melting ice watered dormant shrubs, washed clean the outside porches, fell on unaware heads, on cars, and on bicycles. If LaRochelle had been in order, it might have sounded like music. But LaRochelle was not in sync with the world, and the sounds of melting snow quickly turned aggravating.

The sun set on Christmas Eve. Raindrops turned to icicles and the streets began to glaze. People rushed home. With a winter storm approaching, it would be best to be indoors, safe from the weather and anything else that might wander into the city. Monsignor Jean-Paul Meric was scheduled to say midnight mass. The cathedral would be filled, storm or no storm.

At eleven-thirty, he came downstairs. He was about to leave the rectory for the church when the phone rang. His moment of private meditation shattered, he hesitated, deciding if he really wanted to be disturbed. Reluctantly, he made his decision, and entered his office to answer the phone.

"Monsignor Meric."

"Jean-Paul, Bishop Vasai."

A twisted strand of emotion ran through Meric. It had been six days since he had requested information on David Proust. He had never expected to hear from Vasai during the holiday celebrations. With the thought of a reprieve for at least today and tomorrow, a certain peace had come over him.

"I have some news for you, Jean-Paul."

Meric tightened his grip on the receiver and pushed it closer to his ear. "Yes, Your Excellency."

"After your sermon tonight," Vasai said slowly, tantalizingly slow, "I want you to announce to the congregation that you are being elevated in the church. From the moment the bells chime the midnight hour, you will be forever called Bishop Jean-Paul Meric of LaRochelle."

What poet or orator could describe the emotions of a man born into a middle class French family in the late 19th century with a future that might include an apprenticeship in a relative's tailor shop? Not a handsome or charming child, Meric had been a plain, slightly awkward boy who had had trouble making friends. He had pushed to be liked. Sometimes, too hard. The

111

early years, unkind, remained so during his formative period when men were separated from merchants.

Only one place had offered him refuge. A place where he could revel in solitude among icons far greater than mere dreams. No one in his family had fought his declaration to enter the seminary. It was as though they knew he had chosen a place for himself where he would be safe.

And that was all Jean-Paul Meric had sought. A place to be safe. Finding a needed outlet for his pent up energy, he worked and worked hard, never resisting the rules and, with time, slowly rose above his peers. A Monsignor at fifty-five, and now, at sixty-five when most men dreamed of leisure hours and a retirement check, Jean-Paul Meric was to become a bishop. A molder of religious theology that might effect the next thousand years of history. Was it any wonder he beamed as he said midnight mass to a congregation of his peers on Christmas Eve, 1938? No, not his peers, he corrected himself. Not any longer. Only those who served from the same position of power he now held could rightfully call themselves his peers.

***

Antoine Curvise buttoned his collar. Tonight he was dressed in his black suit—his vestments. He would attend midnight mass, not as a physician, but as a priest of the Roman Catholic Church. For the first time since becoming a priest, the feeling of exhilaration and pride failed to raise his spirits. For the first time, he felt ashamed of his vocation.

This is not my church, he had argued with himself. My church is kind and gentle, unafraid of scandal. We are too strong, too powerful to let any demon come between us now. Five hundred years ago, a hundred years ago, maybe. We might have faltered a bit. But not now. Not in this day and age.

Slipping on his suit coat, Curvise looked at his watch. It was a quarter to twelve.

The knock on his door was soft, barely audible.

"Come in."

Stillness. The knock came again. Curvise found it necessary to open the door himself. He had expected to see one of the nuns or a hospital attendant in need of his services. He was wrong.

"Father Antoine Curvise?"

Curvise's eyes widened. Was the light in the room playing tricks with his vision? Standing before him, the black-hooded priest partially hidden under a robe looked deformed, even grotesque. A wave of fear rose and surrounded him.

"Yes," he forced himself to say. "I am Father Antoine Curvise."

"I am Father Zigman Bronski." A hand appeared from beneath the sleeve of the coarse robe. Curvise looked down and the sight of it made him want to turn away. The index finger was missing. A portion of the little finger had been severed. Scars lined and criss-crossed the upper portion of the palm. Almost reluctantly he reached out and grasped the hand, expecting it to be cold and hard. He was surprised to find it warm and firm. Not at all frightening.

Bronski held their handshake. "You need not be afraid," he said. "I come with an invitation for you, Antoine Curvise, to join us in serving our brothers."

For the past week, it had been easy to say yes. Curvise had said it a hundred times. Now, staring into a demon's face hidden under a hood, that same "yes" was difficult to find.

"I have no choice in the matter, do I?"

"You are under no obligation to accept this invitation. If you choose to come with me, it is of your own free will."

Bronski released Curvise's hand. He was free. Free to make the choice he thought he had made long ago. But the affirmation would not come. He remained silent.

The hooded priest sensed Curvise's fear. It was not the first time he had run into the emotion. "No harm will come to you, Father Curvise. Your services are needed. Can you refuse the pleas of your sick and hurt brothers? Can you refuse the cries of help from your own kind?"

Curvise looked up sharply, but his guest's face remained hidden. The ancient voice remained silent.

"Yes," he finally managed to say. "I'll come with you."

It took but a few minutes to pack his belongings. A battered valise that had once belonged to his father—a gift when he had left for the seminary—held all of his worldly possessions.

"Should I leave a note?" was said and forgotten at once. He had no idea what he would have written. He put on his topcoat and, without looking back, followed Father Bronski from his room.

Outside, the cold air reverberated with the strains of Handel's "Messiah" echoing from St. Margaret's Cathedral. The midnight mass had begun. The street was deserted. Those residents of LaRochelle not safely tucked away in their apartments were inside the church. There would be no witnesses to his departure.

Two sets of footprints marked the walk from the small apartment Curvise had lived in for the last fifteen years to the street and a waiting automobile.

Covered in the same black hood and robe as his guide, the driver stayed silent. The car door opened. Curvise's mind closed.

He should have declined the offer, he thought suddenly. Bronski had given him a choice. Was it too late to turn back? He started to ask and thought better of it. He had committed himself. To what and where, he had no idea. But, if nothing else, he was a man of his word. A man of honor.

They drove quickly out of LaRochelle. The highway to Paris was empty and deserted.

He should have been frightened, but the emotion would not come. Was it because they were priests? Priests like himself? If that were his reasoning, it was surely unsound. David Proust was dead and dead at the hands of these men. Yet, Curvise felt no fear.

"Who will perform my duties at the hospital?" he finally asked. It was the first time during this entire interlude he had remembered his patients.

"Bishop Meric will have a new physician in the morning," Bronski said. "Lean back and relax, Father. We have a long journey ahead."

Curvise corrected his host. "You mean Monsignor Meric."

"Bishop Meric, Antoine. At the stroke of twelve, Bishop Meric."

Curvise laughed lightly. "I have put my own neck in the noose, I see. The church has a new prince tonight. At what cost I wonder?" He leaned back into the seat and made himself comfortable. His life was in God's hands now, just as it always had been.

Bronski had no idea what his guest's rantings encompassed, but he was used to that. "You're in no danger, Father Curvise." Sometimes it bore repeating.

***

No sun would shine on Paris today. The snow had stopped falling at four in the morning leaving the city cold and empty. Christmas was a holiday when children were the only ones required to awaken early.

The car stopped on a side street just a few minutes walk to the train station. Curvise awoke with a start. His face and hands were cold. During the night, someone had covered him with a blanket.

Opening his eyes was difficult and, aided by the milky light of dawn, he wished he had kept them closed. Bronski's face was more disfigured than he could have imagined. The hooded priest's right ear was gone. Old scars and freshly healed gashes lined the nut- brown skin. Under the priest's left eye, a vicious wound had been inflicted at one time, and left to heal on its own. His nose was bent, broken more than once.

Bronski heard the startled sound from Curvise and automatically readjusted his hood. "Not a pretty sight."

"What happened, Father?"

"Gifts from the children," Bronski said nonchalantly, as though the many scars inflicted on his body over the past thirty years were nothing more than the pain of a splinter.

Their driver opened the back door. Curvise and Bronski stepped into the street.

"I haven't introduced you. Father Emil is our driver."

Emil stuck out a hand. Automatically Curvise's gaze fell from the priest's face to his extended hand. It was whole. Relieved, Antoine shook it quickly. "It is nice to meet you, Father Emil."

"My pleasure, Father Curvise. We have heard so many good things about you I feel as though I already know you." Emil grinned. His front teeth were missing. Although not with the same intensity, he, too, carried scars on his face.

Emil opened the passenger side of the front door and dropped the keys to the floor, then pushed the lock and slammed the door closed. "We don't have much time. The snow forced me to drive much slower than I like." He picked up Curvise's valise and walked away.

"You're just leaving the car here?" Did these people do nothing normal, Curvise wondered.

"Its owner will be by shortly to retrieve it," Bronski told him. "Shall we, Father Curvise?"

"Yes, of course."

***

The train from Paris to Zurich was slow, and it stopped constantly. In a private compartment, the three priests ate breakfast and dinner. Father Emil enjoyed the scenic wonders. He never seemed to tire of watching the landscape go by, Curvise noted.

In Zurich, the station was cold and dark. The three men had to quicken their pace to make their connecting train to Vienna. Sleeping accommodations had been arranged in advance. While Father Bronski and Emil slept, Curvise stared into the darkness. His thoughts and emotions changed with every click of the wheels against the tracks. He knew he was in no danger with these men, yet he had asked where they were going and received no reply. At times confusing, he was beginning to realize he really did not care. As the train pulled into Vienna, he finally dozed.

115

Once again, their connections with yet another train were close and perfectly timed. They boarded the express to Budapest.

The ancient cities of Europe were just a blur. No time to see the wonders of man's vivid imagination and spirit were allowed. The one striking sight Curvise could not help noticing in each city they passed were the crowds of soldiers—warriors being assembled for battle. He thought of François Martine. His friend's predictions of a coming war grew more vivid than ever. Of course the world itself was more vivid outside of LaRochelle.

The afternoon sun was gray and hidden behind heavy clouds. Budapest looked dismal and tired.

"How are you feeling, Father Curvise?" They were the first words Bronski had spoken since leaving Vienna. His silence had been appropriate. Curvise had not missed the idle chatter of strangers.

"A little tired." He could still feel the swaying train in his legs even though he stood on the solidly built station platform.

"Could you walk for a while, about twenty minutes?"

"I'm sure I can."

"Wonderful!" Father Emil exclaimed. He grabbed Curvise's valise and started toward the exit.

"Where are we going?" Curvise asked again, although he really did not expect an answer.

"St. Mark. We can rest there until the train leaves this evening," Bronski said.

"Where does the train take us?"

"Kosige. It's just over the frontier in Czechoslovakia."

Curvise had never heard of the city, if indeed it was a city. They had passed through a hundred small towns, villages and hamlets with names that, at times, had seemed unpronounceable. The urge to ask if Kosige was the end of their journey came and went. It no longer mattered.

At the rectory of St. Mark, they were met by the pastor of the ancient cathedral. Curvise was not sure if they were greeted grimly, or simply with awe. One fact was obvious—the priests of St. Mark held Father Bronski and Father Emil in great respect. Visiting dignitaries from the Vatican itself could not have received a more solemn and dignified reception. It was almost as if the Disciples of Christ had entered the great cathedral.

Curvise could not have known the respect held for Fathers Bronski and Emil were twofold. Of course there was admiration for the priests' dedication and care of the brothers. The other reason was simple human frailty. Each of the priests at St. Mark knew that in the future they might end their days under the care of men like the black-hooded priests who stood before them.

***

The evening train to Kosige wound its way through the Carpathian Mountains, slowly at times, precariously at others. Snowdrifts, like great blankets, covered the sides of mountains. A bright moon cast a hypnotic trance over the observers of the cold world outside.

It was almost equally as cold inside the train. Curvise tried to sleep, but it was useless. He tossed and turned and finally lay on his back looking up at the pitted ceiling of his compartment. His thoughts were varied and many, at last coming to rest on Monsignor . . . He corrected himself. *Bishop* Meric. He felt sorry for Jean-Paul and, at the same time, understood his weakness. After all, David was dead. Nothing he or Meric did or discovered now could change that fact. For a moment though, Meric had been his own man. It was something Curvise now regretted. But then, was he any better off than Jean-Paul for his actions? He was bound for a place beyond existence. He had no idea if he was a prisoner, a servant of the Lord, a priest, a physician, or simply a man who had spoken out and, for his courage, was destined to pay an unknown price for his words. Apathy slowly sunk into his fibers. Whatever he was destined for, he must accept with the knowledge that he had decided his own fate.

The train chugged and struggled up the mountains, finally coming to a stop at Kosige. Overnighting at St. Sophie was not necessary. A car was waiting for them.

"Greetings, Father Curvise." This priest was also hidden deep inside his black hooded robe, not to hide his disfigurements, but to protect himself from the bitter cold. His feet, like Bronski's and Emil's were protected only by sandals.

Curvise shook hands with an obviously jovial man. He was not surprised to see the priest's face, although concealed beneath his hood, bore the now common scars.

"Father Curvise, our chef, Father Ehrick."

They did not linger. The cold was biting. Inside the car it was a little warmer, but most of the heat was directed onto the windshield. With a roar of the engine, four priests began the last leg of the journey. All of them were going home, but only one of them did not know where that was.

Sitting in the back of the auto, Curvise stared out of the ice-glazed window. The road up the mountains was rough. Tall pines and spruce lined the road blocking the abyss that lay just beyond the rutted drive and the sun. It was as if nothing but gray were allowed in this part of the outside world.

"We'll be home soon, Father Curvise," Bronski said. "I'm sorry for not telling you where we're going just as I must apologize for my midnight arrival. It is simply a matter of timing. As you can see from your journey here, transportation keeps its own schedules. Had you been in Paris instead of LaRochelle, I would have been able to knock on your door at an acceptable hour of the day. However, your acceptance of our invitation comes with unusual circumstances. Out of habit, I have remained silent. As I'm sure you have gathered from our appearances alone, we deal with brothers who are unruly at times."

Driving with both hands firmly on the steering wheel, Father Ehrick did not take his eyes from the road, but he laughed at his friend's description. "Well put, Zigman."

"While the majority of the priests who come to us are children, a few are, shall we say, angry at times. We try to cater to their needs. You might say we're a hospital of sorts."

"Or an insane asylum," Curvise said.

"One might call it that, yes. We prefer to call it the Institut d'Infantiles," Zigman said.

"Am I an inmate?" Curvise asked.

Both Ehrick and Emil laughed.

"No, Father Curvise, you're our new physician. And I might add, you come highly recommended," Bronski said.

"I don't understand."

"You will shortly, Father," Ehrick called from the front seat, laughing once again.

***

What little bit of sun managed to break through the overhanging clouds reflected strange and eerie shapes that engulfed the car and its passengers. The drive had taken most of the day. It was much quicker in the spring and summer, Ehrick commented. Rounding a curve, the car slowed and seemed to crawl into a hamlet.

Ehrick did the honors. "This, Father Curvise, is Litz, Poland. The Institut d'Infantiles is just beyond this quaint little village."

As they drove past the log houses and a few stores, the inhabitants of Litz stared at the passing car. "Another poor soul destined to scream at night," an older woman commented sadly to her husband. Thinking of the coins he would soon be making, he answered happily, "Another poor soul to feed and clothe."

Hidden away in the Carpathian Mountains, Litz, Poland rested near the border of Ukraine. It was not far from the Czechoslovakian border, not far from the frontier of Hungary. It was situated where nationalities meant little, and only one's ability to communicate was of value. It was a hamlet that, for all intents and purposes, had been self-sufficient for over a thousand years. It served the Institut. Its livelihood depended on the priests who lived and were confined there. The origins of these rough and devout people were buried as deep as the foundation of the Institut itself. Some said they were the descendants of the Roman garrison that had built the first fortress here two thousand years ago.

It was a fact the old ruins of the Institut had been the farthest point of the Northern Empire. Over the centuries, the original foundations were built over with new foundations and, in time, those were destroyed and rebuilt. Why anyone would want to conquer these inhabitants or lay claim to this desolate area was a mystery. Having no mountain pass, it held no strategic value. It was just a hamlet in the middle of the Carpathian Mountains, without worth.

Since its constituents' conversion to Christianity and the founding of the Holy Roman Empire, the Institut had served the priests of Europe in many ways. A shelter. A seminary. A monastery. Slowly, over the centuries, its isolation and heavy walls had brought it into its present use.

From Hungary, Czechoslovakia, Romania, Russia, and all of Eastern Europe, priests unable to care for themselves had been brought to the Institut d'Infantiles to be served by the Brothers of Mercy. This small but noble organization had, for the last seven hundred years, cared for the senile and insane with love and devotion.

Gazing through the smeared windshield, Curvise caught a glimpse of his new home—a fortress complete with spires and walls that matched the trees in height, but not in beauty. The closer he got, the more imposing the Institut became. From a distance, it had looked like one huge stronghold. Now, as they neared their destination, he could see it was a series of buildings—stones three feet thick in the rampart that surrounded the entire estate. One section of buildings looked as though they had begun life as a castle. Huge towers spun into the sky emulating the peaks of the mountains that survived as a background.

Approaching the gates, Ehrick honked the horn once. The iron portals began to move slowly, their hinges unused to such demands. Above the entranceway, Curvise noticed a stone carving, at least three feet high and across, depicting Archangel Gabriel conquering Satan. The detail was fluid—the workmanship superb. It gave him a feeling of hope.

Ehrick drove the car into the courtyard and parked in a converted stable. Horses had recently occupied the building Curvise noted as he stepped from the car. The rusty creak of damp iron drew his attention back to the gate. Two black hooded monks—they reminded him of the wooden characters built into massive tower clocks that continually performed the same ritual day after day, on the hour, every hour—closed the doors. The stone artist had been at work on this side of the entranceway also. This time it was Satan who stood victorious over Gabriel.

Bronski followed Curvise's gaze. "A reminder that things don't always go as we plan," he said.

Curvise shuddered as loneliness overwhelmed him. Studying his surroundings did nothing to help. They only made him feel small and insignificant. The courtyard was at least a hundred yards in each direction. The towers were barely visible from where he stood and, yet, he knew they were giants he had seen miles away. In front of him, a four story red brick building held hundreds of windows. In a slight way, it resembled a picture of a Russian army barracks he had once seen. To his left, was an older building constructed with large cut stones. This one contained only a few windows. To his right, another building stood, supported by massive beams of centuries old wood. It was only two stories high, but it seemed to stretch forever.

"If you'll come with me, Father, I'll show you to your quarters," Bronski said. Curvise picked up his valise and obediently followed.

Fathers Ehrick and Emil walked towards another building—a dark, foreboding building with bars across each window.

The building Bronski led him towards was ornate although the place had fallen into some disarray. Glass in a few of the windows on the third and fourth floors was broken, but whiffs of pleasant smoke came from several chimneys.

A sharp gust of wind blew Curvise off balance and he sought to regain his stability and composure. The stones of the courtyard were coated with a sheet of thin ice. He would have to be careful, he thought as he hurried after Bronski who stood, waiting patiently, at the bottom of the steps.

Absently, Curvise counted the stairs leading to the landing. Six steps. The wide expanse of porch took four strides to cross. The heavy doors of the building swung open with surprising ease.

Inside the building it was warmer. The entrance was a grand lobby that spread out in all directions. Corridors led left and right and on either side of the foyer a circular staircase rose to the upper floors. It had once been the hunting lodge of a 13th century Polish nobleman, Bronski told him. The edifice was made of cut stones; huge wooden rafters supported the high ceilings. The walls were decorated with exotic woods. Odors of fresh bread, aged wood, and disinfectant intermingled in the entranceway.

Bronski stopped in the middle of the lobby. Pointing to his right he explained: "Our wards are here." He turned and began walking left. "Our living quarters and the dining room are on this side of the building. Your room is here." He stopped at the first door to his left and opened it.

Curvise walked inside. The room was plain: a bed, armoire, desk. Bronski opened a second door. "Your medical supplies are in here and this area can act as another office if you wish to use it as such." A fire burned in the hearth. "We live a Spartan existence, but we have all we need."

Curvise put his valise down and sat on the edge of the bed. He was suddenly exhausted. "It will be more than adequate, Father Bronski. Thank you."

"If you're hungry, Father Ehrick will be more than happy to fix you something to eat. There's always a pot of coffee on in the dining room. Is there anything I can get for you now?"

"No, thank you. I'm tired. I think after a night's rest I'll feel better."

"As you wish, Father. If you will excuse me, I have to look in on my children. I'll see you in the morning."

Finally alone, Curvise lay down on the bed, too tired to even take off his shoes. His head pounded from the travel, the excitement, or was it the fear of not knowing where he was? With an effort, he removed his top coat and shoes and then laid back down. Warm under the heavy covers, he quickly fell asleep.

CHAPTER TWELVE

The mist was thick, tapping at the window. Antoine Curvise sat up with a start. For a moment he had no idea where he was. Climbing out of bed he was amazed at how stiff he felt. His legs and arms were sore from sleeping in his clothes. The fire had gone out. The room was cold enough for him to see his breath. Slipping on his shoes and topcoat, he opened the door. The corridor was empty, but the smell of coffee caught his senses.

"Good morning, Father Curvise," Ehrick called, seeing him come into the dining room. "Sit anywhere. I'll bring you some coffee."

Curvise glanced around. It could seat at least a hundred. Easily. There were six long tables lined with benches and chairs scattered about the cavernous room. He sat near the fireplace. The warmth eased the pains in his back, legs, and everywhere. He hurt all over. Father Ehrick brought him a steaming cup of coffee.

"Did you sleep well, Father Curvise?" The priest joined him by the fire.

"Yes. I must have been exhausted." Curvise sipped his coffee. "Mmmm. This is very good. Thank you." He studied Father Ehrick. There were a few scars, but no missing fingers. "Your French has an accent I cannot place."

"I am from Germany," Ehrick said. "Do you speak German?"

"Yes."

"Excellent. It is helpful to know more than one language here. Our brothers come from different places and speak differently, but we can always communicate in the language of our church."

"Have you been here long?" The coffee was thawing Curvise out. He was starting to feel alive.

"Over thirty years," Ehrick said, then hesitated. "It doesn't feel that long."

"Have you always been a priest?"

"Oh no. I studied at the Cordon Bleu. I wanted to be a great chef. I have this passion for food." He looked around as if what he'd said was a great secret he had decided to share with only Curvise.

Curvise nodded. He knew the feeling. His passion had been medicine.

"How did you end up here?"

Ehrick smiled. "I came because I was needed. I was called, like you and most of the brothers here."

"I am correct? You are a priest?"

"Yes. I saw my future as a chef one day. Making beautiful creations to be gobbled down by those who could not appreciate the joy or the love that had been set before them. Almost overnight, it became a metaphor for my life. Spending the rest of my days as a chef was no longer what I wanted. I knew there was more in life to experience. After a few years of wandering, I joined Christ. It has been a decision without regrets."

"Good morning, Father Curvise," Father Emil called out upon entering the dining room. "I hope you're feeling better this morning?" He helped himself to a cup of coffee and joined the two men at the table.

"Yes, much better. Thank you."

Emil's arrival signaled Ehrick that the priests who had labored through the night would soon be coming to eat. "If you'll excuse me, I have to start cooking. May I bring you some breakfast, Father Curvise?"

"No, thank you, Father Ehrick."

"You'll be missing a treat," Emil said. "Ehrick always bakes sweet rolls on Tuesday. Bring an extra one Ehrick, just in case Father Curvise is tempted."

Ehrick smiled and hurried to his kitchen.

"He makes the best *pączkis* I've ever had."

"Pączkis?"

"Polish doughnuts," Emil said. "They're filled with jelly and they're delicious. I'm afraid you'll find our everyday conversation sprinkled with a host of foreign words. Do you speak any other languages, Father Curvise?"

"German and, of course, Latin," Curvise answered. He was still working on pączkis.

Ehrick returned with a plate and six round, sugar-coated cakes. Emil took one and offered it to Curvise.

"No. Maybe a little later, thank you."

"A little later will be next Tuesday. The brothers won't leave a single one."

Emil took a bite. Curvise could see red jelly drip down on the plate. Reluctantly he picked up one. It was still warm and he took a small bite. Then a large one. Emil smiled. Ehrick laughed.

Priests began to trickle into the dining room. Emil introduced some, while others, he suggested, would be met as they made their rounds. Ehrick was kept busy hurrying from the dining room to the kitchen. He must have made hundreds of pączkis, Curvise thought, seeing large plates being carried out one right after another.

"This is very good," Curvise commented.

"You are welcome to more," Emil said working on his fourth.

"Next Tuesday. I am sure I'll appreciate them more then."

Curvise finished his second cup of coffee and watched with amusement as his companion slowly wet the tip of his finger and ran it around the edge of the plate, harvesting the last granules of sugar from his breakfast. With nothing more to keep Father Emil at the table, he excused himself just as Father Bronski walked into the dining room.

"Good morning, Abbot," Emil acknowledged as Zigman Bronski filled the seat he had just vacated.

It was as if the seasons had changed. The differences between the two priests, Curvise was surprised to find, could be felt with all of the senses. Already, he missed the warmth Father Emil had taken with him.

Bronski interrupted these thoughts with polite conversation. "You slept well, Father Curvise?"

"Yes, thank you." But Curvise had little patience. He wanted to wait, but the question burned his lips. "Father Bronski, this is where you brought Father Proust? David?" It was a hard question considering he was not sure what kind of an answer he would get.

"Yes, it is," Bronski acknowledged.

"I'm here because I inquired about him, is that not so?"

"Partially, yes. For the most part, Father Curvise, you are here because Monsignor DeValier passed away not too long ago. Physicians are difficult to …," Bronski paused, trying to find the right word, "recruit. As I said last night, we live a Spartan existence here. We don't complain. It's our duty. Our absence from society and its luxuries is no great loss. Physicians, however, are another matter. And electricity. We could use electricity."

"What brought Monsignor DeValier here?"

"From what I understand, he came under the same circumstances as yourself."

It suddenly became clear to Curvise like a sunrise after a storm tossed night. "Michael Proust is entombed here. Not in the Vatican beside David, but here," he declared.

"Partially correct," Bronski attempted a grin. It was not a pretty smile. One could not even call it handsome. At best, Curvise decided, he would not call it grotesque.

***

"Hello Antoine." David Proust looked through the bars of his cell at his friend.

Stunned, speechless, Curvise could only stand and stare at the man before him. Slowly, the realization of the moment began to dawn on him. "You're alive?" It was obviously a question that did not need to be asked, but there had been no chance of its denial. Curvise reached through the bars to grasp David's hand. His gesture was stopped by an iron gate.

"David, why are you locked up like a common criminal?" Curvise turned and repeated the question to Bronski. "Why is he locked up like a criminal?" The expression on his face reflected his pain.

"It is a custom we use to protect ourselves, Father Curvise, as well as our children. But as you can see by looking at me, it is not always adequate."

"Surely you don't think David would harm you?"

"David is here because this is where he needs to be."

"Open the door. Open the cell," Curvise demanded. Just as suddenly, he relented. "May I sit with my friend?" Perhaps it would be safer to seek permission. David appeared to be fine, yet . . . Why did an iron gate bar his way? What reason could there be for these bars?

"Certainly, Father Curvise."

He was surprised when Bronski unlocked the gate. It would not do to lack faith now. Hesitating only slightly, Antoine Curvise stepped into the cell. Behind him the abbot shut and locked the door. The click of the tumblers falling into place echoed inside Antoine's head. Although it was cold, beads of sweat formed on his forehead.

"Call me when you finish, Father. I'll be just down the hall." Bronski left the two men to their private reunion.

"You have nothing to fear, Antoine." David's voice had grown soft with the absence of conversation.

Curvise was embarrassed. It showed. He stood awkwardly in the middle of the cell, unsure what his first words should be. "I'm sorry David," he apologized. "I just can't believe it's you. We were told you had passed away."

Proust's grin never faltered. It was good to have company. Someone from his past who cared about him.

"Yes, I know. It's not a pleasant thought to know one is dead, but it's one I deserved." His smile faded a little. "Please sit down." He pulled over a straight-backed chair. "I'm afraid I don't have many comforts to offer you, but the chair is better than my cot. As you can see, this is the extent of my furniture." David perched on the edge of the bed. "Well now, how are you, Antoine?"

Curvise could not answer. He was here, in the middle of nowhere speaking to a dead man. At the moment, trivial conversation seemed out of place.

David's smile reappeared. "I don't believe I've ever seen you unshaven before. It was a long journey, I know."

Antoine rubbed his chin. The stubble stung his fingers.

David did not give him the chance to answer. "I'm glad you're here. I knew you'd come." He hoped Antoine did not hear the hint of sadness in his voice.

"Why are you confined?" It was all Curvise could think to ask.

"I'm not confined. I'm here for my penance. I was confined in LaRochelle, only there I did not know why."

"Sister Mary Franza is dead."

"Yes, I know," David said quietly. "I knew the minute she died. The pain was the worst it had ever been, as badly as if Camille and Louisa had combined their torment." He sighed. "No one else will suffer her fate, Antoine. Here, confined, I am harmless. No one suffers but me."

"I don't understand this, David. Do you know what's troubling you?"

"I told you, Antoine. I'm possessed. My actions are not my own." David's voice was steady as if his comment were the most natural thing in the world. "The brothers here know how to control the demon inside me. As long as I'm in this cell, I can harm no one."

Curvise shook his head. "Surely you don't believe that, David. There are no demons."

David laughed. "You seem to have changed your opinion a bit, Antoine. If I remember correctly, it was you who suggested to Bishop Vasai that I was possessed. And rightly, I might add."

"No, you may not," Curvise said crossly. "I only mentioned the possibility to the Bishop to show him how preposterous it was. To set up a defense. He saw through it right away. He even asked me about it."

David's steady gaze refused to let Curvise evade the truth, even about himself. He looked up, unsure of what he would see in David's eyes. They were calm, accepting, forgiving. Perhaps the look Jesus would have given Judas.

"You are right, David. At one time I did believe you possessed, but not now! Look at you. You're healthy. You've gained weight. You speak with a serenity most men can only dream of attaining." Curvise stood up suddenly. "How could I have been so wrong?"

David stood and laid a gentle hand on Curvise's shoulder. "You did the right thing, Antoine. Whether you want to admit it or not, those women died because of my dreams—my nightmares. I wanted . . . I tried to kill myself so that I might suffer in Hell with them. Now, when the day comes that I join them, at least it will not be by my own hand. For that, I have you to thank." He retreated to sit cross-legged on his bed. His smile had returned. "It's not so bad here. Once you get used to the food, the cold, the loneliness."

"Father Curvise," Bronski stood in the doorway.

"Yes?"

"We've had a small accident." Zigman unlocked the gate.

"I'll be back to see you later, David." Curvise hurried from the small prison cell.

"I'm glad you're here, Antoine." David's voice was light, but even moving away from the cell, Curvise could hear the heavy tumblers click as Bronski locked the gate.

***

"What happened?" Curvise examined a gash below the priest's elbow. "It looks as if someone tried to cut off your arm."

"One of the children," Zigman said. "Father Petro forgot to use caution. He was busy with other duties when it happened."

Curvise sutured the wound and bandaged it tightly. It would not be the only scar that would deface the old priest. "I'll want to change the bandage and look at that again tomorrow morning." He dismissed the priest and washed his hands. "I think, Father Bronski, that it's time I visited these children of yours."

"Yes," Bronski agreed, "it is."

***

Curvise, his mind reeling from the sights he had seen, sat at the dining room table, trying to find some peace. His first visit to the children had been a horrifying visit to Hell.

The "children" of the Institut were, for all intents and purposes, exactly that. Men so devoid of any decency that during the day they were chained to a wall by their ankles and wrists. Only in that way could they be cleaned and fed safely. Men who would and did, at every opportunity, strike out at their hosts. Dangerous men. Forced into straight jackets at night, they slept without harming themselves or others.

"They're not to blame," Bronski had said. "They've committed acts that are in all of us. Usually man is capable of suppressing such feelings. Some

127

are not. We don't judge. We just try to comfort."

Curvise had had no reply. If it were a test of his compassion, then, at that moment he had failed. He saw no earthly reason for men who were so blatantly antisocial to be kept alive. "That one man would have killed you had he not been chained to the wall," Curvise had said, remembering one of the children who, aggravated beyond his endurance, had struggled to get at Father Bronski.

Bronski had rubbed the place where his ear used to be. He shrugged his shoulders. "Our friendship began in the seminary. We were ordained at the same time and served the same parish in Warsaw many years ago. I remember we had been in the rectory and Father Koisk complained he wasn't feeling well. He went upstairs to rest and I went to bed a little later. I have never again heard such a scream as the one that awakened me that night.

"Searching the rectory, I found Father Koisk in the cellar. He had decapitated the housekeeper—an old woman. I found him devouring her flesh.

"With the help of the other priests, we subdued him." Bronski had closed his eyes against the memory. "You see, I understand how you feel more than you may know. I came to the Institut to take care of him. Father Koisk is my friend.

"That was thirty years ago. He still hates me and wishes me dead."

"He did that to your ear?"

"Yes, but it wasn't Father Koisk, you understand? It was the demon inside of him." Bronski had opened his eyes and looked at Curvise. "He hasn't forgotten I was the one who deprived him of his feast."

Curvise had looked away.

"But that is the nature of us as men. We care for the insane and for those who are incapable of taking care of themselves."

"The old men . . . Why are they here? Who are they?" Curvise's memory could not shake the sights of the senile, aged men unable to function at even a basic level. On some of the blank, staring faces they had passed, the men's bluish white skin was stretched tightly. On others it hung as waddles on pigeons. Fresh linens were instantly soiled like the diapers of infants. Bedsores were prevalent—an accumulation of long periods of idleness. The stench of the aged was a wilted flower rotting in the noonday sun.

"As you can see, many of the functions we take for granted fail us as we grow old. At the moment, we have forty-five men in these wards. Some are not so bad. Others are worse. We do what we can for them. Patience and understanding are the best medicine we can administer, unless you have a cure for aging."

128

Bronski's humor had gone unnoticed.

Yet Curvise had found compassion. He smiled, remembering. Bronski had introduced him to a bedridden priest. "Father Curvise," he had said, "I would like you to meet Cardinal Yozkin."

A Cardinal of the church in poverty! The idea had seemed ludicrous to Curvise. It was only after Bronski had also introduced the next pale white body as a Cardinal that he saw the truth.

"It is the least we can do to make their days comfortable. All of our brothers are Cardinals, Princes of the Church," Bronski had told him. "Of course, you are not obligated to address them as such."

"It would be my pleasure, Father Bronski. A pleasure and an honor."

Forty-five princes of the most wealthy religious organization in the world existed within the confines of the Institut d'Infantiles. They lived under Spartan conditions through cold winters and insect infested summers. They were cared for by men who belonged to a religious organization Curvise had never known existed.

He shuddered from the cold, but not as badly as before. Already he was getting warm from the men around him. Warm inside the way religion was supposed to make you feel.

He was home.

CHAPTER THIRTEEN

François Martine returned from his holidays on January 5, 1939. The time spent in London had done nothing to ease the conversations he had had with Curvise before his departure. While in England, he had sought out prominent psychiatrists and clergymen, hoping to find an answer to Antoine's theories on demons. For a short while, it had been fun and interesting listening to the Brits trying to solve his hypothetical problem. In the end, he had chastised himself for even thinking he would find a reasonable explanation. As he had known all along, the English were more inclined to believe in the supernatural. Dottering imbeciles, he thought, but he thought that often. That was his general opinion of most of the world outside of France.

Martine's concern for Antoine had not lessened. In fact, as his holiday wore on, it had grown. He had refused to consider any notion in his mind that Curvise might be correct. Demons did not exist. Possession by spirits of the netherworld were mere concoctions by weak willed individuals fed by a foolish religion. Yet, he knew David Proust to be a strong willed man. But, there was always the fact that David was a priest. A man given to believing in the spiritual world. A man who lived beside Curvise in a world of demons.

Returning to LaRochelle, anxious to sit down and discuss world events with Antoine, and hopefully forget this past year, Martine walked into the Catholic Hospital with a bounce in his step.

"Good morning, Sister Grace." He greeted her with a smile and jaunty salute.

"Good morning, Dr. Martine." It was her usual reply, but without her usual smile.

Walking towards Curvise's office, he saw Mother Superior Monique coming his way.

"Good morning, Mother Superior," he said gaily with another rakish salute.

"Good morning, François," she answered as she passed him in the hall.

He had actually taken two steps before he realized what had happened. Mother Superior had not called him François since he had joined the

130

Communist Party fifteen years ago.

"Mother Superior, is everything all right?"

She had turned at the sound of her name and now bowed her head at his que stion. If he had not known her, Martine would have sworn he saw a tear in her eye.

"Father Curvise has been . . ." She stopped to draw a breath, still finding it difficult to believe. "Transferred to another hospital."

She began to walk away. Martine hurriedly fell in step, keeping up easily with her small strides.

"Where?" He did not give her time to answer. "When did he leave?"

She shook her head. "I don't know. All I know is that he's been transferred."

Her answer brought Martine to a stop in the middle of the hallway. Monique continued her walk towards the lobby.

This could not be, Martine thought. He hurried to Curvise's office and, without so much as a knock, barged into the room. Seated behind the desk was a stranger.

"Where is Dr. Curvise?" he demanded angrily.

Startled at this unexpected intrusion, Father LaBella took his time in answering. "And who are you, sir?"

"Dr. Martine," François said, calming a bit. "I'm sorry for the intrusion, but it's very important that I know where Dr. Curvise has been transferred."

"I'm sorry, Dr. Martine." Father LaBella took off his glasses and placed them gently on the desk. "I don't know."

Stunned by the news of Antoine's departure, Martine hurried to the rectory of St. Margaret. Someone knew where Antoine was and he was determined to find out as soon as possible.

"*Bishop* Meric?" Martine sat in Jean-Paul's office, again stunned. He wondered briefly if he were still on holiday and dreaming this nightmare as a result of all the horrible English food he had eaten.

"It is not the policy of the church to give out information on our priests." Meric's voice was forceful. He had slid easily into his new role of authority.

Martine knew the futilities of arguing with the church. His standing was very low. He had no hope of recovering any information from the newly elevated Bishop. Getting up slowly, his steady gaze caught and held Meric. "I intend to find out where Antoine is, Jean-Paul. For the sake of this institution that has endowed you so grandly, he had better be alive and safe."

With that promise, Martine departed and left a sputtering Bishop behind his desk, full of authority and no one to command.

***

131

"Will you listen to me, Defont?" Martine had swallowed his pride and gone to the one man in LaRochelle he thought could help him find Antoine Curvise.

"Inspector, Dr. Martine. It's Inspector Defont," Edmund said, enjoying this feeling of superiority. It was an emotion he did not allow himself often.

Martine bowed his head and held his tongue. He wanted to tell Defont he was nothing but an overstuffed bureaucrat whose claim of friendship for Curvise was as false as the Inspector himself. Instead, he said, "Inspector Defont. I am sure you are aware Antoine Curvise has been reassigned by the church."

Defont nodded.

"I would like to find out where he is."

"Other than the fact that Antoine was the only person in town who would speak to you, why?" Defont fought to keep a straight face. This was not a humorous situation. He had already made his own discreet inquiries as to the whereabouts of Dr. Antoine Curvise, but had discovered nothing. It was maddening. Edmund Defont saw—he *felt* the connection between Antoine's reassignment and the three women's suicides. In his heart, he knew Curvise had the answers he sought. He also suspected Dr. Martine knew more than he was willing to tell at the moment. But he would. And, in the process, Defont would exact his revenge for the years of humiliation he had suffered at the snobbish doctor's hands.

Trying desperately to keep his temper under control, a frustrated François Martine shrugged his shoulders, allowing Defont's barb to miss its mark. He knew if he were going to receive any help from the man, he would have to tell him the whole story. But where did one start?

"I lied to you, Edmund," he began.

Defont said nothing. In his line of work, he had found that being a good listener was essential. Most times, a little bit of encouragement was all a criminal needed to confess to a crime. If he could do that for the thieves on the street, he certainly could afford Dr. Martine the same courtesy. He would stay silent and listen to what François had to say. He would not say a word.

"Sister Mary Franza was with child," Martine began.

"Impossible!" Defont exploded. "I had an independent examination done on her after you finished the initial autopsy. She was a virgin!"

"Yes, she was," Martine agreed. The weight of the world pressed down on his narrow shoulders. "During the autopsy, knowing you would question her virginity, although I did not think you would question my examination," he could not help but add, "I took the liberty of examining her womb. The fetus," he hesitated to use the term, but he could think of no other explanation

132

for what he had seen, "was ten, perhaps, eleven weeks old." Martine risked a look at the policeman. "Do you understand what I'm saying, Defont? I excised and destroyed it. At the time, I thought it best for all involved."

Defont's large frame had grown rigid. "How could you possibly think that? How could you . . ." He took a moment to compose himself. "Why, François? Even if I decide to believe in this fantasy of yours, why would you have tampered with such specific evidence?"

"I don't know why. Maybe to protect Antoine. Maybe," Martine added with a sigh, "to protect David Proust."

Defont pushed himself back in his chair and rubbed his head. It was beginning to hurt. "Maybe we should begin again, François. This time at the beginning with Camille Robéson."

"All right," Martine agreed. "I'll tell you what I know." It was a relief, really, to share the burden. To share the sin.

Edmund Defont relaxed, and this time he did listen to Martine without interruptions. An hour later, the story that had unfolded, ripped and crumpled in his mind. He tried not to believe what he had heard. His church could not be so vicious, so ruthless as to have one of its own put to death! Yet, as certainly as he knew a woman could not be impregnated without a physical encounter with a man, he believed David had driven those three women to their deaths. He found he could not doubt Martine's story, but did he believe it? It made no difference which way he turned. Whether he chose to view it as a truth or a lie, he was still lost. There was no case against David Proust. How could he go to his supervisor with this story? This evidence? This insanity on his mind?

The questions that had lined up during Martine's tale now found their way into the conversation, insisting upon logic. "Camille Robéson. She was a virgin with no child inside her?"

"Correct."

"And the same was true of Louisa Markey?"

"Yes."

"Sister Franza, she was a virgin also, yet she was definitely carrying a baby?"

"Well, it would have never been born."

"Don't play semantics with me, François. There was a child?"

Martine nodded. "Yes."

"She committed suicide after she heard the news of David Proust's death."

"Yes."

"And Antoine told you Sister Franza knew she was carrying David's child?"

"Yes."

"How did she know?"

Martine sat back in his chair. "That Edmund, is what I believe Antoine now knows. That is why we must find him before the church does away with him."

"I've already made inquiries into the whereabouts of Father Curvise and was told it was none of my concern. When a man takes the oath of priesthood, he literally gives himself to the church. The church can do as it sees fit with this man. It has no obligation to keep us, or anyone else, for that matter, informed as to where their priests are assigned." Defont studied the priggish doctor. "Why are you telling me this now François, other than the fact you're worried about Antoine?"

"Because I didn't know the whole story until shortly before I left on holiday," Martine snapped. Why didn't this stupid policeman just help him like he had requested? But losing his temper would not resolve the situation. "I made inquiries while in London, trying to get to the bottom of this. Now it can hurt no one. The three women are dead. David is dead. And I believe in a short time, we will receive notification of Antoine's death. I have told you everything I know about this matter, Inspector Defont. If you won't help me find Antoine, I'll find someone else. I refuse to let my friend be sacrificed on the altar of his murderous church."

Convinced of Martine's sincerity, Defont had formed the outlines of a plan, but first he needed to know just how far Martine was willing to go. Was he willing to risk his own life?

"If what you've told me is the truth—and I'm not saying I believe you—but *if*, to investigate this matter further could put my life as well as yours in danger. If we assume someone in the Catholic Church is capable of murder, we must then assume they have already killed two people who were our friends. Would they hesitate to remove us, François? If Antoine is already dead, what will we gain by putting our lives on the line?"

Martine stared at the big man who sat across from him. "Honor and justice, Edmund. Two values around which we both have built our lives."

"All right," Defont began slowly. "I don't know if it will work, but this is what we're going to do." Once again he sat straight, almost rigid in his chair.

***

"I have a warrant for the arrest of Father Antoine Curvise." Defont handed the summons to Bishop Meric. Meric refused to acknowledge the paper and the warrant fell silently on top of his desk. He glared, first at Defont and then Martine.

"A complaint has been filed against Father Curvise," Defont said. "Withholding information on the whereabouts of a fugitive is a crime. You are required, by French law, to give me any assistance you can in this matter." He had not been sure he could carry through with the charade. He was relying on the Bishop's weakness as a man—a man he knew to be as pliable as his flesh. It was a surprise to find Meric had a backbone.

"I don't know what game you're playing, Inspector, but you can rest assured I'll find out. When I do, your supervisors will be informed. You have no authority here." Meric spoke with a firmness that surprised both men. "What has happened to you, Edmund? Have you succumbed to this man's," he glared at Martine, "ungodly depths? I have known you for many years and I tell you sincerely, I do not know where Father Curvise has been transferred." He stood and extended his arms. "Arrest me if you dare, or get out of my house. I have said all I'm going to about this matter."

Martine felt as if they had been beaten. He started to leave, but stopped when he heard Defont's low voice.

"I know about Father Proust, Your Excellency. I know about Sister Mary Franza and the two young women, Camille and Louisa. I'm not the only one who will suffer the consequences you threaten."

Meric sat down.

"I don't want to arrest Father Curvise. I merely want to know where he is." Defont's voice changed from running water to the hard gravel of a riverbed. "If I have to, I'll inform the newspapers of these incidents. You must understand that I'm determined to get to the bottom of this.

"You know me, Jean-Paul. I am a good and honest man. The last thing in the world I want to do is harm my church, but I believe the Bible says our God is a just God. That's all I'm looking for—justice. I'll have it served even at the cost of my career. And yours."

A grudging respect sprouted inside of Martine. Perhaps he had misjudged Edmund all these long years. Perhaps there was something to the man and his bullying way, as long as he was on the right side.

"I honestly don't know where he's been sent," Meric said.

This time Defont believed the Bishop. This time the priest's voice carried defeat. It was time to press for victory.

"I believe you, Jean-Paul, but someone in the church does know. I want you to find out. I need you to find out. It's very simple. Get me the location of Antoine Curvise and I'll ask for nothing more."

Meric picked up the warrant and handed it back to Defont. "I can't promise and it will take some time, but I will try. Whether you believe it or not, I, too, care about Antoine Curvise."

***

Bishop Jean-Paul Meric waited until he was sure Edmund Defont and François Martine were gone. He even went so far as to look down the hall. It was empty. Closing the door, he returned to his desk and dialed Cardinal Vasai's private number. He had only been a prince of the church for three weeks and already he was feeling the pressures of his office. There was no one to blame but himself. Curvise's transfer had caught him off guard. Reveling in his new title, he had tried to give it some honest thought, but failed. It had been easier to suppress his guilt and he would continue to do so. In his own way, Bishop Jean-Paul Meric also refused to suffer any consequences.

"Your Excellency. Bishop Meric here. We have a slight problem." He hesitated as the shadow of a thought raced across his conscience. He chased it away. There were no murderers inside the church. Only frightened men who feared for their positions of power.

Meric meticulously explained what had happened and Vasai listened patiently. Just as patiently, he told Meric he would see what he could do. The newly elevated Bishop could expect a return phone call when Vasai had the requested information in hand.

***

"I can't believe Jean-Paul doesn't know the whereabouts of Antoine," Martine said to Defont as they walked back towards the offices of the Sûreté.

"Why would he have to know?"

"Isn't it obvious? He sold Antoine out for his promotion to Bishop."

"I don't believe that. I've known Meric many years. He's not the greatest priest I've ever known, but he's certainly not a traitor," Defont bristled. "Just because you snub everything Catholic, François, is no reason for you to make such a lunatic proposal. Meric is a man of God. He would not behave in such a manner."

"He'll never tell us where Antoine is, Edmund. I would bet my life on it." Martine refused to budge, especially when he knew he was right.

"You may have already placed that bet, Doctor. If what you've told me is the absolute truth."

Martine found Defont's grin slightly terrifying. It was a while before he spoke. "Surely you don't believe the church would have us killed?" His question was hesitant. His moment of courage had come and gone.

"I don't know. I'd like to believe it's what it claims to be—a peaceful organization, but then . . . Think of this, François. If what you've said is the truth, that Sister Mary Franza was with child, and that unborn child was not so much human as—how did you put it? A grotesque apparition ....

"A virgin giving birth, François. The last time that happened was one thousand nine hundred and thirty-nine years ago. The Catholic faith is based on the virgin birth of Christ. The Immaculate Conception produced our Lord and from Him came our religion. Our beliefs. The entire realm of the empire of the Catholic Church. All of it rests on this one deity.

"Imagine yourself Pope. The faith you lead stands in jeopardy. One or two men have, by a quirk of friendship, stumbled upon another virgin birth. Would you allow this to be made public?"

Martine did not answer and Defont fell mute as they walked down the Rue Amelot. Death was something to be feared. Each of them struggled in his own way with the inevitability of facing that final day. Heroes were young men. They were getting old. Life became a little more precious with each passing day. Unfortunately, they had opened the door and, though neither sought to close it out loud, they both thought silently of ways to slam it shut again.

CHAPTER FOURTEEN

The clanging of the phone startled François Martine. He had just finished with his last patient of the day and was looking forward to a nice meal and bottle of wine. The past two months had wreaked havoc on his nerves. He had talked to Defont three days ago. The policeman had wanted to go back and see Meric, to put, as he said, a little more pressure on the Bishop. Martine had declined. He had argued that these kinds of things took more time. "Let's wait a few more days," he had said. Now, a few more days had come and gone. He hesitated before reaching for the receiver.

"Hello."

"Antoine Curvise is in Litz, Poland." On the other end of the line, Defont's voice sounded very excited and very close.

"Poland?" In comparison, his own voice sounded weak.

"Yes. Litz. He's been assigned to a hospital there." Defont was unable to contain himself. "Are you busy?"

"I just finished with my last patient. I was going to Marcille's for dinner."

"Good. I'll meet you there."

"That would be fine. And Defont," Martine said before hanging up the phone, "do remember to wear a fashionable tie."

***

"Meric called me a few minutes before I called you." Defont poured a glass of wine for Martine and then himself. "To tell you the truth, I never expected to hear from him again." He sipped the Chablis and then plunged ahead. "Poland. Can you believe it? Poland, of all places!"

Martine was more cautious. "And you believe this, Defont? You honestly believe Antoine is hidden in the outer reaches of Poland?"

"I believe he's in Litz, François. Meric had no reason to lie. Why would he?" Edmund was exasperated. "Damn you, François. You wanted to know. Now you do." His eyes narrowed as he eyed his dinner companion. "What are you going to do about it?"

Martine sipped his wine and thought about what Defont had just asked. What are you going to do about it, he asked himself? Knowing where Antoine was—that he was alive—should have settled his restlessness. But it had not. There were still too many unanswered questions floating through the air.

"What do you suggest we do, Defont?"

The Inspector shrugged his massive shoulders. "I haven't given it any thought. Are you suggesting we travel to Poland to verify Antoine is alive and well?" It was a safe suggestion, Defont thought. Surely not even Martine . . .

Courage swept up, and curiosity was on high. Martine placed his nearly full glass gently on the table, but his eyes sparkled as if he had finished the whole bottle. "Yes, Defont, yes I am. That's a wonderful idea! In fact, too wonderful to waste. We should get started as soon as possible. I'll take care of the expenses."

His reply caught Defont off guard. A look of consternation crossed the policeman's face. Suddenly, he was in an uncomfortable position.

"I have responsibilities here, Martine, as do you. Or have you forgotten? We can't just up and leave for Poland."

Defont's hesitation was all the convincing Martine needed. "I can and will. We started out to find Antoine, and now that we know where he is, I'm going to find him. Your passage is paid, Defont. You can tag along if you have the nerve." Martine finished off the wine and poured another glass.

Defont was torn. It would be nice to put an end to the controversy that had dogged him since the deaths of the three women, but he did not expect to find the answers in Poland. If anything, he expected only to see Antoine Curvise. But, was that so bad?

The determination that had steered his life since his earliest recollections had begun to falter. He could not let that happen, especially in front of someone as imperious as Martine. Even before he spoke, he found himself nodding in agreement.

"Yes, I think we should pay a visit to Litz, but I'll pay my own way, Martine. When do you want to leave?"

"I'll have my agent make the arrangements. We can leave as soon as he gets our tickets."

The taste of adventure lingered inside of François Martine. Poland was a wild place! Gypsies and thieves thrived in the dark country. Hitler was shaking his fists, demanding Danzig be returned to Germany; threatening to invade the Poles if it were not. Adventure still abounded inside Martine, along with the agonizing questions that lingered from his last conversation with Antoine Curvise.

Defont held out his glass. "*Nostrovea*, Dr. Martine."

"*Nostrovea*, Inspector." The clink of the glasses was tiny and small. It sealed the fate of the two men more firmly than each could suspect.

***

It was the last Sunday in March when Defont and Martine boarded their train for Berlin. Tucked under heavy overcoats and hats, they had been warned by Martine's travel agent the area they were traveling to was in the Carpathian Mountains. It would be cold and probably snowing when they arrived. Forewarned, heavy clothing and boots were packed in their suitcases.

Before leaving LaRochelle, Martine had a surprise visitor. Bishop Meric came to his office.

"When you see Father Curvise, François, please tell him I'm sorry. He'll understand." Meric looked into the doctor's eyes. "I hope this puts an end to this matter once and for all. It has caused more trouble than should ever have been allowed."

Martine looked up quickly, his eyes bright with the future. "As Inspector Defont told you before Jean-Paul, all we wanted was to know where Antoine had been sent. We won't bother you again."

And you won't, Meric thought. He had gone to Dr. Martine's office to warn him. To tell him that to enter the walls of the Institut d'Infantiles was to imprison oneself for eternity. He had not known that fact when he had allowed Curvise to be sent there. And so, repenting, he had wanted to warn François and Defont. But he did not. He had checked up on the two men. Having lost contact over the years, he was surprised to find neither had a wife or family left in LaRochelle. At times, God moved in mysterious ways, and, he reasoned, this was one of those times.

***

Both Defont and Martine had visited Germany after the Great War. It had been devastated. Traveling though the country now surprised them both.

"I can't believe the progress they've made," Martine commented several times after seeing a column of soldiers moving down an empty road, the machines of war following them. The cities were clean and prosperous. People smiled and laughed, enjoying life. It was a sharp contrast to the dour faces of the French countryside.

Berlin was a circus that grabbed at their lapels and pulled them into its festivities, making departure difficult. Reluctantly they boarded the train for Cracow, leaving behind the fresh and vibrant Germans and replacing them with the sour faces of the Poles.

In Cracow, they boarded a local train to Sanok. From there, they had to hire an auto to get them to Litz. "And even then I'm not sure you'll be able to get there," Martine's travel agent had told him. "It's in the mountains and may be impossible to reach with the snow."

The agent had tried to find out something of the area's history for Dr. Martine, a valued customer, but could find very little. All he had been able to discover was that it was a most inhospitable place. The residents tended to be clannish and close-mouthed. Some farms prospered in the valleys. Cattle and pigs were raised along with cabbage and potatoes. "How anyone survives is anyone's guess," the agent had commented. "Why on earth do you want to go to Litz? Especially now?"

Why on earth indeed, Martine thought as the train pulled into Sanok. Already he felt the stares of the locals on the back of his neck. In his opinion, the Poles were nothing but criminals and cutthroats. Lazy oafs, too strong for their own good and too mean-tempered for the good of Europe. He mentioned this to Defont.

The Inspector had eyed him momentarily. "Wouldn't you be in a foul mood if you had to live here? It's not the nicest place in the world."

It took an effort to secure a ride across the mountains into Litz. The stationmaster eyed them suspiciously until Martine mentioned they were going to visit a priest. His attitude had changed noticeably. He knew someone who could take them. Over his objections, Martine had given him one hundred francs and the new silk shirt he had purchased in Paris. It confused Martine, this oafish Pole did not seem to want his gifts. Maybe they would prefer to steal it, he thought.

"I've never liked the Poles," he commented to Defont once again. "They're thieves."

Defont said nothing. Over the last five days, he had begun to get a better understanding of Martine. He found he had never really disliked the little man. He had just never understood the arrogance that kept him from being friendly just as he had never understood the coolness Martine had shone towards him. The doctor was not a bad fellow, but he could certainly grate on a person's nerves. Nothing pleased him, it seemed. Nothing was priced to his satisfaction. Nothing was ever good enough. His only redeeming feature was his love of France and all things French. At least, Defont thought, that was something on which they could agree.

***

The truck bounced and shook, rattled and seemed to threaten at any moment to fall apart. Backfiring and sputtering, it slid and shimmied over the frozen gravel road. The driver growled his name with a guttural roar of Polish. Martine leaned back as though assaulted. "I beg your pardon," he said with an arched eyebrow.

Their driver smiled a coarse smile—one that did nothing to alleviate the worries his passengers now entertained. It was obvious to both Defont and Martine that their driver was not afraid of a fight. His face bore the light tracings of the battle-scarred. His nose was delightful in its asymmetry. His breath smelled of sauerkraut and onions.

"Greatcoat," he again bellowed in his normal tone of voice. "Just call me Greatcoat. Everybody else does."

It fit. The bear of a man was wrapped warmly in a woolen German greatcoat he had acquired in the Great War. He was a burly, unshaven, uncouth Pole who understood some French and occasionally asked a question concerning Paris or Marseille. He claimed he had a cousin who lived in Marseille. It was hard for Martine to picture the man having any living relations who would claim him.

Squeezed between two oversized men, François Martine felt like a child. Greatcoat had told them the journey would take about three hours. That had been four hours ago. Now, when they asked how long they still had to travel, he answered with a toothless grin: "Don't worry. Just a short while longer. Perhaps one or two hours. No more."

Martine had just about decided that when someone told him "don't worry," that was precisely what he intended to do.

The road was desolate and surrounded by high snow banks and dark trees. Several times deer ran in front of the truck. Each time the animals appeared, Greatcoat tried to run one of them down—smacking his lips in anticipation of venison, and muttering Polish curses when he missed a potential meal.

Dark shadows slunk ahead of the car. Defont was surprised to find they separated into a family of wolves on the hunt. The pack stopped their stalking long enough to watch the truck roll past. One snarled, long and lean. Even from the truck, Defont could see the hunger in its eyes.

"A bad place to break down, yes?" Greatcoat asked and then allowed his laughter to fill the vehicle.

It was late afternoon when the trio finally arrived in Litz. The truck stopped at the local post office, backfired once and fell silent.

Greatcoat had asked them no questions concerning their visit to Litz until now. He was not a man given to curiosity. "Next week, I'll take you back to

JOHN WARMUS

Sanok. "Who are you seeing?" He helped Martine with his suitcase.

"A friend, Father Antoine Curvise." Martine looked around. Litz was anything but a town. It was not even a village in his opinion.

"You come to see the priests?" Greatcoat asked. He made the sign of the cross and took a step away from the doctor. They would not be going back to Sanok. Pity, he thought.

"Where's the hospital?" Defont had decided to ignore the strangebehavior of their driver. It would do no good to worry now.

Greatcoat pointed down the snow-filled track that cut through Litz. The road was wide enough to turn around the horse and wagons that still provided transportation around the borough.

"It's not far. You can walk."

And they did. Suitcases in gloved hands, steeling themselves against the bitter and biting air, Defont and Martine began to trudge the direction Greatcoat had pointed. In their doorways, bundled up couples stared as the two men passed. No one said a word. No one at all.

"This is a strange place, Edmund," Martine said through a blast of steam from his mouth. "I get the feeling we're being eyed for the pot."

"It does seem different," Defont agreed. "Have you noticed? There are no children." Every town, every village they had passed through had been filled with the offspring of the Poles' lust.

"You've only to look at the women to know why," Martine countered. "I was always under the impression Polish women were very beautiful. At least those who had a little of us in them." His attempt at humor failed.

"Sometimes we think too much of ourselves, François, although I'll admit whatever nationality the French blend with does acquire a certain beauty. But, for myself, I prefer good French stock."

Martine laughed and coughed into the cold air. "Somehow I can't see you with anything but good French stock."

"That must be it." Defont pointed to long stone walls that were partially shrouded in heavy mist. "It's unbelievable! Like a castle or something." He stopped in the middle of the road. "Isn't this a rather strange place for a hospital?"

Martine was occupied, staring at the monolithic ruins. They had to be over six hundred years old he roughly estimated. "Hospital?" he asked absently. "Oh yes, it is a strange place to have a hospital."

Standing just outside the gates, the true size of the Institut was incalculable. But it was certain, the structure was immense. The gates alone stood at least five meters high and another five wide. There was no knocker. Defont pounded on the hard frozen wood several times before they heard the clang of iron being moved—a chain being dropped to the ground. The left side of the twin doors swung open just far enough for a man's head to be seen.

"How may I help you?" the black hooded priest asked in Polish.

Defont asked if the gatekeeper spoke French. The priest replied that he did and again asked, this time in French, "How may I help you?"

"We are looking for Father Antoine Curvise," Martine said. "Is he here?"

"I'm sorry. The name is not familiar." Father Emil started to push the gate closed. Defont leaned against the door, his weight an immediate obstacle.

"We were told Father Curvise was here. We've come a long way. You can't just shut us out. Who is in charge?" Defont asked firmly. "I want to talk to whoever is in charge."

Again Father Emil tried to spare Antoine's friends. "No, no, there is no Dr. Curvise here. You are not permitted to enter. Please, please, go away."

Martine caught Father Emil's error. "Who said he was a doctor? Antoine Curvise is here and I demand you let us in."

Father Emil had the privilege of being the first to feel the wrath of François Martine. Reluctantly, he opened the gate and stepped aside. "Yes, he is here. Do you enter this house of God of your own free will?"

It was a strange question, but who knew what religious rites were practiced here in the wilds of the Carpathian Mountains.

"Yes," Defont answered.

"Of course," Martine huffed.

"Then you may enter." The gate swung open wide enough for the two men to enter side by side.

"Well it's about time," Martine whispered to Defont. "I really thought the cretin was going to let us freeze to death in the middle of the road."

Defont ignored the remark. He was too busy trying to see what could not be seen. Trapped by the high walls, the shroud of mist that had covered the upper portion of the mountains and surrounded the building was in full bloom within the Institut's courtyard.

The gates were closed and chained. "If you follow me, I will take you to Father Curvise." Father Emil led the way into the main building.

Inside it was a little bit warmer. Martine shed his overcoat. Defont simply undid his buttons. Their robed guide seemed as comfortable inside as he had outside in the cold. He was certainly more comfortable than either of the newcomers.

Leading the way down the corridor, Emil stopped in front of a plain door. "You may put your suitcases in here," he said to Defont. "And you sir," he said to Martine, "may put yours in the adjoining room."

Martine's attention was captivated by the twin spiral staircases that ended two stories and many feet above his head. "This is amazing. I've never seen anything so entrancing this far from civilization." His words were meant for himself rather than those around him.

"François, over here," Defont called for his attention. "Your room."

Martine threw his overcoat on the bed, set his valise on the floor and once again joined Defont and the priest in the corridor.

"Would you gentlemen care for some coffee?"

"Yes, very much so."

Defont followed their guide down the corridor to the dining room. Martine lagged behind, his head turning to look at the art that adorned the walls. So much beauty in so little civilization! It would be nice to spend some time here, he thought. Enough so he could study the intricacies of the artists as well as their work.

***

Martine and Curvise affectionately hugged and slapped each other on the back. Defont warmly shook Curvise's hand. Each in their own way was genuinely happy to see the other.

"How in the world did you find me?" Curvise asked. He sat and gestured for them to do the same.

"May I get you some coffee, Father Curvise?" Father Ehrick asked. "And perhaps a refill for your friends?" He had enjoyed watching the camaraderie between the three men.

"Yes, please," Martine made the request for them all. "That would be nice."

"Do you have any bread?" Defont asked sheepishly. "I'm starving." His stomach had been rumbling for the last four hours.

"We're having beef stew for supper. As soon as it's ready, I'll bring some out for you," Father Ehrick replied happily.

"So tell me. How did you find me?" Curvise asked again. This time his voice lacked the same enthusiasm his earlier question had implied.

"Edmund got your whereabouts from Bishop Meric," Martine said. "Oh, by the way, Jean-Paul asked me to ask you to forgive him. He feels guilty about your being here."

"He shouldn't. I brought this upon myself." Curvise turned to Defont in amazement. "How in the world did you manage to get this out of Meric?"

"We threatened to expose the whole story," Defont said "At least the

145

story I heard from François."

Curvise laughed, but it was not a happy sound. The two newcomers glanced at each other nervously.

"I'm sorry. The irony just struck me as appropriate." Curvise glanced past his two friends towards Father Bronski. "Gentlemen, I'd like you to meet the Abbot of the Institut d'Infantiles, Father Zigman Bronski."

Martine winced. Defont stared.

Bronski had long ago learned to take no notice of people's initial reactions to his face. "Inspector Defont. Dr. Martine." They shook hands. "I hope you will enjoy your stay with us." Reluctantly, Zigman Bronski welcomed them home.

CHAPTER FIFTEEN

"Your patients aren't the only ones here who are insane, Father Bronski. You must be also if you think you can keep me here against my will." Martine sputtered and complained. Hearing the news that he and Defont were to remain in the Institut had driven him to pace the dining room with these intermittent outbursts of indignation. "Just how do you intend to stop me from leaving?" At last he came to rest, perching on a stool just opposite the Abbot.

"I have no intention of stopping you, Dr. Martine," Bronski said with regret. "The matter is not in my hands. If it were, I would be most happy to bid you a fond farewell." He looked at Defont. "No attendant here is given to violence. We come to serve. Some of us are chosen. Others volunteer and spend their lives serving those in need. But even they can't leave. It matters not how or why you came. Once inside these walls, you are not permitted to leave."

"This is ridiculous," Martine exclaimed. "For God's sake, we're not living in the Dark Ages. How do you intend on stopping us?"

Defont had given the matter some thought. The news of their incarceration had not come as a great surprise. Since they had arrived in Sanok and spoken of traveling to Litz, they had been shunned. Greatcoat's sign of the cross, the cold hard stares of the inhabitants of Litz as they walked through the town, the wolves slinking beside the roadway, hungry and vicious . . . It all seemed *right*.

"And you, Edmund. You just sit there as though you're not involved. Surely you don't believe this?" Martine turned on his fellow Frenchman.

Defont scratched his chin glancing first at Martine and then at Bronski. "We'd never get past Litz, François. If we did, it would be a miracle. And even if we performed that miracle, wolves or bandits would finish us before we could return to the civilized world.

"Bishop Meric was not bullied into giving us what we sought, François. We talked ourselves into this predicament. So you see, it's a useless battle you are fighting, Doctor. Expend your energy elsewhere." For the moment,

Defont was resigned to being a prisoner.

"Father Bronski," Defont called for the priest's attention once again, "I'm curious. Dr. Martine's travel agent knows where we are. I've informed my supervisors of my itinerary. How will you prevent them from launching an inquiry into our whereabouts?"

Curvise had been painfully silent during his friend's discovery of their imprisonment. Now he steeled himself to speak. "If you had waited a few more months, until summer perhaps, before coming to find me . . ." He hesitated, searching for the right words. "Notification of my death would have been forthcoming," he finally said.

"This is ridiculous," Martine exclaimed again. "You're not dead." He stopped and looked from Curvise to Bronski. "You'll have to kill us all if . . ." He stopped again and looked back at his friend. His confusion was evident.

"It's just a ruse, François. I'm not about to die. At least I hope not, but the outside world has to believe I have. Just as I'm sure Father Bronski is planning both yours and Defont's unfortunate demise."

For once in his life, François Martine was silent, his mind a blank. He stared at Antoine and Edmund, but avoided the steady gaze of the abbot.

It was Defont who gathered the information presented to him and made the logical deduction.

"Father Proust! David! He's alive?"

"Yes." Curvise smiled.

"David's alive? Here?" Martine's agitation returned as did his quick steps.

Defont put his hand on the doctor's back. His face carried an expression of relief. "I knew my church was not capable of murder, Doctor."

Martine shrugged off the policeman's hand. "But it's capable of imprisonment." He stopped his pacing and sat in the nearest chair. The fiery resolve that had carried him through life, and had kept his back straight as a rod, suddenly faltered and vanished. He slumped, leaning his arm on the table in front of him. A chill rose and spread through him, not unlike the diametric kick of warm brandy. He shuddered and closed his eyes, beaten.

Father Ehrick carried a tureen of beef stew from the kitchen and placed it in the center of the table. "I hope you enjoy this." He retreated and quickly reappeared with a basket of freshly baked breads.

Hunger overriding all the events he had heard and been a part of, Defont ladled out a heaping portion into his bowl. Grabbing a loaf of bread he sniffed appreciatively. "If you'll excuse me," he apologized as he began to eat. "I'm famished."

Martine looked from Defont to the stew. The smell tickled his nostrils and calmed his anger. Up until that moment, he had not realized how hungry he was. "How is it?"

Mouth full, one hand clutching a small loaf of bread and the other holding a spoonful of stew, Defont could only nod. Which he did, vigorously. Father Ehrick beamed with pride.

Reminding Defont of a woman at a garden tea party, Martine helped himself to a small portion of stew and tasted it with tiny sips. His mouth pursed into a sour grin. He broke off a small bite of bread, dipped it in the gravy and chewed the morsel with a bit more enthusiasm. "I suppose it's adequate," he said with a sigh.

Father Ehrick's grin faded, but it returned completely as he watched Martine finish off a second helping.

After dinner, full and exhausted, Defont, Martine, and Curvise sat at the table and sipped coffee.

"I'm sorry I dragged you into this mess," Curvise finally said. He felt responsible for his friends' confinement.

"No need to apologize, Antoine," Defont soothed. "I won't say I'm happy about this, but at least we'll find the answers to the questions we left in LaRochelle. How is Father Proust feeling?"

"He's fine."

François Martine had returned to his sulking ways and sat silent and moody even as he listened to the conversation around him.

"When may we visit with him?" Defont was anxious to question David.

"Tomorrow morning after breakfast. I'm afraid you'll find he's still a bit of a puzzle. Physically, he's fine."

"This is an insane asylum," Martine blurted.

"Yes," Curvise said. "But there's more to it than that. There are men here who suffer mentally, but there are men here who simply suffer from old age."

"And they are being held against their will?" Martine's eyes went wide with concern.

Defont looked around. The room was empty. The priests had eaten and gone about their other tasks.

"When the time comes François," he said quietly, "we will also leave. In the meantime, I suggest we do nothing to arouse suspicion. From the looks of these priests, I would venture a guess they're not afraid of violence. Please, be patient."

It was the first encouragement Martine had received since hearing of their incarceration. He looked at Curvise for confirmation that escape might be possible. "Is it feasible? Dare I hope?" he asked in a low voice.

"I don't know, François, but, if it is, I will help you all I can."

"You'll come with us."

"No. This is my home now." Curvise's voice was soft. "I didn't have to come here. I was asked to volunteer and I did. The Institut had need of a physician. Me."

"You can't believe that. You were forced to come just as David was," Martine said hotly.

"No, François, I was not forced. Nor was David. He came because he didn't want any more young women to die on his account."

"Then he's responsible for the deaths in LaRochelle?" Defont asked.

Curvise grew suddenly nervous. He rubbed his hands together and looked about the room. When he spoke, his voice was tight and strained. "In a way.. . If you believe what he says."

Defont put the priest on the spot. "Do you believe what he says, Antoine?"

"I don't know, Edmund. I just don't know. You'll have to judge for yourself."

"He's not violent?" Martine made it a question, no longer sure who or what David Proust might have become.

"No. He honestly believes he was responsible for Camille's, Louisa's, and Sister Franza's deaths. Yet, I know for a fact he could not have been anywhere near any of them. I *know* he couldn't have done what he says he did."

"Tomorrow should prove to be an interesting day," Martine said, finishing the last of his coffee. Already he was leaving behind his sulk and taking an interest in his predicament. "I wonder how I'm to die?" he mused. "Something befitting a man of my stature. Perhaps a duel? Yes! I would like that. Assassinated by an outraged husband." His eyes took on a heroic gleam. He would have continued the fantasy, but Defont's laughter interrupted him.

"You're laughing," he pouted. "Why?"

"I, too, was picturing your death, François. I don't quite imagine it to be as noble as you do. I think perhaps your obituary would read: 'Dr. François Martine, a mildly competent doctor, recently passed away when he consumed some poisonous *champignones*.' Yes, that's it. I think your heroic battle should be against bad mushrooms."

Martine stalked from the room, but not before giving Defont a parting shot. "You're a peasant, Edmund. Nothing but a common peasant."

Defont only laughed that much harder. It took him more than a few minutes to catch his breath.

Unable to laugh earlier, the subject too serious to allow humor, Defont's wit finally caused even Curvise to smile, but he still found sympathy for his friend. "You're too hard on François, Edmund."

"He deserves it, Antoine. If you had been in LaRochelle listening to him go on and on about my friendship with you, or rather my lack of it. Just so he could find you. The little rooster even had me so convinced about this sordid matter I threatened Bishop Meric with jail. And now, here I am, together with François for eternity, ourselves in prison, and it suddenly dawns on me to ask the question, why?"

Defont waved his hands. "I came here looking for answers. Forget the three suicides. Think only of Father Proust. A man possessed. He dreams and women die. He's here in an asylum and even if I left tomorrow, who in the world would believe this? I don't believe it any longer."

"There is more to this than meets the eye, Edmund. Much more as you will discover in time."

"Time. I seem to have an abundance of that now, don't I? At least inside of these walls.

"How did you die, Antoine?"

"Automobile accident," Curvise said slowly.

"There will be many sad faces in LaRochelle when the news of your demise is made public. It's too bad you cannot attend the funeral, eh? Now me on the other hand, I fear not many will mourn my death or Dr. Martine's passing either. It's sad, is it not?"

"Sadder still if it were true."

"Something to ponder in the long nights ahead." Defont stood. A snowstorm of crumbs fell from his vest. "Good night, Antoine!"

"Good night, Edmund."

***

"Dr. Martine! Inspector Defont!" David practically screamed a greeting from his cell. His face was lit with the same excitement he had shown when Curvise had first appeared at the Institut. The three men shook hands between the bars while Bronski fumbled with the key to the door.

"Why do you keep him locked up?" Martine asked Bronski in no uncertain terms.

"It's my desire, François," David said.

With the door now open, Bronski placed three chairs inside David's cell. "Call me when you've finished. I'll be down the hallway a bit."

The friends sat in a circle: David cross-legged on his bed surrounded by Defont, Martine, and Curvise ensconced on straight-backed chairs. At first they simply grinned at each other, content to savor the delight of finding David resurrected.

"I can't believe you've come this far just to see me," David said. He was glad to see his old friends although he could not understand why they were here. He eyed Dr. Martine's natty appearance. "What happened to your face, François?"

Martine fingered the three cuts on his chin. "Shaving with cold water is barbaric and decidedly most unpleasant."

It did not seem the time for complaints and an awkward silence filled the cell. Curvise fell back on his daily routine. "How are you feeling this morning, David?"

"Fine. I tried to dream last night, but nothing. I feel fine."

Martine's curiosity had to be satisfied. "Why do you insist on being kept in here, David? This building must be a thousand years old."

"Older, François. It was built by a Roman garrison in the year 28 A.D. Or at least that's when the foundations were laid. It's been renovated often over the centuries."

"How do you know?"

"Father Alphonse told me. You'll have to speak with him, François. At one time, he was an archeologist. A renowned scholar of Roman history." David smiled. "Did you know this was the northernmost outpost of the Holy Roman Empire? It's been in use since the time of Christ and Caesar."

A glint from Martine's eyes highlighted his interest.

"Please don't think me impertinent," David said. "I'm really very happy to see all of you, but why are you here?"

"Don't you know?" Defont asked.

David sighed. "Yes, I guess I do. You want to know. I wish I had the answers." He bowed his head. "I wish I knew." He looked at Defont. "Have you come to arrest me? Am I to be tried like a common criminal?"

"No, David. No crime's been committed. We only want to know how you knew about the young women's deaths."

David shook his head. "I don't know. I just knew. My dreams, I suppose. My nightmares. I don't know, Inspector, but I do know no one else will suffer because of me. I'm safe here." He patted the thin mattress on which he sat and looked about the room. It was obvious to everyone he was content to live within his four walls.

***

"What's wrong with him, Antoine?" Defont asked. They had left David

Proust to the misery of his self-imposed guilt. He had told them everything he had remembered, but it was not enough. "When I listen to him, I have to believe he was in each of the young women's rooms. When I examine the facts, I don't see how it could be accomplished, and yet," Defont returned to the beginning of his circuitous logic, "his descriptions match their rooms perfectly. How is that possible?"

"He told you how he knew," Martine interjected.

They were in the dining room. The walk from the garrison to the lodge had been long and cold. Sitting around the table, David was very much on each of their minds.

"He's possessed. His spirit rose over the roof tops of LaRochelle and entered each girl's room." Martine's face had an ugly smirk. "This is your religion, Defont. Don't you believe in demons and spirits?" François paused only long enough to let his jibe hit home. "Look around and then ask yourself that question again. My God, man! This is the twentieth century. There are no demons left in this world. David was never in those girls' rooms. He's insane."

Defont let Martine's temper tantrum wash over him. "Whether that's true or not, insanity doesn't explain how David could describe each of the three, not one, mind you, but three different rooms so perfectly. And," the policeman countered, "how do you explain the child you say was inside Sister Mary Franza? Was it put there by a spirit?"

Martine had no answer. He was lost, staring down into the black depths of his coffee.

Defont shifted his attention back to Curvise. "Now that we've all been apprised of what Dr. Martine thinks about this situation, what do you make of it, Antoine?"

It was a question Curvise found impossible to answer. Instead, he was honest. "In the short time I've been here Edmund, I've visited David every day. I'm more confused now than ever. You ask me what I make of this. I honestly don't know what to tell you."

"He needs competent psychiatric help," Martine interrupted them. "Any fool can see that."

Curvise let the remark go by, but Defont could not.

"Are you volunteering, Dr. Martine?"

"Yes, yes, I am. If I'm to be stuck here, I might as well make the most of it. Eventually, this could prove to be enlightening to the psychiatric community."

"It could also be harmful to David," Curvise said. As much as he respected his friend's abilities as a physician, he was not as sure of Martine's self-taught psychiatric expertise.

"I have to agree with Antoine," Defont said.

"Yes, of course you would." Martine waved him off angrily. "What do you know? Where have you studied? I studied at the Sorbonne. That's not good enough? Fine. Tell me where you're going to find a competent psychiatrist in Poland, and even if you do, how do you expect to get him here? Remember, once he enters this place, he can't leave."

"I wasn't belittling your abilities, François."

"Don't apologize, Antoine," Defont interrupted. "He's going to do what he feels like no matter what we say. Am I not right, François?"

Martine rubbed his chin thoughtfully, wincing when his fingers scraped the small shaving nicks. "You two seem to have forgotten that I feel the same affection for David as you. I would do nothing to harm him."

"You're right, François. I apologize," Curvise said.

Martine nodded, accepting his vindication. He looked at Defont. "Well, Edmund, I'm waiting."

Defont glanced at Martine and then at Curvise. "It looks like our obnoxious little doctor is back," he said. "It's a shame, don't you think, Antoine?"

"Oaf," Martine said rising from the table and stalking from the room. "There's nothing I loathe more than having to deal with an uncouth oaf."

***

"Our church does this to its priests?" Defont asked, standing in the doorway of the ward. "It just casts them aside?" He shook his head. "How sad, Antoine. How very sad."

"It's not as bad as it may seem, Edmund. They're not, as you said, cast aside. They're well taken care of here. Their brothers look after them."

Defont watched two black robed priests lift an ancient body of skin and bones while a third assistant cleaned the incontinent priest of excrement and other bodily debris. They balanced him on legs too brittle to stand as a clean sheet was placed on the bed. Gently, he was returned to rest.

"It evens out," Curvise said. "Yes, our church assigns these men here so these priests, they're saints you know, can watch over them. These men are dedicated beyond anything I could ever have contemplated. I feel honored to count myself among them."

"Yes, I believe it is an honor," Defont said. "Excuse me, Antoine." He joined the two working priests who were laboring to hoist yet another bed-ridden patient. With his great strength, he easily lifted the frail body of the

154

sick man high off the bed.

Curvise turned and walked away.

"Your friends are most extraordinary, Father Curvise," Bronski said as he joined the physician in the dining room. Defont and Martine had been confined for only two weeks, but the impact they had made with their determination to be useful could be counted in years. "But I am sure you are already aware of that."

"Yes, I am, Father. I only wish they didn't have to feel like prisoners here." Curvise looked into the scarred face. "Isn't there something you can do to help them?"

Bronski rubbed his hands together, lingering where his index finger should have been. "If it were in my power, I would release them immediately."

"Have we been declared dead?"

"You have. I've held back on your friends." Bronski shrugged, giving Curvise a spark of hope. "I've tried to figure out a way to let them go. It's just not in my hands. If they enter the village, they'll certainly be shot. There's an outstanding reward for the capture of anyone from the Institut who is not authorized to leave. I know it's archaic. It is an old rule, never rescinded. As you well know, we're an embarrassment to the church. Especially the children. Not so much now, but in years past, madmen, the aged, and the senile were embarrassments best kept under lock and key."

"I appreciate your honesty, Father Bronski."

"Ah, there you are, Bronski." Martine burst into the dining room. "I've been looking for you." He joined the men at the table without pause for breath. "Those men in the dungeon—it's disgraceful. I demand that you unchain them immediately."

"There's nothing in this world I would rather do, Dr. Martine. But if I did, everyone would resemble me. They're very dangerous."

"Of course they're dangerous! Wouldn't you be, chained to a wall? Confined to a straight jacket? My God man, if you treat people like animals they'll become animals."

"François, you just can't let them roam free. They are dangerous, not only to us, but to themselves as well." Curvise came to Bronski's defense. He was well used to Martine's tirades.

"I know, I know. The least we can do is pad their cells so they aren't confined like livestock."

"Pad their cells with what?" Bronski asked.

"Wool. Cotton. There's a storeroom upstairs with hundreds of old mattresses. We could use them."

Bronski thought about Martine's suggestion for a minute. He liked the sound of it. "I think we should try Dr. Martine's idea. We'll try it on Father Kiosk."

"You can't do that, Father Bronski." Curvise's reaction was swift.

"We will. If it works as Dr. Martine seems to think, what better way to find out?"

"Of course it will work. I'd stake my life on it."

"It's not your life that will be in danger, François," Curvise scolded. "If you insist on allowing this, Father Bronski, then try it first with Father Reigers."

"Which one is he?" Martine asked.

"He's in the cell next to Father Kiosk. He has a bladder control problem," Bronski elaborated.

Martine made a face. "Yes, I remember him. He urinated on me yesterday. I went in to talk to him and he peed on me. And I'd just put on a clean robe that morning." Martine seemed to consider Curvise's choice. "Okay, we'll try it on him first." He looked at Bronski. "Is that all right with you, Father?"

"As you wish, Doctor."

"Good." Martine slapped his hands together. "Now I can eat with a clear conscience. What's for supper?"

"Beef stew," Curvise said.

"Beef stew again! We've had beef stew since the day I arrived. Is that all Father Ehrick knows how to cook? I don't mind being dead, but I'll be damned if I'm going to spend eternity eating nothing but beef stew." He headed for the kitchen, yelling as he went: "Father Ehrick, I need to discuss something with you."

Bronski shook his head.

Curvise smiled.

"Has he always been so . . . rambunctious?"

"For as long as I have known him, yes."

CHAPTER SIXTEEN

The last storms of winter were relentless. Days went by without a hint of sun. Snow fell and fell until the days stumbled upon each other and lost their meaning. Bitter winds blew the traces of civilization away and drifts piled high against the outside walls of the Institut. It became almost impossible to reach the garrison from the main building.

Father Alphonse suggested they use the passageway under the courtyard. With Martine and Defont's help, he opened the rusted door. Rats squealed and ran under their feet, disturbed by humans for the first time in many years.

"Are you sure this leads to the garrison?" Martine asked, shivering. He hated rodents of all kinds.

"Yes. It ends in the old cellar," Alphonse said happily.

"What old cellar?"

"Under the garrison, there's an unused cellar," Alphonse explained. It was where the nobles hid during times of attack."

"Oh." The prospect of old cellars and tunnels that had not been used in years was not appealing. The idea of appearing a coward in front of Defont was even less so. "Well, what are you waiting for, Edmund? Let's go." Martine gave Defont a light shove from behind.

Defont entered the spider-webbed passageway cautiously, his torch held high over his head. Martine steered Father Alphonse through the door next, content to bring up the rear. The rats scurried about, clinging to the rough hewn walls. The floor was littered with their excrement. "It smells awful in here," Martine said. "This will have to be cleaned."

"Yes," Defont agreed from his point position. "And I know just who's going to do it."

The journey seemed to take forever, but, like all trips, it came to an end. With a mighty shove, Defont managed to get the aged door opened. A cavernous room spread out before him. Alphonse and Martine, like the rats, scurried out of the tunnel.

Father Alphonse held his torch high and looked around the huge room. "Now, if I can just remember where the door to the staircase is," he said, wandering about and looking lost. "Ah, here it is."

Three torches shone their feeble light on this latest obstacle. It did not look inviting.

"It will take more than the three of us to break that door down," Defont said. He pounded his fist against it a few times. "It must be a foot thick and it's reinforced with iron."

Martine edged close and grasped the ring that served as a knob. He gave it a quick turn and sharp pull. The door swung inward. "Any civilized person, Edmund, knows that doors of this type weren't meant to be broken down. Doors like this were meant to be graciously opened."

"Well done, Dr. Martine," Alphonse called.

Defont did not care to comment.

***

It took some doing, but Martine managed to gather a few of the overworked priests together and have the tunnel cleaned. As is the case of things that add comfort to souls, the storms ceased. Snow became rain— gentle spring showers at first that would in time turn into torrential downpours. The tunnel would be used, but not with any regularity until winter once again gripped the Carpathian Mountains.

The padded cell was finished. Father Reigers was unchained and put into the protected room. Martine beamed as the madman fell down, got up, and stumbled around the room, without damage.

"It works! Just look at how happy he is," Martine told the priests gathered about him.

The next morning the mattresses were torn to shreds. Father Reigers lay unconscious, his head bruised and battered from where he had pounded it on the bare walls the mattresses no longer covered.

"It would have worked if he had been put in here immediately upon his arrival," Martine said. Shrugging his shoulders, he walked into the cell to administer to the fallen priest.

***

For an hour or more each day, François Martine talked to David Proust, probing into the inner consciousness of his patient. Probing deeply in search of a key that would unlock David's thoughts. He started a journal, writing down every word David said during their sessions.

Days turned into weeks and then months, stumbling and crowding each other until time became one long moment. Fog shrouded the courtyards and blanketed the mountains beyond the high walls. Truth came in periods of incoherency, followed by brief spells of mystical gibberish. As the weather grew warmer, David became uneasy.

***

"Will you listen to this," Martine said excitedly. Sitting at their table in the dining room, Defont was content to eat his supper and ignore the doctor's soliloquy. On the other hand, Curvise was very interested in what his friend had to say about David Proust. So much so that he had to fight to remain objective.

"His goal is to stimulate a woman into having the son of God," Martine read aloud from his journal. "Can you believe it? Stimulate a woman. Not physically, but spirituality."

It was fitting, Curvise thought, that Martine would fixate on the anatomical inconsistencies of David's outbursts. It did not seem to bother his energetic friend that Proust spoke of having the *son of God*. That is my fixation, he thought.

"In LaRochelle he told me he was a messenger, but of something or for someone he could not comprehend. I'm trying to remember, but I don't believe David ever actually said he was a messenger of God," Curvise said.

"Well, he's said it now," Martine said with flourish. "He has no other purpose in life, or so he believes. He even believes once his task is complete, he'll simply die."

Father Bronski entered the dining room in time to hear Martine's last remarks. "That is what Monsignor Michael Proust also believed."

"Who?" Martine's question was sharp.

"I told you about Michael Proust in LaRochelle, François," Curvise reminded his friend.

"Yes, I remember your mentioning something about him, but . . .?"

"He was here," Bronski said. "In the same cell where David now resides. For over thirty years."

"You knew him?"

"Yes, of course. He died in 1935. He told me quite sincerely that if he had been allowed to complete his task, his death would have come at its completion."

Martine was aggravated and excited at the same time. "Why haven't you told me this? Did he suffer the same symptoms as David?"

"Yes," Bronski said, stepping away from the table. "I'll be right back."

Martine turned his curiosity on Curvise. "Did you know of this, Antoine?"

"Only that Michael had been here and suffered the same malady as David. I didn't mention it to you, François. I did not want to prejudice your opinions."

"Prejudice my opinions! My God, Antoine. This could be a hereditary defect we're dealing with. What else should I know that I don't?"

From the corner of his eye, Curvise saw Bronski return to the dining room. Instead of answering, he waited until the abbot had placed a thick leather bound book next to Martine.

"This is Monsignor DeValier's journal," Bronski said, reclaiming his earlier seat. "He compiled these notes over the thirty years he and Monsignor Proust were here."

Martine fingered the edge of the book. He wanted to open it and begin reading immediately.

"It is to be sent to the Vatican. Obviously, I have not yet done so, but in time it must be shipped there. Hopefully, it will shed some light on the problems you now face with Father David."

"What do you think is wrong with David, Father Bronski?" Martine asked his question, but before Bronski could answer, he re-asked it. "Rather, what did you think was wrong with Michael Proust?"

"He was possessed," Bronski said emphatically.

Martine and Curvise stared at the abbot. Even Defont, who had feigned disinterest throughout his meal, looked up with sudden attention.

"Was an exorcism performed?" Martine asked.

"Yes. Several times, in fact. But the demon's grip was too strong on Father Proust's soul. It was terrifying to see. Michael suffered greatly. A man of lesser convictions would have given into temptation and stopped fighting. Monsignor Proust fought the demon until the last day of his life."

"But it's not a demon!" Martine exploded. "It's an inherited mental illness. David Proust is not possessed. He's simply insane."

"What does that make the children then, Dr. Martine?" Bronski asked. "Are they not insane? Or are they possessed? Their insanity is obvious, is it not? Or have you forgotten your experiment with Father Reigers?"

"Of course I haven't. But there are different forms of insanity. Mental illness. Not all of them are incurable. Some can be reversed with time and the proper medical treatment. Many forms of mental illness go undetected. A man can live a somewhat normal life and still be . . ." He did not want to use the word 'crazy.' ". . . unbalanced."

"You're a prime example of that theory, Dr. Martine," Defont said sarcastically.

"Of course I am. We all are. We all suffer from some form of mental illness. That is," Martine smirked, "those of us who have intelligence."

Defont smiled and changed his tactics. "Does that include taste also, Doctor? I see you haven't eaten any of your beef bourguignonne."

In the hopes of variety, Martine had attempted to show Father Ehrick how to prepare his recipe for beef bourguignonne. He had even gone so far as to boast of his accomplishment.

"Personally," Defont continued, "I find it tastes very similar to the beef stew Father Ehrick always makes."

Unfortunately, Defont was correct. No matter what one called the meal, it still tasted like stew.

"You're a peasant, Edmund. Your culinary tastes are locked in the soil. Dirt would satisfy you." With that, Martine picked up the leather bound journal and swept from the room.

***

Settled in his bed, Martine prepared to read Monsignor DeValier's journal. Opening the pungent cover and reading the first page he was struck by the similarity of the storm that had struck LaHarve in 1905 and the one that had hit LaRochelle in 1938. Michael Proust had fallen ill on his 35th birthday. So had David. Both Prousts had suffered illnesses that, while not considered life-threatening, were persistent and reappeared sporadically. Chills ran up his spine as he read of the suicide of a young woman. And then another.

Tormented screams came from the garrison. The children were talking to ghosts tonight.

As a reader who mouthed every word, Martine's throat became parched and dry. The journal was uncomfortably heavy on his stomach. He got out of bed and slipped on his robe. He would sit in the dining room under the light of more than one kerosene lamp. It would be much better for his eyes than his single flame.

Entranced by the writing of DeValier, he did not notice when Father Ehrick passed through the dining room on his way to the kitchen. He did stop long enough to thank him for the coffee a few minutes later. His eyes burned, but he could not put the book down. He finally shut the journal when Defont and Curvise joined him at the table for breakfast.

"You look awful, François," Defont commented.

"I feel awful," Martine said wearily. He ran his pale hands through his hair, but it did nothing to improve his appearance. The beard stubble on his face itched and his blood shot eyes were incapable of focusing.

"Have you been reading all night?" Curvise asked.

"Yes, and what I've read so far is frightening," Martine said somberly. "David's uncle, Michael Proust suffered the same—not just closely related—Antoine, but the very same symptoms David has expressed. The events started on the same date. No wait. Not the same date, but on each man's 35th birthday. David believes he was responsible for impregnating three women. Virgins. Michael Proust believed he had stimulated two—both of whom were found dead. Suicides."

Defont had not paid any attention to Martine until the doctor's last statement. "Suicides? Where?"

"In LaHarve," Martine answered. "Verifiable, I would think?"

"When? I mean, in what year did they occur?"

"1905."

Martine looked at Curvise. "Monsignor Michael languished himself in David's same cell for thirty years."

Curvise winced. The thought of living in confinement for thirty years hurt. It hurt just as much to think David might have to suffer the same fate as his uncle. "Why?" It was all he could think to ask.

"His faith. Nothing more. Michael Proust believed he was possessed and, as a man of immense faith in Christianity, he refused to believe otherwise." Martine paused for a moment. "Like David, Michael Proust believed himself to be the messenger of God sent here to . . ." Martine stopped.

"What, François?" Curvise prompted.

"To impregnate a female with the son of God." Martine yawned. "I'm sorry. I am very tired."

"Does he say how?"

"He said the same thing as David. To stimulate one of the Chosen."

"Is that all?" Curvise asked.

"That's all I've read so far." Martine yawned again. "Now, if you'll excuse me, I really must get some sleep."

Curvise and Defont watched their friend leave the room. Breakfast came and went, but neither man had an appetite.

"You've been very quiet about all this, Antoine," Defont said. "You and I both know none of the women in LaRochelle were pregnant. I know Dr. Martine insists Mary Franza was with child, but her lab tests came back negative. She was a virgin. How could that be?"

"Without having seen what François says was a child, I would hazard to guess it was a cancerous growth, perhaps. A tumor of some sort."

"Not his imagination?"

"No. He told me he destroyed it to protect me."

"Protect you from what? You're not responsible."

"Me, being the church. For a man who professes a great dislike for religion, sometimes I think François is more devout than I am."

Defont started to laugh, but stopped. "Or me. For years, since I was old enough to accompany my parents to church, I have prayed to the statues inside of St. Margaret's, prayed to the stone images of God and his saints. Religion was nice and peaceful. The church was warm and comforting. I can't say I ever lost my faith, but coming here has certainly jolted it into reality."

"In what way, Edmund?" Curvise was curious. His own beliefs had taken a turn lately.

"For one thing, the way the priests are hidden away here. Justice should have taken the lives of the murderers. Instead, the church hides them. And the others. They're not murderers. They've committed no crime and don't deserve to be here. Yet, the church hides them, too. If it weren't for the brothers who labor so diligently to care for them, I believe I could hate the church."

"Would you respect your church more, knowing it had people like the children serving God?"

"Respect? I don't know. Like you, I was taught there's a difference between right and wrong. Our church teaches us to be honest and forthright. Then it hides its own sins here. It's an understandable weakness, but our religion should have no weakness."

"And how would you treat a case like David's?"

"I'd try to do what you did. Get him competent help. You believed that was what was going to happen. Instead, well, here we are. Dead. A white lie. A venial sin which is easily forgiven.

"What I don't understand, Antoine, is why the church is so afraid to let David freely speak his mind? Are they really that frightened? How can he hurt them?"

"That's it!" Curvise exclaimed suddenly. "That's exactly what's been bothering me, Edmund, only I haven't been able to put it into words such as you have. This fear of demons, possessions, spirits, and ghosts. They may or may not be with us, but if they are, why hide them? And if they aren't, why hide someone like David? It makes me believe there's more, so much more to this than we're allowed to know. I struggle, trying to see what harm would have come to the church if David had been allowed to seek help. And, if necessary, pay for whatever crimes he may have committed. And I can't.

There is no harm. None at all."

Defont shrugged away Curvise's mention of social punishment. "No crime was committed, Antoine. Who could accuse David of committing a crime? What did he do? Dream?"

***

David tossed and turned, his sleep unpeaceful. He soared over the walls. *Look there. Gabriel struggles against a devil etched in stone and time. He could see where the winds had almost weathered away the little finger of the Archangel's right hand.* David was lost, struggling to find his zone of safety. With limited powers, he could only dream in a fixed place in time. There was no anger. No hate. No emotion at all at being turned back. Only the desperate need to finish his task. But other dreams mingled and twisted from his thoughts into memories he could not claim.

The room was clean, cool, and white. People moved about, friendly and smiling. Ape-like creatures wandered freely. It was a laboratory, but like none he had ever seen or imagined. "Who are you?" he asked, not in a scream of terror, but with a voice filled with curiosity. With awe. And the answer had come.

"What is a name? You may call me God."

***

The deeper François Martine read into Monsignor DeValier's journals, the more convinced he became that David and Michael were and had, indeed, been possessed. Nothing else could answer all the questions that had been raised. From what he had learned from reading Freud and Jung, no listed mental illness fit the description of David's malady. If he claimed to be God, well, that could be explained. If he lusted only for sex, *that* could be explained. If he sought blood, was violent, wanted only to destroy things ... if he hated his mother or father . . . if he hated the things near to him—the church or anything—hate could be explained.

The irrational thoughts David spoke of were not irrational. Abnormal as the contents of his conversations had been, there was a logic to them that seemed to be just out of Martine's reach. Nothing made sense. It was . . . irrational. Was David possessed or did he simply possess a power of which men had always dreamed?

Martine examined the notes he had taken on the talks he had had with David and found the line he was looking for. There it was in his own hand-

164

writing. A quote from Father David Proust: "I am not of this earth." Now, where had he heard that before?

***

The spring rains turned into summer flowers. Birds fluttered and swooped over the ramparts building their nests. The sun occasionally broke through the overhanging shroud and cast its light inside the walls of the Institut. As August neared its end, a plague of insects descended on the Institut. Biting flies and blood-sucking mosquitoes came in swarms. No one was spared their viciousness.

"For three months I've listened to David and read DeValier's journal. Three months," Martine said wearily. "If I believe what I've read and listened to each day, I'd have to diagnose myself as having a mental breakdown."

It had been over a month since Martine had joined Curvise and Defont in the dining room for supper. He had been so engrossed in his studies he had lost track of time and his friends.

"Why don't you eat, François?" Curvise suggested gently. "You look haggard."

A bowl of stew sat in front of the prim doctor. Flies lined the edge of the bowl. Absently, Martine brushed them away.

"Yes," Defont chimed in, "eat your stew before it kills the flies. No, wait. Is it beef bourguignonne? I get confused with all the gourmet meals we have here."

"We had chicken yesterday," Curvise said. "I didn't see you here, Edmund."

"Father Ehrick brought me some in the ward. It was delicious, yes?" Defont grinned at Martine. "Did you eat yesterday, François?"

"No. Unless it is done properly, chicken is for peasants." Martine tried to hide his disappointment at missing the meal. Beef stew had grown common and unappetizing. He raised the spoon to his lips, but set it back down without thought, his mind elsewhere.

"Have you read H.G. Wells, Antoine?" he asked.

"Yes, I have."

"Is he still alive? Do you know?"

Curvise blinked at his friend's seemingly random questions. He knew Martine better than to believe this conversation would lead nowhere. "I'm sorry, I don't know. Why?"

"I'd like him to meet David. Maybe send him Monsignor DeValier's journals. They both remind me of his futuristic stories."

"Why not write one yourself?" Defont said.

"Because no one would believe it coming from me." Martine sighed. "I'm not sure anyone would believe it coming from Mr. Wells, but one might well *accept* the idea. That would be enough." Martine pushed the stew away. "David Proust is a man who believes he is here to cause the birth of the son of God, although not necessarily a new Christ. He tells me God is simply a name—not the deity we," he corrected himself, "you worship. God is a traveler from some distant planet." He stopped and waited for their laughter. None came. "David says it's true that this God created us in His own image. Not from clay. Not though evolution. But through some feat of genetic engineering." Martine let out an embarrassed laugh. "Genetic engineering. Those are David's, no, wait. Those are God's words." He wondered whether to continue, and was surprised to find both Curvise and Defont waiting for him to proceed.

"Where did He come from?" Curvise asked hesitantly. Putting his question into words gave this absurd idea reality. "Did David say?"

Martine shook his head. "I don't know. David and . . . I don't know. In the first place, I'm not really sure God's an individual. When David speaks of Him, he tends to use plural pronouns. They do this. They do that. David tells me he knows they are not of this earth. He says he knows this because he now knows his purpose." Martine sat up even straighter than before. "The child of God is destined to return to his origins. In order to do that, he must be born."

"Jesus answered, My kingdom is not of this world," Curvise said softly. "John 18:36. It's a quote from the Bible."

"I know that, Antoine," Martine said indignantly. "Just because I don't pray to your God," he stopped in mid-sentence unsure just what he believed. "Just because I am no longer Catholic, certainly doesn't mean I don't remember the catechism lessons I was taught as a child. Jesus was the Son of God, born into this world by the Immaculate Conception. David believes he is here to produce another."

"The Madonna," Curvise said. "The virgin with child."

"Exactly. Camille Robéson, Louisa Markey, Sister Franza. All virgins with child except," Martine raised one skilled finger in the air to emphasize his point, "not one of them was chosen."

"The Chosen People of God," Defont whispered almost to himself. He recalled his investigation into the backgrounds of the victims. "The Jews."

Curvise looked up sharply. "You told me Camille and Louisa both had a grandmother who was a Jew. And that Sister Mary Franza's mother was a Jew. All three of them had dark skin, dark eyes, and black hair. Jewish traits."

Martine and Curvise exchanged glances.

"The Jews claim to be the Chosen People of God," Defont said. "The Bible shows Jesus with blue eyes, blond hair, and fair skin. But Mary was a Jew." Defont stopped, feeling as though his words were sacrilegious.

"What else did you learn?" Curvise asked, not wanting to change the subject, but to delve into it more deeply.

"Just a minute," Martine said. "I made some notes." He reached into his robe and pulled out a bundle of crushed papers. With precise movements, he straightened them on the edge of the table.

"This is from DeValier's journals. *The creatures were brought to the house of God where they were given the images of God and His fellow travelers.*" Martine turned the paper over. "*The child was almost like them except it was black.*" Martine hesitated, again expecting ridicule. His audience expressed only interest. "*Images were again given to the creatures and, in time, the descendants of God were born.*" Martine continued. "*God chose the people who could reproduce Him, and He made a race that would stimulate the Chosen into bearing His son.*"

"Have you mentioned any of this to David?" Curvise asked.

"Yes. He says he dreams of a place that's white and clean. A laboratory here people are busy, but smiling. A place without anger. He's adamant about that part."

"What about this genetic engineering?" Curvise's mind fired with the possibilities those words created even as they were beyond his conception.

"He has absolutely no recollection. Sometimes he speaks to me as if he's a different person. No, that's not really right. It's more as if he's speaking with someone else's knowledge. As you know, Antoine, I jumped on his terminology right away. I mean, can you imagine . . .?" Martine eyes danced with ideas, but he brought himself back to the present with a shrug of his thin shoulders. "When I asked him about it later, he had no idea what I was talking about."

"What is this gene engineering?" Defont asked.

"There! That's exactly what David said to me when I asked him about it." Martine's look was one of vindication.

Curvise answered Defont's question with one of his own. "Are you familiar with Mendel?"

"No."

"He was a scientist who studied heredity using the common pea for his experiments. He found, through genetic engineering, breeding the same pea family again and again produced hundreds, thousands of peas that looked and were exactly alike."

"But there was a flaw," Martine interjected. "I'm not sure of the mathematics, but in certain specific generations, Mendel's pea produced a mutant. That was his real discovery. No matter how many times Mendel crossed the same plants, he inevitably ended up with mutations."

"We can do this with humans?" Defont could not grasp all that had been placed before him. He was a studious man. A man for which logic held a great deal of power. Flights of fantasy were hard for him to envision.

"No, Edmund. We're a long way from ever being able to reproduce ourselves exactly." Curvise hesitated and glanced at his friends. "Or are we? When I spoke to David's father, he told me David and Michael were exactly alike. Naturally, I assumed he was referring to their mental and spiritual aspirations. Now, I'm not so sure."

"Bronski," Martine exclaimed. "He was here when Michael Proust was incarcerated. He's been here thirty years. Michael came in 1905. He couldn't have changed that much over the years."

"But surely, if he had seen a resemblance he would have said something," Defont said.

"Father Bronski is not one to volunteer information, especially when it concerns the sometimes not so explainable happenings inside these walls. Father Alphonse has been here almost as long. I wonder if he knew Michael Proust?"

"He's on duty in the wards tonight. We can ask him at breakfast tomorrow," Defont said. His curiosity had been pricked and itched like a wound trying to heal. "What else can you tell me about this genetic engineering?" He was eager to learn.

"Don't tell me we've struck a nerve and woken a sleeping giant in your head?" Martine chided lightly. "Don't tell me you have a brain that actually seeks to gain knowledge."

Defont felt the barb. "Unlike you, François, I had no choice when I was a young man. I was not given the opportunity to attend the university. I had to help my family survive. I'm sorry I've never had the same opportunities life has provided you."

"Well put, Edmund," Curvise said.

Martine refused to look at the Inspector. Defont was right. An apology was due. "I'm sorry, Edmund. I was just being me."

"Forget it. Tell me more about genetics. Especially the part about mutants."

"As I said. I'm not sure of the numbers," Martine began to teach who he discovered to be a rather apt pupil. "But Mendel proved no matter how pure the strain of genes one combined, inevitably a mutant would appear. Three generations? Seven? I'm not sure." He looked to Curvise for help. "Do you remember, Antoine?"

"No, I'm sorry."

Defont pondered what the cocky doctor had just told him. "I've always been amazed and mystified by human beings. For instance, we're all basically alike in so many ways—our strengths and other physical attributes. There are millions of us walking and talking, doing the same things all over the world. Are we the peas Mendel produced? The people in the garrison, chained to the walls . . . are they the mutants? Or is it that the children of the Institut are simply a different set of peas?" He looked at Martine. "Edison, Voltaire, Caesar, Christ? Are they the real mutants on this earth? Do you understand what I'm trying to say?"

Martine's eyebrows went up. He looked at Curvise and then back at Defont. "I've never thought of the geniuses in the world in that respect, but yes, I'd have to say that's a possibility." He thought about it for a moment. "A distinct possibility."

The men had touched upon a subject close to Curvise's heart. He had always wondered why some men, as Defont had said—men like Edison—stood above the rest of the world. He had never once thought of associating their brilliance with mutations.

"DaVinci, Mozart, Alexander," he said slowly. "Men who, if one thinks about them, can only be visualized as different. Men not of this world."

"Exactly," Defont said, adding his own candidate to the list. "What about Marconi? How, in heaven's name, did he devise the means, or even conceive of the notion of transmitting voices over wires? Through thin air?"

"Pasteur, Madame Curie," Martine added. "Where did the dreams that became their discoveries exist before their creation?"

"Don't forget Copernicus," Bronski said startling the three men out of their individual reveries. "I'm sorry, I wasn't eavesdropping. I just happened to walk in as you mentioned Pasteur." He sat down next to Martine.

François pounced. "Tell me, Father Bronski, is there a resemblance between David Proust and his uncle Michael?"

By habit, Bronski folded his hands in a position of prayer. He gazed down the hall and out of the window at the dark outside.

"Tomorrow you can judge for yourself, Dr. Martine. Monsignor Proust is entombed in the catacombs under the very place where we now sit."

CHAPTER SEVENTEEN

"My God! The resemblance is uncanny." Martine's torch shook with excitement.

Curvise and Defont stood behind the smaller man, staring at the mummified remains of Michael Proust. He had been in his sixties when he had died, but there was no mistaking the similarities between the corpse and David.

"Who embalmed him?" Curvise asked Bronski.

"Father Alphonse."

Martine touched the glass that separated him from the body. Michael Proust, and maybe a hundred more—Martine could not tell— were entombed behind glass to preserve their likeness for posterity. Niches chiseled into the stone sides of the room had become their final resting place. "And the glass? Is that Father Alphonse's work also?" Martine asked, thinking how nice it would be if he could spend eternity in these catacombs —preserved forever.

"Yes," Bronski said. "This is his domain. There are more, but they have lost their substance over the centuries. Father Alphonse informs me this place is a natural preserve. The air and lack of humidity—it's like being in an ice box. It keeps our brothers alive."

"Well, I can definitely see a strong family resemblance between the two," Defont said. "When you came here, Father Bronski, and first saw Michael, and then when David came, did you see more than just a strong resemblance?"

Bronski looked at the remains of Michael for a minute or two, remembering him fondly. Father Proust had suffered, but he had never lost his will to live or die as a priest. "It was as though I was looking at my old friend arisen from the grave," he said. "David is Michael's reincarnation."

Curvise stared at the body. There was no mistaking the likeness, but something nagged at his thoughts. He could see it, but he could not put his finger on the idea. Maybe later, he thought. "Well, I'm convinced, but I'm not sure of what," he said. "Have you seen enough, François?"

"No. If you don't mind, I'd like to stay down here for a while." The latent archeologist had come to life.

Counting the thirty-four stairs as he climbed them, Curvise held his torch over the edge of the upper landing. The light did not reach the floor, but cascaded along the walls, illuminating, for seconds at a time, the ghastly remains of those who had served and been served in the Institut d'Infantiles.

***

Curvise and Defont walked slowly across the courtyard. The early morning was one of the few times the insects were at rest. A light breeze fluttered and threw about leaves and pinecones. A chill was in the air. The first day of September and autumn was on the wind.

"You met David's father," Defont said.

"Of course! That's it," Curvise interrupted his friend, stopping in the middle of the courtyard. "I met David's father, and there was absolutely no similarity between him and his son, or Michael, for that matter. Absolutely none!"

Defont retraced the steps that had carried him past Curvise's stationary figure. "Surely there had to be something?"

"No, Edmund. It was like two different people. Alain Proust is short, about François' height. Stocky, with heavy eyebrows and dark eyes. There was no resemblance at all. His complexion was the same as ours. David is fair-skinned."

"From his mother's side of the family then?"

"I suppose that's possible. I never met Mrs. Proust, but I'd bet my life she bears no resemblance to David."

Curvise looked into the haze that hid the sun. A strong gust of wind swirled through the courtyard, biting at the hems of the two men's robes. Suddenly, a different chill was in the air. They made the next round on their morning walk in silence, lost in the confusion of concepts beyond their imagination.

At last, heading back to the main building, Curvise tried to find other points of interest besides David Proust.

"How is Cardinal Horck doing, Edmund?" The old priest had been almost at the point of vegetation until Defont had arrived. He should have been dead.

Defont smiled. "Yesterday, he called me a son of a bitch. It's funny how a man, a priest, remembers words like that. But he's alive Antoine, and I'd rather he cussed us than to lie in his bed counting his breaths until death."

"You have a gift, my friend. People gravitate towards your kindness. You would have made a marvelous priest." Curvise tried to remember the last time he had complimented Defont. He could not.

Defont laughed. "It's not a gift. It's my size. I think I must frighten people. Not here, of course. One has only to look into Father Bronski's face. If that doesn't frighten them, I certainly won't."

Curvise lowered his head against a sharp wind and a desire to ask the question that had persisted in his thoughts since Defont's and Martine's arrival at the Institut. He had started to ask it several times, but never had. Now he would.

"Why did you come, Edmund? And please don't tell me it's because François nagged you into tagging along."

Defont reached for the handle of the door, but made no move to open it. "I've asked myself that very question a hundred times. I still have no answer—and maybe that's why I'm here. To find the answer." He pulled the door open. "There's one thing of which I'm quite sure. I have no regrets."

Curvise nodded and walked into the main building. "Neither do I," he said softly.

Defont followed closely. There was something on his mind. "A priest . . ." he began and then stopped to try again. "No, priests don't have these kinds of thoughts. These are the thoughts of a layman. Have you ever thought of killing someone, Antoine? More than one?" he asked.

There was no hesitation in Curvise's answer. "No."

Defont shook his head, a lumbering bear worrying a freshly caught salmon. "I didn't think so. Sometimes at night when I'm in the wards, I stop and look at the Cardinals as they lie helpless in their beds. Almost invisible. So emaciated. So white. I think perhaps I would be doing them a favor by putting a pillow over their faces and sending them to heaven." A tear rolled down Defont's cheek. "Doesn't God see these men suffering?"

"I'm sure He does. It's not our place to decide when men die, Edmund. Sometimes I think these men would have been dead long ago if not for the Institut itself. There's an air, a serenity here. It's almost as though we've left the face of the earth and traveled to a distant planet. We're in a world of our choosing. What more could any man ask of God?"

"God," Defont said. "What if what David told François is true? What if God is just a man's name? Would that bother you, Antoine?"

"I don't think of God as a man or spirit. Categorizing Him would not bring me any peace. He simply is." Curvise sighed, knowing that was not what his friend needed to hear. "I guess if I had to explain myself, I would say He is an idea. A way of life. Man or spirit makes no difference to me. It is His words that rule my days."

Defont nodded his head. "You would have made a fine priest, Antoine," he echoed his friend's earlier remark and walked away.

"I see I'll have to teach Cardinal Horck some new epitaphs for you, Edmund." Curvise smiled at his friend's back. The melancholy of the earlier moment had gone, brushed away by the reminder of a good way of life.

***

Making a mental inventory of his meager supplies occupied Curvise for his entire walk back to his office. Winter would bring a new wave of illness, but Bronski had assured him it would be no problem getting the medical supplies he needed. Now, as he moved between the glass bottles of tinted syrups and small vials of clear medicines, between instruments of health that would so soon become archaic as the world moved forward into knowledge, he tried not to think about David. It was impossible.

He sat behind his desk and faced his chair towards the window. Peace could often be found by simply staring out past the gate, watching the villagers of Litz deliver wood for the Institut's many fireplaces. Great piles of weathered logs and loads of spiky kindling were placed in obscure funeral pyres along the inside walls. It looked to Curvise as if the Institut were preparing for some ancient pagan ritual instead of winter in the mountains. But he knew better. The bins in the basement were already filled with potatoes, cabbages, carrots, and onions.

The Institut was more than an asylum for the sickness of man, Curvise suddenly realized. It was a part of the countryside. The town of Litz depended on it for survival. The old bushas repaired the ripped and tattered black robes of the priests. Each morning housewives labored in the cellar, washing the soiled sheets and pillow cases, dependent on the few coins they received for their labors.

From the neighboring farms, the Institut bought vegetables. The farmers' cattle, sheep, and chickens would be slaughtered when the weather froze. It was a primitive society that survived without any modern conveniences. It would be nice to have such things as electricity and a telephone, but Curvise found he did not miss men's inventions. In fact, he had found he did not even miss the outside world.

***

The calamity of war—anticipated, predicted and dreaded—had been going on for a week before the news reached the Institut d'Infantiles.

In his office, Curvise happened to catch, out of the corner of his eye, the shadow of Father Bronski as the old abbot hurried across the courtyard toward the gate. He did not look away as Bronski closed the gates and walked slowly back to the building, mouthing and gesturing words Curvise could not hear.

"Germany and Russia have invaded Poland. France and England have declared war," Bronski said slowly. Sadly. "It's not our concern," he added. "We are in the hands of God. We'll continue to do our work regardless of what mankind imposes upon itself."

So it was that the inhabitants of the Institut heard that the world was at war again. The news came and went, taken with the same resolve as any other. It was only a slight stumble in man's walk to the future.

***

Curvise had expected Martine to break into a rage and sing France's national anthem. It surprised him when Martine shrugged it off with a single comment: "It will be over in a few months. No need to get upset."

"How can you say that? For years, I listened to you expound on this coming war. Now you sit there and act as if it's nothing."

"What else could it be, Antoine? Wars are easily started. Any fool can produce one," Martine said. "What I'm working on will make any war look foolish."

"What are you doing, François? You and Father Alphonse are always in the catacombs. Have you found something we should know about?"

"I don't know yet. Maybe in a few days." He changed the subject. "Did you know Father Grebsky is an artist? He sculpts the most wondrous pieces."

Curvise did not have to think to place Father Grebsky. He knew him by sight. "His left hand is mangled. Smashed in a door by one of the children."

"Yes."

It was difficult to leave the conversation with that word. Martine was not a man to contain a project in which he was involved. The way he viewed life, if something were important enough for him to take an interest in, then it was certainly important enough to be shouted to the world. It was very difficult to keep this secret.

Cup of coffee in hand, Defont joined them. He looked tired.

"You're working too hard, Edmund," Curvise advised.

Defont ignored the comment and turned on Martine. "I see you've come up from your ghoulish hive, eh?"

It was an insult Curvise was positive Martine would not let slide. He did. Curvise looked at the two of them, wondering. Defont would not meet his eye.

"Just a few more days, I hope," Martine said.

"No, Doctor," Defont corrected him. "No hopes. In a few days—yes."

"Yes," Martine answered quietly. "I'm sorry, I must be excused. I have to get back to my work."

Curvise waited until François had left the dining room before he turned on Defont. "What's going on here, Edmund?"

"Nothing."

"No, not nothing. If it were nothing, you wouldn't look so tired."

Defont glanced around, making sure Martine was gone. He was about to share the little bit of Martine's secret that he knew.

"François has borrowed Father Grebsky to help him with some project. He's practically been living down in the catacombs. I've been working Father Grebsky's shift."

Curvise was bewildered. "What's he up to now?"

"I don't know. He won't tell anyone. He, Father Alphonse, and Father Grebsky keep themselves locked up in the tombs. Ah well," he shrugged, "as François says, maybe we'll know in a few days . . . I hope."

***

And it was only a few days. Four days later, Curvise, Bronski, and Defont walked down the stairs, past the basement and into the catacombs that had become Martine's domain. Curvise was surprised to find even Father Bronski had been kept in the dark.

Martine greeted them at the bottom of the stairs. A proud patron, he was about to show off his latest discovery. Without a word, he led them into the catacombs. His excitement was contagious. Curvise felt a chill that had nothing to do with the cool air beneath the Institut.

Martine stood in front of the newcomers—Father Alphonse and Father Grebsky on each side. Then he stepped aside, unveiling for his friends the secret that had kept him walled inside the catacombs for many long weeks.

"Sweet Mother of God," Defont exclaimed, looking at Martine's project.

Curvise was speechless.

Only Bronski did not appear to be overwhelmed. But appearances are often deceiving.

"Can you believe it? Five! Five perfectly preserved dead men, and they all look like the same person," Martine exclaimed. They had left the catacombs and returned to the comfort of the dining room. "Exactly alike," he reiterated.

His were the only words yet spoken. The shock of seeing David reproduced through five generations had been too much for words. Under the living lights, under the comparative warmth of the dining room, the men's thoughts began to thaw.

"Two of them are Prousts," Martine said. "It's inscribed in stone under each of their resting places. The other three aren't related by name at all."

"I don't doubt that, Doctor," Bronski said. "Three out of five men . . . born over a period of three hundred years and not even related . . . That they should look so much alike. It's not . . . ."

"Not holy, Father?" Martine finished his sentence.

"Yes."

"We asked why the church was so afraid of David that they couldn't afford to have him in the outside world—even under qualified psychiatric care. I think this is the answer to that question," Martine said smugly.

"This has to be an error," Curvise ventured.

"No, Antoine. There is no error. Father Grebsky is more than a competent sculptor. Before joining the church, he studied art diligently. His reconstruction of each face is based solely on the bone structure of each man. He did not create these faces. He merely brought them back into view." Martine's attention shifted to Bronski. "Were you aware of this, Father?"

"No," Bronski defended. "Of course I saw the image of Michael in David, but the others who passed away before my time ...." He shook his head. "I had no idea."

"What we were discussing a few weeks ago—Mendel and his reproduction of peas—does that apply here?" Defont asked.

"It would, but only if the parents had remained exactly the same through each generation. So, to answer your question, no, it couldn't be done. With peas, yes. With humans, no."

"But there has to be an explanation." Defont stopped. "The answer is in David," he said softly.

Martine beamed at the Inspector as if he were a star pupil. He smoothed his hair and almost absently dusted off his sleeve. Leaning forward, he drew his audience closer. "That's what I believe and, I think I can say without contradiction, that is what we all believe." François straightened. "What you say is particularly true, Edmund. The answer is *in* David. There's only one way to get the information we now seek." Once again he leaned forward. Everyone around the table did the same. Martine's voice, when he spoke, was barely above a whisper. "We must let him complete his task."

No one spoke for the longest time. It was as if to speak and break the silence would give credence to what they had just heard.

176

"It's out of the question," Bronski finally said, starting an immediate chain reaction.

"That's insane," Curvise agreed. "What are you thinking, François, to even suggest such an act?"

Only Defont remained silent.

Martine reveled in the controversy that surrounded him. His eyes flashed as they glanced into the faces that belittled him. His back was straight and his head high. He waited until his friends had ceased their condemnations.

"You still haven't given me one positive reason why this shouldn't be done. Oh, you can denounce me, but I'm telling you what you already know. If you want the answer, David must be allowed to impregnate a Jewess. The child she bears will be the new Christ."

"This is blasphemy!" Bronski roared in Martine's face. His own countenance had gone from civilly scarred to a vivid red, slashed by old wounds that would not be forgotten. "Sacrilegious nonsense. You are nothing more than a heretic!"

Martine was unshaken by the abbot's outburst. He had expected it. In fact, he would have been disappointed had the insults not been hurled. It was necessary that they be said, if only to clear the air. Father Bronski was the most fitting person to voice them. It was also fitting that the truth be uncovered.

"You can deny it all you want, Father Bronski, but in your heart you know I only speak the facts." Martine waited until Bronski's breathing calmed. "How long have you known the truth?" he asked.

With a sigh, Bronski slumped in his chair. He closed his eyes and tried to find some peace within. He could not.

"For many years. Monsignor DeValier told me," he finally said. "As a matter of fact, he suggested the same solution you have professed."

"I thought so," Martine acknowledged without bitterness. "When I didn't find it in his journals—oh, he alluded to it, but he could never bring himself to use the words. To actually write it down."

"I can't believe what you're saying, François," Curvise said. "How did you come to such an outlandish conclusion?"

"It was really quite simple, Antoine. I read the Bible. Luke, Chapter one, verses 26 through 32 speak of the Immaculate Conception, the birth of Christ. *"And the angel came in unto her, and said, Hail, thou that art highly favored, the Lord is with thee. Blessed art thou among women. And when she saw him, she was troubled at his saying, and cast in her mind what manner of salutation this should be. And the angel said unto her, Fear not, Mary. For thou hast found favor with God. And, behold, thou shalt conceive in thy womb, and bring forth a son, and shalt call his name JESUS. He shall be great, and shall be called the Son of the Highest.'"* Martine smiled. It was a direct quote. Not even Bronski could find fault with the Bible.

"If you'll quit forcing yourself into ignorance just because you don't like what I'm saying, I know you will understand why I suggested what I did. We have the opportunity here to witness the birth of the man you call Lord. The founder of this religion. And to find out why he wishes to be reborn."

"So he can return to His Kingdom," Defont said, his voice soft as sheep's wool.

All eyes turned to him.

"Don't you see? David said He only wanted to return home. And he said His home was not of this earth." He looked up. "His home is up there somewhere."

Bronski's face had again grown red. "No!" he practically shouted. "A thousand times no! You can say it for eternity, but I refuse to believe it."

"What are you afraid of, Father Bronski? Surely, your faith is strong enough to witness the birth of your own savior?" Martine's voice was very clear.

Bronski's anger became controlled energy. His eyes narrowed to slits and he looked as though, at that very moment, he could stab François Martine through his traitorous heart. With an effort, he spoke civilly, but his words dripped venom. "How would you do this, Doctor? Abduct a young girl—a Jew—and throw her in the cell with Father Proust? My faith in my savior is not in question. It is my faith in people such as yourself that is in doubt." He stormed from the room.

Undaunted, Martine turned to his remaining audience of two.

"He's right, you know," Curvise said.

There it was. An obstacle too large for him to move. "Yes, he's right," Martine agreed. "I hadn't thought it through that far, but I'm right, too." His eyes pierced Curvise's. "Doesn't it bother you that this church, this holy institution of saints and popes and what-nots, built by a simple man, is now frightened of seeing Him again? It does me. I find it unconscionable that the Catholic Church could be frightened of what the new savior might think or say about how His teachings have been prostituted for wealth. That is, if He could even recognize the religion of Christianity. Personally, I don't believe He would even care. Like Defont said, I think He's only interested in finding His way home."

Curvise sighed. "I don't understand you, François. Even if He were born, tell me how He could get off this earth. Have you a magic rocket or some sort of H.G. Well's space vehicle you've been building in the catacombs?"

Curvise felt uneasy even speaking in such terms, but he was unable to let his friend's theories go untested. "I don't understand your logic."

"I don't either," Martine acknowledged. "But look around you, Antoine. Thirty years ago we were bound to the dirt. Now we can fly. We drive automobiles. We listen to the radio and send telegrams over wires as thin as our hair. Thirty years of progress. Created for whom? For what? Is it possible that the mutants Edmund spoke of—the Edisons, Marconis, Einsteins. Is it just possible they're not mutants at all, but a special breed of people who have in them the same genetic engineering David claims to possess?" Agitated into movement, Martine jumped to his feet and walked to the head of the table.

"Damn! Why is it so hard for you to imagine? You accept other ideas without question." He took a seat. "Tell me, Antoine," he began again, attacking from a different angle. "How does a man conceive of something like a light bulb? Or of transmitting our voices across wires and then, the very air we breathe while the rest of us have to be taught to tie our shoes? Who are these people? What is the purpose of all this? To better our lives?" Martine leaned forward, punctuating the air with a stabbing finger. "I think not. I think . . ." He sat back in his chair and relaxed, confident now his words would be heard. "I think their purpose is to someday, through God, provide the means for Him to go home."

"You say, 'through God.' Do you believe if He is born again He will have the knowledge to take us beyond our present state?" At last Curvise was showing signs of wavering. "Will He be a . . . mutant?"

"I don't know, Antoine. It's all speculation, although it's based on a great deal of fact. You've seen the evidence yourself down in the catacombs. I'm not sure I would call Him a mutant, but I definitely believe He won't be like us. How different He might be, I can't say. He may hold the knowledge of the universe in His hands or He may just be a preacher like Christ. I don't know, but I do know this. We have the opportunity to answer those questions." Martine held up his hand before Curvise could protest. "I know. I know. We can't just abduct a Jewish girl, but if we could . . . If we could."

CHAPTER EIGHTEEN

Short dreary days fell, one upon the other. The first winter storm blew down the Carpathian Mountains. Rolling thunder echoed through the nights. While the world powers made war, a skirmish of sorts was taking place inside the Institut.

"Have you seen Father Bronski this morning?" François came storming into the dining room, glaring at the priests who sat quietly eating their breakfast. They had all gotten used to Dr. Martine's outbursts and paid little attention to the man when he threw a temper tantrum. They were actually mild compared to what most of the priests experienced in their daily routines.

"Now what's the problem, François?" Curvise asked.

"He's locked me out of the catacombs. Can you believe it? He's locked me out." He sat down heavily. "There's more down there and he knows it. He knows if he lets me down there, given time, I'll uncover all the secrets he's buried."

"What more can you discover, François? Why not let it rest? We've received word Poland has been defeated. The Germans now occupy the country west of the Vistula River. The Russians have taken control of the east."

"War." If he had been a barbarian, Martine would have spat. As it was, he made his feelings quite explicit in that single word. "Let them take it all. What is it about? Land? Who cares who the master is?"

"If it were France, would you be so willing to concede?"

"Hitler won't invade France. France will invade Germany and, when she does, Hitler will be defeated. I don't worry about Hitler or the German army." Martine spied Bronski coming into the dining room and waved in his direction. "I'd like a word with you, Father," he said sourly.

"May I get a cup of coffee first, Dr. Martine?"

"Eh? Yes, of course." Martine got up. "Allow me, please." He poured Bronski some coffee and set it gently on the table in front of the abbot. "Now, can we talk?"

"What's on your mind, Doctor?"

"You know perfectly well. I want the catacombs opened," Martine said, emphatically. Without giving Bronski a chance to argue, he added, "When you confined us, and you have, I agreed to abide by your rules here. One of those rules was that I would have access to all of the Institut. Now, I find myself locked out of a portion of your palace. Have I broken any of your rules?"

Bronski took time for a sip of coffee before answering. "No, Dr. Martine. You have not broken any rules. In fact, you are right. I was wrong. The catacombs are open."

Martine sputtered into thin air. "Why didn't you say so instead of letting me make a fool of myself?"

"Don't you wish Edmund was here right now?" Curvise asked Bronski. A slight smile played around his lips.

Bronski remained expressionless.

"What is that supposed to mean, Antoine?"

"It was just a thought, François."

"Father Bronski." Father Emil hurried into the dining room. "Greatcoat is at the gate. He says it's important that he talk to you at once."

Bronski left the table without a word.

"François, did I hear Father Emil say 'Greatcoat?'" Curvise asked. "Who or what is Greatcoat?"

"If Defont were here, I'm sure he'd tell you, Antoine," Martine said with a smirk. Then, seriously, "David seems to be more agitated lately. Have you noticed, or is it just me?"

"No, it's him. He's become very high strung."

"He needs to be out of that damn cell. There's nothing physically wrong with him, but there will be if he continues to just sit and go soft." Martine waved to Father Alphonse and changed the subject. "Father Alphonse is going to teach me to embalm," he said proudly.

"Then you will have your patients at every stage of life," Defont said, coming up behind Martine in time to catch the last of the conversation. "After you kill them, you can bury them." He laughed.

Curvise smiled.

Martine ignored the remark.

"Is that why you've been visiting the wards more often, François?"

Martine eyed Defont evenly. "I just assumed when you passed away, you'd want your old friend, François, to be the one to prepare your mortal remains. It would give me a great deal of satisfaction to stuff your worthless hide into one of these tombs."

Uninvited, goose bumps rose on Defont's arms and he shivered. "That's not funny, François."

"I guess, my dear Edmund," Martine said with a smile, "that all depends on which point of view one takes."

Curvise interrupted the repartee. "Who's Greatcoat?"

"Greatcoat? Oh yes," Defont was happy to answer. "He's the gentleman who drove us here from Sanok. He delivers the mail and brings in supplies for Father Bronski."

"Gentleman!" Martine exclaimed. "He's nothing but a rogue."

"Have you met him, Antoine?" Defont asked.

"No. Father Bronski's out by the gate talking to him now."

"He's a strange fellow and, like François says, probably a rogue, but an honorable one."

"Honorable? I suppose. Honor among thieves," Martine mumbled.

"He's not a thief. I've spoken to him several times. He may not be what one might call totally legitimate, but he's certainly no thief."

Martine was surprised to find Defont had been out doing things in which he was not involved. "When did you speak with him?" he demanded.

"When I went to Litz with Father Bronski."

"What? How did you get to go outside these walls?" Martine was as close to awestruck as he had ever allowed himself to get.

"We're allowed to visit Litz as long as Father Bronski accompanies us." Defont grinned at Martine's discomfort. "Were you aware of that, Antoine?"

"Yes, but I haven't been yet. I just haven't been able to find the time. Eventually, I hope to visit the town."

"They're a strange lot. Cold and very clannish. I was actually afraid when I was there. I wouldn't venture into their midst alone," Defont said seriously. "They hold the priests here in very high regard. This is the closest they come to religion. Father Bronski is almost like their spiritual leader, but I didn't see anything resembling a church. And Litz is, as you commented when we first walked through, François, childless. At least I saw none."

Defont's remark that he had been frightened surprised Martine. He had always carried an image of Edmund as fearless. For some reason, the thought made him feel better about himself.

Bronski never mentioned what his conversation with Greatcoat was about and no one ever asked.

***

The winter fell heavily on the mountains. Isolated, the Institut d'Infantiles continued on its way. Two new children came from Hungary, but they were no longer classified as madmen. With the war, insanity had become indistinguishable outside the walls of the Institut.

"Cardinal Karlick passed away last night," Defont said sadly. He looked out the window. The courtyard was buried under snow. "He was ninety years old." Decidedly, he opened the door and stepped outside. Curvise followed.

"It's cold," he finally said.

"Yes, it is."

"How's David?" Father Proust had fallen into some sort of depression, refusing to eat. Refusing to talk. To sleep. He sat in his cell and stared out through the bars, seeing nothing. Defont, Martine, Curvise—all three men had tried to bring him out of his shell, but had failed.

Defont took a deep breath of chilled air. "Do you think we should consider Martine's proposal?"

"Which one? He has so many." But Curvise knew which proposition Edmund meant. He had given the idea of having David complete his task a great deal of thought lately. Defont did not answer his question, so he asked another. "How?"

"Well, to start with, it's not as if we have to, as Bronski so indelicately put it, throw a girl in the cell with David. All she really has to do is be here. In the Institut." Defont pointed to the main building. "I know it's crazy Antoine, but what else can we do? I refuse to just sit here and watch David deteriorate into . . . well, you know what I mean."

"Yes, I do. You're not the only one who has harbored such thoughts, Edmund. It's just that I come up short when I think about the girl." Curvise stopped. He could not bring himself to ask how they could bring a Jewess into the Institut to be David's whore.

"It can be arranged, Antoine." Defont offered no further explanation.

Curvise asked for none."And if we did? And if it failed? What if she commits suicide? We've not only doomed ourselves, Edmund, but we've doomed another's soul to Hell." Curvise shivered in the cold. "Besides, I still have hope that you and François will be allowed to leave."

"Leave? To go where? Back to France? Don't forget, Antoine, Martine and I are dead just as you are." Defont gazed at the sky. "Besides, what is there to go home to? I have no one in LaRochelle. Neither does François. This is not such a bad place to spend the rest of our lives. To be needed. As a matter of fact, I enjoy being here. I've never known this kind of peace. Were it not for David, I would even say tranquility."

"Have you spoken to François about this?"

"Yes. And of course, he agrees. It was his idea in the first place. It's Father Bronski who needs to be convinced." Defont shuddered. "Let's go back inside." He held the door for his friend. "We were hoping you might see your way to speak to our dear abbot." He stamped his feet to rid his sandals of snow.

Curvise rubbed his hands together, trying to get the feeling back in them. "I have no influence over Father Bronski, but if you really think it's best . . ." his voice was reluctant, "I'll talk to him. That's all I can do."

"I'm not willing to sacrifice a life to save David," Defont clarified. "I'm sure David would gladly give his own life to save me or anyone else for that matter. I believe he's that kind of a person. Because of his selflessness, I know I wouldn't hesitate to offer up my life for his. If only it were that simple, eh?

"I was skeptical when Martine first suggested this, but the more I listened to him and to David, I can't see any other solution. If we do nothing, David will suffer great pain. Eventually he'll simply wither away as his relatives have done." A sudden burst of enthusiasm issued from Defont. "Think of it, Antoine! A virgin birth. The possibility of the baby being the new Christ child. And us, here. His admirers. His apostles."

"I have thought of it, Edmund, and also what it would do to the church we now serve. I can't help feeling they wouldn't look kindly on this matter."

"Have you read Mien Kampf?"

"No," Curvise said slowly, surprised by the question.

"You should, Antoine. Herr Hitler has outlined his plans for Europe most clearly. I don't know what's going to happen, but if he succeeds in what he's written, he'll rid Europe of the Jews."

Curvise was stunned.

"Ironic, wouldn't you say? The Jews, the Chosen People, wiped off the face of the earth. Is Hitler a mutant, Antoine? His claims the Jews have spoiled the earth could be true. They're not welcome in most places, but what if? What if he's aware of David's task? What if his plans to kill all of the Jews succeed? There will be no more Chosen Ones. And this child David is trying to bring to life will never come.

"We've talked of the genius of great men who have contributed to the world. We haven't spoken of the monsters who periodically arise. Is it possible this God David speaks of erred and allowed bad genes to reproduce?" Defont stopped, unable to continue. He felt what he was trying to say so strongly he was unable to find the right words of expression.

"But to think of killing all the Jews in Europe, Edmund! That's insane. There are literally millions here. It would be impossible."

"They've already started," Defont said. "Greatcoat told me the Nazis have begun building camps in Poland. Hitler's "Night of Crystal" is still fresh in most of Europe's minds.

"I'm not a fanatic about my religion. You know that Antoine, but I'd hate to think we had an opportunity to bring peace and enlightenment back into the world and were afraid to take a chance. I'd hate to think we were unwilling to sacrifice our lives. It seems like such a small price to pay to see the future in our Lord's hands."

"Have you presented this argument to Father Bronski?"

"I've tried. He refuses to listen."

"Do you believe what Greatcoat told you about the killing of the Jews?"

"I don't know, Antoine. It's hard to comprehend the magnitude of what he says. I don't disbelieve him. But I'm here behind these walls, living life differently than most of the world. If I were some other place, seeing the streets filled with people going about their lives, I wouldn't, I couldn't believe it. But here, knowing what we know." Defont shrugged his shoulders. "What can I say?"

"Then it's true," Curvise said. Sitting behind his desk, he had asked Father Bronski if the rumors Greatcoat had whispered to Defont had any substance. Bronski had nodded his head. Curvise found the idea that one man could hate an entire race of individuals so much that he planned their demise, beyond his understanding.

"I only know what Greatcoat tells me. I have no reason to not believe him. However," Bronski said weakly, "it is not our concern."

"How can you say that, Father? What has happened to us? A madman plans to murder the Jews of Europe and you say it is not our concern?" Curvise felt betrayed. "That's not the compassion and love our Lord taught us. What's wrong with our religion, Father Bronski? Has it become so callous that the life of a Jew means nothing? What then? The life of any human being?"

"I have no love for the Jews," Bronski said. "What befalls them is their punishment. I haven't killed any of their kind, nor do I carry that intent."

"You don't have to pull the trigger of a gun to kill, Father. You have only to stand and watch." Up until this moment, Curvise had not been totally convinced of the validity of Defont's arguments. Now it was plain that to not help David in his task would be a great error. If his church had grown so calloused it was unwilling to speak out on behalf of the Jews, it was no better than Hitler himself. In fact, it was a worse offender. For good or bad, Hitler had been born into who he was. The church had chosen to be in league with a tyrant. That choice had been made with only one purpose in mind—to save the grandeur of its religion.

"I want you to reconsider your attitude, Father Bronski. It's not indicative of our Lord's teachings. Nor is it an attitude befitting this institution."

Curvise's sudden attack left Bronski bewildered.

"This is not the Vatican," Curvise continued. "Or some grand cathedral in Venice or Madrid. There's no wealth here except what we bring to this place. The men who labor to serve their brothers put up with primitive conditions. They are true believers in our Lord.

"I was like the rest of them before coming here," Curvise confessed. "Perhaps I didn't lust after power and recognition as much as some, but those faults were inside of me. Up until this very minute, I have always counted your arrival to offer me a chance to serve here as the moment of my salvation. Now you tell me you are no different than the rest of our church. Well, I won't have it! I don't believe it. We are not afraid of the future here. I want you to find your courage, Father Bronski. David needs your help."

***

Martine and Defont sat across from Curvise in the dining room. They had finished their supper and were drinking coffee. A stillness had befallen the Institut—a stillness that crept and crawled over the cold stone floors and entangled the footsteps of those who tried to avoid its presence. It had been just over a month since Curvise had spoken to Bronski about the Jews. It had been just over a month since David had last spoken. He ate, but just barely enough to keep him alive. His face was shallow and drawn. His lips had chapped and, when he moved them in silent conversations, they split and bled and grew black with scabs. But his eyes were the most disturbing as they grew blank and unfocused, staring past the bars on his door.

François Martine had tried to lure David from his cell. Coaxing, cajoling, threatening. Nothing had worked.

Another year passed into history. Christmas and the new year passed without a song of celebration.

"If David dies, I'm holding Father Bronski personally responsible," Martine said. "His adamant refusal to listen to our prescriptions, no matter how he feels about them, is tantamount to murder."

"You can't hold anyone responsible for what's happening to David," Curvise argued. "He's simply lost the will to live. It's not a crime." He looked to Defont for support.

"What's a crime now?" the big policeman said absently.

Father Emil ran into the dining room, his face flushed from the exercise. He was breathing heavily. Snow coated the hem of his robe and covered his feet.

"Dr. Martine. Come quickly. It's David." With a sharp intake of breath, he turned and ran back toward the garrison.

Martine was up and running before either Curvise or Defont could react. A moment later they were at his heels.

***

"David!" Martine exclaimed.

"Hello, Doctor," Father Proust said. He was standing by the bars. "Where have you been? I'm hungry and I haven't seen you for a while." He turned and looked at Emil. "Are you okay, Father? You ran out of here so fast."

Emil nodded.

Curvise and Defont stepped into view.

"Antoine. Edmund. Is something wrong?" David asked.

"Not now," Curvise replied. "Are you feeling better?" It was all he could think of to ask.

"Was I sick?" David seemed confused by all the attention.

Martine laughed. "Was I sick?" he repeated, wiping perspiration from his forehead. "Father Emil, will you please get David some of Father Ehrick's famous beef stew?"

"And some bread," Defont added.

"Right away." The priest hurried off, leaving the four friends together.

Martine unlocked the gate. "Would you like to come out here to eat, David?"

"No, but it would be nice if all of you came inside and kept me company. Antoine. Edmund. François." David waved his arm in invitation.

Defont gathered three chairs and placed them around David's bed.

"I feel so tired," David said.

"That's from lack of eating," Martine informed him. "You haven't eaten properly for the last five months."

"Five months! Has it been that long?"

Martine glanced at Curvise.

"Where have you been, David?"

David looked up sharply. "That's a strange question, Antoine. Did I leave my cell?"

"No, I just thought you might have remembered where you were."

"I've been right here," David said, looking past Curvise. "Hello, Father Bronski."

"Father Emil is on his way with your supper, David. May I borrow your three friends while you eat? Father Emil will keep you company for a while."

"Yes, of course," David said, gracious as always.

The girl was frightened. Her companion sat and stared at François Martine with empty eyes. Although both Martine and Curvise had tried to keep their examinations brisk, it was unnerving having to verify the two girls were virgins. Both doctors were happy to complete their duties.

Martine took Urbana by the hand. "You needn't be frightened," he said. "You're safe here. These men are Catholic priests. They won't harm you. Neither will I." He smiled.

She forced a smile back.

"There, that's better." He patted her hand affectionately, then shifted his attention to the other girl. "Are you still frightened, Sabina?" Martine still held Urbana's hand. He still smiled.

She nodded only once, but her dark eyes flashed alive if only for a second.

"How old are you, Sabina?"

"Fourteen."

"And how about you, Urbana?"

"Thirteen."

"Well then." He let go of Urbana's hand. "I should refer to you as young women instead of girls."

Curvise watched the exchange without envy. Martine had a way with women of every age. Young ladies, still shy, gravitated towards his fatherly ways. Older women swooned over his debonair manners. It was not surprising to find both girls had relaxed a bit.

"Are you hungry?"

"Yes," Urbana said quickly. Sabina nodded her affirmation.

Waiting for Martine to finish his interviews with the young women, Defont had stayed in the corridor just out of sight. He stepped into view when he heard Martine call his name.

"Yes, Doctor?"

"Would you please take these young ladies to the dining room and see that they're fed?"

"Certainly, Doctor."

Sabina got up from her chair and was quickly at Defont's side. Her tiny hand slipped into his large one. Urbana followed, but refused to share her handshake as she had with Martine. In the back of the room, Bronski and Curvise watched as each girl unconsciously chose her surrogate father.

Martine wiped his face with a rag. Getting up from the chair, he glanced down the hall and watched the two young women being escorted by the oversized Inspector. He shook his head.

"I know this was my idea, but now . . . I'm not so sure it's the right thing to do." He turned and looked at Bronski. "I've forgotten how innocent young women can be."

"It had an immediate effect on Father Proust," Bronski said. "He was your original concern, Doctor."

"Yes, yes, I know." Martine was uneasy, agitated.

"I don't like this, François," Curvise said.

"You also, Father?" Bronski said, his insinuation clear. "It's not too late to end this," he added.

"No," Martine said adamantly. "We started this and we must finish it."

"François, think of what you're saying. They are just children," Curvise argued.

"Yes, they are children, but Father Bronski is right. Their effect on David was astounding. I don't like this any more than you, Antoine, but we must continue. What alternative do we have?"

"Father Proust will die true to his beliefs as his ancestors have over the years. The young women will be returned to the camp Greatcoat purchased them from and in time, they also will die," Bronski said.

"You're not afraid to die, are you Bronski?" Martine asked, suddenly angry. He did not wait for an answer. "And because you're not afraid, you think everyone else should look forward to death. Well, I'm afraid to die and I'm afraid to let my friends die. I don't wish to see harm come to those young women. And if it is at all possible, none will. If what we theorize is true, one will become pregnant. The other will simply be her companion. But both will live." He stopped and rubbed his forehead. "If we're wrong, what harm has been done?"

"What harm has been done to whom?" Bronski asked. "To us? To them? To our souls? Indeed, what harm?

"I have done what you requested, Dr. Martine." Bronski looked at Curvise. "It was your request also, Father Curvise. What happens now is out of my hands. At least for the moment." He walked to the door. "Father Ehrick has prepared a room for each of the girls down the hall. And, by the way, they cost fifteen francs a piece."

"Thirty francs," Martine mumbled. "Isn't that what Judas was paid?"

"Yes," Curvise said softly. "Thirty pieces of silver."

189

CHAPTER NINETEEN

"I visited her last night. I saw her clearly." David rubbed his eyes and spoke slowly. "I knew she was here the moment Father Bronski led her through the gates." He looked up at Curvise. "It all became clear, Antoine. For a fraction of a second, but it all became clear."

"What became clear?" Curvise was surprised to find David so exceedingly calm. At the very least, he had expected the younger man to be distraught over his actions.

"I'm sorry for the young women in LaRochelle, Antoine. You know I never meant them harm. It was frightening at first. I shouldn't have been confused, but things weren't as they should have been. God had not taken into account the enormous proliferation of his images."

"Why do you say God as though He is not God?"

"That is what He is called. Like I am called David and you, Antoine. It is simply a name."

"Who is He?"

"I don't know. I can only see briefly, and even those images aren't clear. It's like my memory is not functioning with all of its resources. Does that make sense?"

"Yes, it does."

"When the child is born, I'll pass away." David continued to try and explain what he knew, what he felt. "It doesn't bother me. I've fulfilled my task, my mission in life." So sure, a minute later he stopped and asked his friend for assurance. "Had I not, would I have spent years suffering nothing but torment, Antoine?"

"From what Father Bronski tells me, yes. You would have suffered. Greatly."

"Why was I fighting this? Do you know?"

"From what little I understand, David, I believe it stems from your ardent desire to be a priest. Your beliefs in our religious teachings were so dominant, any deviation from what we, as priests, considered normal, you saw as evil. As far as you knew, those thoughts were trying to destroy

190

everything in which you believed. Maybe it was an error on God's part. He did not foresee there could be men as strong as you and your uncle who would suffer any fate but the loss of their faith.

"Do you know why you succeeded now, David? With this woman?"

"She was one of the Chosen."

"But why? Do you know what made her special?"

"No, but the child will know," David said. "The son of God will have the answers."

***

In a few days, Curvise knew David would not remember any of this. As it had been in LaRochelle, only days after the young priest's tryst, his memory faded. A safety mechanism installed by God? Curvise no longer cared. At least now David would not awake in pain for his mistakes.

Curvise walked across the courtyard. Defont and Martine had been up all night, watching the two girls. Curvise wondered if they knew what had happened. Or if it had. He stopped and looked up at the gray morning sky. The snow would be melting in another month or so. Spring would arrive, but not until late April. It stayed cold here longer than it did in France. He shook his head and hurried forward. The weather was only a diversion. If the truth were set before him, he would have to decide. To believe David was to enter a world of insanity. Not to believe him was to remain locked in the superstitions of the past. Insanity was everywhere, it seemed. Logic and reason had very little use behind the walls of the Institut.

***

"Sabina," Martine said excitedly.

"Are you sure?" Curvise asked. He still was not sure whether he harbored hope for or against the event.

"Her clothing. She folded her clothes neatly, just as Defont said she would."

Curvise looked around the dining room. "Where is Edmund?"

"Sleeping."

"And why haven't you gone to bed?"

"I'm too excited. Sleep! Sleep is for peasants. Don't you feel the magnitude of what is happening here, Antoine? Or perhaps I should say, what has already happened?"

"David reaffirmed what he told you earlier, François. He said he will die when the child is born."

"You don't believe that," Martine said.

"If I don't believe that, then how can I believe anything else he has said?" Curvise left the table to pour himself a cup of coffee. The buffet was a large, solidly built piece of furniture that rarely held anything but a constant supply of clean cups and coffee. Having filled his cup, he turned to look at Martine. "We did this to save his life. Not end it."

Martine joined his friend by the buffet. "We did this to spare David the same suffering his family has endured for centuries," he said gently. "He won't die." But his voice did not ring with confidence. "Come on, let's sit down and have our coffee like normal gentlemen. Like men without worries." He led Curvise back to the table, surprised by the weakness he felt in his friend's arms. "Are you losing weight?"

"I haven't been eating much lately. It's been hard to keep an appetite."

Martine looked up sharply. There was more to Antoine's statement than the emotional strain of simply being David's friend. Curvise's eyes were dull, the pupils large and slow to react. Automatically, he reached for his friend's wrist and checked his pulse. At least it was normal.

"Will you please stop mothering me, François. I'm fine. I just haven't been hungry lately," Curvise protested.

"All right," the physician in him gave in grudgingly, "but make sure you eat. The last thing in the world I want to do is embalm you." Martine tried to make his words sound light, but failed.

"I was surprised when I first met Sabina and Urbana. Their French was excellent, but," unwittingly, Martine felt that anyone civilized enough to speak French properly would certainly live a fine life, "I really couldn't get over how thin they were. And frightened," he added.

"Can you blame them, François? Edmund tells me the Germans have built camps for no other purpose than the extermination of Jews. What in the world is happening?"

"Where did you hear such nonsense?" Martine said hotly. He was more than a little shocked.

"From your friend, Greatcoat."

"Well, that explains it. And he's not my friend."

"He bought those girls from the Germans," Curvise said. "Have you read Mien Kampf?"

"No. I don't read trash," Martine huffed. "And besides, women have always been for sale in certain European countries. Of course, you wouldn't know about such things."

"Is it that easy? You simply purchase a woman like you would a loaf of bread at the local bakery?" François was right. Curvise knew little of the secular world and its customs.

"Yes. Mind you, not in France or Belgium. But in Poland, Czechoslovakia, and other Slavic countries women are considered worthless. And cheap. Especially the Jews. It didn't surprise me at all to find Bronski had purchased those two girls. What did surprise me was that he had paid so much."

Curvise shook his head and closed his eyes. He had no reason to doubt Martine's words. It was just a shame that human lives were held in such low regard. How would he feel, he wondered, if he could be bought and sold for no more than the cost of a yard of cloth?

"How is David feeling this morning?" Martine snapped Curvise out of his melancholia. "Does he remember last night?"

"So far, but I don't expect that to last. He told me he saw her clearly," Curvise said. "He's changed dramatically."

"How do you mean?"

"He's alive. He's hungry. Very much aware of his surroundings. Willing to die when the child is born."

"Will you please quit saying that? David's not going to die."

"How can you be so sure, François? If I remember correctly, you were the one who so adamantly insisted a woman couldn't become pregnant without physical contact from a man. Have you changed your opinion on that?"

"For the moment, no."

"A few minutes ago you were excited about ... how did you put it? 'What has happened and what is happening.'"

"I am, but we have to wait. At least until . . ."

"Until what? Until her stomach begins to grow?"

"Why do you insist on twisting everything I say? If the girl's pregnant, it will be a miracle. If she's not, what have we lost? The son of God?" Martine repented. His voice softened as his confusion became evident. "It was all so easy when it was just a thought, Antoine. An idea. Today, in the light, it confuses and frightens me. A miracle.

"I don't believe in miracles, Antoine." Martine pushed himself from the table and reached to help his friend rise. "Of course, you must come with me. It is time to examine our two young ladies again. If this is to be a miracle, we're going to damn well make sure we have proof that's exactly what it is!"

***

Martine knocked gently on Sabina's door and waited until she bade him enter.

"How are you feeling this morning, my dear?"

"Hungry." By habit, she began to unbutton her blouse. For the last two months she had been examined daily by both Drs. Martine and Curvise. There was no reason to believe this morning would be any different.

"No, no," Martine stilled her motions. "You don't have to undress today." As easily as the buttons had been undone, they were again fastened.

"How are you feeling? Have you experienced any discomfort in the morning? Nausea? Extreme tiredness? Anything that's not quite normal?"

"No. Mostly, I'm just hungry. All the time." Sabina shifted nervously. Dr. Martine's questions had her worried. "Is Urbana sick?" Perhaps that was why he was so concerned.

"No, she's fine," Martine assured her. "We're going to move her bed in here with you so you can have some company. Would you like that?"

"Oh yes," she exclaimed. Until now, the two girls had been kept separated, seeing each other only for short periods of time when they met in the dining room. "Does Urbana know yet? I'd like to be the one to tell her." Sabina hurried to the doorway, but Martine stopped her.

"Please, sit down for a moment. I have something to tell you first."

Obediently, Sabina sat. Raised by a strict father, she was comfortable being subservient to the commands of men. Martine noticed and, without having known her father, respected him.

"Do you know why Dr. Curvise and I have been examining you every morning?"

"No."

"Do you feel any different? Inside?" He patted his belly. "In your stomach."

"You asked me that earlier." She pouted slightly, frustrated at not being able to please him. "Mostly, I'm just hungry."

"But do you know why you're so hungry?" Martine persisted. He wanted to blurt out she was going to have a baby. Didn't she understand? But the fact she might not, caused him to take a gentler, more circuitous route.

This time she shook her head. Her eyes were large and, in her anxiety, she swung her feet against the chair legs, kicking first the right side and then the left.

Martine placed a restraining hand on her knee. "Do you remember the dream you told me about that first day? The one you had your very first night here?"

Sabina blushed and looked down at the tops of her battered shoes. "Yes,"

194

she whispered shyly. Embarrassed. She had seen her mother and father do the things she had told Dr. Martine about. It had been a small house she had shared with her brothers and sisters. They had all seen what went on in their parents' bed at night.

"Do you understand how a child is created? Made?" Martine added. He could feel his face flush. It would be so easy to attack this from a clinical point of view. If only Sabina were older. If only things had happened in a "normal" sense. At least then he could have explained this thing through cause and effect.

"Yes." Sabina refused to look at him. Martine considered it a blessing.

There was no way around it. "You're going to have a baby, Sabina," he finally said.

"Is that why I'm always hungry?" Legs now stilled, her nervous energy found an outlet in her twisting hands that refused to lie calmly in her lap.

Martine had expected an outburst of guilt. Shame. Remorse. The last thing he had expected was this curious acceptance.

"That doesn't upset you?" Perhaps he should have asked how it made her feel. But at that moment, he didn't want to hear that she was hungry.

"No," she said sadly and sighed. She had disappointed him again. One small hand reached out and touched the doctor gently on the cheek. "It's all right," she said, not knowing what she said at all. But it was enough. Martine looked up and smiled.

"Yes," he said, "it is."

"Does that mean I can eat now?"

At this, François Martine laughed out loud. "Yes, yes. By all means. Let's go feed you."

Sabina jumped from her chair and grabbed Martine's arm. "Will Monsieur Defont be there?" she asked coyly.

"Yes," Martine said, only a little envious. "Unfortunately, yes." He could not understand the child's affection for Defont. The Inspector's size alone should have intimidated someone of her stature. But, as she had confided in him weeks ago, Defont made her feel safe. Martine supposed if one looked at life through a child's eyes, it made sense.

***

Zigman Bronski sat alone in his room, tapping his finger on the top of his desk. He had followed the daily activities of Dr. Martine and Father Curvise closely. Now that there was no longer any doubt the young Jewess was with child, he felt compelled to write his superiors at the Vatican. Confused and bewildered, he tried to organize his thoughts into some coherent form of communication. Before Monsignor DeValier had passed away, he had told Bronski of Michael Proust's illness. The abbot had later read DeValier's journals, but had dismissed the words as the ravings of a madman.

Father Zulisky, abbot of the Institut d'Infantiles before Bronski, had taken him into the catacombs and shown him the remains of the dead. The old man had mentioned that one day someone like Michael Proust would come, claiming to be the angel of God. When he arrived, (not if, Bronski remembered) the prescription was clear. Confinement, deep in the garrison, away from the wind.

He had thought it strange at the time—how could he not? But one did not question authority. Not even the fact that it had taken almost thirty years surprised him.

"We don't judge here, Zigman," Zulisky had told him. "We only obey our vows. You must remember the children who come are mad. They will speak evil and curse our Lord. We cannot be allowed to judge. We only serve them as we would wish to be served.

"You will hear strange and mystifying words. You have only to remember they are words Satan has put into the mouths of our brothers. They are not to be taken seriously, for to do so would give them credence. But," Zulisky had cautioned him, "there may come a time when you feel something has happened that is out of the ordinary, even for this place. Only when you believe our religion is truly in danger will you report to your supervisor. His name will change over the years, but you will always know who he is."

In the ten years Bronski had served as abbot of the Institut d'Infantiles, he had not once written anything to the Vatican except standard reports. Most of them dealt with finances and roll call, reports of those who served, new arrivals, and the names of those who had died. Now he was forced to write a report he did not understand. A report that, after he read it, would make him look as crazy as one of the children. Still, it had to be written. It had to be sent.

He opened the Book of Records and ran his finger down the list, stopping at the last entry. He had been informed of the new Director of the Department of Religious Antiquities. He began his letter: *Your Excellency, Lord Cardinal Vasai . . .*

***

On his way to the garrison, Martine had just stepped into the courtyard when he saw Defont running his direction from the front gate. The policeman, Martine thought, looked rather like a large scarecrow, waving his arms about wildly in the spring air. He stopped for a moment, and then decided to continue. Defont was always doing something not quite normal. While it was not a way of life he could comprehend, it seemed to help the Inspector better relate to the children. Martine continued on his way until he heard Defont call out his name.

Reaching the doctor, Defont clutched at his side and gasped for breath. Martine watched complacently. There was nothing he could do for Edmund and, truth be known, he was enjoying Defont's discomfort just a little bit. He still recalled the running soccer player who had bowled him over so many years ago.

At last he grew impatient. "Come, come, Edmund. I don't have all day to stand here and listen to you wheeze."

Defont straightened with difficulty and took a large breath. "France has been invaded," he began. "Germany has invaded France."

***

François Martine sat at the dining room table, visibly shaken. His pale face was even more ashen than usual. In his wildest dreams he had never thought Germany would invade France. He had always known the two countries would clash, but France, France would be the invader. The conqueror. The idea of Nazis on French soil made him sick to his stomach. Tears formed and fell from his eyes.

"Come on, François. You know how news reaches us here. In all probability, the Germans have been beaten by our fine French army." Defont was trying hard to perk the doctor up, hoping he could do the same for himself. "Greatcoat says it's been over two weeks since they invaded." He loved France as much as Martine and although the news was depressing, it was not quite as earth shattering as Martine's emotions led one to believe.

Curvise sat with his friends and stared into space. The pain he felt was real. Not for French soil or his homeland, but because it was eating away his insides. "There's nothing we can do, François. France will survive."

The animosity between France and Germany was as old as Europe itself. French children were raised and taught to fear and despise the Hun, as Martine had been. Just as he had been taught that the French were superior to the Germans, to all of Europe, he still felt that way now.

His mind refused to calm from its cyclone of disturbing thoughts. He must leave immediately! Who would stop him from rushing to defend his homeland? Certainly not the ignorant oafs of Litz! He would simply demand

Bronski release him so he could join the battle to save his country.

Father Bronski joined the three men. Wrapped in his own worries, he, too, found time to be concerned for France.

"I have decided to release you from your confinement," he said to Martine. "You and Edmund are free to leave."

Bronski's words surprised Curvise. It was not like the abbot to bend the rules. Something was wrong.

Martine did not think so. He grasped Bronski's hand and shook it vigorously. "Thank you! Thank you," he said, and wiped the tears from his eyes, glancing at Defont in victory. "Did you hear? We're free!"

Defont only stared at the abbot. "And Antoine?"

Bronski shook his head. "He is to remain here. I'm sorry."

"I won't leave without Father Curvise." It was simply said, but left no room for argument. Still, Martine tried.

"Edmund! What are you saying? We can leave and fight with our country. Antoine understands. After all, he's a priest. Antoine, tell him."

"It would make me very happy to see you leave," Curvise said, and winced. The Phenobarbital he had injected last night was wearing off.

"No," Defont said.

"Then why?" Martine demanded. "Just tell me why?" He was angry and disappointed. "We came to find Antoine. To make sure he was alive. We've accomplished that and now, now that your country needs you ...." Martine pointed to Curvise. "You can see for yourself he's fine."

"Are you fine, Antoine?" Defont asked. He did not wait for the priest to speak. He could read the pain in his friend's eyes. "Look at him, François. Look at him and tell me he's fine."

Slowly, Martine looked at Curvise. Instantly, his vision cleared. He knew immediately that something was wrong with Antoine. Something was terribly wrong.

***

"How long has the pain been so intense?" Martine asked as he finished his examination.

"Three or four months. What does it matter, François? I'm dying. I know it. You know it. There's nothing we can do." Curvise struggled to sit up in his bed. "I'll talk to Edmund. Convince him you and he should go back to France."

"Yes, yes. You do that. And after you've convinced him to leave, then you can convince me," Martine said, preparing an injection of Phenobarbital.

Holding Curvise's arm, he noticed both old and new needle marks. "Has it been helping?"

"The pain comes earlier each day."

"Do we have any morphine?"

"No."

"I'll see if we can get some." He pushed the needle into Antoine's arm. "I've given you a larger dose than you would have administered to yourself. You should feel better soon."

"If you don't leave now, Bronski will never let you go." Curvise laid back on the bed, awaiting the effects of the injection.

"You might as well save your breath, Antoine. I'm not leaving."

"Then be careful, François."

"Of what?"

"I don't know. It's just a feeling I have. I wouldn't trust . . . I would watch Father Bronski very closely."

"I don't understand, Antoine." Martine was sure it was the medication that had set his friend off on this tangent. Mood swings tended to be a normal side effect of the drug.

"I think Bronski offered you your freedom so he could be free to rid himself of Sabina . . . and the unborn child." Curvise's words were hesitant. Ashamed at his skepticism, he was still unable to ignore his feelings.

It was a while before Martine spoke. "I can't believe he would do such a thing, Antoine. He's dedicated to the church. A bit unusual, I agree, but to think he would murder. I find that hard to believe. Even Bronski knows one of the ten commandments is 'Thou shalt not kill.'"

The drug took its full effect and the pain eased. Curvise's thoughts again became clear. "François, think about what we've started here. We have a young girl, a Jew who is pregnant, yet she's a virgin. If this experiment is allowed to continue until its conclusion, we will have witnessed an Immaculate Conception. Do you really think the lives of two Jews and two Frenchmen will stop Bronski? Don't your realize if this child is born, he no longer has a religion in which to believe?"

"Is that how you feel?" Martine asked, walking to the door to bar any uninvited visitors. He did not want to be interrupted. "If you were in Bronski's shoes, what would you do, Antoine?"

Curvise studied his friend carefully. It was important Martine believe what he was trying to say.

"François, there are fanatics in all walks of life. More so in religion. Take David for instance. He would have languished here—for what? Twenty years of suffering just so he could remain true to his vows? I've never felt that strongly about anything, not even my religion. I believe in my faith, but not to the point of murder. As a matter of fact, I'm looking forward to seeing this child. His birth won't affect my belief in the Savior at all. But, is Bronski able to say that? I don't think so. This is all he has. I don't think he'd hesitate to become a martyr."

A sharp knock jolted Martine away from the door. He opened it cautiously.

Defont barged into the room. "How are you feeling now, Antoine?" He did not wait for the reply, knowing Curvise was apt to be less than truthful in this matter. "Is he any better, François?" His worry showed on his face and in his voice.

"He's better now, thanks." Martine closed the door, securing the three men inside the room. "Antoine, have you mentioned your feelings to Edmund?"

"No, the idea suddenly came to me when Bronski offered to let you and Edmund leave."

"What idea?"

"He has some notion Father Bronski wants us to leave so he can . . ." Martine stopped the foolish thought with a shrug of his shoulders.

"Kill the child," Defont finished for him.

Curvise nodded his head.

Martine let out an audible sigh.

"As soon as he spoke, I felt that was his real motive," Defont said.

"Then you've both gone mad," Martine commented.

"Maybe," Defont acknowledged. "I don't know. As with Antoine, it was only a thought that briefly entered my mind. I don't want to believe it, but it's there.

"I was just talking to Father Bronski a few minutes ago, François. I asked him if we left, would we be able to take the two young women with us."

Both Martine and Curvise held their breaths. The answer was too important to miss.

"He said it was out of the question."

They resumed breathing.

"He said they would be in danger if they left the Institut."

"From whom?" Martine wondered aloud.

"Bronski didn't say and I didn't bother to ask. Still, I hate to think he'd resort to murder. I find it hard to imagine him that cold." Defont defended Bronski cautiously. "I'm not so sure about Greatcoat," he added.

Curvise walked to the door. "I have to visit the wards." He opened the door, but did not leave immediately. "I don't know. It's probably just my imagination. But please, be careful."

"I'll be with you in a minute, Antoine." Martine watched his friend shuffle down the hall before once again closing the door and trapping Defont in the room. "Antoine is very sick, Edmund. He has cancer. The disease has eaten away most of his insides already."

Defont was physically stunned. He took a step backward, away from the bad news, and sat awkwardly on the edge of Curvise's bed. "Cancer?" *No! Not cancer! Antoine was too good a man. Too kind. Too . . . necessary.* "Are you sure?"

Martine nodded.

"Does he know?"

"Of course."

Defont jumped to his feet, ready to race after Curvise and protect him from the world. He could not understand Martine's apparent lack of concern. "Why did you let him go? Why don't you keep him in bed?"

"Bed won't help him, Edmund. Let him do his work for as long as he can."

"Damn it! Isn't there something you can do?" But Defont knew there was not. It made him angry. "How long does he have?"

"Three, maybe four months. By then he will be nothing," Martine said sadly.

"Will he live long enough to see the child?"

Martine did some quick calculations on Sabina's due date. He shook his head. "She's not due until December. I don't think Antoine will live that long."

"Can't you keep him alive until the child is born?" *Cancer was incurable.* "At least until the child can touch him?"

"There are no miracles in medicine, Edmund. I don't think Christ himself could cure cancer. If I thought it would help, I'd pray for him."

Martine moved to stand beside Defont. "We must let him do what he wants, Edmund. Do you understand?"

Defont nodded.

"And I want you to move into the room next to Sabina and Urbana. I refuse to believe anyone here would harm them, but let's be safe just the same."

"Yes," Defont agreed. He was still hoping Martine might be wrong. Maybe Curvise would live long enough to be cured by the coming Savior. "We must make sure the child is born."

"Can Greatcoat get us some morphine? For Antoine. It will ease the pain."

"I'm sure he can," Defont said and then repeated, "I'll make sure he can."

***

Greatcoat delivered the vials of morphine on the same day he delivered the news of France's surrender to the Nazis. No one cared any more.

CHAPTER TWENTY

Another summer wrapped its humid fingers around the mountains. Rains brought the insects and a steady buzz of flies, mosquitoes, and rumors that filled the air. With the fall of France and the Netherlands, all eyes turned east. The Russians would be next on Hitler's forward march. Russia, with its Bolsheviks and Jews.

Martine stepped into the morning mist. He watched Defont, Sabina, and Urbana walking around the courtyard. He had given her implicit instructions she was never to go out of her room unless Defont was with her. Her door was to remain locked at all times. As in the past, she had raised no objections and asked no questions.

Curvise got weaker with each new day. Still managing to make his rounds, the time he spent in the wards grew continually shorter and shorter.

David grew stronger, although his mind had closed on the task. He could no longer remember, or even think about what had transpired. It was something that had simply not occurred, as if a genie had gone back in time and erased the past for Father Proust alone. His cell door was left open, and once in a while he came out and helped the priests care for the children. But, not often. Locked or not, his security rested within his confinement.

During the summer, new Cardinals usually came to the Institut, but the summer of 1940 had yielded no newcomers. If Greatcoat were to be believed, none would come. The Nazis were arresting even the priests.

"Are you going to the garrison, Doctor?" Bronski came out of the main building.

"Yes," Martine said. He continued to watch Defont and the two girls, knowing the abbot did the same.

"There's no need for Edmund to guard the girls," Bronski said as if he had read Martine's mind. "No one here would harm them."

"You're right, Father," Martine said. "No one here will harm them." He turned to face the abbot. "You know about Father Curvise's condition, I assume?"

"Yes. It is very distressing."

Together they began to walk toward the garrison.

"When I asked you and Edmund if you wished to leave, I had no ulterior motives, Doctor. I know you think otherwise, but I can assure you, I did not."

"It's funny to hear you say that, Father. I didn't believe you had either." Martine smiled politely. "But why did you make such an offer at that particular time? Didn't you know Antoine was sick?"

"At the time, no. But I would have made the offer anyway. I've known many Frenchmen in my day, Doctor. I know the devotion they carry for their country often borders on fanaticism. I don't understand it, but I must respect it."

They walked in silence for a moment. Curvise had been and was on Bronski's mind. Without him, the Institut would have no physician. "Are you going to stay with us, Dr. Martine?"

They took several more steps before Martine answered. "Are you asking me to volunteer to serve my brothers?"

Bronski laughed. "Yes. Yes I am."

Martine stopped and studied the abbot. He was being presented with a business deal in which each partner could receive something of value. "I will if you give me your word those girls are safe."

"I know you don't understand me or this place Doctor, but I can say, without fear of contradiction, I have never killed anyone. Nor do I intend to."

"Even when you know what might happen if the child is born?"

Bronski looked around. "This is my home, François. When the child is born, will He make this better? Worse? My life is here. We have no wealth. As you know, we don't even have a chapel. We don't pray except in our hearts and minds. I am devoted to my religion and my church. As Father Curvise has said to me, 'nothing will change.' No one can change our beliefs. I live by the rules and vows I have sworn to uphold. It's the only life I know."

He stopped and then said, "The child will be like you and Edmund. Like the two girls. He will be a part of," Bronski spread his hands wide, encompassing the entire courtyard and beyond, "this. He can never leave. You understand, Doctor?"

"Yes. I was afraid of that."

"If he is the resurrection of our Savior, then he will have only us to serve."

"Yes, but is it fair to keep both of the women, Father Bronski? Urbana has done nothing to deserve this incarceration for the rest of her life." Martine argued to save just one.

"She is better off here. If she left, I'm afraid she wouldn't survive very long in the world. What Greatcoat has told us . . . It's happening. I'm afraid it will only get worse."

"Your adherence to the rules is most aggravating, Father Bronski," Martine said without humor.

"Yes," the abbot agreed. "And your constant disregard of the rules is, shall we say, equally aggravating." But he conceded a bit. "As she gets older, we'll talk about it."

It wasn't much, but Martine took it as a concession.

***

Propped against his pillows, Antoine Curvise was able to see outside into the courtyard.

"It's hard to believe it was only a year ago I saw those same people bringing in the crops from their farms and gardens," he commented hoarsely. "I think I'd like to try and sit in the chair for a while."

It took all of his strength to get out of bed, and even that was not enough to make it to the chair. Urbana had to hold him, to help him walk and sit down. The pain had intensified so that even the morphine no longer stopped the wrenching agony. Curvise had lost almost forty pounds, when he could have afforded to lose none. Urbana handled him easily.

"Dr. Martine said you weren't to get out of bed," she chided. "He'll holler at me if he finds you sitting here." She twisted a strand of her long hair, weaving it in and out of her fingers.

"Does he really holler at you?" Curvise asked, forcing a smile to his face.

Although it no longer reminded Urbana of a grinning skull, she still wished he would not make the effort. She could tell it exhausted him. "No, but I'm worried about you." She had conscientiously taken over the job of Curvise's guardian from Father Emil who was kept busy in the garrison. She liked the dying priest.

"Don't worry. My suffering will be over soon."

Except when he talked like that. For a moment, she looked as if she might cry. "Please don't say those kinds of things," she said, taking his hand in hers.

He gave her a squeeze. It took all the strength he could muster. "I'm sorry we brought you here, Urbana. So very, very sorry."

"Why?" she asked with surprise. "Don't you like me?"

"Of course I do. You're a wonderful young lady."

"Then don't be sorry. If it weren't for the priests, I'd be dead by now."

"All right," Curvise relented. "Then I'm not sorry. I'm glad you are here." And he was. "Does that make you feel better?"

"Yes. Lots better. Does it make you feel better?"

Curvise smiled and began to talk to her. She liked it when he asked her questions. Some days he had been too tired.

"Where did you live?" It was nice, Curvise thought, to have someone to speak with of things other than pain and death.

"Brunn. That's in Czechoslovakia." Urbana made herself comfortable at Curvise's feet.

"Did you like living in Brunn?"

"Until the soldiers came. After that it became difficult."

"Where did you learn to speak French?"

"In school. We were taught French, Polish, and German," she said proudly. "I was supposed to begin learning English this semester." She frowned quickly at the loss.

"Where are your parents? Your brothers and sisters?"

"The soldiers took us all to Slavkov to build a camp." She began to twirl her hair. "It was very hard."

"And Sabina? Did they take her family, too?"

"Oh yes. They took all the Jews. At first we thought it might be nice to build such a big place, but we soon found out it was hard work."

"Do you know what kind of a building, what kind of a camp you were building?"

Urbana shrugged her shoulders. She had not cared. When the work became strenuous, she had lost interest simply doing as she was told. "A camp. It was clean and very big."

Curvise shut his eyes. Greatcoat had said it was a camp built for the sole purpose of exterminating Jews. That the condemned had been brought in to build their own mausoleum . . . It was a statement he still could not bring himself to understand.

Urbana watched him a moment to make sure he was not praying. She did not like to interrupt the Father when he was at prayer. Finally, Curvise opened his eyes, but he had no more questions.

"Will you please go back to bed now, before Dr. Martine sees you sitting up and yells at me?"

"In a little while," he promised. "I just want to sit here for a little while longer."

***

Martine heard the clatter of wooden wheels on the cobblestones. From the window he had a perfect view. Four brightly colored wagons pulled into the courtyard. Horses stomped their hooves and threw back their heads, whinnying, hungry and tired. A fifth wagon was coming through the gate.

Father Alphonse came up behind him. "Gypsies," the priest said.

"Gypsies," Martine repeated.

The gypsies would be gone tomorrow morning. They had traveled from Yugoslavia on their way to Poland. Along the way they had picked up, like discarded pieces of trash, the new princes of the Institut. The Rommies were well paid servants for the priests of the Institut.

Father Alphonse made the sign of the cross. "I'd better give them a hand," he said sadly. When the gypsies came, they brought the sick priests with them. The last time they had come, he had prayed he would never see them again. His prayers had not been answered.

***

Curvise saw the gypsy wagons pull into the courtyard. At first, he thought it might be a circus. His interest was piqued.

Urbana had been standing close to the window, but backed away when she saw the nationality of the strangers.

Curvise noticed her change of mood. "Are you afraid of the gypsies?"

"Yes," she told him seriously. "They steal children."

Curvise sighed. The child was so young, and yet she had already learned to label people.

The gypsies stole children. The Jews killed them. He wondered briefly how the world had labeled the French. "They won't harm you," he reassured her. "Help me stand, please." He wanted to get a better view of the courtyard.

Leaning against Urbana's shoulder, Curvise watched as several priests were helped out of the backs of the wagons. Up close, the buggies were not as pretty or as colorful as he had first thought. The dust of the roads, the wear and tear of a harsh life had faded them, or was it his eyes? He blinked and saw Defont carry a man into the building. Each of the newly ordained Cardinals needed some kind of assistance.

"There, you see. The gypsies are just delivering the sick to the brothers here." He tried to sound upbeat, but failed.

An announcing cough came from the doorway. "I thought I told you to stay in bed, Antoine," Martine said. "And you," he turned dramatically on Urbana, "didn't I tell you not to let him out of bed?"

The small girl cowered behind the frail priest.

"Now François, it wasn't her fault. I insisted she help me." Curvise hobbled to his bed. The pain inside was fierce. And constant. Like an old friend who refused to leave his side. "Why do you insist I die in my bed,

François?" He tried to smile, but the pain overrode his intentions.

Urbana was at his side instantly. Better next to a dying priest than a doctor who yelled. She helped Curvise back in bed and adjusted his pillows so he reclined just enough to be able to see out of the window.

"I told you he would holler," she whispered.

"What secrets are you two sharing?" Martine moved across the room in quick strides. "Are you talking about me?" He smiled, then took Curvise's hand in his. "I don't want you to die in bed, Antoine. I just want you to have some peace."

He extended his other hand to Urbana. "I was just teasing you. I'm not mad. You may do whatever Father Curvise requests."

Relieved, she took his hand and joined him at the side of the bed.

"Did you see the gypsies, Antoine?" He did not wait for an answer, but turned to Urbana. "Would you get me a cup of coffee from the dining room, please?"

"Yes, Doctor. Would you like some coffee too, Father Curvise?"

"No, no thank you."

Both men watched as the quick feet of life left the room.

"Why are you always frightening her, François?"

"Children need to be frightened. How else can they tell the difference between what's good for them and what's not?" He laughed. "I try to frighten you, but you're too old. You don't listen." He patted Antoine's hand.

Curvise tightened his fingers around his friend's. "Take care of her when I'm gone." He was surprised at the depth of his feeling. He had never known the warmth and affection women brought to men. He had never had their softness to lean on before.

"Never mind that talk. You needn't worry about Urbana or Sabina. I have an understanding with Abbot Bronski. They will be well taken care of."

Martine walked to the window. "Did you see the wagons? I think they're rather colorful and exciting. Just think of it, Antoine! To wander over the face of the earth. No rules, no governments, no army. Just being free."

François Martine stood and watched the brightly dressed women standing around while their men assisted the sick priests from the wagons. He pictured himself—a bandanna tied around his head, his horse nuzzling his shoulder, the air blowing on his face. There would be mountains and rivers to cross. Adventures.

He turned away from the window. "Antoine . . ." he started to say. Then closed his eyes, fighting back the tears.

It tookFathe Alphonse four days to prepare the remains of Father Antoine Curvise. Martine could not bring himself to assist or even go anywhere near the catacombs where his friend would be entombed for eternity. Curvise's death had left a large empty place within him. No Requiem Mass had been said. No bells had tolled for Antoine's passing. At the Institut, death was looked upon as a relief from the suffering of mankind. Although its grief was surely felt, it was never mourned. It was, one might almost say, anticipated.

***

Sabina's belly grew with each passing month. Her face had taken on the kind of glow young women exude while in the position of motherhood. Weight was stored and her sallow appearance had turned to one of health and color. Urbana found comfort in assisting her friend. They could be seen walking around the courtyard holding hands, full of giggles and talk. Even the snows did not deter them. Every morning, sun or snow, they could be seen walking in the world.

"Why do you insist Sabina walk in this terrible weather?" Defont demanded of Martine. His pent-up fatherly instincts had risen to protect this child he felt was being sent to him. "She'll catch her death of cold out there."

"The best exercise for an expectant mother is walking. Don't ask me why, Defont. I can't quote you medical journals, but I can quote you common sense. Walking is the perfect exercise." Martine reached for a pączki, his fourth. The cold weather had created an appetite in him.

"But does she have to be outside? It's freezing out there." Defont would not give up.

"The cold will kill any germs that might come her way. In good health, she's actually safer outside than she would be in here." Martine's words were difficult to understand. His mouth was filled with jelly.

"How much longer before the child is here?" It was a question Defont asked every day.

"Another month. I've told you before, she's due sometime around the middle of December." Martine's eyes narrowed in wicked amusement. "Or has your memory become so short you can't recall from day to day?" Delicately, he wiped sugar from his mouth and sipped his coffee.

"Don't you worry, François?"

"Of course I worry, but what can I do? Be like you, a nervous hen who goes around pestering anyone who will listen? Asking the same questions day after day after day?"

Defont looked abashed. "Am I really that bad?"

"Worse."

"Well, someone should worry," the big policeman pouted. "It might as well be me. Perhaps," Defont started the sentence and then let it die, pretending to consider his words but, in reality, waiting until he had Martine's interest. Then he began again, his voice but a whisper. "Perhaps, I would not worry so much if only . . ." The friendly insult changed to a real desire. "I wish we had a better doctor. Antoine," he added.

"I wish the same thing, Edmund. The very same thing."

Father Ehrick came out of the kitchen with a pitcher of cold milk in one hand and a tray of pączkis in the other. The tray on the table where Martine now sat was empty. The doctor decided he could eat one more, but when he reached for another, Ehrick pulled the tray aside.

"These are for the mother," he said sternly.

"And what's in the jug?" Defont asked.

"Fresh milk from the village," Ehrick said, walking quickly away. Knowing Defont's love of fresh milk, he responded before the question was even asked. "No! I told you. These are for the mother."

"How's David lately?" Defont asked. He had been so busy in the wards that he had had little time for visiting.

Martine rubbed his chin in a gesture Defont instantly recognized as a sign of confusion. "I don't know what to make of David anymore," he said. "It's as though his mind is slowly shutting down. Everyone around him is fading from his memories. At times, he looks at me as if I'm a stranger."

"Is it possible what he told Antoine will really happen? That he'll die when the child is born?"

"If he does, it will be because he's willed himself to die and not for any other reason," Martine said hotly. His anger was not directed toward Defont, but himself. He did not want to believe David's death was imminent, but he could not bring himself to deny the possibility.

"If David . . . if you can believe David's responsible for Sabina's condition, why can't you believe he'll die when the child is born?" Defont argued and then offered, "I believe he will. To believe one is to believe them both," he added sadly.

Father Ehrick returned and sat down beside the Inspector. He had decided that the question that burned in his mind as well as the other priests at the Institut had to be asked. "Is it true, Doctor? Is Sabina a virgin?"

"Yes," Martine said. "It's true."

"And the father of the child she carries is . . .?"

Martine frowned. "I don't know for sure."

Ehrick nodded his head. "The Virgin Mary, it is said, was brought into fertility by an angel of God—his messenger here on earth. Is it possible the messenger has returned?"

Defont looked at Martine, anxious to hear his reply.

"Do you believe the Virgin Mary was the mother of God's son?" Martine asked. He was still unwilling to commit to anything at the moment.

"Yes, of course," Father Ehrick smiled. "I would think you would also, after what has happened here."

"Yes, but don't you find it strange . . .?" Martine stopped. "Never mind." He had been about to ask Father Ehrick if he found it strange a woman could be pregnant without a man present, but the priest had already answered the question.

"Why do you find it so hard to believe in the Immaculate Conception, Doctor?" Ehrick asked. "The fact it is about to happen again should be ample proof it occurred once before."

"But doesn't it shatter your faith?"

"Heavens, no. It reinforces it. It simply means God is still alive and with us."

"You don't think it will destroy the church?" Defont asked.

"How could it? After all, this is the religion Christ founded."

Martine laughed. "The religion Christ founded has been dead for centuries. What we have now is a monster that thrives on wealth, ignorance, and fear."

Father Ehrick studied Martine for a moment or two, his indubitable smile still in place. "Yes, that may be true. Out there. But here, this is still the religion Christ founded."

"Well said, Father Ehrick," Defont exclaimed happily. "What do you say to that, François?"

"If God is present here, he would bring me a pączki," Martine replied sharply.

Just as smartly, and without a word, Father Ehrick reached up his sleeve, pulled out a pączki, and handed it to Martine. "I have some milk in the kitchen for you, Edmund. Not that you need a bribe to believe in God."

It took only one glance to see the expression on Martine's face. That alone was enough to make Defont believe in miracles. The sound of his laughter filled the dining room.

CHAPTER TWENTY-ONE

The German conquest of France, Belgium, and the Netherlands had come so fast, so easily, so *right*. The ancient ruins of Europe crumbled into dust, and covered senile and inept leaders who had for so long depended upon their reputations to hold office. The old Barbarians were dead. Long live the new.

An already archaic and inefficient mail system was further damaged by the war. What used to take three months to cross the borders of the European states, now took six, if it was delivered at all.

The package was ripped and tattered, smeared with greasy dirt and the fingerprints of hundreds of hands between which it had been passed. The return address was barely legible. By the time it reached the Vatican, and finally the mailbox of Cardinal Vasai, almost six months had passed.

Father Giuseppe Rossini, new to the Cardinal's staff, struggled with the filthy packet. Like the mail, the priests who served inside the temple of Rome were slow and inefficient. The strict codes and order had been misplaced for the time being. War played havoc with everything and everyone. The Catholic Church was no exception.

Vasai had returned to Bordeaux as a conciliatory emissary to appease the Germans. The church would not support the Nazis, but neither would it denounce them. The old battle-scarred veterans of the religious wars now walked and talked of appeasement, of order, of patience. .... Of the sword of justice finally being laid to rest.

In a time not too long ago, any correspondence arriving from the Institut d'Infantiles had been immediately forwarded to the Cardinal who headed the Department of Religious Antiquities. Unfortunately, no one had informed Father Rossini of this procedure. Cardinal Vasai was due back in the Vatican next spring. It was only four months away. Not so long when one considered how long the letter had been in transit.

Cardinal Vasai had been receiving more mail than usual lately. The war had brought out hundreds of Christians seeking aid. Charities asking for funds. Refugees seeking asylum. This Institut was no different. Giuseppe was sure the packet contained a request for funds. That was the extent of the mail nowadays. Everyone wanted money. Sometimes Rossini wondered how people had the courage to regard their holy church as nothing but a bank. He put the packet in the bottom of the desk and closed the drawer.

***

Father Zigman Bronski paced the long corridor nervously. He had expected an answer by now. In his report, he had specifically requested instructions on how to deal with Sabina and the impending delivery.

His emotions rose and fell with every step. Surely his superiors would not let this birth happen. While it was not a decision he could make himself, Bronski knew his promise to François Martine had only been a half-truth. He was fully prepared to sacrifice his soul to eternal damnation if he were ordered to do so.

He covered more ground. Why hadn't they answered his letter? Did they not care? Did they simply think it was the rantings of yet another priest gone mad? Or did they feel as Father Ehrick who had said the child's birth did not matter? That it only proved God was still alive?

It did not really matter how the Vatican felt, Bronski decided. What mattered was that they tell him how he should feel.

***

Edmund Defont sat on the edge of David's bed, his face twisted with pain and emotion. Since the moment Sabina had gone into labor, David had lain in his bed almost completely comatose, except . . . Defont was sure the priest's eyes, staring up at the ceiling, saw past the barriers of mortar and stone. He corrected himself again. It was no longer David Proust who lay unmoving on the thin mattress. Defont felt it as well as saw it. David had passed away a few months earlier. The young priest had lost all recollection of his past. He had recognized no one and spoke haltingly and often incoherently. There was no longer any pain, but there was no pleasure. He lingered, waiting for the end. Or, Defont wondered, was it simply a new beginning?

Still, it hurt. David Proust had been his friend. And, just as the ache had overcome him at Antoine Curvise's death, David's passing would also bring him pain and remorse.

Like a soft wind, the moment came and went. Unobtrusive as an apparition, Father Emil appeared in the doorway. Defont glanced up for a second. It was enough time for a life to enter the world—and leave. David Proust's soft breathing stopped. Defont touched his friend's wrist and waited to feel the pulse. Nothing. The emptiness of the man before him filled Defont with loneliness.

David had taken his last breath—the infant, its first. The cry echoed through the dim halls and rooms of the Institut, claiming life.

***

After clearing the breathing passages, Martine slapped the newborn only once. "It's a boy," he announced. But that was not a surprise to anyone, even himself.

Reluctantly, he handed the child to Father Ehrick who had won the honor of giving the child its first bath. Warm water and alcohol were at the ready.

"You do know the proper way to bathe a baby?" Martine asked skeptically.

Ehrick smiled. François had spent all of last week teaching him how to hold a child just so, what temperature the water must be, how gently he must cleanse the new skin. It was not so different than the care he gave to the children, only this helpless person was so very tiny.

Conscious throughout the delivery, Sabina smiled weakly. "Is he all right, Dr. Martine?"

"He's perfect," Martine said with accomplishment and a little bit of awe. Motherhood had always amazed him. Inevitably, women who had spent hours, and sometimes days in the constant pain of labor, never thought to question their own health.

He reached down and gently smoothed Sabina's long black hair—blacker now and damp from her sweat. She had changed since he had first laid eyes on her. Her thin sallow face was now round and full of life. Dark eyes that had stared emptily and afraid, now glowed with hope and energy. In the short period of time she had been at the Institut, she had been transformed into a woman. In stark contrast, Urbana was still a child.

"He's absolutely perfect," Martine repeated affectionately. "And so are you."

Sabina closed her eyes. "Where is Monsieur Defont?" she asked wearily. "Does he know?"

"He'll be here soon, I'm sure. You rest and don't worry. I'll tell him he can wake you if you're sleeping."

Martine had no intention of doing anything of the sort, but perhaps the new mother would rest easier if she were not afraid of missing her bumbling friend.

Urbana had held Sabina's hands through her ordeal. Now that it was all over, she found it hard to move. Fright had frozen her muscles. But at last she began to breathe normally, letting out a small sigh.

Martine looked up and smiled. "You can relax now, too."

But she could not. Her hands still shook and her face was pallid, although her eyes were wide and curious. This had been her second encounter with womanhood. The painful menstrual cramps and frightening flow of blood had been a terrifying shock. And now this. She wished for a moment she could be a man. Anything but what she was—a frightened child in a world of men.

Martine sensed her fears. Reaching for her hand, he pulled her to him and gave her a reassuring hug. "You were a tremendous help, Urbana. I couldn't have done it without you."

She relaxed in his arms. He gave her another brief squeeze and then a gentle push. "Now, go and see what's taking Father Ehrick so long."

Her shoes made small clicking noises against the stone floor as she ran towards the dining room, a little girl again.

***

Driven by the cry, Zigman Bronski retreated to his room. Kneeling in the center of his small enclosure, he clasped his hands in prayer. Torn by his beliefs in the church and its sacraments of devotion, he asked God for guidance. For a sign to tell him what to do. He tried to believe what he had told Martine, but he had lied, buying time and hoping for direction from his superiors. Hoping for a miracle that would see the child and its mother struck down.

He had wanted to act on his own, but could not. The years of servitude to his religion had deprived him of any initiative. His failure to receive instructions also cast doubt on his fears. Did their silence mean he should do nothing? Was it possible the Vatican did not believe him?

But believe what? Bronski wondered. That a young Jewish girl had given birth to a new Christ?

Had he not been taught there was only one Christ? And that Christ had already been born into this world, one thousand nine hundred and forty years ago? There was only one conclusion left to draw. He had allowed a Jewish girl to give birth to the very anti-Christ the Bible had predicted would destroy the world. The child should have been destroyed immediately, but having written for a directive, Bronski was powerless to do anything but wait. It was up to the Vatican to decide. Then it would be up to him to act.

His report had been clear. He had left no doubt as to what he would do, if ordered. *So why hadn't they answered?*

Zigman Bronski retreated to the wards. The thick stone walls of the Institut blocked most sounds. Some, like the constant screams of the children at night, refused to be contained. Their tormented thoughts and ideas struggled to pierce the heavy stones and solid woods that lined the rooms and corridors. But, for the most part, a man could think and talk without fear of being overheard.

He helped the priests finish changing the sheets on the Cardinals' beds before retreating to the opposite end of Ward One. A buzzing in his head like a winter mosquito sparked a thought. The idea was simple. Later, he would attribute it to his prayers for guidance.

A child had been born to a Jewess in an insane asylum in the middle of the wilds of Poland. Bronski's thoughts began to circle. The child had been born to a *Jew* who now resided in the middle of a war zone. This person of *Jewish origin* was trapped where Nazi troops combed the area looking for— for *Jews* to exterminate.

Patience, he told himself. Patience—the material that had built the Holy Roman Empire and the substance that held the priests together. Patience—the virtue of good, and the sin of evil. His patience had paid off. The Lord God had heard his pleas for help. In the end, patience would solve his dilemma. All he had to do was wait. Time and events would take care of his problem.

The weight that had rested on his shoulders slipped and fell to the floor, soundless, like the snow that fell in the courtyard.

***

"Look! Look! He's reaching for my finger," Defont exclaimed, wagging his index finger in front of the baby's face. Tiny hands groped for Edmund.

"He can't see yet," Martine said. "His eyes are still closed."

"But he's reaching for my finger. Look," Defont demanded. A hand so small as to disappear within Defont's curled little finger grasped and held it. "He's got it. What do you mean he can't see?"

"He just sees shadows," Martine said, trying not to sound excited.

Sabina laughed and handed the baby to Defont. "He likes it when Monsieur Defont holds him."

Defont lifted the baby over his head and stared into his eyes. "They're blue, like water."

"There's no color yet," Martine said. "Don't you know anything about children, Edmund?"

"I know what I see." Defont brought the baby down, kissing it on the forehead. "How soft and sweet," he whispered.

Exasperated, Martine gave up trying to convince Defont he was making more of the baby than nature allowed. It was easier just to ignore the man.

"Sabina, have you decided what you're going to name the child?"

"Yes, I have. I'd like to call him Adam."

Martine closed his eyes and tested the name silently on his tongue. Baby tugging at his nose, Defont peered over the top of the child's head.

"Why Adam?" Martine finally asked.

"He's my first, just as Adam was God's first. I . . . I thought it appropriate. Don't you like it?"

"Yes." Martine pronounced the word as if someone had asked him to rule the world. "I like it. I like it just fine."

"Look," Defont called. "He's smiling at me."

"That's gas."

"Gas for you, François. It's a smile for me," Defont said with a laugh.

Sabina finished eating and reached for her baby. "Enough for me," she said. "Now it's time for him." She stopped and started again. "It's time for Adam to eat."

Defont handed her the child. "Go to your *maman*," he said, easing his finger from Adam's grasp. "He didn't want to let go! Did you see that, François?"

"Yes, yes, I saw," Martine said peevishly. He was more than a little envious of Defont's easy ways with the child.

Unlike the Inspector who had wanted a child or, as Defont had put it once, "a houseful of children," Martine had been quite content living his life without such interruptions. In François' opinion, only an ignorant fool would continue to clutter the earth with fodder for the cannons of war. That thought alone helped squelch the jealousy he had felt earlier.

"Let us go to the dining room for coffee Edmund, and give the mother a chance to feed her baby in peace."

***

Defont broached the subject first.

"Did you see the fine work Father Alphonse did on David?"

"I was down in the catacombs yesterday," Martine replied. "It's eerie, you know, to see six complete replicas of one man."

"Is he the last?"

"I'm not sure, Edmund. I was just thinking. I seem to recall Antoine mentioning David's brother and two more sons."

The two men looked at each other for a moment.

"But David's task is complete," Defont said. "There's no need . . ."

"No need for what?" Martine stopped him. He suddenly began to laugh. Not at something funny, but a rather cruel laugh as one might when he discovered the joke was on him. "I just thought of something, Edmund. I'm the only person alive who can verify this Immaculate Conception and now, of course, it is no longer verifiable."

"I don't understand, François. Everyone at the Institut knows."

"Knows what? That what Antoine and I have said was a fact is an absolute truth? When Sabina went into labor, I took her virginity surgically so the water would break properly." Martine laughed again. "Under the circumstances, given the fact I am a doctor confined to an asylum, would you believe me?"

The expression on Defont's face mirrored his thoughts. "If I didn't know better," he said softly, "I'd think you were crazy. Isn't there some way you could verify whether or not Adam is David's son?"

Martine rubbed his whiskered jaw. "A blood test would give a strong indication of whom the father was."

"A blood test?"

"The procedure is quite simple, really. We'd need a sample of David's blood and the child and, of course, Sabina's."

Interested, Defont leaned closer.

"Theory tells us if the father has, for instance, type O blood, and the mother type A, the child will have either the type O blood of his father, or type A blood of his mother. However, the child would not, under any circumstances, have blood type B. In addition to this evidence, the blood may be further typed as to a negative or positive RH factor. Positive parents would produce a positive child."

"The blood doesn't mix?"

"No, it maintains its integrity."

"Then, let's test the child and Sabina. Compare their blood types. Do you know what type David was?"

Martine shook his head. It was obvious he was disappointed.

Defont's own hopes sank, only to rise quickly. "If the child's blood is not the same type as Sabina's, would that prove anything?"

"Nothing, actually. It would show us the boy's genetic heritage is derived from his father. But, before you go any further with this Edmund, I do not have the facilities here to type blood."

Defont sighed, frustrated. "Then why did you bring it up?"

"I didn't bring up the subject," Martine bristled. "If I remember correctly, you did. Besides, what is it you were hoping to prove?"

"That the child—that Adam—is not related to either Sabina or David," Defont said, softly.

"Edmund, we know he is not David's child."

"Yes, we know that. David told us—what he thought in his nightmares and his fantasies—things which you have now stated are facts. Things which, if they are facts, could be proven if the child had a blood type different from Sabina and David."

"Theoretically that statement should work. But not in this case. If David were the angel he claimed to be, created by God, then would it not make sense that God's child and David would both be blessed with the same blood type?"

It was a logic Defont could not conquer. "What else then, François? What other tests are there that you could perform?"

"None. Although, I suppose time will be a test in itself. In time, the child should come to resemble at least one of his parents. A boy usually resembles his father."

"Adam has blue eyes and fair skin. He has light hair—just like David."

"Yes, yes, yes," Martine answered in exasperation. "I agree with your words, Edmund. Adam does not resemble Sabina. He not only resembles David, but the others interred in the catacombs—at this time."

François Martine hated to agree with Defont on this subject. The big man plunged into theories with no background. The contentious policeman had not spent hours journalizing Father David's every word. Nor had Edmund spent the time that he, François Martine had, comparing DeValier's journals to Curvise's and his very own notes about this subject matter. *He* was the one who should be putting forth valued hypotheses. Besides, a week was much too early to tell what the child would look like as he grew. The boy's skin could darken, matching Sabina's olive hue as could his hair and eyes.

"What difference does all this make?" Martine asked crossly.

"You were the one who said it, François."

"Said what? What words are you putting in my mouth now?"

"They are your words, François. You asked me who would believe the word of a doctor confined to an asylum." Defont shifted his bulk. "And you were right to question it, don't you see? I certainly would not believe you. I have lived through this experience, but had I not François, I would think you were crazy."

A shadow touched the corner of Martine's eye. He glanced up and saw Father Bronski standing in the doorway.

Defont followed Martine's gaze. "Father Bronski." He waved the abbot over. "Join us, please."

Bronski did as Defont requested, but it was not with any happiness. His face reflected the darkness he had first foreseen at the birth of the child. The prophecy that proclaimed Armageddon, the end of the world, had begun its course of destruction. A course preordained and set into motion by the birth of the anti-Christ—the destroyer of the world—the child he had allowed to be born onto this earth.

Defont and Martine knew the doubts and agony Bronski suffered. The abbot had made no secret of his feelings towards the child and its mother. They did not know he only waited patiently for orders.

An awkward silence surrounded the three men.

"Have you seen the child?" Defont broke the silence innocently. Curvise's words were still fresh in his mind, warning him to be wary of the brooding abbot. Was Zigman the fanatic Antoine had supposed? Perhaps he should have stayed silent. Defont knew only that if Bronski gazed down at the child, a helpless infant, his heart would melt. The priest's animosity would be vanquished. How could it not?

"You delude yourself, Edmund. There is no child here."

Bronski's words, soft as butterfly wings, were not nearly so pretty. Still, they gave Defont hope. If Bronski could not see his way to accept the child, then perhaps it was better that, in the abbot's eyes, there was no child. At least then there could be no danger.

"You're a fool, Bronski," Martine struck out savagely. "How can you deny what you know is fact? You, a man who has suffered so that your brothers would not. You, who have lost fingers and been struck by the insanity that lives here. You, a man whose heart is as great as any saint. How can you sit there and deny the existence of this child?

"Shall we add the name of Zigman Bronski to the list of those who crucified the first Son of God?"

"What would you have me do, Doctor? Rip off my robe and denounce my Lord? Would you have me join you on your knees in front of this false prophet? Should I simply give up the years I have walked in God's footsteps, tear down the church and all its beliefs to join this . . .?" Bronski paused with a caustic smile. "What will you call this new religion of yours?"

Defont's commanding voice interrupted the volatile situation. "That is not what Dr. Martine implied, Father Bronski. I'm sure you are well aware of that."

"It is what he meant, Edmund."

Bronski returned his attention to Martine, but his voice was more controlled. "I did not believe in this coming until you, Dr. Martine, showed me the error of such thoughts. I was unaware of the others hidden in the catacombs until, once again, you showed me what my brothers had fought to suppress for so many years. They fought and died to keep this evil from being born. It was my weakness that allows him life."

Defont twisted suddenly. Had the abbot said "allowed" or "allows?" Again, Curvise's dire warnings flittered sharply through his head.

"I cannot change that gentlemen," Bronski continued, "but I can swear to you that this life shall forever be confined within the walls of the Institut."

"Yes," Martine acknowledged calmly. That was another argument he had not yet won. "You've made yourself quite clear on that point. But how can you be so sure this child is evil, Zigman? David said nothing that would lead us to believe this child wants anything more except to return home. Those are the very words written in Monsignor DeValier's journals. I know you have read them. I can show them to you if you wish. So, I ask you again Father Bronski, how is it you have decided this child is malevolent?"

"It is written in the scriptures, Doctor. The anti-Christ will come. The devil's spawn will signal the beginning of Armageddon. The world will be engulfed in fire and brimstone." Bronski turned his level gaze on Martine. "If someone tells you the snake will bite, do you believe him, or do you sleep with the snake? We have been warned, Doctor."

Curvise's weakened voice in Defont's ear—*"There are fanatics everywhere, Edmund. I do not trust him. Be careful."*

"We would be fools," said Bronski. "I have been a fool not to heed such good advice."

"But you didn't know, Father Bronski. You said so yourself just a few minutes ago. It does you no good to accept blame when you are blameless." Martine changed his tactics. "When Monsignor Michael Proust was here, alive and suffering, claiming to be an angel—the messenger of God, did you believe him?"

Bronski lowered his gaze. "No, I did not believe it possible."

"You didn't believe what was possible?" Martine pushed gently before playing his trump. "Another Immaculate Conception? If you do not believe it possible now, how could you believe it happened before?"

"I don't know."

"I think you do. At least I think your church knew it was possible. For what other reason would they drive men to suffer the anguish of insanity rather than allowing them to fulfill their obligations?

"You, Father Bronski, more so than anyone or anything I have ever related to religion, represent the real meaning of Christianity."

Defont blinked. Bronski glanced up, confusion evident in his silent expression. Martine obliged him with a benevolent smile. Arguments could always be won with words, if one's opponent listened to the truth.

"Love. Love of your fellow man. And compassion. That was all Christ wanted for those around him. For everyone. Here, within these walls, compassion is practiced every day. Kindness and understanding are a way of life. Outside these walls, men are constantly killing each other. Even if they don't put a knife to someone's throat, they learn to despise their neighbor.

"You talk of the devil. The evil is not here, Father Bronski, nor is it in the child. The only sinister attribute I have experienced within these walls is ignorance.

"You have been fortunate to witness what I sometimes hesitate to call a miracle, but there can be no other explanation for what has happened. If it happened once, why can't you believe it could happen again?"

Bronski's reply was sharp against the soft question François Martine had imposed.

"What gives you the right to judge my religion? Or my church, Dr. Martine? You, who adhere to your communistic beliefs. You, who professes God does not exist. Do you change your attitudes that easily, Doctor? Now you seem convinced God is here."

"I haven't changed my opinion about the God to which you and the rest of the Christian world bow. For me, He is still a figment of misguided minds. But my opinion of Jesus Christ has changed dramatically. You have read and heard what Michael Proust said over the years he was confined to the Institut. I know you heard what David said. What if, Zigman, what if those words were the truth? That Christ was but a man trying to return home? Not a god, except, perhaps, he called himself by that name. Can you allow yourself to think that clearly? That freely? Or are you to be the one who hounds Him until He is nailed to the cross again? Are you that frightened, that unsure of your own beliefs?"

Defont sat in silent wonder. Amazed at Martine. Envious of Martine. In awe. François had the ability to take the very thoughts he had had in his own mind and transform them into ideas with strong convictions. If only they had convinced the abbot. Instead, they had angered him.

"My beliefs are ones that have survived time and adversity, Dr. Martine. They are etched in the rock upon which Christ built His church. They will not be torn asunder by a pseudo-intellectual like yourself or anyone else.

"I will agree with you on one point, though. I was a fool to allow this to happen. You asked how I could acknowledge the Immaculate Conception then and not now. It was that very conviction that led me to believe it could not happen again. I was wrong. May God forgive me. I was wrong and I will suffer the consequences of my actions. As will you." Bronski turned his rage on Defont. "And you, Edmund. And the child. You shall not be set free to bring this scourge upon the world. Of that, you may be sure."

Defont and Martine watched the abbot stalk from the room. Their discussion might have been enjoyable had it taken place between philosophers with time on their hands, and not reality, but an illusion.

"One can only imagine how Christ must have felt when he was brought in front of Herod," Martine commented sourly. "To stand before such lords of ignorance without a chance in the world of convincing them he meant no harm."

"But what if Bronski is right, François? What if Adam is here to destroy the world?"

Martine cocked his head to one side and glared at Defont. "And what will he do that we haven't already done to ourselves, Edmund? Start a war? Must I remind you one is already taking place? Will he bring about hunger? Disease? What? How can a child destroy what little we have left of this planet?

"Bronski thinks only of his church. Frankly, I would not care if all the religions of the world were exposed for what they really are. If the child can bring about that kind of destruction, then I say more power to him."

***

Outside the walls of the Institut, the snow built and packed into a barrier of ice, locking the forlorn place into hibernation away from the destructive forces that roamed Europe.

Zigman Bronski retreated to his room. The serenity that had carried him through life had suddenly been shattered. Yes, he knew he had been a fool for letting Martine and Curvise convince him to accept David's pleas for help. How could he have been so blind? So ignorant? Why had God failed to warn him? Why had God failed to send him a sign, a word from the Vatican to end this child's life? What forces were at work that prevented him from hearing from his masters in Rome?

He buried his face in his hands. Why was he so weak and too afraid to carry out the task he knew to be his? Had not Abraham been willing to sacrifice his own son without question? It would take only the flick of the knife to bring back the sleep he needed.

Restless and in need of something to do, he opened the bottom drawer of his desk and pulled out the Book of Records. The old, leather bound book held the names and dates of the thousands of priests who had come to this place to die. He had failed to timely enter David Proust's death. It was a matter with which he quickly disposed. Under David's entry, he scripted the date of the child's birth. It no longer surprised him to find his hand shook as he completed the entry.

CHAPTER TWENTY-TWO

The winter storms receded grudgingly. Sacred holidays passed unobserved and long forgotten. A new year came and no one cared. For centuries, life in the Institut had been gauged by death—by how many children arrived and how many were buried.

"Look François, he's a genius," Defont called out. "Already he wants to walk." Adam hung on to Defont's fingers, supported just above the floor. His little legs tried desperately to move across the cold wood. The child was six months old.

François glanced from Defont to Adam, then returned to his coffee. He was tired. He had been up all night with one of the Cardinals. "There's nothing unusual about that," he snapped.

Martine enjoyed watching Adam grow and expand his limits, but he was not about to let Defont know that. It would have been easier to agree with the policeman's boasting if it had not been so constant. It was as if no one but Defont realized Adam was special. Sometimes, Martine admitted to himself, he bent over backwards not to see the unique things the boy did just to aggravate Edmund.

He shook his head as he watched the big man and the tiny child playing. Defont the protector. Defont the teacher. Defont the nursemaid. A stranger would almost certainly believe Defont to be the boy's father.

Martine watched as Defont raised his arms, bringing the boy level with his face. Adam kicked happily, feet running in space.

"He'll fall," Martine shouted. He could not help himself. Any fool, even Defont could see the boy was going to hurt himself.

"Not with his grip, François. He's as strong as any Frenchman." Defont tossed Adam into the air and caught him as he fell towards the floor.

Martine looked away. "Now I know why you never had any children," he said sarcastically.

Tucking Adam safely in his arms, Defont joined Martine at the table. In his lap, Adam squirmed into a more investigative sitting position. Tiny hands reached out to grab a spoon or the cup filled with hot coffee.

"No, no," Martine said gently, moving the cup out of the way. "That will burn you."

"Look at him, François! His curiosity is boundless."

"All children are curious, Edmund."

"Not like Adam."

"Not like Adam," Martine mimicked. "You make him sound as if he is the only child you've ever held."

"Not the only child, François, but no other has been as alive as he."

Adam wriggled out of Defont's grasp and crawled onto the table. It was evident he was intent on reaching the cup Martine had so recently moved.

"Look, he wants the coffee."

"Will you be laughing when he burns himself?" Martine asked angrily, grabbing the cup and moving it even farther away from Adam's outstretched hand.

"Put it down, François. He won't burn himself."

"I will not put it down, Edmund. Just because you, an adult with a child's intelligence, would not burn yourself, does not mean Adam's curiosity will not place him in harm's way. I swear, Edmund, perhaps Adam is smarter than you."

"Put the cup down, François," Defont insisted gently. "Right in front of him. He knows it will hurt him because you have told him so. He understands."

Martine hesitated, but the sureness of Defont's convictions made him curious. Slowly he placed the cup before Adam, ready to snatch it away at a moment's notice.

Adam reached for the hot cup, touched the cool handle and crawled back into Defont's arms.

Martine was speechless. Any other child would have turned the cup over, scalding themselves with the hot liquid.

Defont stood and hefted Adam to his shoulders with a practiced motion. "Come on Adam, let's go outside." He smiled at Martine. "As I have told you often, François, he is a most unusual child."

***

Sabina came out of the kitchen wiping her hands on her apron. She had put on weight carrying Adam and had taken some of it off. Since she had begun helping Father Ehrick in the kitchen, she had put most of it back on in the places that cause most women to suffer. She rose early each morning to feed Adam and then to start the fires in the ovens. Ehrick was teaching her to cook.

"Would you care for some breakfast, Doctor?"

"No, not today, Sabina." Martine smiled up at her. "Please sit down. You look tired."

"Not tired," she said softly. "Worried."

Martine was instantly alert. "Worried? About what?"

Always soft, her voice became softer still. She glanced around the room to make sure no one else was present. "Father Bronski," she breathed. Unconsciously, she reached up to twist her hair between her fingers. Martine recognized the nervous habit she had picked up from Urbana.

"Has he said something to you?"

"No. That's just it. Why does he avoid Adam and me? Have we done something to him?"

The problem was not a problem. It was, Martine thought, a blessing in disguise. The further away Bronski stayed from the child, the less apt he would be to wrap himself in the dark side of his religion. He reached for her hand.

"You've done nothing to Father Bronski, Sabina. His enmity is brought on by his own ignorance. He simply refuses to understand."

"Understand what?"

Giving her hand a quick squeeze, Martine let go and leaned back in his straight-backed chair. Consciously, he avoided her eyes as his words attempted delicacy. "How you came to be with Adam."

"Do you understand?"

Martine met Sabina's gaze and her question. "To be absolutely honest with you, not as well as I think." In the past, they had touched only briefly on the subject. It was not something they freely discussed.

"It was not something I wanted to do, Dr. Martine. Rather, it was more of an obligation. I'm not sorry, nor am I guilty of any wrong-doing. It was preordained I should bear Adam."

It did not pass unnoticed that Sabina did not say "her child" as most mothers would have in describing the birth of their son. It made Martine think she knew exactly what had happened and why. Although he hesitated to ask, the subject was open, and he had to pursue the matter.

"Do you know why you were picked?"

Sabina shook her head, although her denial did not silence her words. "I think it had something to do with the fact I'm a Jew." Searching for confirmation, she smiled. "I'm familiar with the Bible, Dr. Martine. Jesus' mother was a Jew, like me. Is that why Father Bronski dislikes Adam and me?"

Her insight was deeper than Martine had given her credit for realizing. "Do you think Adam is a Jew?"

"At first, when he was inside of me," Sabina blushed and patted her stomach, "I was certain. Now, I'm not sure. He's not like any Jewish child I've ever seen." She rolled her eyes and looked up at the ceiling. "He's not like any child."

The consummate interviewer, Martine kept his questions short. "How do you mean?"

Sabina wrung her hands together, glancing about the room nervously. "The infants I've seen in my family cling to their mothers and refuse to let go." Her hand went to her breast. "When I feed Adam . . . it's difficult to explain. He takes nourishment, but no pleasure. It is as if he has no need for a mother's love. As soon as he's finished, he starts to fidget. He looks around for Monsieur Defont, or anyone else for that matter. Father Ehrick. Father Alphonse." Sabina paused before voicing her insecurity. "Am I being silly, Dr. Martine? A jealous mother?" She laughed suddenly. "The roles have been reversed, have they not? I am being the clinging child while Adam wants his freedom. Sometimes I feel if he didn't have to eat, I would never see him."

Martine forced a fatherly grin on his face. In his experiences with young mothers and their babies, it was as Sabina had said. Infants clung to their mothers' arms and screamed like the devil when given to a stranger. He had no answer for her. It was easier to take another tack.

"Were you frightened when he was conceived?"

"Not then, no. I was so scared when I went to bed that first night." She looked up at him. "Of you and the others. But the dream was reassuring. The angel appeared and told me I was to bear the Son of God." She stopped and turned away, embarrassed at the exhilaration she still felt over an erotic dream that had occurred so seemingly long ago.

"Did the angel say why he came to you?"

"I was *chosen*," she said, the dream still vivid and real in her thoughts. "I was chosen to bear the Son of God."

"Are you sorry?"

"No," she said hesitantly. "No, I'm not sorry it happened, but I do worry. After all, they killed the last Son of God, did they not? I couldn't stand and watch Adam be crucified."

Again, Martine noticed Sabina called her child by name, as if he were an entity who did not belong to her.

Confusing thoughts filled the doctor's mind. He had taken from Sabina what her young lover should have and brought a child into the world. He had witnessed this miracle and yet, only a short time later, doubts constantly sprang into his thoughts. Had he been deceived? Had he and Antoine Curvise been so caught up in proving the Immaculate Conception a reality or a falsehood they had seen only what they had wanted to see? Had David somehow slipped past a sleeping Defont and reached Sabina's bed in a moment of passion?

No, it was impossible. He could not deny what he had seen and felt. The experience had been too great. It was too sad to have been just a dream. Too exhilarating to have been a nightmare.

***

Winter passed slowly. The snow became heavy rains that soaked into the ground and puddled, finally refusing to be absorbed. And still they fell.

As had become his habit, each morning after Sabina had fed Adam, Defont came to take the child and walk the corridors, cooing and whispering softly to this miracle of woman. Freed of motherhood for a short while, Sabina would accompany Urbana to the dining room for breakfast. The two girls generally had the place to themselves and lingered, as women do, talking about things of interest to themselves. At times, Dr. Martine joined them. But the morning was for Edmund and Adam.

Passing the wards, they would stop and visit the priests who took a special delight in creating their own melody of coos and soft whispers. Occasionally, one of the Cardinals would struggle to smile and stare with eyes that almost looked alive.

Martine bristled when Defont brought the child into the wards. He claimed it was because he did not want Adam exposed to the sights and sounds of the aged. He refused to acknowledge that a great deal of his temper arose from the fact that he coveted the affection Defont already had. Everyone in the Institut shared in the joy of the child, but no one, not even Sabina could surpass the affection Defont had developed for Adam. At times they were inseparable.

It amazed Defont, the things a child could do to a grown man. Adam, with his bright blue eyes, always looking. *François be damned!* Defont was sure the boy understood the things he pointed out to the child. Always smiling. Reaching out with his tiny hands to touch the men who lay before him.

Since the first day, Defont had never again questioned Adam was the Son of God. On a day when it was raining particularly hard, he had carried Adam into the catacombs and placed the tiny hands on the corpse of Antoine Curvise. He had not expected a miracle, but it would not have surprised him

229

had one occurred. Maybe in time, he thought. Maybe next year.

Then, one day, summer approached and the rains stopped for a few days. Defont was proud to share Adam with the outside world. The Inspector strolled past trees and explained how they grew. Adam reached out and caressed the rough bark. Defont pulled the summer leaves within reach and explained their individual shapes. Adam crushed the green life within his tiny hand.

"Softly," Defont had whispered, and Adam had let go, watching the twigs spring back and forth in the warm air. Perhaps it was just Defont's imagination, but he could have sworn that, just as Adam was investigating the world, Mother Nature had stopped to look at the beautiful child.

A mosquito bite brought him back to reality. Or was it the sounds of cannons being fired in some distant place that made the birds and insects stop their singing and look toward the heavens?

CHAPTER TWENTY-THREE

Lord Cardinal Armand Vasai had spent the winter in France, trying to come to grips with the surrender of his homeland. His nerves were frayed, exposed by what he had witnessed in France. In Paris, Jews were being rounded up and shipped to *somewhere*.

He had refused to believe the rumors. His beloved France, conquered, stood like pillars of salt. But why not? Had he not preached appeasement? Patience? The pride and warrior spirit the French had believed they possessed, although the world had known otherwise, had finally been exposed. The Nazis had not only kicked France into the ground, they had made them grovel and stand helplessly by while French citizens were rounded up and shipped to *somewhere*.

That somewhere was something Cardinal Vasai simply refused to believe. Like a ripple in space, when a single man realizes he is not the image he has so long believed; that moment, when faced with death, he crumples to his knees and cries; the ripple in space, magnified by millions, becomes a wave that rips and opens a vast emptiness in a world already a void of despair. France, beloved France, fell to her knees and cried to live.

Lord Cardinal Armand Vasai escaped from France seeking the serenity, the grandeur of Rome. The pomp and ceremony of the Vatican was the only balm he could imagine to soothe his ego. Instead, the city-state only returned him to reality. He hated Rome and the Italians. He despised the smug, oily grins these cardboard conquerors had painted on their faces. And he abhorred their food. They were nothing but barbarians, cooking everything in olive oil! Had they never heard of butter?

Standing before him at his office door was a small swarthy Italian—a monsignor at that. "Where is Father DeLoch?" Vasai demanded, rising to the pinnacle of his stature as a prince of the church. "And who are you?"

"Monsignor Giuseppe Rossini, Your Benevolence," the middle-aged priest answered with all the reverence he could muster.

"Where is Father DeLoch?"

Rossini spread his arms, an absurd caricature of Christ crucified. "I do not know, Your Excellency."

It was not what Vasai wanted to hear. "Why are you here?" As of yet, Vasai had not heard the pontiff's edict replacing the secretaries of the Cardinals at the Vatican with members of his own staff.

At the urging of his confident, Cardinal Emanuel Gaston, the pope felt he had good reason for distrusting his lords in waiting. Rumors abounded his princes had coddled up to the Nazis and Fascists. Deals were being made to insure the sanctity of the church. Clandestine meetings were being held in the dark cafes of Rome. Pius would make sure the church would survive, but not at the hands of traitors. His warning, his retaliation was that only Italians would stand between his Cardinals and the lay world.

"I am your secretary, Your Excellency." Rossini bowed. His feeling for this overstuffed Frenchman was successfully hidden behind the dour look on his face.

"By whose authority?"

"His Holiness." Instantly, Rossini no longer attempted to hide his contempt. Did this pompous Frenchman think he had requested this post? As had many others, he had been ordered by the pontiff's senior advisor, Cardinal Gaston, to assume this position. It was a position that would successfully keep men like Vasai out of the mainstream of the Vatican's affairs.

The threat now exposed, Vasai, like France, crumbled. He was beaten and had no recourse but to accept this . . . spy. Yes, Vasai decided. That was what this little man before him represented. A spy for the pontiff. Distrust had spread to even the gates of heaven.

His demeanor did not change. The facade he presented to Rossini was still stiff and unyielding. Searching frantically for the words to take command, Vasai realized there was nothing he could say. He turned and walked through the alcove that led to his office.

Reaching for the doorknob, Rossini's hand flashed and beat him to the gilded handle. With swift, sure movements, the Monsignor opened the door and bowed, allowing his master entrance.

Father DeLoch had never opened the door for him, Vasai thought. Maybe this was not such a bad idea, having an Italian for a servant. It seemed to be their best feature.

"Your mail is sorted and waiting on your desk, Excellency." Rossini closed the door behind him. He knew his part. Humility was a game he had always dramatized well and would continue to do so until he got what he wanted out of life. "May I get you some refreshment? Coffee?"

Vasai sat down behind his desk. Three piles of smudged and dog-eared envelopes stared up at him. "Some coffee, yes," he remarked absently.

Rossini disappeared into a small kitchen while Vasai looked over the mail. The first pile contained requests for funds from the many charitable organizations throughout the world. They came like flies in summer.

Rossini reappeared, carrying a silver tray. A sterling silver coffee pot and china cup rode quietly in his hands. He poured the coffee with grace and added the one lump of sugar he knew Vasai took. The cup was placed at Vasai's elbow with a bow.

"I took the liberty of sorting your mail, Your Excellency. This pile contains requests for monies. This one, from your congregation throughout France. This last one is from the religious organizations you command. They are personal and I have not opened them."

Vasai followed Rossini's words with his eyes. The first two piles he noted, had indeed been opened—their letters paper-clipped to the outside of the envelope for easy access. He approved. He no longer had to awkwardly fumble with a letter opener. Yes, he definitely approved. Father DeLoch had simply brought him his mail and unceremoniously dumped it on his desk.

"Is there anything I should read in here?" He waved his hand over the first two stacks.

"Nothing of importance, Your Excellency."

"Remove them, please." Vasai reached for his cup and took a luxurious sip of hot coffee. It was strong and rich, the way good French coffee should be.

Rossini deftly scooped up the unwanted mail. "Will there be anything else?"

"No thank you, Monsignor. You may go." Vasai's acknowledgment of Rossini's position sealed their relationship.

The letters requesting assistance and monies had been a large part of the bothersome mail Rossini had removed. No pangs of conscience would attack Vasai today. He had been spared the cries and pleas for help from the outside world.

Relaxing in his overstuffed chair, he reached for the top envelope in his remaining pile of mail. The postmark of the smeared and dirty envelope jumped out at him. *Litz, Poland.* His hand began to shake. His brief moment of serenity had passed.

A flood of memories swept over his thoughts. It had taken him almost three months to be free of the guilt he had suffered at Jean-Paul Meric's insistence David Proust had been possessed. It had taken a heavy toll on his health. His interview with Father Proust who had calmly sat in the small room insisting he was an angel, insisting he was here to bring back the Christ child, was not forgotten as easily as he had dared hope. If it had not been for Antoine Curvise, he might have believed the poor deranged priest. But at Antoine's insistence, he had tried to get David admitted to a psychiatric hospital. His communiqués with the Vatican had been overruled. *"We will take care of this matter."*

Litz, Poland. The last time he had said those words were to Monsignor Meric. They still tasted sour. At the time, he had thought both Proust and Curvise dead. He knew better now. David was alive as was Antoine and those meddling fools, Edmund Defont and François Martine.

His elevation into the College of Cardinals had opened many doors. Doors best left tightly closed. Sealed with wax, they had been boarded up to avoid any crack in the facade of the Catholic religion. Was death preferable to confinement if the confinement were in an asylum for the insane? Vasai was still undecided.

He had strutted about his new office while Cardinal Emanuel Gaston opened the doors of information. Only then had he blustered—it could not be true! Preposterous! Impossible! Surely the church doesn't believe in such ancient nonsense! But Gaston would have none of his arrogance.

"You are the head of this department, Armand. Read the history of this place and judge for yourself if our fears are justified or not. But be warned about the truths that will be revealed. The Institut is as old as this church."

Vasai had spent the luster of his elevation to Cardinal in the archives, reading the history of the Institut d'Infantiles, retching in pain and wallowing in the macabre manner in which his brothers were treated. Reading these forays into the past not only enlightened him, they, by their hand, caused his spine to tingle with fright. Insanity, possessions, deranged men who wandered the mountains deep in Poland claiming to be God. Claiming to be His messenger. Chained to walls for years on end. Murderers and perverts who, in a moment of weakness, snapped the vows of love and charity and ripped open the lifeless bodies of their victims. What manner of priests were these monsters? What had happened to their gentle spirits and loving hearts? What demons walked beside the towering walls of the Vatican, waiting to engulf a passing soul?

Eyes stinging from candle smoke, he had read of Monsignor Michael Proust, a priest who had languished for thirty years in the bowels of this most ungodly of God's places. It was to be David Proust's fate as well. The mere remembrance brought a pang to his heart and made his hands shake.

There was little glue left on the back of the envelope. Not nearly enough to keep the communication at bay. Still, Vasai left the letter unread while he remembered.

"We have guarded against this evil for over a thousand years." Cardinal Gaston's words echoed in his ears. *"It is not our imagination that we stand vigilant against this evil. It has tried to make its presence known on earth many times."*

That accounted for the swift action taken against David Proust.

"It never came from the same family before. It is desperate for birth. When you mentioned David Proust, we knew it was attempting to come to life again."

Slowly, Vasai lowered his eyes and read the letter. It took a few seconds to correlate the dates. If what Abbot Bronski wrote was true then . . . then it was alive. It had been born.

It was not possible for the ruination of his church to rest on his head. No! While he had scoffed at Gaston's warnings, he had followed the Cardinal's prescribed regulations regarding this matter of angelic conception.

Only after assuming this position did he realize how important that single phone call had been. Only after pouring over the dog-eared reports in the archives did the true value of his information become tangible. In the last three hundred years, the child had attempted to be born six times. No, he corrected himself. Not six. Five. If what Abbot Bronski had written was true, the child was alive today. He had failed to keep this force from life.

But it was not his fault! Abbot Bronski's letter should have been forwarded to him immediately. Father Rossini's failure to keep him abreast of the matter had caused this lengthy delay. The war and its disruption of services . . . A hundred reasons why this slip-up had occurred chased through his head stopping only long enough to be examined for believability—not truth.

He should have stayed in Rome instead of traveling to France. France was no longer a power. No longer a viable force in world affairs. Why had he wasted time in France? A host of petty circumstances had taken him away from his duties at the Vatican, and now he was going to have to pay the price.

Damn Bronski. Why hadn't the abbot simply eliminated the problem? Why was another's incompetence forcing him to face the pontiff and explain how the anti-Christ had come into being? Oh, he was not to blame, but Pius would never call this disaster anything but Vasai's failure.

He rang his secretary.

"How long has this packet been here?" Vasai kept his anger in check. It would be best not to antagonize anyone until he knew exactly where he could place the blame.

Rossini took the well-traveled envelope and studied the postmark. "Sometime in September, Your Excellency."

Vasai cringed. Rossini's Italian accent drove him slightly insane. "Were you not told," he began righteously, "that any communications from Litz, Poland were to be brought to my immediate attention?"

Rossini bowed a little, assuming what he hoped was a perfectly acceptable semblance of humility, and tried to look aghast. It would have been easier if he had cared.

"No, Your Excellency, I was not."

"Well, I'm telling you now. In the future, you are to make sure when a communiqué from the Institut, or even Poland, arrives, it is brought to me immediately." Vasai punched holes in the air with his index finger. "If I should be away from the Holy See, you will forward it to me wherever I may be. And you will do it immediately."

"Yes, Your Excellency."

"That will be all for now."

Giuseppe Rossini returned to his desk, his face flushed with an embarrassment that quickly turned to anger. Was it his fault no one had informed him of procedure? No. The secretary he had succeeded, Father DeLoch, was at fault. But, of course, Rossini thought snidely, after being anointed an Archbishop, how could one be expected to remember all the rules of the Vatican. There were too many. Too many rules, too many regulations, and too many Frenchmen.

Returning to his duties, he was surprised to see Cardinal Vasai hurry from his office without so much as a glance in his direction. Vasai had rushed out of his office without informing his secretary where he could be reached. It was, Rossini noted with self-satisfaction, a blatant violation of the Vatican rules.

***

Turning a corner, Vasai walked quickly down the Gallery of Maps. The pontiff's chambers waited at the end of the hallway. He could see the massive double doors, the two Swiss guards, and the damnation he had to face.

Already he could feel Cardinal Gaston's dark stare. The man was always present, taking notes, gathering information, passing along his disdain. There would be no love lost between these men of the cloth. Even when Vasai was on top of the world, Gaston could ruin his day with a word.

Armand hesitated. It had been a spur of the moment decision to personally request an immediate audience with the pope. Had he lost his mind? Who, but an idiot, would knock on the door of their executioner without an alibi for committed deeds or, at the very least, someone else to blame? Still, this situation had to be handled immediately.

The Swiss guards looked on, impassive to his plight. Vasai longed for the days in Bordeaux before he had ever heard of Father David Proust, even as he now longed for the security of his office. Perhaps, he decided sagely, it would be better to go through proper channels.

He entered his outer-office quietly with all the decorum he could muster. He paused outside his office only long enough to issue an order. "Father Rossini, please get me an appointment with His Holiness as soon as possible." His voice was calm, calmer than he could have imagined. He wished he could say the same for his conscience.

Armand Vasai had entered a world that contained the last vestiges of the Dark Ages. A world that still shook and rattled with myth and superstitions. Demons still wandered the night warded off by prayers and wooden relics.

He had grown up fearful of the night and the strange happenings that occurred under its cover of darkness. As his body grew and his mind expanded, pushing the superstitions further and further back into memory, he found he still could not let go. Try as he might, the old ways—whispers as secrets by old women and craggy men—still haunted him when the sun went down.

Get hold of yourself! He breathed deeply and tried to still his restless nerves. He was an intellectual now. Not prone to the realities of old wives' tales. Not given to harsh curses for protection against evil spirits. Spirits were for children. And fools. He saw the world as it was—lusting, greedy, mistrustful, and dishonest. It was obvious, was it not? Even here, where men were supposed to be of the highest quality, above suspicion and reproach, had he not been tethered to an Italian spy?

As if the thought were clairvoyant, the phone on his desk rang. "Yes, Rossini."

"His Holiness can see you next month."

"Next month is not good enough. I need to speak to him immediately." Vasai was adamant.

Rossini was just as adamant. "I am sorry, Your Excellency. It is impossible."

Instantly, his secretary's worth diminished. Vasai hung up the phone without a reply.

The intellectual slipped back into the past and became a superstitious old man. For an hour, he wandered the path of the primitive savage fearful of every movement—of every sound—frightened by the unknown.

The sharp knock on the door brought him back to reality.

Rossini entered. "Lord Cardinal Gaston wishes to see you."

"Cardinal Gaston? Yes, send him in." Vasai stood. He had not needed to. It was simply a reflex from his days as a bishop. Gaston and he were equals now. He started to sit back down, but Emanuel Gaston had already entered the room.

Gaston was a dark man in body and temper, but it was an anger he used wisely. He was young, only forty-one—a meteor on the rise, a candidate to succeed some distant pope. His position now, as advisor to Pius, made him a feared and envied man by those who sought power. He sat down and, with a slight, almost invisible wave of his hand, signaled Vasai to do the same.

Rossini stood in the doorway.

"That will be all, Monsignor." Vasai dismissed his secretary before taking his own seat.

The two Cardinals stared at each other for a few moments. Who would speak first? By rights it should be Gaston. Was he not the intruder? By rights it should be Vasai. Did it not make sense to assuage Gaston, the man who had access to the pope?

Gaston pulled out a cigarette and lit it, deliberately placing the spent match on the edge of Vasai's desk.

"His Holiness regrets he cannot see you, Armand. His calendar is full as I am sure you are aware. He has asked me to intercede for him and, if possible, handle your problem." Gaston spoke in Latin, refusing to use French, although it was a language in which he was well-versed.

Vasai did not miss the Cardinal's veiled barb. What right did this moron have to call him by his given name? Normally, he would never presume to be on familiar ground with someone he considered an enemy but, as the Bible said—an eye for an eye.

"Problem, Emanuel? I have no problem." Vasai's words were spoken *too* quickly.

Gaston took a long drag on the cigarette, slowly expelling the blue smoke. He adjusted his glasses on the bridge of his nose and gave the Cardinal a look Vasai could only take to be one of disgust.

"Your request for an audience with His Holiness was simply your way of making a social call, Armand?"

Vasai stiffened. To agree would lessen his chances of an audience. "My business with His Holiness is personal," he finally said.

"Then you have no need of my counsel. Or the counsel of the pontiff. I'm afraid he does not have time for idle chit-chat." Gaston started to rise.

Vasai realized he had been left with no choice. "Wait." He picked up the letter from Bronski and handed it to Gaston, waiting impatiently while the Cardinal quickly read the contents.

Gaston placed the letter on Vasai's desk. He crossed his legs and blew smoke across the room, oblivious to Vasai's anxiety. "What advice do you seek?"

Confused, Vasai fought for the words that would encircle Gaston in his crisis. "Was this not what you warned me about? Is this not the evil you so easily spoke of a few years ago?"

Gaston's black eyes pierced Vasai. "Again, I ask you, what advice do you seek? You are not so dim-witted as to not know what must be done. Take care of the matter, Armand. The solution is simple."

"Simple! How does one simply order a murder?"

Gaston shrugged his shoulders. "That is your concern. This is your responsibility, and belongs to no one else. I am sure you will find a way."

"My concern, Emanuel? My concern? Yes, then I will handle it my way." Vasai crumpled the letter into a ball and tossed it into the wastebasket beside his desk. "If it is only my concern, then I have taken care of the matter."

Gaston took another long drag on his cigarette. If he was disturbed by Vasai's actions, it did not show. Only his words expressed his displeasure.

"Your position here is a most enjoyable one I would think, Armand. You lack for nothing. Your responsibilities are almost nil." His sharp eyes flickered to the wastebasket before returning their steady gaze to Vasai's face. "You are a member of a small, but esteemed group of men who enjoy coffee served on silver trays and the adoration of their congregations. Your church has given you everything and asked for one small duty in return. Now that the time has come for you to act upon your obligation, you choose to waver. If you are incapable, I am sure we can find another to take your place."

The insult was loud and clear as it echoed through the room.

"Do what must be done."

"Do not talk to me in that manner, Gaston. I will not stand for it." Vasai jumped to his feet and glared down at his adversary. "Are you so calloused as to simply snuff out the life of a child?"

"No, Armand, I am not. It is not I who will do this act. Nor is it you. The means have presented themselves in the form of Abbot Bronski. You have simply to give your permission—bestow your blessing. No blood will stain your hands."

Vasai slumped back into his chair. The harshness of Gaston's words was difficult to digest.

"Don't be a fool, Armand. This is not a pleasant task, but something that must be done. I won't remind you it should never have come about. It was the failure of Abbot Bronski to safeguard his ward. He is to blame. Not you or I.

You have simply to inform him this matter must be eradicated.

"It will be done, regardless, if you or someone else sits in that chair."

Vasai's veneer sagged. Gaston was correct. He knew it. "The matter will be handled, Emanuel."

Gaston looked around for a place to put out his cigarette. Finding no ashtray, he used the dregs of Vasai's cold coffee. The live coals hissed and were instantly silent, a requiem for the deed about to be done.

"There was never any doubt in my mind, Armand. I knew you would see it was your place to do what was right."

Armand Vasai watched the scarlet robes of Cardinal Gaston disappear behind his closing office doors. Right or wrong, he knew he had no choice. To allow this child, this fearsome infant to mature, could bring down the very walls of the Vatican. It had been prophesied. But why, he lamented, did it have to occur on my watch?

He reached for a pen and paper, hastily scribbling, *Kill him.* Before the ink had dried, he crumpled the paper and dropped it in the wastebasket.

He tried again. *Eliminate the evil.* It sounded so . . . ugly. There had to be a way to say what had to be said with some delicacy—some decency. Bronski knew the child was evil. The abbot was willing to destroy it. He only wanted *Confirmation,* Vasai thought. Confirmation—the ceremony that bestowed on a young man the knowledge he needed in life. Now it was a word to end a life.

Vasai started to sign his name and hesitated again. His signature would be an indictment for the future should the letter fall into unfriendly hands. Again, he crumpled the paper. This message could not be sent by written word. He needed time to think. To devise a plan that would keep his name from being recorded beside the name of Herod Antipas, the Jewish king who had ordered the murder of all first born sons to preserve his own throne.

He glanced at the calendar. June 22, 1941. Summer had just begun, and the child was not even a year old. It could not be any danger yet. Besides, it was confined to a most secure place. Vasai needed time to think. To spare his ancestors this shame.

Shame!

"What shame?" Vasai said aloud, slamming his hand on the top of the desk. "It is not a shame to defend one's home. This is my home and I will defend it with all of my resources."

He stiffened his back and sat up straighter. He was not Jean-Paul Meric. He was not a weak man. He liked Meric, but he would not be like his old friend.

He rang for Rossini.

The idea had come out of the blue. Back in the Vatican for only one day, and already the intrigue of lifetimes had surrounded him. But not for long. If Rossini was, as he figured, a spy for the pontiff, he had not only solved the dilemma of the child, but his own dilemma as well. The solution was so simple he would have acted on it even if Father DeLoch were still his secretary. But—and it was a delicious *but*— the fact Monsignor Rossini was to play such a large part in his plan tickled Vasai. He would send Rossini to the Institut to find out just what this child was. Investigate! And, if necessary, Rossini could relay the command to Abbot Bronski to— *say it—say it! Kill* . . . destroy the usurper of this grand old religion.

"Sit down, Father Rossini. I have a mission which I feel I may entrust to you." Vasai turned on the charm of the French. "Our department has several dioceses scattered throughout Europe. Old cathedrals which have withstood the ravages of war and age and which hold many priceless relics. St. Sophie in Czechoslovakia, St. Basil in Romania, St. Andrew in Hungary, to name only a few. A monastery in Poland. Venerable institutions that have served us well. To better understand our responsibilities, I have decided to send you on a fact-finding mission to catalog our holdings and suggest whatever you wish to help us preserve these monuments."

Slightly bowed in a position of servitude, Rossini straightened as he heard Vasai's words. His eyes lifted from the floor to meet Vasai's countenance. For a moment, he felt Vasai's equal, but only for a moment. The cold hand of reality reached out and gripped the back of his neck. The countries Vasai had mentioned were not friendly places. Especially after the news he had recently heard.

"I am at your service, Your Excellency. I will go and do whatever it is you wish." He stopped and tried to see some intrigue in his master. On the surface, he found none. "Did you have any particular place in mind you wish me to visit first?"

"I have given this a great deal of thought. I believe the best place to begin our knowledge would be with the monastery in Poland. In the town of Litz, to be exact." Vasai spoke softly, not wanting to frighten his secretary. His intentions refused to have their desired effect.

Rossini looked up, his eyes shining like a deer's caught in the headlights of a car. He knew little of the Institut, having been told only recently to report to Gaston any communications that came from there. Still, a chill ran up his spine. Instinctively, he had known that was where Vasai was going to send him. "Isn't it dangerous? I mean, Poland? Isn't Poland dangerous for priests?"

"Dangerous? What do you mean, dangerous?"

241

Rossini fought off his fright and the urge to smile. "Your Excellency is unaware of the latest news, I presume?" His question was cautious.

"What news, Father Rossini?"

"Herr Hitler has launched an invasion of Russia." Rossini tried to keep his exuberance hidden. "At the moment, I would surmise travel to Poland would be impossible."

The news did not shatter Vasai. Outwardly, he seemed unfazed. "I had not heard. Thank you for bringing it to my attention." The Cardinal appeared to consider the information he had just received. "Yes, Father Rossini, I am quite sure you are correct. It certainly appears travel to Poland would not be expedient at this time. It is of no matter. We will simply wait for a more opportune time." Vasai smiled at his subordinate. "We have time on our side, Father."

CHAPTER TWENTY-FOUR

It was drizzling on the last day of October when Monsignor Giuseppe Rossini boarded the train for Kosige, Czechoslovakia. The German army had sliced through the Russians so easily, so quickly, it had given them no chance to come out of this monstrous invasion with anything less than a defeat. Fortress Europe was only a matter of time.

Inside the Vatican for the last four months, euphoria existed. The godless devils were about to fall. The vast empire of Catholic Russians was again to be in the pontiff's hands.

Unaware he was not privy to the library that chronicled this secret place, Rossini had tried to find something, anything about the Institut. He searched the dusty records of the archives. He poured over faded books, records, and anything that might give him a hint of what this Institut, this monastery in Poland, had that was so valuable to Cardinal Vasai and the Department of Religious Antiquities. All he had found were the records of the priests who had been sent there. Names and dates going back to the 12th century. His curiosity overcame his reluctance. He would go, under orders, only to better his position in the Vatican. One had to suffer occasionally to achieve a lofty goal.

Rossini now saw his future inexplicably tied to Cardinal Vasai. When he had reported to Cardinal Gaston the news of his impending journey, a coolness had settled over their relationship. What Rossini had taken as a sign of respect had, in reality, been contempt. Gaston's spy had been discovered, and Vasai had deftly outmaneuvered him. Rossini was no longer of any use. Monsignor Giuseppe Rossini would not be returning from the Institut.

***

It was snowing when Rossini stepped off the train in Kosige. It snowed the week he waited for transportation to be arranged for the final leg of his journey.

He had been received coolly by the priests at St. Sophie until he had informed them of his final destination. Their attitudes had changed considerably when he had mentioned the Institut. The priests had become . . . He hesitated, trying to categorize his hosts' emotions. They had held him almost in awe. There was no doubt he had instantly won their respect. They were emotions a lowly Monsignor was not used to seeing in the power hungry Vatican where men strived to be seen and recognized.

He wandered through the ancient cathedral, biding his time, searching for the relics and wealth Vasai had said were there, yet found nothing to indicate the parish was anything but impoverished. It made him wonder just what the monastery would be like. The Institut d'Infantiles. An Institute for Children. Just what kind of children? He had no idea.

"Your transportation will be here this morning, Monsignor," he was told after being awakened with the dawn. Shivering in the cold room, he dressed quickly, and hurried outside.

Standing like a statute, doing his best to look inconspicuous, he waited for the car that was scheduled to pick him up. It was an hour late already. The collar of his black overcoat hid his ears and the lower half of his face, but did little to keep the biting cold from seeping into his bones. Every few minutes he stamped his feet to rid his shoes of the snow and keep his circulation moving. He was not a person who enjoyed the cold crisp air.

Rossini grimaced as parts of Vasai's orders echoed through his head. *"Just follow my instructions,"* the Cardinal had ordered. *"Tell Abbot Bronski to eliminate the problem. It's a very simple assignment, Father Rossini. Is there something I've said you don't understand?"* At the memory, Rossini bit his tongue, even as he had then. Vasai's voice still grated on his nerves.

Occupied with his torment, Rossini had not seen the car pull up and park. He did see the driver, almost a boy, get out of the car and open the passenger door. As though shaken from a dream, he realized his ride had finally come. He hurried from the corner of the cathedral where he had hidden into the comfort of the waiting sedan.

"Father Rossini?" the driver asked.

"Yes," he said, climbing into the front seat of the cramped vehicle. He slammed the door a little too hard. It was the only expression he allowed of what he thought about being kept waiting for so long and in such a precarious position. He would never let anyone know they had caused him to suffer. Shifting uncomfortably, he struggled to adjust his overcoat. The heater inside the car was working, but the warm air it blew was inadequate against the frigid outside temperatures.

Two more priests were in the back seat. Wrapped tightly in an overcoat, one slept while the other stared out of the side window. Rossini watched the second priest for a moment, wondering what the man was seeing. It was obvious, even to him, that this priest was oblivious to his surroundings.

No one spoke.

After a moment, Rossini found he disliked the silence. "How long will it take to reach the monastery?"

The driver looked at him queerly. "Monastery? We are going to Litz."

"Yes, of course. That's where the monastery is." He shifted so that he could talk to the priest in the back seat. "Are you traveling far?"

"To Litz."

"And your friend?" Rossini nodded towards the sleeping priest.

"Yes, he's also traveling to Litz." The stranger blinked rapidly and seemed to remember his manners. He leaned forward and extended his hand. "I'm Father Rojia." Gently, almost cautiously, Rojia placed his hand on his companion's knee. "This is Father Mihika." His voice was tinged with a sadness Rossini could not hear.

"Will you be staying long in Litz?"

"Yes, I believe so." Rojia sat back and looked at his friend. "I think we will be there for a long time. And you?"

"Monsignor Rossini."

"And you, Monsignor Rossini? Will you be staying long?"

"No. I have some business to conduct at the monastery and then I return to Rome."

"As I said," Rojia repeated, "My friend and I are going to the Institut. I don't recall it ever being labeled a monastery before." Now that he had begun, he spoke easily.

"Yes, of course. The Institut d'Infantiles. It was a monastery at one time I believe."

"Very possible."

"Are you familiar with the Institut?" Rossini asked.

"Yes, of course."

Rossini looked perplexed. How was it the priests here knew of the Institut, and in Rome it was only a vague place? A monastery off in the mountains of Poland? "Have you ever visited the Institut before?"

"I'm afraid I would not be sitting here had I visited the Institut before," Rojia said, adding to Rossini's confusion. "How is it that you are going to the Institut, but you don't know what it is? Aren't you going to serve?"

"To serve?" Rossini said, surprised. "To serve who?"

"Our brothers, of course. The Institut is a hospital, Monsignor Rossini."

"A hospital?" Rossini exclaimed. The icy hand that had reached out to touch him in Vasai's office again tried to put its cold fingers around his throat. Something was wrong. Why would Cardinal Vasai send him to a hospital? What kind of relics would be kept in a hospital? What kind of problems could the abbot of a hospital have that required a specific directive from the Vatican? The desire to open the door and jump out of the car swept over Rossini. Beads of sweat formed on his upper lip. He straightened out and stared ahead at the mountains that loomed in the distance.

Within minutes, he calmed down. He had nothing to fear. He was only going to investigate relics for Vasai and deliver a simple message. "There are children at this hospital?" he inquired, remembering Vasai's request he speak to Abbot Bronski about a child.

Father Rojia leaned forward. "The Institut is a place for priests who have become ill. For the elderly who have no place to go."

Rossini's confusion grew. Every question he asked added to his puzzlement. "Why are you going there?"

"My friend has fallen ill. I'm going to take care of him."

Rossini turned to look at the old priest again. "What sort of illness is afflicting him?" Once the words were out of his mouth, he realized he was not really sure he wanted to know the answer.

Rojia leaned back in his seat. "He is ill. That's all."

"I . . . I don't understand," Rossini stammered. "I was told this place was a monastery." He glanced at the old priest again. The blanket that had covered him had slipped, exposing the straight jacket that confined him.

Rossini's eyes widened in terror as Father Rojia pulled the blanket back up around his friend's shoulders. Rossini looked away, leaning his head on the cold window pane that separated him from the real world. Something was wrong here. Very wrong.

The car picked up speed and struggled up the snow-lined road. The mountain shadows began to engulf the vehicle and its quartet of passengers. Tires crunching through packed snow, wind whistling through ill-fitting windows, the swoosh of the windshield wipers trying desperately to keep the window clear, the nagging hum of the defrosters—all of these things kept Rossini on edge. Envious of the priest who slept, he leaned his head against his window and tried to fall asleep. The jarring, bumpy road would not allow him the escape.

The drive from Kosige to Litz, not long in miles, was hours of difficult traveling. The twisting, narrow road made speed impossible. At best, frozen rains had made the road's surface precarious. The driver was constantly downshifting, then revving the engine until it became almost a melody. By that lullaby, Rossini managed to fall asleep for a few hours. The day passed without incident, with only the steady rise and fall of the car's engine and the whirl of the clutch to break the afternoon's silence.

In the shadow of dusk, Rossini stirred. Outside the car, a gray shroud hung over stark black trees. To his right, a broken display of rock wall and boulders lifted to the heavens. To his left, there was space, dotted only by the tips of the tallest trees. The gorge that kept the road they traveled narrow and dangerous was deeper than clouds would allow him to see. *If* he had been interested.

This is the most colorless place I've ever seen, he thought. And the most uncomfortable. Stretching his back and neck, he was jolted by a scream. The entire car began shaking violently.

At first, the scream sounded far away like something one might hear in a nightmare. It took Rossini a few seconds to realize it was coming from the back seat. Feet kicked out, jerking the front seat forwards. Rossini's head bounced off of the windshield.

In the back seat, Father Rojia struggled desperately to keep Father Mihika from kicking the driver. Rossini could do nothing to help. Their driver braked cautiously, but even at the slow pace they were traveling, the car skidded and fish-tailed. Rossini watched as the driver fought the wheel, turning it first one way and then the other. The car behaved as if possessed, spinning in half arcs that allowed Rossini a brief glimpse at the deep crevice that edged the roadway.

Then his attention returned to the violence at hand. The deranged priest suddenly kicked out, striking him in the jaw. A trickle of blood ran down his left check. Father Mihika lunged forward, his teeth bared in cannibalistic savagery. His eyes filled with hate.

Father Rojia knocked his companion backwards and, for a brief moment, Rossini no longer had to fear having his throat bared to a predator's fangs. Still, Father Mihika's feet kicked. Rossini tried to grab them and caught one ancient ankle that twisted and turned in his grasp as the other leg kicked freely. How could a man so old, so confined, have so much strength?

Suddenly, one wicked blow connected with the back of the driver's head. He slumped forward, dazed.

The car was in the center of the road and moving slowly. Its slight skid to the left was a minor movement compared to the violence inside. Rossini dodged another kick. He had no time to notice the changing view.

The car swerved and veered towards the embankment. Towards the edge of the earth, Rossini thought as he noticed and tried desperately to reach the wheel. It was a race he could not win. Touching the hard, cold plastic, he twisted the wheels just moments after they left the road.

There were no witnesses as, in slow motion, the car arced into space and plunged down the straight side of the mountain. It bounced once, before bursting into flames, and then tumbled like a glorified sun to the bottom of the gorge.

The fire smothered and died. Black smoke filled the air, fighting for existence and losing to the heavy thick snow that fell across Europe. It would be spring before the automobile was found. The remains of the passengers— bits and pieces left by the wolves—would not be enough to identify those who had died in the accident. It was a story that would be told a million times across Europe in that first winter of the second world war. Bits and pieces of humans left in the snow. Not nearly enough left to identify.

CHAPTER TWENTY-FIVE

Spring, 1951

"I'm tired, Andre." Those had been the last words Alain Proust had spoken. There had been no profound explanations on the mysteries of the universe. No startling epitaph to be inscribed on a marble headstone. Alain Proust had spoken only what he felt at that very moment between life and death.

Andre Proust held his father's hand long after the last breath had expired. Partly because he did not want his father to leave. Partly because of his confusion.

He was old enough to accept death. It was never easy. This, he knew from past experience. The accident that had claimed the lives of his wife and sons could have been fate. It could have been bad luck. It could have been explained in a hundred different ways, none of which would have brought them back.

Andre Proust held his father's cold hand, trying to understand what forces were at work against his family. Why had they suddenly been chosen to suffer? What exactly were their sins?

It had started long before he was born.

His uncle, Monsignor Michael Proust, had died unexpectedly young. Everyone had accepted it as the will of God. His brother, David, another Proust who had dedicated his life to God, also died abruptly. Andre remembered that moment clearly. He could close his eyes and, in an instant, be in the living room of his father's house, watching Alain Proust open the letter from the Vatican and read its contents. It had still been *an act of God*, but, this time, acceptance had not come so easily. Against his family's wishes, his father had traveled to LaRochelle to talk to David's friends, his son's doctor, and the parish priest.

The warm family relationship between father and son, grandfather and grandchildren began to cool. The questions death had brought to the surface went unanswered. It was easier to avoid the confrontation between religion and reality. Easier for family members to travel separate ways. Excuses abounded for the lack of warmth and love that had once filled their lives.

Suddenly, Andre had felt unwelcome in the home where he had been born and reared. He had spent many sleepless nights trying to discover why his father had turned against him. Was it his love of physics? He had offered to give up his studies and assume management of the Proust vineyards. It was an old argument he had tried to make right.

Surprisingly, his father had turned down his offer, encouraging him to follow his heart and pursue his love of the strange, natural world that existed just beyond sight. "Don't waste your life here, Andre," Alain Proust had commanded.

If only the subject had been closed with those words. Instead, arguments between father and son began to break out constantly. The old man no longer wanted him around. Leave Bordeaux! Leave France! Those were the words that were used. Andre never understood his father was only asking him to run away from whatever evil haunted the Proust family.

Determined to give her children the heritage they rightfully deserved, Andre's wife had, at first, supported his angry refusals to leave his homeland. Each outburst had only severed father's and son's ties a bit more. Proud people hurt more easily than they surrendered. But one walk had changed all that. Andre remembered it like it was yesterday.

His father and his wife had taken a walk in the gardens. When Malett returned, her face was pale and drawn. Her spirit, her fire, burned to cinders. "Let us leave this place," she had whispered, and Andre had not refused. He could not bear to estrange his own family.

A teaching position had been arranged for him in America at the University of Tennessee in Knoxville. At first, he had not understood why this place had been chosen, but he found out in 1942 when he was recruited to work in Oak Ridge at the new atomic facility. His predisposition towards atomic physics had sealed his fate. He had packed up his family, the silent wife who refused to give an explanation why she had chosen to desert him in his fight with his father, and his two obedient sons. They left France in August of 1939. He had not returned since.

Oh, he had tried. The outbreak of the second world war came just as Andre had finished moving into his new home. He had not yet begun his tenure at the University.

The news of the war tore at his loyalties. Surely, Malett would understand his need to return and defend his—their homeland. He was wrong.

The letters he had written to his father had been answered—every single one filled with Alain's pride that his son had gone to America. *"France is no longer your home, Andre,"* the old man had written in shaking script. *"If you love me, stay away. Make America your home."*

And he had. Andre had not seen his father in over ten years. Now that he had, he was reluctant to let go of the cold hand.

"I'm tired, Andre."

The funeral should have been grand—filled with mourners who had loved and respected Alain Proust—a man who had loved his community and his country. A man who had worked feverishly to keep his vineyard intact and prosperous. It was not. Alain Proust's funeral was a small solemn affair that lowered his remains into the ground with very little ceremony.

***

"Your father died destitute. There is no wealth, Andre." The Prousts' family attorney spoke gently. He had been a pallbearer at the funeral. "He asked me to give you this."

The cream colored envelope held no interest for Andre at the moment. It was far too weightless to carry the words father and son had left unsaid between them over the years.

"How could my father have died in poverty?" He had not come back to claim the Proust lands that had been in the family for centuries, but that they no longer existed was a shock.

"The Proust vineyards—all of your father's property—were confiscated by the French government and distributed to the poor. Your father was accused of being a collaborator."

"Accused, but never convicted," Andre retorted angrily. *Damn this ugly rumor!* "I am well aware of the accusations made against my father. And the fact you did nothing to defend him. Wasn't he supposed to be your friend?"

"He was my friend, Andre. Your father wanted no defense. He refused to offer any." Monsieur Gibault stroked his thin white goatee between liver-spotted fingers. "He did not wish to divide France more than she already was. You say you are aware of certain accusations. Perhaps you are not aware of the entire story.

"Your father collaborated, but not for the reasons of which he was accused. The money he made selling wine to the Boche was spent to defeat them. To feed the poor. To support the resistance. Yet, when the war was over, the fools your father had kept alive turned against him, calling him a traitor and demanding his death.

"But, as you said, he was never convicted." Gibault looked across his wide expanse of desk at the son of his friend. "We can make a case to try and regain your family lands, but it will be costly."

"I don't want the land. I don't want anything from France."

"Yes, of course. You live in America now. You have no guilt, no skeletons in your closet as France does. It will not be necessary for you to face your neighbors. To hang your head when you pass someone on the street you know is a coward or a traitor. You have that advantage, Andre. You may simply leave. Taking your case to court would only drag you into our contrition. It is for the best we let your father rest in peace."

"My father had a final request, Monsieur Gibault. His last wish was that I return his brother, Michael and my brother, David to the soil of France to be buried beside him in the family plot. I can't imagine why, considering the way his homeland has treated him. Has the government left him enough French soil for that?" Andre could not contain his bitterness. He had not only lost a father, he had lost a man of courage, a man he had never known. A man who had given everything to his country and, when that was not enough, had had what little was left shamefully taken from him.

***

Standing on the street corner just outside Gibault's office, Andre opened his father's estate, a single envelope, and stared at two startling similar death notices. The exactness of the events that had claimed the lives of two Prousts—two priests, thirty years apart—did not immediately disturb him. According to the letters, both David and Michael were interred in the Vatican. Good, he thought. That would make his task simple. He could be a dutiful son and, in a short time, be back in Oak Ridge, away from a country he would never again call home.

The church would give up its priests for the cold dirt of France. Andre knew that as certainly as life. Even in America, living in the Bible-thumping Baptist south, he still practiced Catholicism. Faithfully. The one constant in his life had been his church. He knew they would support him in carrying out his father's last wish. How could they not?

***

"I am sorry, Monsieur Proust," the haggard priest shook his head. His apologetic smile was ruined by more than the visage of his uneven and discolored teeth.

This was Andre's second visit to the Department of Mausoleums and Graves. For a week he had been juggled from one department to another by the spiritual caretakers of the Vatican. His quest to recover his brother's and uncle's remains had begun in this very same, small, dusty alcove seven days ago. Longer than God had taken to create the world. Would he spend the rest of his life searching for two graves on a continent that had recently buried millions?

Since his first visit, he had inquired at the Department of Records, Department of Deaths, of Burials, of Saints, of Martyrs, of priests missing for reasons unknown. He had listened while priests, monsignors, bishops, and archbishops tried to explain they had no records of either Father David Proust or Monsignor Michael Proust. He had heard their words as they rationalized the letters he carried with him must have been written or, at the very least, sent to his father in error. He had pretended to pay attention to the feeble excuses of how his church had no records of two of its servants. The simple task of retrieving two corpses had become a quagmire of religious mistakes.

Andre's patience was wearing thin. Frustrated, he lit another cigarette. Already five butts littered the floor at his feet.

How could the Catholic Church lose two of its priests? Dead priests at that. It was not as if he were searching for two particularly mobile persons. Moreover, the church was an organization that kept records dating back hundreds of years. Complete records of ancient times throughout recorded history. It was known for its precise and documented truths. Why had it so suddenly become incompetent?

Once more he pulled out the letters, the very ones his father had shown Antoine Curvise years earlier, and waved them underneath the priest's nose. "According to these notices, both my brother, David, and my Uncle Michael are buried here." He chose his words carefully. He was having a difficult time keeping calm. "These announcements were obviously sent from here." The watermark of the Vatican was too notable to miss.

The priest's leathered face remained emotionless. He shrugged. This man could show him documentation written by God and it would do no good. "I'll check the records again, Monsieur Proust, if you insist. I have checked them twice, but I will check them again. However, I can assure you there are no priests carrying the Proust name entombed in our catacombs."

Andre read both of the letters again. He had them memorized, but he was too tired to trust anything to chance. "Maybe the months are wrong. Did you check the entire year?"

"I do not know how to answer you any more, Monsieur. We have no records of your family being buried here."

Throwing down his half-smoked cigarette in disgust, Andre crushed its life with a savage twist of his heel. "Who else would have any records pertaining to the dead?"

"You might try the Department of Religious Antiquities." It was not an answer guaranteed to please Andre Proust, the priest thought, but it would remove the foreigner from his department.

***

Back in his hotel, Andre angrily paced his room. He had wasted yet another day with members of his religion. It would have been impossible to believe the incompetence of the Vatican had he not been on the receiving end of this lesson in futility. It made him wonder how the church had survived one thousand nine hundred fifty-one years. Was it because they were Italians that made them ineffectual? No, the French would have fared no better.

He hated himself when he thought like this. It was a throwback to his being born a Frenchman—that feeling of superiority where none existed. It had not taken him long to become Americanized—proud, efficient, quick, and thorough. He had found the work ethic of his adopted country far superior to the rest of the world. How he wished for that competence now.

Three phone calls later, he had the telephone number of the Department of Religious Antiquities and the name of its department head—Cardinal Emanuel Gaston. More phone calls later than he cared to count, he was still unable to secure an appointment with even the Cardinal's secretary. As much as he hated to admit it, if he could not find his brother and uncle soon, he was prepared to give up. He had nowhere else to go.

Why he had suddenly thought of going to the American Embassy for help he would never know. Perhaps it had occurred to him as he sat on his bed, waiting for an archaic phone system to connect him to the outside world. At just that moment, when he felt like a foreigner, it did not matter. What mattered was, the idea made sense.

***

"Please, come in and sit down, Mr. Proust." The assistant ambassador's aide was tall, young, and eager to help.

Andre explained his problem, not expecting the assistance he requested any more than he knew why he had come. He was desperate, and acting that way. One thing he had learned in the United States was that Americans, sometimes standoffish in their own land, were often eager to help one another abroad.

The aide wasted no time in getting on the phone and making a few calls. He spoke quietly, but directly into the receiver, scribbling notes and occasionally giving Andre an encouraging nod. Finally, he hung up the phone for the last time.

"I don't know what help this will be, but I did manage to get you an appointment tomorrow with the Director of the Department of Religious Antiquities, Cardinal Gaston. Would you like me to make a note of that for you?"

"Yes, thank you." Andre was pleased. He had not spoken to a Cardinal as of yet. He had not even tried. That was another trait of the Americans. Go to the top.

He thanked the assistant ambassador's aide and shook hands. Because of this man's help, he would be able to end his futile mission in style—with an audience before a Cardinal. Andre Proust held no false hopes he would find his missing family members. He only knew that now, he could feel like he had really tried.

CHAPTER TWENTY-SIX

"Monsieur Proust, please be seated." Cardinal Gaston gestured to the Louis XVI chair his predecessor, Cardinal Vasai had brought to the Vatican. Vasai had left a wealth of French antiques for the perpetual spirit of his church.

Andre ignored the opulence and refinement that surrounded him and came directly to the point. "I wish to reclaim the remains of my relatives," he intoned mechanically. He had repeated the phrase so often every time he saw a priest the words sprang unbidden to his tongue. He took the letters out of the envelope and placed them on Gaston's desk.

The Cardinal made no move to pick them up. He did not even glance in their direction. Instead, his eyes were locked on his guest. *Proust.* The name came back into his memory with a bitter taste. "I was asked by His Holiness to grant you an audience, Monsieur Proust." He leaned back in his chair, fingers laced tightly to encompass his girth. "Might I ask why you wish to see me?"

"As I stated before, I am looking for the remains of my brother, Father David Proust and my uncle, Monsignor Michael Proust." Andre spoke more harshly than he had intended.

"Then you should inquire at the Department of Mausoleums and Graves."

Andre wanted to laugh. He would have had the business he was on not been so serious. Never had he witnessed such a comedy of errors. Never had he known so many responsible people who were irresponsible. "I've been there. I've been to a number of different departments this past week, and always I am told to go to another department. Frankly, Cardinal Gaston, I am getting a little tired of this runaround."

"I'm sorry. I don't understand."

"Maybe if you read the letters you could reach an understanding." Gaston's smugness irritated him, but Andre remained calm. He had grown quite capable at repressing his temper over the past week.

Gaston shifted, but not in the direction of Proust's letters. Reaching for an ornate box on his desk, he took out and lit a cigarette before offering one to his visitor.

"No, thank you."

"They're really quite mild," Gaston intoned. "I have them imported."

Andre watched silently as the Cardinal closed his eyes and drew in a lungful of pungent smoke, expelling it in a thin stream directed toward the ceiling. He could almost hear Gaston's unvoiced dominance.

Seemingly unaware, Gaston again pulled the smoke deeply into his lungs, but this time he exhaled towards Andre's face. The insult was clear.

"We do not bury our brothers here, Monsieur Proust. We are only caretakers of religious relics and artifacts. I'm afraid I don't know how I can be of any help."

"Neither do I." Andre retrieved his letters from the edge of the desk where they remained untouched. "You . . ." *pompous, arrogant, self-serving bastard.* Andre left his angry words unvoiced. They could be better used when speaking to Cardinal Gaston's superior.

"I am sorry I wasted your time, Your Excellency. Obviously you cannot help me. I see I have no choice now but to seek an audience with His Holiness. Good day."

"One moment, please."

This conversation was not going the way it should, Gaston thought. Pius had charged him to take care of this matter. It would do him no good to fail. He had lost his position with Pius over accusations of his association with the Nazis. Had Hitler won the war, he might well have been in line to succeed the pope. As it turned out, he was fortunate to have the position he held. Fortunate he had not been prosecuted. Fortunate the church still wielded enough influence to keep its house in quiet order.

"Please, sit back down, Monsieur Proust."

Against his better judgment, Andre returned to the chair.

Emanuel Gaston leaned back in his chair and pursed his lips several times in rapid succession. It was, Andre thought, as if the words about to be said were not the words Gaston wished to say. He waited.

"Maybe if you start at the beginning, Monsieur Proust. I might be able to help you."

Andre told his story. Again.

This time Gaston pretended to read his caller's letters, although he had no need. He knew exactly where Andre's family was interred. He had known since the Proust name had first been mentioned. When he spoke, he did so expansively. "Yes, yes. These letters were sent by this Department, but why? The truth of the matter is that the war has played havoc with us as it did with everyone in Europe. The letters were sent from here, but by whom? Why? I'm afraid I cannot help you."

Gaston quickly continued his placation before Andre's temper flared. "I understand your desire to fulfill your father's last wishes. I will gladly take you through our extensive network of catacombs and cemeteries to search for your brother's and uncle's final resting places. We have put many of our brothers to rest over the years. Unfortunately, our records are not as accurate as they should be."

For the first time since his arrival, Andre heard words that gave him a moment of comfort. Why hadn't someone simply told him this before?

Gaston was quick to notice Proust's resolve weaken. It was obvious his guest could be handled. "A thought has just occurred to me, Monsieur Proust. It is just a vague idea, but possibly one that might explain why you have been unable to locate your family members. Just one moment, please." Gaston buzzed for his secretary. "It may be your brother and uncle had, at one time, been assigned to this Department. If that is the case, we may have a record of them somewhere."

The office door opened, quietly admitting the Cardinal's secretary. "Your Excellency."

"Monsignor Briska," Gaston turned his attention to his subordinate, "take these letters out with you and return in ten minutes." The Cardinal gestured magnificently with his finely ringed hands, and spoke in Latin, confident Andre Proust could not understand the language of the church. He smiled, condescendingly. Surely, Monsieur Proust must know he was doing ... would do ... everything in his power to assist the young man in fulfilling his dead father's last request.

He looked sternly at his secretary. He wanted no mistakes. "Ten minutes, and not a moment sooner."

Andre fought to keep his expression neutral, not believing what he had just heard. Obviously, Gaston was unaware he was proficient in this ancient language of priests and scientists. Even if he had not been, he would have recognized the stall for what it was. Why, he wondered. Why was he being put through this charade? What had the Prousts done to the church to deserve this kind of treatment?

"I have asked my secretary to check our files. Hopefully, we will find an answer for you."

"I appreciate your help, Your Excellency." Andre kept his voice humble. Gaston was playing him for a fool. So be it. If he could not get the answers he wanted here, Andre would find someone who knew—someone who had known the Proust family before the war when their vineyards were rich and their tithes abundant. "Is it possible your predecessor might know of David?"

"It would be quite possible if Cardinal Vasai were still here. I am sorry to say he suffered a debilitating stroke some years ago."

The mention of Cardinal Vasai opened a flood of memories for Andre. Vasai had been the bishop of Bordeaux. A close friend of his father's.

"Did he pass away?" Andre hoped he did not sound too interested.

Gaston bowed his head in benediction. "No, but it is only a matter of time before God calls him home. I understand he suffers greatly."

Ten minutes later, *(Andre was sure he could have set his watch by the secretary's appearance)* Gaston interpreted his underling's failure to find anything to connect the Department of Religious Antiquities to David or Michael Proust.

"As I said earlier Monsieur Proust, during the war we lost many of our records. Our files. The Germans spared us nothing. I am truly very sorry, but unless we have more specific information, I'm afraid there's nothing I can do to solve your dilemma. We have thousands of priests buried in the catacombs in and around Rome. Without more details, it will be almost impossible to find your beloved family members." Gaston spread his hands in a weak imitation of Jesus beckoning the children into his arms. "Be content in knowing their resting place is with God, wherever they might be."

Andre sighed and took the letters from the Cardinal. "Thank you for trying, Your Excellency. I appreciate your efforts." He shrugged his shoulders helplessly. "I guess I might as well give up. If you should ever come across any news of my family, please get in touch with me." He attempted a pained smile.

"I am truly sorry for your dilemma, Monsieur Proust, and yes, if news should be found, I will most certainly be in touch."

Gaston extended his ringed hand. Andre found it was all he could do to kiss the hand of such a liar.

***

It was not anger that dogged Andre Proust as he made his way out of the sanctimonious enclaves of the Vatican. How he wished it had been. Anger could be expressed.

Disappointment? No. Maybe. But why?

Confusion. Yes, he was confused. He had only come to find the remains of his family and take them home. To bury them beside his *maman* and *papa*. Why was his church hiding their corpses? Why had his church lied?

Angry? Yes. Disappointed? Yes. But mostly determined. Andre Proust walked away from the Vatican determined not to rest until he had found his brother and uncle.

He had always intended on returning to Bordeaux, but with David and Michael. Only yesterday he had been ready to skip France entirely and depart for America. If only Gaston had realized he understood Latin, and had stepped out of the room to give his secretary false orders, Andre would have believed the Cardinal's many excuses. He would have given up, but now . . .? Never.

***

St. Peter's Square was filled with holiday visitors. They lingered in small groups staring up at the Cross of Truth on the dome, taking pictures of marbled statue saints, and hoping for a glimpse of their pontiff or their princes—of the men who exuded the righteous way to live. Andre suddenly felt embarrassed for them . . . and himself.

"Monsieur Proust." The old priest from the Department of Mausoleums and Graves reached out and touched his arm, breaking the spell of anger and self-pity. "Have you found your relatives?"

Andre blinked and focused on the priest. He wanted to scream, *NO! NO! You and your kind have hidden them from me*! Yet, his anger dissipated.

"It has been taken care of," he said calmly. "Thank you."

"Good. I am glad to hear such good news." The old priest seemed more than happy. He was relieved.

"I was hoping to see an old family friend, Cardinal Vasai, but he no longer resides here I'm told."

The old priest's face brightened. At last! Someone he knew. "The cross of age has borne its weight across his shoulders, I'm afraid. Sadly, it is a fate we all must endure."

Andre was unsure how to ask his next question. Fate intervened.

"If you return to France, you may visit him," the old priest continued spewing information. "He is in a hospital in Bordeaux."

"Thank you," Andre said politely. "If I return to France, I will make it a point to stop in and pay my respects."

If. The word almost made him laugh. The church owed him. If collecting meant he must return to Bordeaux and find Cardinal Vasai, Andre Proust meant to extract full satisfaction for his labors.

***

The suspicions that had haunted Emanuel Gaston since Cardinal Vasai had assured him the matter in Poland had been handled, suddenly rose anew.

That should not have been the case. The matter had been handled. Armand had stopped him in the hall one day and quietly brought him up to date with, *I have sent Monsignor Rossini to the Institut. He carries my instructions for Abbot Bronski.* Unbidden, a grudging respect for Vasai was born. He had not only taken care of the child, he'd rid himself of Gaston's spy. It was almost too perfect.

The Department of Religious Antiquities had not heard from the Institut in over ten years. The war and its raging battles had completely isolated the asylum. The defeat of the Germans and the subsequent takeover by the communists had further isolated the ancient establishment. Still, Gaston was confident the Institut existed. If it had fallen, he would have known. The gypsies who once again traveled the dirt roads of the Carpathians reported the Institut d'Infantiles was still standing—still serving the needs of the priests. So why did he continue to worry?

Gaston pressed his intercom button impatiently.

"Yes, Your Excellency?"

"Is Father Yorick still at St. Basil?" Gaston wondered briefly if his voice sounded as scratchy as his secretary's.

"Yes, Your Excellency."

"I wish to send a message to him. As soon as possible."

"Yes, Your Excellency."

Gaston's network of SS and gestapo agents recruited during Hitler's regime had proven a valuable source of information for both the church and the Nazis. With the defeat of the Reich, many of Gaston's agents were helped to escape the sometimes quickly moving Soviet armies. By transforming them into priests, many were spared torturous confinement in Siberia. A number had made their way to South America. A few had remained behind to keep the Vatican informed of the communists' intentions.

It had only been recently that Pius had ordered him to disband his network of spies. Against the pontiff's orders, he had been forced to keep a few of his agents behind the Iron Curtain. Trapped. Father Yorick had grown impatient and belligerent of late. He wished *(demanded)* to be brought out of communist Romania. Gaston had dared not. Now, suddenly, an opportunity to rid himself of a nagging doubt and a nagging spy had presented itself.

SS Untersturmfuhrer Heinz Streck, now known as Father Sven Yorick, had been one of his most dedicated agents. A man with no scruples except when it came to saving his own neck. A man proficient in the art of killing.

The thought came unbidden. "Why would I think I needed Yorick to kill?" Gaston did not linger over the concern. He had learned the will of God was oftentimes hidden. The fact this nagging suspicion persisted *(the child is alive)* was enough divine intervention for him. He would send Yorick to the Institut. If Vasai's original plan had failed, Father Sven Yorick would finish the task—and gladly, Gaston was sure.

If Abbot Bronski had possessed the true strength of his church, if the child was dead, and Yorick's involvement had been unnecessary, well . . . Gaston chuckled at his cleverness. The walls of the Institut were impenetrable. Yorick would live his life in true service of the Lord. And, for Gaston, another link to the past would be severed.

***

Andre Proust walked slowly through the grounds of the Sanitorium de Acula. The cobblestone path lined with blooming trees and shrubs was well manicured. A freshness lingered in the air. The nuns he passed were cheerful and starched. One could hear them as they walked by.

The bright clean building ahead of him had been donated to the church to serve as a hospital for the sick and aged. The east wing had been reserved for those men of the church holding power. Mere priests were not accepted. Only the aristocrats were served. The rest of the Sanitorium de Acula were reserved for the wealthy who could well afford the exorbitant fees the hospital charged. It was a place for stature, not men.

"I understand, Monsieur Proust, but I must reiterate. Cardinal Vasai is ill. The stroke he suffered left him partially paralyzed. His faculties no longer function. It would be an embarrassment for him to have an old friend see him in his present condition." The director of the sanitarium dressed as impeccably as he protected his wards.

"I do understand. I have no wish to embarrass a family friend. I only came because my father and His Excellency were good friends. As a matter of fact, it was Cardinal Vasai who married my parents. Of course, he was only a priest at the time.

"Tomorrow I go back to America. I'm only sorry I could not have come sooner." How easily the untruths fell from his lips, Andre thought. Without guilt. If the church could lie so frequently, why shouldn't he?

"You come from America? Such a long way. Still, I am sure a visit from a member of his parish could do the Cardinal no good."

The director did not sound as sure as he had a moment ago. Andre pushed his advantage. "On the contrary, it might make him feel better. In America, they have found quite often a visit from the past can instill new life." Vasai was in his mid-seventies and beyond new life, but it could not hurt to pacify this priest of power when a miracle might yet occur. Andre held his breath.

The director hesitated slightly. *What harm could it do?* He smiled. Andre exhaled.

"Very well, Monsieur. You may visit with Cardinal Vasai. But only briefly. Don't be disappointed if he doesn't recognize you."

"I understand." It would be a miracle if the Cardinal recognized him. After all, it had been many, *many,* years since they had even seen each other.

Vasai was lying somewhere near the final breath, but not near enough, Andre thought. He remembered Armand Vasai as a large man—towering over his congregation—his sermons booming across the great expanse of the church, reaching into the corners where the sinners hid. The fiery priest's eyes had once flashed with righteous indignation. Now, they were clouded with cataracts, staring out at some distant memory. Spittle had leaked from the corner of the Cardinal's mouth and dried in a milky crust.

Vasai's attendant, an elderly nun, stood as Andre and the director entered the room.

"Monsieur Proust is to have a short visit with his Excellency, Sister."

Obediently, the nun bowed her head and left the room.

Andre occupied the chair she had vacated next to the bed. He held Vasai's pale, wrinkled hand and waited, hoping the director would leave him alone. Crossing himself, he began to pray. Very quietly, the director left the room.

"Cardinal Vasai," Andre tendered as soon as the door closed. "I am Andre Proust. I've come to find my brother, David Proust. Do you know where he is?" There was no response. Vasai lay still, lost in his dreams or nightmares.

Andre tried again, this time a bit louder. "Cardinal Vasai, please tell me where my brother is buried."

The hand, cold and lifeless but a moment ago, contracted in an undeniable squeeze. A voice dry as heat lightning crackled. "Meric."

At first Andre was not even sure the Cardinal had spoken. He moved his ear next to the mouth of the old priest. "Who?"

Again the spark of life, the dry whisper of a voice was heard. "Bishop Meric."

This time there could be no mistake. Vasai had definitely answered Andre's question. The word he had used had been repeated with great effort to the man. Obviously it was not an erratic memory. The word even had a vaguely familiar sound, but Andre could not place it. Who or …. Wait! Meric had been the pastor at the church where David had served. *So, he was a Bishop now.*

"Cardinal Vasai, please. I need your help. Does Meric know where I can find my brother?"

For a moment, Vasai was silent against his sheets and this newcomer who asked him disturbing questions. Then, his fragile mind kicked into play. It had been Meric who had driven him into this lingering existence. Meric's call that had comprised him in a situation where it had become necessary to order the murder of a child. Guilt encircled what was left of his mind like a vulture on the wing. *Murderer, it whispered. Murderer, it taunted, dancing in and out of his thoughts like the flames of Hell.* Until the accusation rose to the surface for Andre Proust to hear. "Murder."

Shocked, Andre dropped the Cardinal's limp hand. "Murder! Who?" He paced a quick step away from the bed, but returned in an instant semicircle. "Cardinal Vasai, who was murdered?"

But the veil had dropped. Vasai had said all he could. A moment later, his blank and guilt-ridden eyes once again stared at the ceiling. The rise and fall of the sheet across his feeble chest grew even more shallow. Andre left while the Cardinal still had life.

***

The drive to LaRochelle was easier than Andre remembered. He had forgotten how pleasant the countryside of France could be on the senses. A spring breeze blew off the bay. Flowers bloomed and spread a blanket of color around the hills and pastures. A few notes of a bird's song filtered in through the open window. In a way, it reminded him of the countryside around Oak Ridge. For an instant, he was homesick for his adopted country. For anywhere and any place away from this mess.

His father had gone to visit Monsignor Meric and David's physician, Father Antoine Curvise after he had received the Vatican's letter informing him of David's death. In his earlier letters, David had written of both friends often. It had been after that visit his father's attitude towards him had changed, Andre remembered. Was there some connection? Alain Proust had grown morbid, his coldness finally driving his son all the way to the shores of America. Even now, a lifetime later, Andre Proust still felt the shame and anger—the loss of his father's love.

What was the city of LaRochelle hiding, and who had been murdered? Andre Proust stepped on the accelerator, anxious to put an end to this experience.

***

The rectory of St. Margaret had changed little over the years. Meric still used the same office he had as the pastor of the parish. He had refused to leave and set up his archdiocese at a more prestigious church. It meant Andre had little trouble finding the Bishop.

"Yes, of course I remember Father David." Meric answered Andre's question almost gladly. He had never completely conquered his guilt at having sent David to his death. He still thought of Antoine Curvise. Dr. François Martine. Inspector Edmund Defont. Men he had betrayed for his church. For his beloved religion. "He was a fine young man. A priest who was destined for greatness." These last words were pronounced with unwitting innocence. "I was deeply hurt when I heard he had passed away."

"Do you know where my brother is interred?" Andre asked without hope.

Meric studied the man sitting across from him, this man who claimed to be David's brother. There was not the faintest resemblance to Father Proust in either the young man's face or stature. David had been tall and athletic with blond hair, blue eyes and a quick smile. Andre Proust was short with deep-set brown eyes. Dark hair crowned his dark countenance. It was an unhappy face. Nothing at all like David.

"Why do you ask?" The Bishop was reluctant to bring up the past.

"It was my father's last request that his brother, Monsignor Michael Proust and my brother, Father David Proust, be put to rest in the family plot."

"Why would you think I would know?"

"I spoke to Cardinal Vasai yesterday. Your name was mentioned. The Cardinal was very ill," Andre explained, "and could not say more than a word or two. However, he did mention you might be able to help me."

"I don't know if it will be possible to bring the bodies home, but yes, I know where your brother is buried." What harm could there be now, Meric wondered. What did it matter? No one other than himself was alive to tell what had happened here. If only he had warned Dr. Martine. Inspector Defont. Maybe they would still be alive. But he had not had the courage to speak out then. Only now, when it no longer mattered.

"Father David is interred in Litz, Poland," he finally said. It was the first time he had said it out loud since telling Edmund Defont where Antoine Curvise had been transferred. It had not burned his tongue. As a matter of fact, he felt like a weight had been lifted from his shoulders. The cross he had borne all these years was gone. "Yes," he repeated, delighted to find himself more whole from his confession, "he was transferred to Poland."

"Poland! Why was he sent to Poland?" Andre's emotions were twisted between confusion and relief. Finding the answer to his original query had done nothing but raise more questions. Did this roller coaster ride never end?

"David went voluntarily," Meric said, almost in defense of some unasked inquiry. It was painful recalling the night the black robed monk had transported the young priest away from St. Margaret's Rectory. David's consent still rang clearly in his ears.

If Meric's words were meant to soothe him, Andre found they only served to confuse him more. He knew the devotion his brother had for the church. If David had been asked to go somewhere by his superiors, he would have.

"Yes, I would never doubt that. David would never shun his responsibility, whatever the church asked of him. But why Poland? What church did he go to serve?"

"Not a church, Monsieur Proust. A hospital."

"But why?"

"Why do we go anywhere? Your brother went of his own free will. I know. I stood in his room that night and heard him agree to go."

"Was he ill?"

Meric blinked Andre Proust into focus. "Yes, it is as you said, Monsieur Proust. Father David was ill. I don't know what kind of illness possessed him. No one did. I only remember he went to Poland voluntarily." Meric looked down at the top of his hands. "A few months later I received notice he had passed away. His heart." Jean-Paul looked up suddenly, his eyes wide with worry his young visitor would condemn him for something over which he had no control. "I had asked Dr. Curvise to check his heart." The Bishop shook his head slowly, chasing away the memory. "He was a fine young man. A fine young man."

Andre interrupted Meric's sorrow. *Curvise.* He was the doctor David had mentioned in his letters. Perhaps if he could talk to him this slowly engulfing fog would lift.

"Do you know where I can find Dr. Curvise?"

"Yes, of course. He went to the hospital shortly after Father David's departure."

"The hospital? The one in Poland?"

"Yes. He and David were very close. It was a terrible shock to hear of Antoine's death."

Andre had become familiar enough with dead ends to know when it was senseless to continue.

"Would it be possible to have my brother's and, I assume, my uncle's remains transferred back to France? Could you make that request for me?"

Meric stared at Andre a long time before he answered. When he did, it was without hope. "No, Monsieur Proust. I am sorry, but I cannot. David is

266

where he belongs. Where he is most comfortable. Your uncle, too. Let them rest in peace."

"I don't seem to have much choice in the matter, do I?"

But suddenly, Andre realized, he did. After coming so far, being led down so many false paths, he was determined to try. "Bishop Meric, this hospital in Poland. Is it a part of the church?"

"It is the church," Meric said sadly.

CHAPTER TWENTY-SEVEN

The tingling sensation was a lit fuse to the coming explosion. Zigman Bronski clutched his chest and staggered towards the dining room, knowing if he fell he would never again walk the long cold hallways of his beloved Institut. Sharp, pulsating pains shot through his shoulder and down his left arm. He placed a hand on the wall to steady himself. To keep himself from death's grasp. Had he been able to stop gasping for precious air, he would have called out for help.

If. If he could get to the dining room, maybe someone would be there. Maybe.

It was funny in a way. He had hated this cold dark place when he had first arrived. He had been a young man then. Now, nearing seventy, he saw his days ending swiftly, with more certainty he would not see another sunrise.

His determination not to die in his sleep had driven him to change his work habits. Now he labored through the night—through the time when death stalked the world. Ironically, the sun had just begun to come up.

Before him, the hallway stretched beyond his dimming vision.

***

Sabina knocked gently, bent and placed her ear to the cool wood of Adam's door, listening. He had become shy, if that was the proper word, no longer allowing his mother to enter his room freely. He was growing up. She wished he would not.

She did not know what made her turn and look down the hall. It took only a glance to recognize Father Bronski. The recognition of his pain was almost instinctive.

No longer worried about preserving her son's privacy, Sabina flung open the door. "Adam, get up. I need your help." She did not wait to see the boy respond to her urgent message.

As if already aware of the crisis, Adam responded immediately, taking time only to slip on his robe and sandals before hurrying after his mother.

268

"Father Bronski!"

Sabina slipped her arms around the abbot and struggled to hold him erect. His bout with pain bent him double, almost knocking them both to the floor. Adam was at her side before she could fall.

For a moment as brief as a reflex, Adam and Bronski's eyes met. It was the first time Zigman had looked directly at the child—this child who was quickly growing into a young man. For that brief moment, the pain in his chest disappeared. Then his eyes closed and he lost consciousness.

***

François Martine finished his check-up of the priest. All through his examination he clicked his tongue as though reprimanding the old abbot.

"Would you mind not making that noise, Doctor?" Bronski's voice was groggy. The sedative Martine had given him was quickly taking effect.

"Noise? What noise?" Martine put away his stethoscope completely oblivious to his own idiosyncrasies.

"Never mind." Bronski closed his eyes, no longer afraid to sleep. "Well Doctor, what is your diagnosis?" It was a useless question, since he already knew the answer.

"You've had a heart attack. A mild one to say the least." Martine pulled a chair over and sat down next to the bed.

"Will I live?" His questions just got sillier, Bronski thought, but he felt compelled to ask.

"That depends on you, Zigman. If you're willing to give up the long hours of work you insist on doing, you might. If you don't . . . well, we both know the answer."

The sedative had swept away the powerful reserve Bronski used to meet each day. All of his trepidations, all of the worries he embraced alone bubbled to the surface.

"How can you ask that, Doctor? How does one give up his labors? Especially now? We have more Cardinals, more children than ever before. We've received no help for so long now. It's been . . . what? Two years. Three?"

It was true. Since the end of the war, the Institut had been besieged with a rush of sick and demented souls, bent and battered bodies. Twisted minds raving that God had deserted them.

When Bronski had first arrived at the Institut, only two of the wards had been in use. Now, four of the large dormitories were filled with crippled and senile Cardinals. And still no one came to help. Where had they gone?

"We're all old and tired, Doctor. How can you ask me to do less than carry my fair share?"

Martine had no reply.

Bronski would not have heard it if he had. The abbot's breathing had, at last, eased and become steady.

"Is Father Bronski going to be all right?" As always, Adam had entered the room without a sound. His presence, though welcome, oftentimes came as a surprise to those who thought they were alone.

Martine answered him truthfully. "I don't know, Adam. His heart is old and tired."

"Why don't you give him a new one?"

"If I knew how, I would."

Martine had grown used to hearing these strange requests from Adam. *Transplant a heart. Impossible*! But not to Adam. "Will it be possible someday?" he simply asked.

"Yes, Dr. Martine. It will."

Martine put his arm around the boy who was now almost as tall as he. Together they walked down the hall.

Each year of Adam's life had expanded his capacity to absorb the knowledge around him. At five, he was speaking several languages. At six, he had followed Martine around for almost a year, watching, learning. He was, in Martine's mind, almost as capable a physician as himself. At age seven, he had sat for hours learning mathematics from Father Alphonse, philosophy from Father Emil, and anything from anybody who had something to give. The boy's ability to learn was phenomenal. He never ceased to amaze those around him, and yet, he was still a child, bashful at times—especially when his mother teased him.

Sabina had grown into a most beautiful woman who, like Adam, had a gift for learning, although not nearly as completely as her child. She was twenty-four now. Martine found it almost sinful that she was confined to the gray cold walls of the Institut. She never complained and, if the truth were known, she would have greatly missed her dysfunctional family. She was, in her own way, a most soothing force with the Cardinals—the woman they had long forgotten; the softness they had never experienced.

"What will happen to us when Father Bronski dies, Dr. Martine?"

"I don't know. I am more than content to live out my days here. As for you," Martine looked at Adam. "You will have to leave."

"Yes, I suppose so," Adam agreed matter-of-factly.

Again, the boy's lack of emotion—whether it be fear of the unknown, the excitement of new adventures, the sorrow of abandoning friends—did not surprise Martine. It was something he had grown used to as Adam matured.

They reached the dining room together. Edmund and Sabina waved them over to their table.

"How is Zigman?" Defont asked with little fanfare.

"All things considered, he's fine. He's resting comfortably."

"Father Regis died last night."

Martine looked up sharply. He tapped a thin finger against his lips as he weighed Edmund's words. "I wonder if there's some symbolic relationship there?"

Defont kept quiet. From the tone of his voice, François was ready to expound on his esoteric theories. Quite honestly, he did not want to get into that kind of discussion at the moment.

"Dr. Martine, why would you believe there was some sort of correlation between Father Regis' death and Father Bronski's heart attack?" Adam's voice sounded thin in the nearly deserted dining room.

"If you gentlemen are going to talk of death, I'm leaving," Sabina announced. "And you, young man. You're supposed to be helping Father Emil in the garrison."

"Yes ma'am, I know. I'll leave as soon as Dr. Martine answers my question." Adam's face was a mask of curiosity. With all he knew, he still wanted to know the answer to *everything*.

"Father Regis murdered his housekeeper many years ago," Martine began.

Sabina shuddered and walked away.

"Father Bronski," Martine continued, "found Father Regis in the cellar of the rectory. They came here together over forty years ago, but they had been friends before that awful night. So you see, their lives were inexplicably entwined. If you and your mother had not found Father Bronski when you did, he would most likely be in the catacombs with his old friend right now."

Adam brushed the hair off his forehead. His blue eyes flashed. "Yes. I suppose it's a possibility. Human lives are occasionally joined together by some bond even nature cannot explain, but I don't think Father Bronski's life is tied to Father Regis. He has another to whom he is bound." Softly he smiled, and walked away.

"Just a minute, young man. What do you mean by that statement?"

"I am very sorry, but I cannot talk to you now, Dr. Martine. I have to assist Father Emil." Adam started to run.

Defont laughed as Martine sputtered.

"It's hard to believe he's ten years old," Defont commented.

"It's hard to believe we've been here over ten years," Martine said with only a hint of bitterness. He could no longer think of any other place he wanted to be, but this life had been chosen for him by circumstances beyond his control. He would never forgive The Fates for that mistake.

"Who would have thought we would have stayed here this long?" Defont said wistfully. "Do you ever think of LaRochelle, François? Of France?"

"No." Martine grimaced at the lie. It seemed he had lost the talent for fabrication. "Well sometimes, but not often."

"I do. I think about how nice it would be to have an entire town at your disposal. We need help, François. There are just too many sick for us to handle alone."

"I know, Edmund. I've asked Father Bronski to hire the townspeople, but he adamantly refuses."

"Why? Can you tell me why? He lets the women come in and do the laundry. Why won't he let the men help us?"

Martine shrugged his thin shoulders. "Shame. He refuses to let anyone but the priests tend to the sick. He doesn't want anyone to see the Cardinals in their humiliation."

Father Ehrick came out of the kitchen and joined the two men.

"He's right, you know." He had overheard their conversation. "We cannot let our brothers be disgraced."

"But it's not a disgrace. They have no control over what they do," Martine argued. "They don't know where they are or who is taking care of them. They're beyond caring."

"But we're not," Ehrick said.

"Talking to you is like talking to Bronski sometimes, Ehrick. Who will take care of the Cardinals when we're all too sick and too old? Will we care who takes care of us?" Martine refused to give up. He had changed, but not much.

"God will provide for us, François. He always has in the past."

"You obviously didn't pay any attention to the Commissar when he was here. He told us God was dead."

The Commissar of the local Polish Communist Party came to the Institut once a year to lecture the priests on the benefits of communism. It was part of the deal struck between the church of Poland and the new government. In return for this act, the communist government agreed not to confiscate any of the church's religious structures as long as they were occupied.

"Yes, I heard him say God was dead. But who am I to believe?" Ehrick's face was unreadable. "Him? Or you?"

Martine's charge into battle was sideswiped. "I don't understand."

"For the last ten years François, you've been telling us the Son of God

272

has been reborn." A sly grin etched itself on Ehrick's face. "Am I to believe Comrade Wesinoliski or the esteemed Dr. Martine?"

Martine rubbed his chin, imagining the gesture made him appear to be deep in thought. "God is not who you think He is," he said finally. "Neither is His Son."

Unconsciously, Defont sighed. This discussion had been going on since Adam's birth. The priests who had lived at the Institut before Adam's unusual conception had, for the most part, stayed away from the controversy. Their lives would neither suffer or be made any easier by taking a stand. The child was born. If it was, as Dr. Martine and Father Curvise had stated, an immaculate conception, what could they do? Adam was a child, albeit an exceptional one. Whether they thought of him as the Son of God, the Redeemer reborn, or just a bright mind in their dark and dreary lives, no one really knew. No one ever said.

Those who came after Adam's birth accepted him as a part of the Institut. Intelligent and happy, the boy was an extra pair of hands to help them in their daily tasks. That was what really mattered.

When asked, Adam had never claimed to be anything. For the moment, he was too busy being just who he was.

On those occasions when his status was argued, those involved in the debate made sure he, Sabina, and Urbana were not present.

Martine had succumbed to Antoine Curvise's theory about the child. Or was it David Proust's? Or Defont who had said the child was a mutant? One of the exceptional humans born over the centuries who, in time, would change the way the world acted. Who would bring a new understanding to the meaning of life on earth. A genius like Edison, Beethoven, DaVinci, Shakespeare, Caesar, Christ. The passing years had obscured the voice who had used the word "mutant." Now, it no longer mattered. Martine believed (*. . . Knew! It is not something as intangible as a belief. It is a fact. I know!*) if Adam was allowed to live, he would achieve great accomplishments for the planet.

Even after witnessing the conception and birth, Zigman Bronski still adamantly believed Adam to be the anti-Christ the prophets had said would come and destroy the world. In the past ten years of his life, in the past ten years of strict avoidance, he had been able to keep both his inflexible attitude and archaic beliefs.

Lost in the mild debates were David Proust's words. *"He is the Son of God. He is here so He may return to His home one day. . . . God is not what you believe. He is just a man and His name is God. We are all His children."*

These words had been written numerous times in Dr. François Martine's journals. Likewise, they were recorded in the journal of Father Antoine Curvise. Defont had heard David utter the statement. The Bible held the words of Jesus: "I am not of this world. One day I will be reunited with my Father in Heaven." But, like all words, they were soon twisted and forgotten.

Edmund Defont accepted Adam as the reincarnation of Jesus Christ as he had since the day he had placed the infant's hands on Antoine. Even without a miracle, no doubt remained in his mind. Thinking about it now, he laughed. He knew who Adam was. One day when they had been walking around the courtyard, he had simply asked the child. Adam had stopped and looked up at the sky.

"What are you looking for?"

"My home, Monsieur Defont."

Early on, Defont had come to accept the boy and his elusive answers. "Do you know where it is?"

"Not yet. But some day I will."

"And when you learn where your home is, then what will you do?"

"I'll return and join my father." Adam had placed his small hand in Defont's large one. "And my friends will be with me."

There was something in the way Adam spoke that convinced Defont the boy knew what he was saying. For a moment, the ex-policeman felt as Simon Peter must have when Jesus revealed to him He was not of this earth. How easy it would have been to fall to his knees and hail this Son of God. How hard it was not to.

Still, his next question had surprised Adam. "You've been here before?"

Adam's answering tone was quizzical. "I feel as though I have. Many times, but when the times were not quite right."

"And if this is not the right time?"

"Would it be impertinent of me to say I'll be reborn?"

Defont had laughed. "You? Impertinent? Never, Adam. Never."

CHAPTER TWENTY-EIGHT

Spring pressed on in its brevity. Hordes of insects swarmed and bred and bit. Rains fell. Flowers bloomed. The farms that had for centuries supplied the priests with their daily bread, once again flourished. The nearly depleted cellars began to grow fat and rich with the harvest. Wood was cut and stacked along the decrepit walls in preparation of the approaching harshness of winter.

Zigman Bronski slowly recovered from his heart attack, but his ability to labor in the wards remained drastically shortened. When allowed, he washed faces, fed bed-ridden Cardinals, held the hands of a few who might remember and take comfort. All minor things Dr. Martine allowed him to do. It was not enough, but it was better to have patience than be a patient. Of that, he was sure. At night he prayed, as he had done all of his life, for guidance and help. For strong arms and young minds to come and relieve the old priests who labored so diligently, not only with their tasks, but with the duties he could no longer perform.

At first, it had been the war. Now, the domination of the communistic regime prevented him from contacting the Vatican and requesting more help. Bronski no longer worried when such worry could accomplish nothing. All the records—the names and dates of death *(one birth)* were in his books. In time, the world would return to normal. Whoever was to take his place would once again renew the ties of this ancient institution with its home in Rome.

***

Busy all night in the garrison, Defont walked slowly towards the main building. His legs hurt. His back ached. Like a barometer of human suffering, the children had been agitated and nervous, crying and screaming since sunset, sensing or feeling bad news, bad tidings. A few days before the Germans had invaded Russia, they had screamed and ranted. Their brother, the Beast, was about to be set free. When Father David died, they had been unnaturally quiet.

275

Nearing the entrance, Defont heard the familiar banging of the brass knocker against the gate. Mixed emotions fluttered across his face.

Outside, a caravan of gypsies and their painted wagons solemnly waited.

It was always a surprise when the gypsies arrived, even more so after the war. As a people, they had been decimated during Hitler's reign. The Nazis had branded them undesirable and unfit to live. How many had been tortured and killed no one really knew. Estimates ranged from ten to one hundred thousand. Gorsoaf and his band had not returned to the Institut since the war had started. They were presumed dead. Still, some of the Rommies had survived, grown and prospered as gypsies were born to do.

The band who awaited admittance were strangers or, as sometimes strangers are, friends. They had traveled from Romania through the ancient Carpathian pathways to bring the priests home. How they knew where the Institut was, no one knew. No one questioned. They came, unloaded their packages of someone else's shame, and departed. Sometimes, they brought news of the world. Other times, they sat silently. Fearful. It was a bad omen, this Institut. It was part of their gypsy lore. Stories told around the campfires said it was a place they had to make a pilgrimage to at least once in their lives to atone for their sins and the sins of their forefathers. Whatever their reasons, they were greeted solemnly.

The arrival of the gypsies meant more children, more Cardinals—more work.

Defont slipped the chain and pushed the gates open wide. Still wet from an afternoon shower, the smell of damp horses filled his nostrils as the tired animals stamped their way to the inner courtyard. The monotonous squeak of rusty wheel bearings kept time to their movements. In the driver's seat, an old man passed the reins through knotted fingers and raised his hand in silent greeting, his face as gray as the Polish skies.

Called by the creak of wood washed clean and warped by the spring rains, Father Emil came out of the garrison and waited to see how many children he would be blessed with today.

From the steps of the main building, Father Alphonse watched, anticipating how many priests he might have to call for assistance. Sometimes the gypsies' load was light. A Cardinal no longer wanted among the living. Sometimes even the children bound for the garrison were docile, their anger spent on the deeds that had bound them for this place. But most of the time it was just not that easy. Father Alphonse sighed heavily. The air was filled with the anticipation of the doomed.

Three new Cardinals had arrived—one angry child for Emil—but each had brought their own guardian! Four strong backs, four strong pairs of arms had come in answer to everyone's prayers. Suddenly, the day was no longer without joy.

A brief hour later, Defont closed the gates and locked them. Secured under his arm, he held a very special gift for Urbana.

The last time the gypsies had come to the Institut, Defont had requested newspapers for Urbana. She wanted to know of the world. Now, almost a year later, that message had been mysteriously conveyed to the gypsies the war had left alive, and the newspapers had come with the priests.

Urbana had hid inside the main building, watching furtively while the gypsies went about their frightening business. With the interlopers now gone, she hurried to the main door unable to suppress her smile. She had seen the bundle under Defont's arm. It was too exciting! Like a young girl on Christmas morning she found herself too delighted to stand still. She danced lightly about the anteroom until the door opened to admit her benefactor.

"You have newspapers for me," she challenged. Denial would have been useless.

"Yes," Defont grinned. He had wanted to hide them. To pretend he had no such gift. To taunt and tease her as a big brother, with a smile. Instead, he gave them up easily. He knew she had been standing at the window watching him.

Urbana took the papers eagerly, hugging them protectively to her breasts. She turned to leave, hesitated, and returned to Defont. Distress was evident in her face, in her every move. Normally reserved, Urbana had backtracked to thank Defont in the only way fitting—with a hug. The only problem was that her hands were full of treasures and she did not want to let go. Not even for a proper thank you.

"Monsieur . . ." she began.

Defont laughed, understanding as he always had. "Go on. Take your papers to your room and hide from the rest of us."

And Urbana ran. Down the hall to her room where she intended to stay until she had read every word of the enigmatic world outside the walls of the Institut.

***

In his office, a single candle burned intensely, casting light on the open Book of Records. Bronski picked up the pen and began to enter the names of the new arrivals. He listed the Cardinals first. Then the priest who, from the day he arrived at the Institut, would be known as one of the children. Finally, with tired satisfaction, he scripted the names of the new brothers—Father

Lintz, Father Pascuale, Father Simon and Father Yorick.

Sven Yorick looked like a priest should. Small in stature, slightly bent, he had soft eyes and thin, wispy hair that belied his hard soul. He was a man who had never instilled fear in anyone with his looks or speech. His voice was soft and reassuring. His mannerisms spoke of a proper gentleman. A perfect example of a man incapable of murder. A perfect example of a fraud. He had been the Komandant at an extermination camp in Poland, but fortunately, not for long. Those who had known him then had long been turned to ashes.

He was supposed to have been taken out of Romania after the war ended, but something had always seemed to interrupt his benefactor's plans. Hesitant at first to venture back into Poland, back into the land of the dead, after a lengthy period of deliberation he decided to accept Gaston's orders. In Poland, at least, he would be closer to Germany. Closer to escaping to the West.

The Cardinal's communiqué had been as short as it had been confusing. *Report to the Institut d'Infantiles in Litz, Poland. See the abbot about a child.* He caught the scent of deception in Gaston's message. Caught Gaston's deliberate effort to remain anonymous.

He had never heard of the Institut or Litz, for that matter. It had taken several days of discreet inquiries to find out exactly where it was. Joining the gypsy caravan in Romania had been a stroke of luck. He did not find out exactly *what* the Institut was until the Rommies gathered around their campfires and spoke in whispers about their destination. An insane asylum in the middle of nowhere! The knowledge did nothing to clarify Gaston's cryptic orders.

A consummate player of parts to suit the times, Yorick knew he would perform his role to perfection. He would work beside the priests in this Institut. He would share their labors and their food. He would wait for an opportune time to speak to the abbot. Exactly as Cardinal Gaston commanded.

***

It was a typically wet spring morning. Having been relieved of his night duties by the new arrivals, Defont joined François Martine in the dining room for coffee. He was happy to be out of the garrison, especially at night. He was happy he would have more time for Adam.

The four new priests had taken duties in the wards. They were quiet, introverted young men who had come from all over Europe to work at the

Institut. How they found out about this hidden place, no one asked. No one cared. They were here, and that was all that mattered.

"Have you spoken to Urbana lately, François?"

"Spoken to her? About what?" Martine grumped. He hated the early mornings. Especially when he was cold.

"She wants to leave," Defont said flatly.

"I don't blame her. She's too young and too pretty to waste her life here."

"She asked me to speak to Father Bronski on her behalf."

"So why are you telling *me*, Edmund? Do I look like our dear abbot?" Martine sipped his coffee. "Why don't you talk to Bronski?"

Defont shifted uncomfortably. "That's not fair, François. Since Zigman had his heart attack, I didn't want to upset him. You know how obstinate he can be. You're as bad as he is." Defont set his coffee cup on the table. "And, well, I wanted to ask him in the right way."

"The right way! The old goat won't hear a thing you say," Martine said crossly. "Mark my words, Edmund. It won't make any difference at all if you ask him the wrong way or the right way." Martine paused, suddenly curious. "You don't really believe there is such a thing, do you?"

"Yes, I'd be interested in hearing that answer myself." Bronski's shadow appeared in the doorway.

Embarrassed, Defont ducked his head.

Martine chose to ignore the abbot. He was used to the old priest creeping up on him. Besides, he had expressed his sentiments to Zigman directly. The words he had said to Defont were not new.

"May I join you gentlemen?"

"Certainly, Father Bronski." Defont shifted his bulk to accommodate the abbot, but the priest chose the opposite side of the table.

"Now, what is it that you wish to ask me, Edmund?"

There were times when Defont could charge into battle without regard to his safety—his life on the line. Times he could speak his mind without fear of contradiction or condemnation. Yet, there were times when he needed to ask his superiors for a favor. These were the most trying of times—the moments that found him tongue-tied and mute. It was a cross he had carried all of his life. It still rested on his shoulders.

"It's about Urbana."

"What about Sister Urbana?" Immediately on the defensive, Bronski's gruff voice matched his mood.

Defont twisted the coffee cup in his hands. "I'm trying to think of the best way to put this—so you'll understand. If you'll give me just a moment . . ."

"He wants to know when you're going to let her leave this damn place,"

Martine snapped, losing his patience with the entire scenario.

"Damn place," Bronski repeated Martine's epithet. "Damn place? Do you think this place is damned, François?"

"For Urbana, yes. She doesn't belong here, Zigman. We both know that, but you're too stubborn to admit it."

"If I remember correctly, she's here because of you, Doctor. You and Father Curvise, and you too, Edmund—all of you wanted Urbana and Sabina to come here. I only carried out your wishes. Or have you forgotten?"

Martine fumed. He had not forgotten. His nights were still filled with his request to witness the Immaculate Conception. They were still haunted by his vision of two frightened young girls condemned to life imprisonment.

"And if we let Sister Urbana leave, Edmund, François, who's next? Sister Sabina? The child?" Bronski had yet to address Adam by his name. "Why not just open the gates and give everyone their freedom. Unchain the children from the walls! Assist the Cardinals from their beds! Tell the priests who have given their lives to our service we no longer need them."

"There's no need for sarcasm, Zigman. I only asked you a simple question with regards to Urbana's future."

"How can I let her leave, knowing what she does?"

"That's just it. She knows nothing. She has no idea what happened here that night."

"You never told her?" Bronski was surprised. He glanced towards Defont for verification.

"She has no idea," Martine repeated.

"Would she leave her friend behind, do you think, François? Or would she walk through those gates and come back with the sole purpose of rescuing Sabina and the child?"

It was obvious Bronski had given this subject much thought. The abbot continued as though he had read Martine's thoughts.

"You are not the only one who sees the anguish in Sister Urbana's eyes. It would give me a great deal of satisfaction to be able to grant her immunity. To allow her to leave." He shook his head sadly. "But it cannot be. As long as the child is alive, she is bound to this place with us."

"She is an innocent victim who is suffering for something over which she has no control, Father."

"Yes, and it pains me very much, Dr. Martine. Much as it pains me that I succumbed to you and your friends' wishes to see this child born. It was not I who sealed her fate, but it is I who suffer beside you."

"I understand your misgivings, Father, but let me ask you. What if . . . what if you were to find out Adam is the Son of God? Jesus Christ reincarnated?"

"François," Defont interrupted. "Stop this kind of talk." Why couldn't Martine realize that, at times, discretion was better than being right. Did he not understand how much Bronski hated the child? That the old abbot only needed an excuse, a viable rationalization to execute the boy?

"No, Edmund, I will not. It's high time we brought this matter to a head. Bronski here believes Adam is the anti-Christ, here to destroy the church. To tear down his religion. Well, I say it's time he faced the truth."

For a man so aged, so fragile of health, Bronski's being radiated power. His scarred and ancient face flushed and filled with anger. "You walk a dangerous path, Doctor. For all of our sakes, I urge you to be careful."

"No, I will not be careful. I've quit being afraid. I'm not afraid to die or spend the rest of my life within these walls. I'm not even afraid of you, Bronski. But damn it! I refuse to let you continue with this myth you've created in your mind." Martine slammed his hands down on the table. "You have condemned Adam from the moment he was born. Not once have you spoken to him—not even to say hello. Not once have you used his name. It is a good name, Zigman. Adam. Say it! Adam.

"Are you so afraid of the child you cannot bring yourself to wish him a good morning? Do you avoid him because you simply do not want to hear the truth—that Adam has never once said or done anything that could be misconstrued as a threat to you or your precious church? Is that where your real terror lies?"

The abbot swayed as he stood, his head reeling from the doctor's words. Perspiration beaded on his forehead and neck, traveling the pathways of his scars. Blackness filled his mind, his soul, threatening to dissolve him. It would be so easy to give in! *That* was how he knew he was in the hands of the devil.

"Sit back down, Father Bronski. You're sick. Your heart is weak." Martine's words were relentless.

"Stop it, François. You go to far." Defont placed a restraining arm on his friend. "Stop it, please."

"No. Let him continue, Edmund. He has a right to speak."

Martine softened his tone, although not his words. "You are dying, as we all are destined to do someday. You've been given the opportunity to meet a most extraordinary person—a young man, ten years old, who can speak to you in a dozen languages. A brilliant mathematician. A child who suggested to me, while you lay unconscious, I should replace your heart with a fresh one so you could live. When I asked him if it was possible, he told me it would be—soon.

"Is that a response of an omniscient god? A god capable of performing miracles? No, Zigman, no. It was only the response of a mind far more advanced than either yours or mine. Adam should be in a university absorbing all the knowledge we possess. He is destined to lead mankind into greatness, not tear down your ancient canons. It is you, Bronski, not I, who walks a dangerous path. You are so blinded by your ignorance you cannot see in whose footsteps you walk. Pontius Pilate. Herod Antipas. Will the history books add your name to that list of murderers?"

The blackness that had formed was as quickly swept away. Bronski's face relaxed. His breathing calmed. There was no reason to subjugate himself to this heathenistic diatribe. He was foolish to even think he might be able to convince a communist like Dr. Martine that he was the one who spoke the truth. Like Jesus in the wilderness, Zigman Bronski simply walked away from temptation without a word.

"What's gotten into you, François?" Defont's voice was hushed. "Are you trying to push Bronski over the edge? You know how he feels towards Adam. He would kill the boy and anyone who stood in his way rather than let him leave the Institut."

"No, Edmund, you're wrong. I don't believe Bronski is capable of killing anyone. Don't you see? If he intended to kill Adam, he would have done so long ago." It was all so simple for Martine. "He certainly could not bring himself to kill the Son of God. Especially when all Adam wants is to go home."

Defont was still uncertain. "Then the question becomes how do we convince Abbot Bronski of that fact?"

"I think he knows. I think he's known since Monsignor Michael came here. David's appearance just reinforced his desire to keep this hidden away in these mountains. It is possible revealing Adam's mission could very well destroy the Catholic Church.

"No, not the Catholic Church. Just a few who fear the end of their beliefs. The church is dying now. If Adam is the Son of God and destined to leave this planet, the coming age of exploration will surely turn the religious community on its head. The superstitions and deities created by the ignorant will be cast aside and replaced with new technologies and saints that will far exceed our imaginations. I believe we are standing in the doorway of a new and glorious age, Edmund. One that cannot help but further our own lives."

"And if Adam fails. Is it over?" Defont asked, suddenly worried. "Is he the last of these sons? The Jews have practically been eliminated, François. Was Hitler one of the travelers who knew of the Chosen People? Was that why he tried to kill them all?" Defont was silent as he realized the enormity

282

of what he had just said. "We must protect Adam at all costs, François."

"That goes without saying, Edmund."

Defont refilled their coffee cups. Their silence was as comfortable as their words. Oftentimes, more so.

"Urbana still carries the seed," Martine whispered at last.

"I haven't forgotten. Maybe that's why Bronski refuses to let her go."

"That is a possibility I had not considered until this very moment," Martine said softly.

Defont leaned back on the bench. "Why are we trying to prove who Adam is? Don't we know?"

"Yes, but does Adam?" Martine asked. "Is he aware who he is?"

Defont shook his head. "Yes and no. He reminds me of Father David at times. He has these flashes. As though all is there in his mind, but it's not in order."

"Of course. It couldn't be. He has to grow. To reach an age. Adulthood. Or maybe the age when this first struck David. He had just turned thirty-five. Adam just has to mature."

"Christ was thirty-three when He was crucified. He knew who and what He was. He looked up to the heavens to ask forgiveness for His executors. He knew He was not dying. He was just . . . waiting to be born again.

"The Catholic religion is a fraud," Defont said angrily.

"No," Martine corrected. "It was built on Christ's words. The fraud you speak of grows only from the ignorance of the men to whom Christ preached. His disciples. Inadvertently they misunderstood what He was saying. And He had no way to tell them the truth—that one day He would leave this planet and return to His own. My stars, Defont! How many times has He been born only to find His life ended by the very disciples He helped to start this damn religion?"

"Is it just our religion?" Even angry, Defont could not throw away a lifetime of teachings.

"No, religion has been with us a lot longer than the life span of the Catholics." Martine glanced upward, his gaze limited only by the wood-beamed ceiling. "I recall reading somewhere about a denomination in India. A cult that believed and practiced conception through dreams. I don't remember what they called themselves, but it was a long time before Christianity was born. The Egyptians believed in a heaven after death. As did the Greeks and the Romans."

"How long have they been here?" Defont asked. What Martine was saying was flying too swiftly over his head. He tried to comprehend it all immediately, but he knew it would take nights of lying awake in his bed to straighten out his confusion. Still, he did not want the learning to stop.

"The best guess, not mine, but those of the scholars, is about ten thousand years ago. Until then, if I recall correctly, there were only sub-humans living on this earth. The cave men. More animal than human. Our . . ." Martine paused to straighten out his thoughts. "No. Not our ancestors." He laughed. "Imagine if our travelers had not arrived here, Edmund. This planet would be inhabited by the colored races. Races living as they had for millions of years. No evolution. No technology. No intelligence. Just raw animals surviving on a pristine earth."

"Are you saying that we're related to Adam? To those who brought him here?"

Martine spread his hands apart on the table. "We're the ones who look to the heavens with longing. Haven't you felt like you didn't belong here? Not just at the Institut, but on this earth? When you look at a Negro, don't you feel some compassion for him. Pity he's not one of your kind? Sorrow he will never possess the intelligence you have? Damn it. I feel that way."

"François, you feel that way about anyone who is not French. Still ... if we accept this, why can't Bronski? The Vatican? The world?" Defont nodded his head, emphasizing each point.

"Fear," Martine said. "Fear . . . plain and simple."

***

A knock came on his door. "Come in."

"Abbot Bronski?"

"Yes, I'm sorry. You are?" It was one of the new priests. Bronski was not yet sure of the name.

"Father Yorick. I've come with a message from Cardinal Gaston."

"Cardinal Gaston?" Another name he did not recognize.

"Cardinal Gaston is the Director of the Department of Religious Antiquities at the Vatican."

Bronski's eyes widened. He now knew why Yorick was here. "Have you seen the child?"

Yorick nodded, but said nothing. Gaston's orders had mentioned the child, but nothing more. Between the men, silence stretched uncomfortably long like a storm on the edge of thunder. An impatient man at heart, Yorick forced the issue. "What is it you wish done?"

The moment of truth had arrived. Here before him was the answer to his prayers—a man willing to be the Sword of God; a man destined to rectify the abbot's sins. Bronski's thoughts were immersed in Christianity at a level

284

never meant for a species as violent as man.

"Kill him." The words were no sooner said than Bronski regretted them, but they were spoken and could not be taken back. Nor would he. "The child is to be killed."

"Is that why I'm here?" Yorick's hand crept to his face, hiding his grin. It was no wonder Gaston had desired anonymity. It was no wonder there was weakness and fear in the eyes of the old priest before him. An order for murder! And from the Church!

In the shadowy world of deception, men like Yorick thrived on the flaws in others. Until this very moment, he had fathomed no idea why he had been ordered to this godforsaken place. Now! Now he could almost see West Germany on the horizon.

"And when is this to be done?"

"You may judge your own actions. I only ask it be taken care of as soon as possible. Every day he lives . . ." Bronski stopped in mid-sentence. The threat of the anti-Christ was something he had to live with, at least for a little while longer, but it was painfully obvious the man before him needed no explanation. Perhaps Father Yorick had been briefed from the Vatican before his arrival. It was not his concern.

"One matter, Abbot Bronski. I wish to be transferred to West Germany when my duties are complete."

Bronski nodded, cautious not to promise too much. "Be careful of Edmund Defont and Dr. Martine. They are the child's protectors."

"If they stand in the way?"

"Do whatever you must, but the child must die." For the third time Bronski betrayed the boy. *And Jesus told Peter: "You will deny me three times before the cock crows."*

"Where does he sleep?" Already Yorick was formulating a plan.

"His room is next to the ward at the end of the corridor. His mother's room is next to his."

The cross, so heavy on Bronski's shoulders for these many long years should have been lifted. Had he not carried out God's will? *Yes, now. With the courage of another.* Zigman found he was no longer surprised to find its weight still crushed him.

Bronski waited for Yorick to ask him *why,* not knowing, not understanding that years of orders, years of giving orders had silenced his avenging angel's curiosity.

Yorick's robe billowed in the drafty hallway as he left the abbot's office. Caught in a sudden gust of air, the door slammed. The candle was doused. Appropriately, Bronski sat alone in a sealed room with only his dark thoughts.

Yorick walked slowly down the corridor glancing into the wards as he passed. It will be a simple task, he thought. The doors to the rooms were never locked. Even now he had only to open Adam's door and step in. How easy. The first night he worked alone in the garrison, he would slip out before dawn and . . . It was always a joy to be asked to do something at which one excelled. He grinned, his thoughts already back in the Fatherland. Back among his people.

CHAPTER TWENTY-NINE

Zigman Bronski tried desperately to sleep. He tried to wash out the earlier thoughts Martine's angry words had put into his head. To give in to the doctor's words, to recognize the child was to destroy two thousand years of Christianity. To destroy what millions had bravely died for. Martyrs who had given their lives to insure the existence of the church. Too many had served, died, and given their last breaths for this wonderful religion called Christianity. Too many to let one or two or five individuals stand in its way. What were five lives compared to those who had come and gone before them?

He tried to forget his own orders to kill. It was hopeless. Rather than spend the night sitting in his room, he walked the corridors praying for a solution.

"If only I had died," he said out loud, standing in the doorway of the first ward staring at the sleeping Cardinals. Staring at himself lying in one of the beds—helpless. "If only our eyes had not met." The child had looked directly at him. He had seen the beauty, the love, the intelligence inside the boy.

A trick! The devil's way of concealing his true intentions. The child waited for him to die. The *devil* waited for him to die, hoping to entice his successor into granting his freedom.

It would not be that way. His diary was filled with the evils the child was capable of performing. He had written that his eyes had seen the birth of this prophesied anti-Christ who lived inside this beautiful child. No, even after he was dead, the child, the man, the devil would still be confined to this place of sanctuary.

Martine and Defont . . . They knew the child could not leave, so now they hoped to persuade him to let the Jewess go free so she could spawn another evil into the world. Never! Urbana, too, would languish here until she died. They would all accompany him into death. What else could he do?

Wandering the halls and wards, Bronski slowly began to lose his mind. Everywhere he looked, he saw the spirits of his beloved church waving to him—beckoning to him to end the misery that dogged his every step. *Atone for your sins, Bronski. It was you who brought the women here. It was you who spawned this evil.*

He had known Father David was the angel, the messenger of God. He had known if he allowed David to act, the results would be what they were. Still, the doubt had existed in his mind. He had refused to believe the truth uttered from the foaming mouth of Monsignor Michael. The insanity had gripped and torn that poor priest to shreds.

He should have killed the infant, but found he was too weak. Now he would pay for his sins. He would not go to his grave without atonement.

***

The cramps brought tears to Urbana's eyes. She had to sit down. For the last week, she had been getting up before dawn to prepare breakfast. She did not mind. Father Ehrick was feeling badly and it was nice to be able to help the man who had brightened her days with his constant smile. Only he and Father Emil seemed immune to the agony and suffering at the Institut. Not really, but it was nice to begin one's day pleasantly.

Not like now. She needed to lie in bed for a day. Struggling, she put away the pots and dishes from breakfast. It was almost four in the afternoon by the time she eased her way back to her room, each small step a jarring misery. Her back and lower abdomen ached with the dark pull of her monthly cramps. Still, it was her fault she was not yet in bed. Had she not dallied reading newspapers she would have been finished by noon. Now she was paying for her idleness.

Halted by a particularly painful muscle spasm, Urbana made a decision. Knowing she would be unable to get out of bed tomorrow morning, she made her slow way back to the kitchen where she scribbled a note asking Sabina to take her chores tomorrow morning—promising she would take her friend's at dinner.

Back in her room, she curled up under her covers, fighting the tears that came with the awful penance she had to pay for being a woman. The only consolation she had was that Sabina understood.

***

Adam had volunteered to help his mother prepare dinner while Father Ehrick was ill. He found the note.

"What is it, Adam?" Sabina asked.

"Urbana isn't feeling well. She's asked you to take her place for breakfast tomorrow."

Sabina nodded in agreement and lit the stove. "Will you cut the potatoes for me?"

"I will if you'll wake me tomorrow morning when you get up. I'll help you make breakfast."

Sabina looked at Adam as only a mother could. She did not understand him, but she loved him dearly with a generous kindness that followed him daily. How had this special person come to be hers? He was never too tired to help. Never too busy to stop and talk.

"You don't have to, Adam. I don't mind making breakfast myself."

He smiled at her. "I want to. Please."

She could not refuse. "Okay," she laughed. "I'll wake you. But first, we have to get through dinner. Potatoes, please."

A few minutes later, in the middle of making biscuits, she gave her son a floured kiss. "You're growing up much too fast."

***

It was almost nine before Sabina and Adam finished cleaning the kitchen of the evening's clutter. The priests who had worked during the day arrived sporadically to have supper, rest, and talk.

Mother and son walked to their separate rooms. It had been a long day. Sabina gave Adam a goodnight kiss on the cheek and messed his blond hair.

"Don't forget to wake me in the morning," he reminded her.

"Are you sure you wouldn't rather sleep?" Even now, she remained reluctant.

"Thank you, no. We have so little time together. I'd rather spend the morning with you."

She sighed and gave him a hug. In her room, she found herself wishing he was still small enough to sleep with her. She missed having him tucked in her arms at night. His infancy had been a great pleasure for her—lying awake and staring at him in the darkness. Listening to his soft breathing as she squeezed him gently to her breasts. Even now she was not sure whether she had been the protector or the protected.

***

Yorick paced the corridor of the garrison—alone for the first time in three weeks. Even the children were on his side, their screams unusually absent.

His was a simple plan. Just before dawn he would make his way to the main building and slip into Adam's room. Oh, so quietly he pictured himself opening the door, his knife at the ready. A single quick thrust through the heart while his hand covered the child's mouth. No noise. No struggle. In a matter of seconds, the boy would be dead. Yorick could then make his way back to the garrison and finish his shift.

It was all so easy. The boy and his mother slept late. It would be hours before they were found. In a week, a month at the most, he would be transferred to Germany.

He made another round through the garrison, stopping at each cell. In the short period of time he had worked here, he had developed a routine that brought him to each cell once an hour. That would give him more than enough time to do what had to be done and it ensured that the children would not miss him. These lunatics had a way about them that defied reason. The slightest deviation from normal would easily set them howling.

***

Zigman Bronski nervously—excitedly—paced his room. He was aware of the schedules of every one of the priests under his jurisdiction. Tonight, Yorick would act. The cross that weighed so heavily on his back would be lifted forever. He could at last die in peace, his responsibilities at an end. He could die knowing he had not shirked his duty. He would not leave the problem of this child, this curse on the world, to his successor. Father Alphonse did not deserve to have this error thrust upon his back.

It would be difficult enough when he found the note with the abbot's confession. Yorick would plunge the dagger into the boy, but Bronski would accept the fact it was he who had killed the child.

The old priest looked at the rope that hung from the ceiling in preparation for him. After he was positive the boy was dead, he would take his own life. And Yorick? Bronski had made sure the man would live out his days at the Institut. In a macabre sense of justice, Bronski found he could not allow the murderer to go free.

***

The alarm rang, waking Sabina for a new day before the old night had ended. It seemed like she had just fallen asleep. Dressing quickly, she thought about how nice it would be when she was finished preparing breakfast to come back and take a nap. For a moment, she thought of not waking Adam, but she had promised. Besides, she liked having him around.

Yorick eased the door open with infinite caution. As he had suspected, no one was in sight. Inwardly, he allowed himself a small smile. He had a thousand excuses ready should he meet anyone on the way to Adam's room, but none of them would be used. Tonight was his night.

Candles burned on either end of the corridor giving one the effect of always walking out of the darkness. Away from the constant restlessness of his wards, away from the outside sounds of mice and singing crickets, attuned so sharply to any movement, Yorick thought if he really tried he could hear the sizzle of the candle wax as it melted. His first step brought him up short. *Jingle.* He waited for the imagined echo to fade. A grimace crossed his face. Reaching into his robe he remembered Emil's keys to the garrison cells. He would have to hold them in his hand to keep them quiet.

This was not a problem. It only meant he could not silence the boy the way he had originally planned. It only meant instead of a thrust under Adam's rib cage, he would have to cut the boy's throat. The windpipe and voice box could be severed along with the jugular. It was all a matter of technique.

Edging along the wall of the corridor which afforded the most shadows, Yorick crossed the main foyer and was in the next hallway with ease. At the doorway to the first ward, he stopped and cautiously peered around the door frame. The priest on duty was dozing in the back. Two steps, and he would be out of view. It would be the same thing at the second ward. Finally, he was just steps from the child's room. He did not see the shadow move towards Adam's door.

***

"Adam, it's time to get up," Sabina spoke softly in his ear. The room was dark, but she knew where every feature of his body lay. Her hand reached out to brush away the hair that habitually fell across his face. "Adam?" She did not see his eyes open, but she knew he was looking at her. "Are you awake?"

"Yes," he said through a yawn.

"Do you want to go back to sleep?" He sounded so tired.

"No, I'm up." He swung his legs off the bed and groped for his robe.

"I'll be in the hall waiting for you." Sabina started to leave.

Outside the door, Yorick waited.

***

Bronski stood in the shadows watching his assassin reach for the door.

The moment he had waited for since the birth of the child was finally at hand. Zigman Bronski, protector of the church. Zigman Bronski, killer of children. No! It was only one child. One evil child who had looked into his eyes and seen his soul *and given him peace*. Why had he looked at the boy? His reason had been stripped away and cast to the floor like a discarded rag. Why had he looked into Adam's eyes? The child was evil. *The child was not!* The realization had been instantaneous. *What have I done? I must be insane.* Had he the time, Zigman Bronski would have fallen to his knees wallowing in self-pity and remorse. But he did not have the opportunity.

***

The door opened too quickly as Sabina pulled and Yorick pushed. Any more quickly and Yorick might have been thrown off balance. Any less quickly and Sabina might have had an instant in which to save herself.

She was surprised, stepping back as a shadow filled the doorway. Instinctively, Yorick plunged the blade into her chest, believing it to be Adam. Who else could it be? As she slipped to the floor, Sabina's scream told him otherwise.

Adam stood quietly at the back of the room. *He is petrified, Yorick thought. He cannot move! How much easier could this be?* The boy's solemn blue eyes followed the assassin's every move. He had not made a sound, but there was noise coming from somewhere.

Even as Yorick started to turn, he felt a pair of gnarled hands about his neck. They were good hands, strong from years of work, weak from years of age. Bronski's hot breath seared his cheek. The abbot's voice was like the broken edge of a mirror.

"Stop it. I command you to stop!"

But Yorick had blood in his mouth and a single purpose filled his mind.

"Run, Adam." Bronski's orders rose in a scream. "Find Edmund." Already his hands were losing their grip.

"Let go! Let go, old man!" Yorick struggled to free himself from the abbot's grip. "What are you doing?" The boy slipped out the door. Yorick struggled harder. If the boy got away, he had no chance of doing the same.

Twisting free of Bronski's grasp, Yorick stabbed blindly. Still slick with Sabina's blood, the knife slipped easily into the old priest's chest. Bathed in blood, but not Christ's, Yorick thought ironically, as he stabbed again and again, almost falling when the old man collapsed against him.

With a backwards shove, Yorick pushed himself free of the abbot's dead weight, jogging quickly aside as Bronski crumpled to the floor.

"Run," Bronski tried to scream as he raised his head a final time and saw Adam running down the hall. It was not enough of a warning. Already Yorick was chasing after the child. After Adam.

"Help," Bronski cried weakly—too weak to be heard. Blood leaked from a cut on his forehead, dirtying his hair and marking his face with the brand of a sinner.

Someone else—someone with power took up his defeated scream. Urbana.

Father Michalowski ran out of the ward. Adam disappeared into Defont's room. Father Zigman Bronski died.

CHAPTER THIRTY

Defont had just gotten out of bed when Adam burst into his room. No words were needed. Running into the hall, he caught a glimpse of a robed priest running from the building. Instantly, his mind had a clear picture of what had occurred.

Urbana's screams did not stop until Defont shook her. With decisive motions, he pulled her into his room. "Lock the door and stay here with Adam until I return. Open it for no one but me."

Back in the hall, François Martine was already hurrying towards the prone abbot. There was too much blood, Defont thought as he ran after the escaping assassin. The doctor was wasting his time.

The front gate was open. The road in front of the Institut was bare. The escaping priest had vanished into the woods. Intent on following, Defont did not hear Father Alphonse's warning to stay inside.

From the tower, the Institut's only bell rang with atonal qualities. Without reason, Defont stopped short at its first note. It was a jarring sound—one that made him instantly glad he had never heard it before.

The policeman's hesitation gave Father Alphonse time to reach his side.

"Don't go any further, Edmund," Alphonse said gently pulling Defont back inside the wall. "He won't get away."

Seething with anger, wanting nothing more than to put his hands on the murderer, Defont was not ready to listen to reason. "He's a priest. He'll get away."

"No, Edmund, he won't. Anyone of us outside the walls of the Institut when the bell tolls is subject to the wrath of the villagers. They will not let him escape."

Within minutes, Father Alphonse was proven honest. The gunshots were barely audible. Short. Quick. *Pop. Pop.* Like the sound buttons make when they fall to the floor. Distant, harmless sounds. *Pop. Pop.* Muffled by the thick trees. *Pop. Pop.* Muffled by the hills. The thick stone walls of the Institut. It took Defont a moment to realize what the sounds were.

"He is being hunted now, Edmund. He will return. One way or another."

Alphonse led Defont back inside the main building. "It is a cruel world outside these walls. Sometimes the cruelty gets inside. Sadly, there is no peace."

***

"Sabina is dead. Abbot Bronski is dead." Martine took a deep gulp of air and tried to steel himself. Failing miserably, he sagged.

There was no one left for whom he had to be strong. The dining room was empty except for himself and Defont. Urbana and Adam had accompanied Sabina and Father Bronski to the catacombs where the dead would await the artistic hands of Father Alphonse.

"I can't believe they're both dead," Martine said. "That they both took the knife to save Adam. Sabina I can understand, but why Bronski?"

"Because his life was bound to another's," Defont said quoting Adam's words. "Bronski's life was not tied to Father Regis as we thought, François, but to Adam's."

Martine raised his head. "He did say that, didn't he? How is he taking his mother's death?" He had not seen Adam since the tragedy.

"It's a funny thing, François. Funny you should ask that just now. I was just remembering his reactions." Defont stood. "Do you want some more coffee?"

"No."

Defont refilled his cup. The fire in the hearth should have been too warm for this time of year, but there was a chill in the room. Sitting back down, he took a sip of the hot liquid.

Martine waited for an explanation. When none came, he prodded his friend. "What did you mean, it's a funny thing?"

"It's almost as if he has no emotion," Defont tried to explain. "He was not angry, afraid, or upset. When he came into my room, he told me Abbot Bronski had been stabbed. He failed to mention Sabina had also been murdered."

"That's only natural, Edmund. Adam was in shock. What did you expect him to say?" Martine was exasperated at Defont's lack of compassion in the face of such a tragedy.

"No, he wasn't in shock. I'd go so far as to say Adam wasn't even upset. His tone was more . . ." Defont searched for the right word. "Informational. It was like he was just delivering the news. No tears. No nothing. Now that I think about it, it's eerie."

"My God, Edmund! Adam's on the verge of becoming a young man.

What did you expect him to do? Sit down and cry? He's no child!"

"But he is only a child, François. He's only ten. We forget that sometimes."

Martine looked at Defont. His friend was right, but he did not want to admit it. "He'll feel the pain when he's alone," he finally said.

"I don't believe he will," Defont rebuked. "Listen." He had just noticed the silence.

"What?"

"The bell. It's quiet."

"They've caught Yorick," Martine announced.

"I hope he's dead."

Martine ignored the vindictiveness of the comment. At the present, he was more interested in the living. In Adam. "What did you mean to imply when you said you didn't believe Adam feels any pain over Sabina's death?"

"Just what I said. I don't believe he has any normal affections for Sabina."

"How can you say such a thing? Sabina was the perfect mother. Loving. Caring. She adored her son. She died for him. How can you even think such a horrible thought?" Martine was incensed Defont had turned so cold.

Defont had no stomach for the argument. "I only said what I thought at the moment. Probably I will be proven wrong."

"Probably," Martine snorted, hating to be content with Defont's concession, but unable to get more. "You are wrong."

Defont got up. His thoughts had already shifted to Yorick. He could do nothing to help Adam's psychological shock, but he could certainly do something to help his own. A little hands-on punishment for the murderer would do wonders for his state of mind—if Yorick were not already dead.

"Where are you going?" Martine asked.

"To the gate. I want to be there when they bring the killer back."

Martine watched him go. Edmund was wrong, he thought to himself. Adam was not a cold uncaring child. He could not be. Compassion was a basic ingredient of the human species. Animals had no compassion, but Adam was not an animal. Could it be Adam's intelligence was so great it precluded him from feeling the normal emotions of pain? Of death? Of the loss of a loved one?

But intelligence required love, Martine knew. The most intelligent of men still carried love in their hearts. To have love was to have compassion. So why didn't the boy cry?

With a sigh, Martine pushed himself up. He had to go to the catacombs and help Father Alphonse. To pass Antoine and David, and maybe stop and talk to them for a minute or two. They would understand Adam's reticence just as he did. He was an intelligent man, far above most men he knew. And he felt compassion. And pain.

***

The villagers of Litz dragged a naked and bloodied Father Yorick screaming for mercy through the open gate. The priest had not been caught without a vicious struggle. His robe had been ripped off; his face smashed by outraged and angry villagers. Chains had been roughly secured around his ankles and wrists.

Defont felt no compassion. The man was a murderer.

It took four of them—Greatcoat, Defont, Fathers Emil and Ehrick to haul a kicking and clawing assassin to the garrison. It was amazing how much strength the small man had. Of course, Yorick thought he was fighting for his life. He cried. He prayed. He pleaded and confessed he had only been following orders. Bronski's orders. Gaston's orders. Everyone was to blame except himself.

Had he known what fate awaited him, he might have plunged a dagger into his own heart. But the murderer, a fiendish beast who roams the dark fearful of being seen, a coward at heart, would never consider taking the one life he held dear—his own.

Chained to the wall of a cell, Yorick screamed at Defont. "You can't hold me. I was only following orders. Unchain me, Father Defont."

"I'll unchain you, you murderous bastard. From life!" Edmund grabbed Yorick by the neck, slowly squeezing the breath from the miserable man. It was fortunate, or possibly not, Greatcoat was still in the cell. He grabbed Defont's hands and managed to pry them loose. "You don't want him dead, Edmund," he said calmly.

"No, you're right. I don't want him dead. I want him to suffer."

Greatcoat escorted Defont out of the cell and left him standing at the door while he returned to their prisoner. "You're not a priest," he accused. "Who are you?"

He received no reply. He really had not expected one. When he and the others had dragged Sven Yorick to the garrison, Greatcoat had noticed the small tattoo on the impostor's shoulder.

"Edmund, are you feeling better?" Greatcoat glanced at the door.

"As well as can be expected," Defont growled. But he was calmer. Meaner. Not so ready to set an assassin free with a quick death.

"Come in here. I have something to show you." Greatcoat grabbed

Yorick's shoulder and exposed the small "SS" tattoo. "He's a Nazi," he confirmed.

"Are you sure?" Defont's clenched whisper sounded loud in Greatcoat's ear.

"Yes. I've seen these men many times. They were the plague of Europe." Greatcoat grabbed Yorick's penis in his hand. "The first thing we should do is remove this."

"You bastard. I'll kill you for this," Yorick screamed in pain as Greatcoat pulled harder and harder still.

"Brother Greatcoat," Father Emil said from the door. "He is a priest."

"No, Father Emil. He is no priest."

Yorick screamed in pain, defying conversation, normal or otherwise. Still, Father Emil's voice of reason was heard.

"He came to us as a priest. We will administer his fate in that manner."

Greatcoat let go and stepped back. He knew the years Yorick would languish in this cell were a punishment greater than any he could inflict.

In his element, Defont now took control of the situation. This man had not worked alone. Assassins were generally paid killers. "Who sent you?" he questioned.

"No one. I came alone."

"I will ask again." Defont could feel his anger on the rise. "Who sent you? Who sent you?"

Father Emil's gentle touch silenced him. "Wait for our brothers, Edmund. You must learn to season your temper with patience."

Yorick spit. They would not kill him. That was all that mattered. "You bastards," he screamed. "Unchain me. You have no authority to hold me." He struggled vainly against the shackles that bound him to the wall. Had Defont been closer, his face would have soon resembled that of the Institut's departed abbot.

Father Ehrick and Father Michalowski came into the room carrying a water bucket in each hand.

Emil tried to calm their prisoner as he had Defont. "It will do you no good to struggle, Yorick. We are here to take care of you."

Yorick spat, hitting him in the face. Unruffled, Emil wiped the saliva away. It was something he had done many, many times in his life.

Father Ehrick tossed the first bucket of cold water on Yorick. It must have felt like a thousand volts of electricity running through his body. He stiffened and hung on the wall. Another followed and another until the four buckets had been emptied. Excrement poured from the prisoner.

The buckets were refilled and the vile secretions washed away. Father

Ehrick brought a rag soaked in vinegar and stuffed it into Yorick's mouth. "He'll calm down soon."

The priests at the Institut knew the soothing effects of vinegar. It was reported in the New Testament that Christ, while on the cross, was given vinegar as a punishment. That was a mistake. The Roman soldiers knew vinegar was used to take away pains inflicted in battle. One had only to apply it to the lips. Its medicinal powers were well known in ancient times. The centurion who gave Christ the vinegar had been falsely maligned. His act had been one of compassion, not hatred.

"Come back when your anger has abated, Brother Edmund. I am quite sure by that time Father Yorick will be happy to talk to you," Emil said with a sly grin.

***

In the true tradition of her gender, Urbana lamented the loss of her friend with tears and screams. She, who was supposed to comfort Adam, instead needed to be comforted. Near hysteria, she was taken to her room by Martine and given a sedative. He sat beside her bed, holding her hand, sharing her grief.

"She was my only friend," Urbana said sniffling and wiping tears from her eyes with the back of her hand. "I loved her dearly."

"You have friends in us, my dear." Martine squeezed her hand. "You're not alone. We all share your grief."

"She was all I had. We grew up together. Our families lived next door to one another. We attended school together. Laughed, spoke of boys, and marched to the camp hand in hand. Who did she wrong to deserve the punishment she received? No one," Urbana cried. "No one."

"I know. I loved her too. She was like my own daughter, Urbana, as you are." Martine wiped a tear from his eye.

"Why?" The young girl stared into the aging doctor's eyes. "Why hasn't Adam cried for his mother?" She grabbed Martine's sleeve and whispered to his face. "He has no emotions, Dr. Martine. He just looked at her as if he had never seen her before. He cut off a lock of her hair. When I asked him why, he told me one day she would be with him again. Then he walked away as if she had never existed.

"What's wrong with him? Why can't he cry for his mother? I love him as if he were my own child, Dr. Martine, but I'll never understand him. Why can't he cry?"

Martine pushed Urbana gently back on the bed. Her eyes closed as the sedative took hold. "Rest. Tomorrow we'll talk again." He leaned back in the chair and held her hand until her breathing steadied into sleep.

Night wrapped itself around the mountains. From inside the garrison, the screams of demented souls filled the blackness with eerie incantations—a Gregorian chant that made the hair on the back of Martine's neck stand up in fright.

After making sure Urbana was sound asleep, François quietly made his way out of her room. He left her door slightly ajar, allowing a sliver of candle glow to enter. Concerned about Adam, he stopped and looked in on the boy.

Adam was sound asleep in the very room his mother had been murdered in earlier. With the events of the day still fresh in Martine's mind, the boy's repose rattled his nerves. Urbana had been right to question the child's reaction. Or lack of it. How could Adam remain so calm in the face of such an ordeal? Slowly, wearily, Martine made his way to the dining room. There he found Defont and Father Alphonse.

"Is Urbana all right?" Defont asked with concern.

"Yes. She's just tired and upset." Martine sat down. "How are you holding up, Edmund?"

"Better than I would have expected."

Martine did not bother to ask Father Alphonse the same question. The priests here took every day in the same stride. They were, in his opinion, immune to disasters as well as anyone on the earth. They had to be.

"I was just telling Edmund," Alphonse said, "that I will assume the role of abbot until a new brother is officially assigned the position. Only because of my seniority."

"I think you will make a fine abbot, Alphonse. What will happen to Father Yorick?"

"He is not a priest, François," Defont said.

"Not a priest!" Martine was surprised. "How did he come to be here?"

"That, Dr. Martine, is what we intend to find out," Alphonse interjected. "Edmund informs me Yorick confessed he was only following orders. Orders given to him by Father Bronski and someone called Gaston."

"I can't believe Father Bronski was involved in this assassination."

Alphonse hung his head. "I agree with you, of course. Especially in lieu of what has transpired this morning. A man does not engage a killer and then try to prevent him from carrying out his job. Especially at the loss of his own life. But until we can question Yorick, we will remain without an opinion one way or another."

Martine looked up sharply. Were they all so blind? Had everyone forgotten Defont had been a police inspector before coming to the Institut?

"Did you question him, Edmund? Who is this fellow who calls himself Yorick?"

"I tried François, but he is too belligerent at the moment. Maybe tomorrow. Greatcoat says he is a member of the SS. Or at least he was at one time. He has the marks tattooed on his shoulder."

"How did he come to be here, passing himself off as a priest?" Martine was confused. He knew little of the SS. Only what he had heard from Greatcoat or read in the few newspapers that came months after they were published. "He must have had some identification. Bronski must have . . ." He stopped and glanced at Alphonse. "Or do you just accept a man on his word?"

Alphonse shrugged his shoulders helplessly.

"What of the other men who came with Yorick? Have you talked to them? Are they who they claim to be?" Martine was incredulous. For a moment, it seemed impossible that anyone could walk into this place and assume the role of a priest without being asked to provide some identification.

"What questions would I ask, Doctor? What questions would you ask? The clergy does not need tattoos or secret codes to prove who we are. We accept help however it arrives." Alphonse's eyes narrowed. "How many people do you know would willingly subject themselves to this place?"

Martine nodded. "So what do we do now?"

"We continue as we have in the past. In a day or two, after we put our brother and sister to rest, I'll write to the Vatican and seek their guidance in this matter. In the meantime, we'll continue as normal." Alphonse rose. "Now, if you'll excuse me, I must rest. It's been a most trying day."

Martine stood with the new abbot, looking deeply into Alphonse's eyes for a sign of imminent death. He found none.

"I'm fine, Doctor. Just tired, although I do appreciate your concern." Alphonse paused before leaving the room. "Tomorrow you will help me finish our task, yes?"

"Yes," Martine agreed sadly.

***

After leaving the dining room, Father Alphonse returned to his room and tried to rest. He was not immune to the death or suffering that transpired here. He hid his emotions. Why burden others when they were suffering themselves? He tried to sleep, but failed miserably. His thoughts circled and refused to end.

Walking the hallway until his legs tired, he was not surprised to find he had stopped in front of Bronski's room. They had been together for over forty years. He hesitated. About to walk away, he changed his mind. Afterwards, he wished he had kept the door shut. Locked. Bolted. After all that had happened, he was not sure how much more grief his spirit could handle. For an instant, he understood the total anguish that had driven his friend to consider the damnation of his soul.

"Zigman, my friend." Alphonse quickly stepped into the room closing the door behind him. Thankfully, the hanging noose disappeared in the darkness. Moving by memory, Alphonse lit a candle. Sitting behind Bronski's desk he read the letter his friend had written.

I'm not long for this world. I have tried to lead a Christian life, tried and now I find I have failed. Do not pity me. Do not mourn. I do not deserve such praise.

At last the Vatican has responded to my concerns about the child. Cardinal Gaston, who I am now informed is our master, has sent Father Yorick to do my bidding. I should have done this terrible deed myself, but I lacked the courage. It was so easy to let the child live. So I gave into temptation. Father Yorick's fate is in your hands.

I know it is my friend, Alphonse, who reads this letter. Until my final decision is overruled, I bestow on you the dubious title of Abbot of the Institut d'Infantiles. My dear Alphonse, you must, at any cost, keep Sister Sabina and Sister Urbana at the Institut. They must never be allowed to leave. The same holds true for Brother Defont and Dr. Martine. It is the laws of our Order, not me, that condemn them.

Forgive me, Alphonse. My mind is black and twisted. I am honored and privileged to have served with you. It is with deepest regrets I will not be able to join my friends in the hereafter, but it is just. I am undeserving to enter the kingdom for which you and my brothers are destined. So I say goodbye, Alphonse. Goodbye, my friend.

Zigman Bronski

***

Sadness engulfed Alphonse. Tears now ran freely down his leathery cheeks. No, he was not immune to death. He did not live life without compassion.

"Your God has not failed you, Zigman. You have entered the kingdom of heaven, my friend, by your final courageous act. God would not let you cast your soul into the fires of Hell. Your singular act in Adam's defense has given you the eternal life you truly deserve."

Father Alphonse removed the evidence of an unused action. The rope would be returned to the stable in the morning. Bronski's letter fed the flame of the candle. He needed time to think. To straighten out the thoughts that stumbled and fell through his mind.

***

Both Defont and Martine needed to rest, but some sense of security kept them together in the dining room listening to the sounds of the night long after Father Alphonse had departed.

"Who is this Gaston Yorick mentioned?" Martine broke the silence. "Why would he want Adam dead?" He looked at Defont. "You don't really think Bronski could have been involved in this, do you?" He had to ask. He needed to be reassured the man they had called Abbot for the last ten years had not hidden some murderous instinct under his robes and religious beliefs.

"How can I, François? Adam said he is alive because Father Bronski intervened. Zigman saved his life. That's not to say Bronski did not bring Yorick here in the first place and then, when the killing became a reality, realized his mistake and tried to set it right. I've seen it happen before. Usually right before the gallows' trap door is sprung." Defont rubbed his hands together. He was suddenly cold. "But I assure you," the policeman's voice was deadly. "I will get the truth from Yorick—one way or another."

Martine had no doubts Edmund would do as he said.

"What I don't understand François, is why Bronski waited all this time. Surely he could have killed Adam a thousand times before now."

"Rules. Devotion to one's cause." Martine said. "Bronski was, if anything, a man devoted to his church and its archaic rules and regulations. It made him, in reality, both sides of the sword. On one side—safe. He would do nothing against the canons of his church. On the other hand, if he had been ordered, I believe he would have had no qualms about thrusting the dagger home with his own hands."

Defont agreed. "Would you say that was true of all the priests here? Us? Alphonse? Ehrick? Emil? Would you believe them capable of killing if they were so ordered?"

"No, I don't think so. Like any organization or business, the church has many men like Alphonse and the others. They are devoted men who work without question, doing what they believe is right. Murder would be morally reprehensible and, as such, make them incapable of committing such an act. But every organization has its fanatic devotees. Men who would forfeit all of their beliefs to carry out an act that could brand them an outcast to most of the world. They see themselves as martyrs who, with the single stroke of the knife, rise above their peers to a place in history. Their blind acquiescence makes these men most dangerous. Yorick is a prime example. Someone ordered him to murder Adam, Edmund. Blindly, he followed those orders. That is, of course, if he's telling the truth."

"And if he is? How do we insure fairness?" Defont, for the first time in many years, was on the scent of justice.

"We don't. How can we prove it? Yorick may confess here, but in a court of law where he suddenly is afforded certain rights, he will deny everything. Justice being blind, he would walk away a free man. Ironic, is it not?"

"Unfortunate is the word I would choose. Unfortunate that, to protect the innocent, we must release the guilty. I've always believed in the justice system of France. I still do. But justice here, in this place is even better. More right. Final. As long as this place stands and the priests are here, Yorick will be chained to the wall to pay for his crimes. Here, justice is not blind."

"That is a point on which I have no argument, Edmund. Even if I had, I am far too tired to continue this line of thought. If you'll excuse me, I'll say goodnight."

"Goodnight. François."

On aching legs, Martine slowly walked to his room. With everything that had happened, with all the questions that had been raised by Bronski's death and the thoughts of revenge that had arisen during his conversations with Defont, the single vision he could not escape was the image of Adam cutting off a lock of Sabina's hair.

Back in his room, he sat down on the edge of the bed and pulled out his diary. For years, he had kept a record of Adam's actions and mishaps in the Institut. It would take several pages to bring his journal up to date tonight.

Sleep threatened to stop his writing several times, but Martine doggedly persisted, not wanting to lose the emotions he felt as he chronologically recorded the events of the day. Two hours later he entered his last remarks. "We have been told someone named Gaston is responsible for Yorick being here. Defont promises he will squeeze what information we need from this fiendish fellow. I cannot help but believe he will succeed. What course of action we will have at our disposal remains to be seen. Hopefully, Father Alphonse will share our need for justice."

He thumbed the diary, stopping at a page he had written the preceding year. It contained a conversation between Adam and Father Alphonse. It had frightened him then as it still did today.

"Why do you allow our brothers to suffer?" Adam had asked.

Alphonse had looked perplexed. "We do not make them suffer."

"You prolong their existence. In so doing, you make them suffer."

"What would you have us do?"

"Euthanasia." Adam's reply had stunned the old priest.

"You would have us kill our brothers to end their suffering?"

"Father Alphonse, is it not our belief that when we die, we are transported to a paradise? There we live for eternity without pain or grief. Is that not what we are taught?"

"Yes, Adam, it is. But to attain our place in such a paradise, we must follow the rules prescribed by our Lord."

Adam had shaken his head disagreeing with the priest. "I can't find that particular rule. The one that prohibits us from preventing our brothers' suffering."

"Thou shalt not kill?"

Martine would have sworn he had seen a slight grin form and disappear from Alphonse's face. A rarity indeed.

"If I understand this," Adam had said, "we must allow our brothers to lie in their beds suffering beyond the age of usefulness. They have no purpose remaining here. They are simply waiting, perhaps hoping to die so they may attain paradise. Is it possible heaven does not exist?"

"Anything is possible, but that is not what we believe. No one can say for sure there is a paradise," Alphonse had replied. "On the other hand, no one can say there is not."

"Assuming there is, will our brothers resent us for having kept them alive instead of hastening their entrance into heaven?"

Father Alphonse had shaken his head. "We've done nothing to deserve their hate. Would you hate me if I defended your life to the point where I was killed? Would you hate me for ending your entrance into paradise?"

"No, because we are all destined to die eventually. On the other hand Father Alphonse, would you hate me if, in that second of time before your life was over, you discovered death was just an end? That there was no paradise waiting for you?"

"No, Adam. Because I believe with all my heart heaven awaits us at the end of our journey on this earth."

"And our brothers feel the same?"

"I cannot speak for them, but I would hope they feel as I do." Alphonse had then turned the conversation around. "Do you believe there is a heaven waiting for us, Adam?"

"I know there is a place called heaven, but I'm afraid it's not the place you imagine it to be. I am sorry, but the priests here suffer without rewards."

"You are entitled to your beliefs. I am sorry yours do not have a happy ending, but only time will tell if we are to be reunited again after we have passed away."

"You needn't be sorry, Father Alphonse. For you, the dream is reality." Adam had turned and walked away.

The book slipped from Martine's hand and fell to the floor. In that moment before he fell asleep, a realization struck his thoughts. He knew what had to be done. Adam had to be proclaimed the resurrection/reincarnation of Jesus Christ. There were no doubts in François' mind. The church had to recognize Adam and present him to the world as the leader of Christianity. The rhetoric of the anti-Christ, that God was dead, Martine realized, had been true. At least up until the moment Adam had been born. But now! Now, God was alive and His son was residing deep in the Carpathian Mountains in an asylum for the insane.

CHAPTER THIRTY-ONE

"If you have a better solution, then I suggest you tell me what it is." Martine grasped Defont's sleeve in his hand. The two men had been taking a walk around the courtyard. At least Martine was. At times it seemed Defont was doing his best to escape the doctor.

A week had passed since Zigman Bronski and Sabina had been murdered. A week since François Martine had been endowed with his revelation.

"Don't you believe Adam is Christ?" Martine asked.

Defont lengthened his strides. "I don't know what to believe any more. Last week you were sure he was from . . . I don't know . . . From there." He pointed up at the gray sky. "Last year he was a genius—a mutant come to enlighten the world. Today you want to insist he is the new Christ. What will you have him be tomorrow?"

"I'm not insisting anything," Martine said. "Edmund, would you please slow down."

"You are insisting," Defont argued, but he lessened his speed.

"All right, I am. But I'm insisting we convince Father Alphonse and the others to . . . We need to ask the church for an Inquisition so they and everyone else can know exactly who Adam is."

"He's a child, François. A bright and, as you have said many times, exceptional child. Brilliant! A genius! I don't have any problems accepting those facts. Why do you wish to make him out to be more? Can't you just accept him as he is and let him be?"

Martine was hurt. He stopped and watched Defont walk away. "I only want him to have what is rightfully his," he called to Edmund's back. "You know as well as I who he is. You were there that night, Edmund. You can never walk away from it no matter how hard you try." Martine continued with sudden insight. "No matter how much you might wish it were not so, no matter how much you wish to keep Adam all to yourself, you cannot deny the boy his birthright. You were there!"

Defont stopped at Martine's words. In a few quick steps, he had rejoined the doctor. "Yes, I was there, François. I sat with David until he passed away.

307

I wish now I had been anywhere else."

"You don't mean that. How could you? You were witness to one of the great acts of mankind. One of the three kings who saw Christ in the manger. You can't just turn your back on the miracle that occurred here."

"It is a miracle you and Antoine claim happened. I cannot honestly say, François." Defont shrugged his bearish shoulders. "If I was asked, I could not honestly testify Sabina was what you and Antoine claim she was."

Although painful, Defont's honesty did not deter Martine. "I understand that, Edmund. I am the only one alive who knows in here," he pointed to his heart, "what transpired that night. I, alone, am the witness to this Immaculate Conception. This birth. You know as well as I David never touched Sabina. He never entered her room. You cannot deny that truth."

"You are right as always," Defont said gruffly. Once again he began to pace the courtyard, Martine at his heels. "What I saw defies what little knowledge I have." He stopped and looked at François. "What good will it do to have this Inquisition? Who will benefit from it?"

"Adam," Martine said looking directly into Defont's eyes. It was easy to read the doctor's clear conviction in his steady gaze. "We have to convince the church, the pope, that Adam is not some evil monster sent here to destroy Christianity. You heard what Father Alphonse said he found in Bronski's office—a report filled with suspicion and hatred for Adam. Innocently spoken words Bronski had twisted so Adam would appear to be against the church. Fortunately, he never mailed those reports. The one letter he did send was enough to have this murderer, Yorick, sent here.

"The Vatican knows Adam was born. They have known for years, centuries that he would come. That's why Michael Proust and the others are entombed here. Hidden away where it was impossible for them to carry out their task. The church has falsely believed if a new Christ were born, He would be born to destroy them. We know that is not the case. As far as I can tell, Adam cares less about the Catholic Church than I do."

"Then why are you trying to save it?"

"I'm not, Edmund. Don't you see? I'm trying to save Adam. We have to convince the Catholic Church he is the Messiah, but that his purpose on earth is not to destroy their religion, but to elevate mankind. If we don't succeed, they, with their twisted notions, eventually will. Is that what you want, Defont? History to repeat itself?"

"How do you propose we convince them?" Defont tried to imagine himself being told Adam was Jesus Christ.

"All of us who were there that night are aware of what happened. Only one of us is still not acquainted with the event. Urbana. What I'm proposing is that I give all the journals—Monsignor DeValier's, Antoine's, mine, and Bronski's to the girl. Let her sit down and read exactly what has transpired. Let her either be convinced it is the truth or let her tell us she finds us all insane."

"You're willing to put Adam's future in the hands of a woman?" Defont was surprised.

"It won't be the first time the gods have entrusted our future to a lowly female. Do you have a better suggestion?"

"No. As a matter of fact, I think Urbana is the perfect choice to judge you."

"You misunderstand, Edmund. It will not be me on trial, but the son of her friend."

"And if she sees the truth, whatever that may be . . . what then?"

"I've talked to Father Alphonse and he agrees with me to let Urbana make this decision. If she sees Adam as Christ, he will write to the Vatican and request an Inquisition into the status of the child."

"And if she doesn't agree? What then?"

Martine screwed up his face in a look of utter despair. "We won't be any worse off than we are now."

"Adam will have no chance of ever leaving here?" Defont questioned.

"He doesn't have much of a chance now."

"Suppose Urbana finds Adam is the Son of God and we have this Inquisition. And just suppose they judge Adam to be the Messiah. What do you think they will do about it?"

"They'll take him to Rome! They'll . . ." Martine stopped, unable to find an answer.

"Crucify him?" Defont whispered.

"That's what they're trying to do now," Martine exclaimed. "If he's accepted, *accepted*, Edmund! They want him dead now because they do not understand him. It is that simple. But if they come to understand him. Enjoy his knowledge . . .

"I am sure there are many men in the Vatican who want Adam dead, but they cannot be the majority. There would have to be more, many more who, when they discover Christ is alive, will rush to his defense once they realize the very man they have given up for dead many years ago lives. How can they not, Edmund? After all, I will swear to them I have seen with my own eyes the miracle described in the Bible. The Immaculate Conception. After that, how could the church refuse to accept Adam as the Son of God? Subsequently, logic would dictate once the church accepted Adam for who he is, why would they want to harm him?"

"That's a question I hope we will not have to answer someday," Defont said as he veered off the circular path and headed towards the garrison.

Lost in thought, Martine walked on. When he realized he had lost hiscompanion, he cut his walk short and followed Edmund. "Why are you going to the garrison this time of day?"

"I want to talk to Yorick again."

Defont was convinced the imposter knew more than he had been willing to tell. It had not been hard for the big man to get his prisoner to talk, but Yorick had spoken in circles, hoping his many words, his many lies would satisfy his jailer.

Reluctantly, Martine tagged along.

***

Defont gripped the iron barred door, pushing what little of his face he could even closer to Yorick. The effect was grotesque.

As Father Emil had promised, the prisoner had calmed and was no longer on the wall. Still restricted, the chains jangled softly, mapping Yorick's position when he moved, but for now they were silent. Yorick sat quietly against the far wall covered in a loose fitting robe, his fight broken by the applications of cold water.

"Do you wish to go in, Edmund?" Emil asked. The old priest sagely watched Yorick for any signs that might signal the prisoner's return to violence.

"Yes, please." Defont stepped aside so Emil could unlock the door.

The door groaned. "I don't think you'll have any trouble with him, Edmund. I'll be just outside if you do."

"Are you coming in, François?"

"Yes." Martine was hesitant.

Emil provided chairs and Martine and Defont sat down in front of the assassin. Wrapped in misery, Yorick refused to acknowledge their presence.

"I want you to tell me again the events that led to your coming here," Defont began harshly.

"Leave me alone. I've told you all I know."

"Yes, I know, but I want to hear it again. Now you can tell me or I'll have you put back on the wall."

Martine had not yet witnessed Yorick's bout with the wall. He knew and had heard of it being applied to a few of the other children. It had frightened him to know of its cruel existence. His school of thought frowned on punishment no matter how heinous the crime, or deranged the inmate.

310

"Please Yorick, tell Monsieur Defont what he wants to hear," he pleaded.

Yorick looked at Martine. For a brief moment their eyes met, but it was enough. In Martine's eyes, he saw the glimmer of his salvation. Weakness. Defont, like Emil and the other three had no weakness. They did what they thought was right, harshly and without compassion. But this man before him was different.

"What do you wish me to tell him, Doctor?" Yorick was not insane yet, but he knew if he did not escape this place, time would slowly wreck his power of reason.

Martine gave Defont a smug smile. It was a triumphant grin of the intellect winning out over the brute. "What do you wish to hear from Yorick?"

"He knows what I want to hear. He also knows I have no patience for him."

"Start at the beginning, Yorick," Martine said reassuringly.

"Yes, Doctor. I was a priest at St. Basil's in Romania."

"I want the truth, Yorick. Not this fairy tale you've concocted," Defont growled.

"Why don't you let him speak, Edmund? You asked him to tell you how and why he came here, yes?"

"I've heard this lie before, François. I know who he is. Greatcoat showed me the tattoo. Now, I would suggest you stop this lying Yorick, or by God I'll put you on the wall and keep you there until you are nothing but a carrot."

"Threatening a man will not get you the truth, Edmund," Martine explained. "A frightened man will tell you anything. Not necessarily the truth."

Torture was the last thing Yorick wanted, yet he knew if he did not tell Defont what he wanted to hear, it was only a matter of time before his tormentor would lose his temper and again chain him to the wall. But if the doctor heard the truth, any chance of gaining his sympathy would be gone. Without the doctor's sympathy, any chance of escaping this dungeon was gone. Yorick decided to cast his lot with Martine.

"I was a priest . . ." he began again.

"Father Emil," Defont called.

"Yes, Edmund." Emil appeared in the doorway instantly.

"We're putting Yorick back on the wall."

Emil disappeared.

"You can't do that, Edmund." Martine's protests were almost a whine.

Yorick watched, his hopes rising. Dissent between his captors was in his favor. Split the ranks and conquer. Never let the enemy fight for the same cause. He would suffer the wall, gladly now that he had an ally.

"This is not your concern, François," Defont said angrily. "He'll hang there until he tells us the truth."

Emil returned with two more priests and, with Defont's help, the four men chained Yorick to the wall. He did not protest, but went as a victim for Martine's eyes to behold. Naked, his chin defeatedly resting upon his chest, he stared at the doctor, pleadingly—until the first bucket of water shocked him into a scream.

"This is barbaric," Martine shouted. "It's inhumane to treat any man like this."

His protests fell on deaf ears. The water splashed with electrifying results. Martine stormed from the cell.

From the corner of his eye, Yorick watched his salvation leave the cell. He knew the doctor would be back. A scream, half forced, half in pain, followed the doctor out of the garrison. If the torment had not been so intense, Yorick would have laughed.

"We'll talk again tomorrow, Yorick," Defont threatened. "Or maybe next year. I'll let you decide."

"You're a bastard, Defont. An ignorant bastard." Yorick lunged at his tormentor. His chains rattled and brought him up short. Spittle flew from his lips like curses, but it did no good. Defont had left the cell. The priests in the garrison returned to their duties as though nothing out of the ordinary had occurred. And indeed, nothing had.

***

"It was barbaric," Martine said, trying desperately to keep his temper under control. He had hurried from the garrison to the main building searching out Father Alphonse, determined to counter Defont's uncivilized behavior towards Yorick.

Trapped in what used to be Bronski's office and was now his, Alphonse could only sit behind the old desk and listen to Dr. Martine's complaint. It was a sight he had secretly enjoyed when it had been Father Bronski the doctor was brow-beating with some cause of justice. Silently, he now asked for Bronski's forgiveness.

"We simply cannot torture men to satisfy our own sense of justice. Fair play dictates we treat all of the children equally. Edmund's attitude is most unsettling. Actually, it's barbaric. Barbaric!" Martine exclaimed. He jumped from his chair and walked towards the door.

Alphonse let out a premature sigh of relief.

Martine stopped at the doorway, then returned to the desk. "What are you going to do about this?" he demanded.

"There is nothing to do, Doctor," Alphonse said with a sigh of resignation. "Whether you wish to believe it or not, the treatment prescribed for the children has worked very well over the years. It may seem cruel to you, but unless you have some other means of controlling violent outbursts, we will continue to use methods I know are effective."

"I'm not disputing the effectiveness of the treatment, Father Alphonse. I'm complaining about the arbitrary use of this method to torture Yorick. There is a difference."

"Your compassion for this murderer, Yorick, is appreciated and recognized as a part of our Christian heritage. Frankly, Dr. Martine, I agree with your attitude in this matter, but if we are to carry out your idea to help Adam, it is imperative we know with whom we are dealing. Edmund is merely trying to find out who sent Yorick into our presence. I found a copy of the letter Abbot Bronski sent to the Vatican."

"What did Father Bronski have to say?" Martine asked.

"He merely asked for guidance. He did inform Cardinal Vasai the child had been conceived. Another letter, penned the following year, asked again for guidance and informed Cardinal Vasai Adam had been born. That letter was not sent and Zigman did not write to the Vatican again. Of course, the war and the subsequent communist takeover of Poland have made communications most difficult. I have asked Greatcoat to find a means of communicating that will insure privacy. In the meantime, we must find out with whom we are dealing. I personally find it hard to believe our church would act in such a murderous way, but we are not infallible.

"By the way, it might interest you to know I have accumulated the journals of our late abbot. When you are ready, you may give them to Sister Urbana."

"Have you read them?" Martine asked curiously.

"Not in their entirety. I'm afraid I do not put much faith in such writings. Father Bronski was—confused about the situation here. But as you are well aware, his final act in saving Adam justifies his life as a priest."

"Yes, I would like to believe we are all given one final act to justify our lives," Martine said. "Unfortunately, the damage we do in the meantime is irrevocable."

***

Martine placed the journal Antoine Curvise had kept before Adam's birth with his diary and subsequent writings of Adam's unusual behavior. Armed with incredulous tomes, he set out to find Urbana. He would present Bronski's journals later, feeling if Urbana read his and Curvise's findings first, it might possibly sway her opinion towards his point of view.

He found her in Ward Two, helping the priests. Her energy was boundless. She worked as hard, if not harder than the men who devoted their lives to the Institut. She had little patience trying to cut corners when it came to the comfort of the Cardinals. She had been like that for as long as anyone could remember. The only permanent fixture missing now was her smile.

Her shift was almost finished. Martine asked her to meet him in the dining room. He had a task for her.

***

"This," Martine patted the leather bound books that rested in front of him on the table, "is what we know of Adam. I want you to read them. When you have finished, let me know. There are more which I will then give you."

Confused, Urbana looked from the books to the doctor. "Why have you written about Adam? All this for a small boy?"

It was a question he had not expected. "Don't you find him to be a bit—unusual? Different?"

"He's intelligent, more so than any child I have ever known," she said. "More so than me about many things." It was a modest admission. One without envy or awe.

"Did Sabina ever tell you how she came to be with Adam?" Martine asked.

Urbana looked bewildered.

"How she conceived him?" he added, trying not to blush. He was far too old for this.

"Is there more than one way?" Urbana asked, suddenly feeling her cheeks redden. "I'm not a child any longer, Doctor," she added.

"Yes, I am well aware of that. These books are about Adam's conception, his birth, and what Father Curvise observed before Adam was born and what I have managed to observe over the years. You will also find reference to Father David Proust. You never met him, but he is very important to this . . ." He stopped. What could he say about David?

"When you have finished reading them, I will ask for an unbiased opinion. Do not worry if you do not understand everything you read. I'll confess, I do not fully understand everything I have written. That," he smiled gently, "is part of the mystery. I know you are intelligent and opinionated.

314

You will read some things that might strike you as derogatory. Keep in mind that whatever you read, it is from the author's point of view and was written as truthfully as he knew how." Martine slid the books across the table.

With a gentle smile, Urbana pushed the books back. "I don't want to read these, Dr. Martine. I don't *need* to read them."

Martine's jaw fell. "Aren't you the least bit interested in what has transpired here?" he asked incredulously.

"No, Doctor. What happened here does not matter. Nor will it change the way I feel about Adam." She smiled softly at his disappointment. "I'm sorry."

***

The next morning Defont awoke early and made his way to the garrison. He had asked Martine to meet him at eleven. It was now only six and still dark. François had disrupted his interrogation of Yorick yesterday. Edmund was determined it would not happen again. The big policeman had sensed the weakness Yorick had seen in Martine. He knew Yorick was counting on convincing Martine he was being mistreated. Of course he was being mistreated! But nowhere near as badly as he had treated Sabina and Father Bronski.

Defont opened the cell. Yorick's look of surprise amused him.

"No, he's not here. I've convinced him of your deceit. It will just be me you have to talk to from now on."

Yorick shivered from the cold. His bloodied wrists had not healed from his last ordeal on the wall. His ankles were chaffed and sore.

"You were doing so well yesterday. Pity." Defont turned and began to walk out of the cell. "I'll be back tomorrow or maybe the next day," he said slowly closing the cell door.

"Wait!" It was an anguished cry. "Don't go." From a defeated man. Restrained into paralysis, Yorick's chest heaved as he fought to catch his breath. When he spoke, it was with a new voice. He no longer snarled like a cornered animal, but whimpered like a dying hare. "I'll tell you what you want to know. But please, please Monsieur Defont. Get me off this wall!"

Defont erased his smile of satisfaction before returning to Yorick's side. "When I am satisfied you have told me the truth."

Yorick would make sure he told the truth. The truth. What was the truth? Yorick tried to put the truth together in his mind. So many lies—so many years. Truth was no longer a reality. He looked at Defont. "My name is Heinz Streck," he began haltingly.

Not eagerly, not angrily, Defont listened to the words that fell from Yorick's mouth. What terrible things had happened in the world while he and François were confined here? What hideous forces had been at work?

Yorick told him everything.

Defont walked out of the cell defeated. For all of his troubles, for all of his conviction there were more people behind this plot to kill Adam than Yorick and his master, he still only had one name. *Gaston.* Who or what was Gaston? It was obvious either Yorick did not know or was bound never to tell.

He passed Father Emil on his way out of the garrison and quietly asked him to take Yorick off the wall. Nothing would be gained by him suffering more.

Emil nodded his consent, pleased Brother Edmund had found compassion for another child of the Institut.

***

At eleven, Defont walked into the dining room. Martine sat waiting for him. A look of consternation crossed his face. He dreaded having to see Yorick hanging on the wall. He was angry at Defont for his inhumane behavior towards his prisoner and determined Yorick would no longer suffer such cruelties.

"Before we go Edmund, I want you to know I will not allow Yorick to remain on the wall. I demand that you take him down and talk to him as a civilized human being. I've already been to see Father Alphonse about this and he agrees with me. As you can see, I'm quite adamant about this."

It was all Defont could do to keep from laughing. "You're right, François. I was wrong. I have already visited our prisoner and had him removed from the wall. So you see, there is no need for your belligerence." His amusement dwindled quickly. Yorick's confession was still fresh in his mind. "Please, sit down. I need some coffee."

A little confused at such an easy win, Martine waited for Defont to return to the table. Something was wrong. His first concern was Yorick. Had Edmund killed the prisoner?

Joining Martine, Defont stirred his drink thoughtfully, biding time until he could think clearly. His hand wrapped around the cup, drawing the heat to his fingers. He wished he could draw it into his soul. He was about to tell Martine what had transpired when he spied Father Alphonse walking into the dining room.

"Father, join us. You must hear this also." Defont continued without fanfare. "Greatcoat was right. Sven Yorick was a priest."

Martine was surprised by the statement. "What do you mean 'was?'" His worst suspicions were about to unfold. Edmund had done away with the prisoner.

"There was a Father Yorick. Unfortunately, he was gassed and cremated in some extermination camp in Poland during the war. The man we know as Yorick is Untersturmfuhrer Heinz Streck. A member of the SS."

Alphonse crossed himself and bowed his head.

Martine's eyes widened. His mouth hung open, but for once he was silent.

"There are maybe a hundred priests scattered throughout Europe and South America who died in the camps. Their identities were taken over by a group of men who serve several masters—one being someone called Gaston."

"That's incredible," Martine exclaimed. "It can't be true."

"Yor . . . Streck has no reason to lie. What he told me today was the truth."

"How can you be sure? Yesterday you refused to believe anything he said," Martine interjected angrily.

"Yesterday I refused to believe a priest could come into this place and commit murder. Those beliefs have been proven correct. Streck is as Greatcoat said—a German, a Nazi, a traitor who escaped punishment for his crimes during the war by assuming the identity of a priest he knew was dead. It was no accident Father Yorick was arrested in Norway and shipped to a camp in Poland. He was chosen deliberately. He served in a small community. Was unknown outside his parish. Like hundreds of others, he was systematically eliminated so war criminals could, if and when the day came, escape.

"That day came, but Streck did not escape. Trapped behind Russian lines, he transformed himself into Yorick and convinced the priests at St. Basil he was one of them. When he could, he contacted Gaston to get him out of his predicament. We caught him before he could escape."

Martine twisted and squirmed until finally he had to turn away from Defont's burning gaze.

"Who else is involved in this hideous plot?" Alphonse asked.

"The only person Streck made contact with was Gaston. If anyone else is involved, he doesn't know who they are. He couldn't even tell me who Gaston was."

Alphonse stared at Defont. He knew who Gaston was, but the pain in his heart would not allow him to share the information he had. How? How could a Cardinal, a prince of the church be involved in these hideous plots? What possible reason could Gaston have to make a pact with the devil?

Alphonse's pain was obvious. His shame stayed hidden. "Who do you suspect Gaston might be?" he finally asked Defont.

"If I didn't know better," Defont said hesitantly, "I'd swear Yorick was speaking of a priest. I don't see how anyone outside of the church could have arranged this. But I can't understand why anyone in the church would get involved with someone as foul as Yor . . . Streck."

Alphonse nodded his head. "I must go. I have work to do." He had to leave before Defont asked him if he knew who Gaston was. It would be difficult to lie.

Both men watched their new abbot leave with a gait much slower than that Alphonse had possessed earlier in the day.

"You suspect Gaston is a priest?" Martine asked, surprised he found it hard to believe.

"I don't know. I do know I'll never find out from Yorick. But it wouldn't surprise me. The more I hear of things that happened outside these walls, the less shocked I am."

Martine sipped his coffee. It was cold. He took the time to refill it before questioning Defont further. "What else did you learn from this fellow, Streck?"

"He was led to believe Bronski had requested." Defont stopped and let out a breath of air. "That Bronski would assist him in this murder. That Bronski had asked for someone to come and kill the Jews."

"Kill the Jews," Martine commented. Almost as an afterthought he whispered, "Two women and a child."

Defont looked surprised. "Is Adam a Jew? I've never thought of him as such."

"Well, he must be. At least half-Jewish. Sabina was. David was French." Martine thought about what he had said. "He doesn't look like any Jew I've ever known."

"Was Jesus Christ a Jew?" Defont asked well aware the Bible was specific on that point. "Is the Catholic Church ready to accept a Jew or even a half-Jew as their rightful leader?"

The solution Martine had received as an inspired thought last week suddenly blew up in his face. Still, he was not ready to give up on the Inquisition just yet.

"I don't think he's a Jew," he said without much conviction. "How could anyone prove he is?"

"Why don't we just say his father was French and we don't know the nationality of his mother?" Defont's sarcasm was blatant. "Come now, François. You're clutching at straws. You can't deny a person their birthright, Jewish or not."

Martine rubbed his chin. "No, I don't think he is a Jew," he finally said.

"No, and I'm not French. And you're Polish."

"Listen. David said the seed, the ovum were genetically transplanted into the Chosen People. If," Martine rubbed his temples, "if Adam is the Son of God—not the God of Christians, but the son of a God who traveled here and implanted his genetic make-up into the Chosen People—the Jews—then Adam would not be Jewish. And, for that matter, not French. David did not impregnate Sabina. Not in the way to which we are accustomed. He merely awoke some primitive instinct in her that allowed Adam to be conceived. If you or I had impregnated her, the traits of our genes and hers would have produced a child with both of our characteristics prominently obvious."

"And you believe this is possible?" Defont asked, growing confused and bewildered at Martine's logic.

"I didn't believe an Immaculate Conception was possible until I witnessed one."

"But Adam bears a striking resemblance, not only to David and Michael, but to the others entombed in the catacombs. How do you explain that?"

"I can't. No, wait. Yes, I can. Antoine told us he had met David's father and there was absolutely no family resemblance between father and son. We talked of this some time ago. There are two Chosen People on this earth," Martine said exuberantly. "Two. One to stimulate God's conception. The other to carry His likeness. David claimed he was the angel of God. The Jews claim to be God's Chosen People. Without each other, God could not be born."

"He did say that," Defont said excitedly. "I remember now. We were sitting right here. You may be right, François. You may actually be right for a change."

"I am right and we will prove Adam is . . ." He let the sentence trail off, closed his eyes and expelled a gust of air. "That Adam, like Christ, is God himself."

Defont could not believe his ears. Over the years Martine had come up with some bizarre statements, but this one went beyond the realm of unbelievability to the edge of complete insanity.

"Do you hear what you are saying, François?"

"Of course."

"Where do you get these thoughts? How can you now claim Adam is God when just a few minutes ago you were convinced he was the Son of God?"

Defont was incredulous.

"Divine intervention. I think, not just for a moment or two each day like you, but every minute," Martine said, his voice rising to a fever pitch.

Father Ehrick came out of the kitchen. He had heard bits and pieces of Martine's and Defont's conversation. It was nothing new. The two men had been discussing or arguing about Adam for years. But something Martine had just said struck a chord in him. Like the other priests, he had debated within himself who or what Adam might or might not be. Of all the brothers, he had spent the most time with the boy. Sabina had brought him with her to the kitchen each morning. As Adam had grown older and wiser, Ehrick had had many conversations with the boy. Conversations that, at times, pressed the edges of reality beyond his limited imagination, but he had never discouraged Adam from talking. From expressing himself honestly. He had grown to love the boy and accept him.

Like all men of religion, Ehrick had studied the Bible searching for the grain of truth that would solidify his beliefs. For most of his adult life, he had simply accepted the Immaculate Conception as fact, just as he had the Holy Trinity—the Father, the Son and the Holy Ghost.

He joined the gladiators at their table. Their arguments were always open to anyone who passed. For the most part, the brothers usually avoided them. Who had time to debate the unknown?

"What you just said, Doctor, about Adam being God and not the Son of God. How did you reach your conclusion?"

"From what David told us. Forget what you know about Christ's conception, Ehrick. David said God, a being he claims was just a man, created a Chosen race—the Jews. Specifically, the women of the Jewish race. David also said God implanted in these women unique ovum so when these women were stimulated by the other Chosen race, God would be born.

"Don't you see. God wasn't implanting his son, but himself. The Father and the Son. One being, yet separated. Add the Holy Spirit and the knowledge it possesses and what have you? One person. One name. God."

Defont and Ehrick stared silently at their educator. Martine continued to hold class.

"When do we receive the Holy Spirit?" Martine asked, and then answered his own question. "At our confirmation. At age thirteen. At that age we are supposed to receive the knowledge of the Trinity."

"What you're saying is, Christ, when He told the apostles the Holy Spirit would ascend upon them was, in reality, saying the Holy Spirit had ascended upon Him. His knowledge was complete. From that grew our rite of confirmation," Ehrick said.

"But when He made that statement, He was older than thirteen," Defont said, unwilling to sit by silently.

"Well, that does leave the possibility time has disrupted the order in which God became God. It is possible the apostles misunderstood what Christ was saying and because of their mistake, assumed all children, as most did during their lifetimes, became men at thirteen. It might well be God will . . ." Martine took the time to correct himself. "That Adam will not know exactly what or who he is until a much later age. Say thirty . . . or any age."

Martine pinched his thumb and finger together as if trying to keep the idea he was expressing from escaping the room. "The rituals of the Catholic Church have been shaped to the times, not to the facts. Am I now correct, Father Ehrick?"

"Yes, you are, Doctor. It is no secret. Do you have a theory on how this came about?"

"If we can allow ourselves to believe just one fact—and yes, Edmund, before you jump all over me, I've said it many times before and even changed the way I've thought about it, but I've never quite gotten it out of my system. We have to believe God came here from somewhere out in the universe. He came here with others to create, to establish His own image in a race of peoples. A civilization. The Bible states this as a fact. God created man in His image."

Defont nodded in agreement.

"Yes, that's true. We believe that," Ehrick agreed.

"Then, it becomes all so obvious. We must forget time as we know it today. Over the course of eons, God was able to take the creatures he found here on earth and implant in them the unique seeds of his kind that would carry and produce his distinct effigy. In other words, infants born in *His own image*. It didn't happen in a few years, but over a long period of time. Maybe a thousand years. Maybe longer. The Bible says Methuselah lived to be 800 years old. God, being infinitely wiser than us, knew if He were to reappear, He could not do so knowing, or rather having the knowledge He possesses immediately. In most cases, a child born who could relate to adults would be branded a demon of some sort and probably put to death. We have already witnessed this as fact. So God genetically devised a method where, over a period of time, His knowledge came into play. Again, Adam is a perfect example. Each year we have watched him grow mentally. Not alarmingly so, but far beyond that of what most of us are capable."

"You're saying we are all children of God, or at least of the creatures created in His image?" Ehrick questioned.

"Yes, we are the images of God. Diluted over an expanse of time but, yes, we are what He created. And His exact image may be found in Adam."

"We are all related to one man," Ehrick said.

"No. David said there were many more who came with God. Even in the Bible, Adam and Eve had two sons who went out and multiplied to create a new race. Where did their wives come from? Who were they? They were the offspring of God's companions. They were the travelers who came here in a time before our imagination. We know we cannot closely interbreed without causing a multitude of imperfections that would eventually kill our kind. God must have known this too, and so came prepared to correct this problem. There may have been thousands of fellow travelers who arrived here." Martine sat back exhausted, but pleased with himself.

"Your theories are most interesting," Ehrick said. "Worth more thought."

Defont said nothing. As far as he was concerned, it had all been said.

CHAPTER THIRTY-TWO

Andre Proust closed his eyes against the sights outside the train too ghastly to see. Warsaw had virtually been destroyed during the last war. Building after building resembled crumbling anthills, the Poles paralleling the industrious insects. Workers searched for bricks, for any materials still whole, hoping to rebuild. And it had not only been Warsaw. Berlin and almost every other small village or town the train rumbled through had been destroyed—inhabited now by the insects man had become.

It had taken Andre almost three months to get a visa from the Polish government. Considering all that had happened in the country, it was not a long time. The Iron Curtain had descended over Eastern Europe. Movement east, but more particularly west, became relatively easy. Refugees poured out of the Balkans in search of freedom—in search of food.

In the minds of people like Churchill and Truman, the communists had gained a chokehold on the conquered nations of Eastern Europe, but that was the only place such domination existed. The communists had very little control over their captives; however, enough to benefit the war-torn continent. Most of the second-rate nations ceased their petty hostilities towards one another. Miraculously, the communists managed to incorporate Europe into one vast homogeneous state. A house built of cards as history would prove.

What did it matter? Meric had told him where David was. Where David's body was buried. Now all he had to do was retrieve his brother and bring him back to France. How difficult could that be? Still, he could not help but wonder. Why had Cardinal Gaston not told him where to find David? Andre was sure the man knew.

Opening his eyes, he glanced out the window. The city, the ruins, had disappeared. Farms and trees had replaced the people who resembled ants. Mountains loomed in the distance.

"Litz. The last I heard, it had been destroyed. Burnt to the ground," the stationmaster told him. "Why do you want to travel there anyway?"

Andre did not bother to answer. "The chargé d'affaires in Paris said it

323

was in the mountains. I have permission to travel there, do I not?"

"Yes. It is very far in the mountains. You must go south from this direction. There is nothing there to see, Monsieur." The stationmaster tried to be polite.

"Thank you, but I must go. I have to see Litz for myself," Andre finally explained. "My brother is buried there and I want to take him home."

The stationmaster looked Andre over closely. This man certainly did not talk like a communist. "What was your brother doing in Litz?"

"He was a priest," Andre said with pride.

Instantly, the stationmaster's attitude changed as if he had just pocketed a sizable bribe. He scribbled something on a piece of paper and handed it to Andre Proust.

"Take this to the building at the end of this street, Monsieur. You can't miss it. Give it to the man there. He will be able to help you get to Litz."

***

From just outside the railway depot, Andre found he could make out a large building in the distance. It reminded him of a church without a bell tower. As he got closer, he realized it had been a church at one time. Fire, or maybe bombs had reduced it to rubble. Only the outer walls were still standing—for the moment.

An elderly man met him at a makeshift door. He was blocking the entrance, but Andre could see over his shoulder. An altar, not a grand or glorious one that reached to the heavens, but a table with a crucifix sat in the middle of an empty room. For a moment, Andre thought he would be denied entrance, but after handing the paper to the old man and watching him quickly read it, he was shown into the church.

"We have to be careful nowadays," the old man said. "Please follow me."

They walked through the church's scarred remains as reverently as through any large cathedral Andre had ever visited, but this one seemed to possess the strength its gilt-covered affiliates lacked. It had been put together with the remains of ruins—the bricks placed one on top of another without mortar. Without proper nuts and bolts, corrugated tin and planks of wood became dividing walls when held in place by rope. It had been built by a people who had not given up hope. By a faith that refused to surrender.

From the rear of the makeshift church another building stood intact, posing as a sentinel for the illicit cathedral.

"This is our school," the old man explained. "At least it was spared the torch. You may stay here until I can arrange transportation for you. A day or two at the most."

They climbed the stairs to the second floor. The small room contained a bed and a small wash basin resting on a wooden crate.

"The bathroom is at the end of the hall. Sometimes the lights work. Sometimes they don't. Don't be alarmed if they go out at night."

"Thank you," Andre said, and reached into his pocket. "How much do I owe you?"

"Your brother served at the Institut. I have no need of your money. It is my pleasure to give you the room free."

Andre blinked. This was a far different attitude than the one with which he had been confronted when he first approached the building. He blinked again. He had not mentioned his brother had served at the Institut, yet this man before him made the statement as if he had known David. It was not a point he could argue. He was not sure if David had served at this institute, but the old man's words lifted his spirits. At least he was on the right track.

"Thank you."

"Are you hungry?"

"A little, but I can wait."

The old man shook his head, denying Andre's refusal. "I'll send something up to eat. It won't be much, but it will fill your stomach for the night."

Alone in the room, Andre put his valise on the floor and sat down on the bed. The springs creaked.

"Why didn't you ask if there was a hotel, you fool?" he berated himself. The village was fairly large. Surely large enough to support a hotel.

He walked to the window. Putting up the shade, he glanced outside at yet another building which stood intact. Dirty and difficult to see through, Andre started to wipe the window clean, but thought better of it. It was probably dirty for a reason. He laughed, feeling sinister and mysterious—a spy behind the Iron Curtain. A clown in a dilapidated building with dirty windows.

A knock on the door pulled him away from his fictional musings. An older woman, probably the old man's wife, entered and handed him a plate of sausage, potatoes, and cabbage. Again, Andre offered to pay, but she refused to take his money. Hungrier than he had thought, he ate his supper and, as the old man had said, it filled his stomach.

There was no place to sit, so he lay down on the bed. It was cold in the room, although not cold enough for a fire. The chill of Poland's mid-October brought a brisk, healthy glow to one's skin, not like the blizzards that would all too soon isolate the country and frostbite the unwary. Andre's brief glimpse of the mountains had revealed their snow covered peaks, and made him glad he had packed an overcoat.

Why would you come to a place like this, David? Why would you be a priest? Questions of his brother occupied his thoughts.

He had always gotten along with his brother. It simply could not be helped. David had been one of those special people—likeable, friendly. Being only a year apart, they had grown up together. Yet Andre knew little of David. During their school year, David had excelled at sports. He had studied little, but had never failed. It was as though he always knew the answers in advance. Conversely, he had had to study hard, spending many long hours memorizing what he needed to know.

After David graduated high school, it came as a surprise to everyone when he had announced he was going into the seminary.

Andre should have known. He should have guessed. David had seldom, if ever, been seen with a young lady. Not that they hadn't been ready, willing, and able to accompany his brother wherever he might go. David had always been too interested in sports. Or was that just his excuse?

After that, David never returned home for more than a few days. He was always on the go. Studying. Learning.

Andre had found his years of labor early in life had paid off as he entered the university. He sometimes thought a block had been lifted from his brain. Suddenly, he did not need to study *quite* as hard, but it was a habit he had acquired while young and one he did not deny. As a result, he excelled.

He had dated, but never seriously. He was not the most handsome of men, looking just like his father—short and squat, fighting a midriff bulge since his early twenties, sporting a dark complexion and the temper to match. Then he'd met Malett. She had captivated his heart and won his confidence.

What a change that had been for Andre! David had always been the handsome one. There had been fleeting glimpses of sibling rivalry where he envied David. More often, he had been happy to just be in his brother's presence. He had never told David about his feelings, and now it was too late to feel anything.

***

"Monsieur Proust," the old man woke him gently. The morning was cold. "We have your transportation."

Andre struggled to open his eyes.

"I took the liberty of bringing you some hot coffee, Monsieur. Your automobile leaves in half an hour. Please, get up."

Andre struggled out of bed. Wrinkled and disheveled after falling asleep in his clothes, he pushed the hair out of his face and reached for the coffee. "I'm up. Thank you."

"When you're ready, come downstairs. The auto will be here soon."

"Yes, I will. Thank you."

Andre finished his coffee and straightened himself out the best he could, brushing his hair, and wishing he had time to shave. As the chill of the morning seeped into his bones, he retrieved his topcoat from his suitcase. Before leaving the room, he left a $10 bill on the bed.

Downstairs, the old man introduced him to his driver. Andre could not help but wonder how someone came to possess such a strange name as Greatcoat, but from the size of the man and the ferocious look on his driver's face, he did not bother to question the christening.

Greatcoat took his suitcase and threw it in the trunk. Reaching for the back door, Andre was startled to find he had company for the ride. What did he care? He supposed getting back and forth to Litz was not as easy as getting around LaRochelle. Or the rest of Europe for that matter. It was even possible he would enjoy the company. Resigned to the adventure, he climbed into the front seat.

"Good morning," he said to the younger man.

"How do you do?"

"Are you going to Litz also?"

"Yes, we are."

For the first time, Andre realized what he had taken for a rank bedroll was another passenger—old and tired and grayer in complexion than the dirty blanket in which he was wrapped. Immediately, he grew silent. The old man was sound asleep.

Greatcoat started the car and, with a jerk and a roar, the vehicle departed the village and headed into the wilds of Poland.

"How long will it take to reach Litz?" Andre asked Greatcoat, his voice low so as not to awaken his fellow passenger.

"Two, maybe three hours. It depends on the condition of the road."

The car sped past what little was left of level ground and began its arduous climb into the Carpathian Mountains.

"Why are you going to Litz?" Greatcoat asked Andre. "You're not a priest."

"No. I'm going to get my brother and my uncle, I hope."

"They're in Litz?" Greatcoat was surprised. He knew everyone in the village.

"I don't really know. I was told they were in the Institut."

"They are priests?"

"They were. They're both dead."

Greatcoat crossed himself. "Then they have peace."

They drove for a while, Andre biting the inside of his cheek at the reckless manner in which Greatcoat sped up the twisting road.

"What's your brother's name?" Greatcoat growled through the silence.

"Father David Proust."

Greatcoat laughed.

"What could you possibly find humorous in that?" It was bad enough that his driver possessed no sense of caution when driving or that he looked like a demon from Hell, but his lack of respect for the priesthood was unconscionable!

"The priests in the Institut—they are crazy. Like him." Greatcoat nodded towards the sleeping man in the back seat.

Andre turned and looked at the young man. "You're a priest?"

"Yes. I am Father Versie. My companion's name is Father Dubich." The young man's voice softened. "He's not crazy, Monsieur. Just old and tired."

Andre glared at Greatcoat. Did this bear of a man have no manners?

"To go to the Institut, you must be crazy," Greatcoat repeated. "They're all crazy there."

Versie reached over and touched Andre's shoulder. "Don't pay any attention to him."

"Then why are you going to the Institut?" Andre asked hesitantly. Instinctively, he felt this could be a dangerous conversation.

"I'm accompanying my friend, Father Dubich. Also, to help the others."

"Yes, and in time, you will be as crazy as they are," Greatcoat prophesied.

"Why do you dislike the men who go to the Institut?" Andre demanded of his driver.

"Me? Dislike the priests of the Institut?" Greatcoat could not help but laugh at the arrogant righteousness of his passenger. When men did not understand, it made them fools. "I like them! Even more, I have a great deal of respect for them. Everyone does. They are the true disciples of Christ."

"But from the way you were talking—saying they were crazy," Andre shrugged.

"They are. That doesn't mean I can't like them. Let me tell you, Monsieur. The priests at the Institut live like hermits—freezing in the winter, plagued by insects in the summer. Do they complain? Do they try to change things?" Greatcoat shook his head and laughed again. "No. As I said, they're crazy."

Inside his topcoat, Andre sat up a little straighter. It was not as he had first thought. It was not as this lunatic driver said. David had not been crazy.

***

Hours of traveling around one curve and into the wind, around the next curve with the wind to the back, around another curve and feeling the wind slowly push the automobile into a slow skid corrected by the next curve miraculously taken at the proper moment, had brought Andre to Litz. Snow lined the streets of the village and covered the mountains. In the distance, the foundation structures of the Institut materialized slowly in the low clouds, coming into focus like a pointillist painting done in shades of gray. A shroud of ashen sky covered the battlements of the institution.

Impatiently, Greatcoat honked the horn twice and then again, giving the caretakers of this place little time to accommodate him, Andre thought. He was in no hurry to see what was on the other side of the wall. Before him, the icons of his church were etched in stone. Gabriel stood atop the devil. It gave Andre a false sense of security.

The gates swung open, and Greatcoat slowly pulled his car inside, creeping by inches past the invisible barrier of the Institut's boundary line.

Father Versie helped his friend from the back seat of the car. Instantly, a black-robed priest ran to give him a hand. Greatcoat opened his door and yelled, "Father Emil, I have one more for you."

He turned to Andre. "This is not a place in which to linger. Get your business finished as quickly as possible. Maybe I can take you back to town."

Ignoring his driver's warning, Andre got out of the car. The automobile backed up and out of the courtyard. On appropriately loud hinges, the gates slowly closed, engulfing Andre in their shadows.

Father Emil approached.

"I've come to see Abbot Bronski," Andre said, obeying Bishop Meric's earlier directives.

"I'm sorry," Emil said. "Abbot Bronski is no longer with us. You must leave." He walked to the gate and opened it just enough for a solitary man to escape.

Andre would have none of it. "Who is in charge here?" he demanded.

"Is there something I can do for you?" Emil's voice returned steel to steel. "I do not wish to sound rude, but we simply don't allow visitors here."

Andre calmed down. "I understand Father, but I am not a visitor. I have come to see . . . whoever . . . about my brother, Father David Proust."

The change in Father Emil was evident. He closed the gate immediately. Slipping the chain through the rings, he locked Andre away from the world.

CHAPTER THIRTY-THREE

Andre stood in the foyer. He was cold and tired. His hand hurt from holding his valise, but he was not comfortable enough, did not feel *welcome* enough to set it on the floor. Asking him to wait, Father Emil had disappeared down the corridor.

A black robed priest walked by, smiled, and nodded hello. On the surface, Andre immediately felt better, although his inner anxieties remained. What had David been doing in this place? What was *he* doing in this place? Restlessly, he fidgeted with his regrets. He should have stopped his search. He would have, had Gaston not been such a pompous idiot. If only the Cardinal had not lied. If only he had gone to see someone else. Someone who honestly had no idea where David had been buried. Perhaps he would not be standing in the middle of a cold entranceway of some primeval fortress wondering what was going on?

Meric's parting words to the younger Proust echoed through his mind. "*It is the church.*"

"*It's an asylum. You know, for the insane.*" Greatcoat's description of the place to which the church had exiled his brother rang truer now than it had in the car.

Andre did not know why David had been sent to this place. He only knew he did not belong, and he wanted very much to leave. He did not see the priest come up behind him.

"Monsieur."

At least the voice was friendly, Andre thought as he turned to meet his host.

"I am Father Alphonse, the abbot here. How may I help you?"

"I, I . . . , Andre stammered, not quite sure how to begin his request. "I've come for my brother," he finally blurted.

Alphonse showed his surprise. "Your brother is a patient here?"

"Yes. No. Rather, he was. He passed away in 1939."

"I'm sorry, Monsieur. I do not know your name?"

"Andre Proust."

Alphonse remembered his manners. "Please, there is no reason for us to be standing here in the cold. If you will come with me, we can sit in the dining room and have a cup of coffee. You may leave you bag here. It will be safe," he said with a smile.

"Oh yes, thank you." Andre set his luggage against the wall. Exhausted, he followed the abbot *(what choice do I have?)*, his hard-soled shoes making tiny echoes that chased him down the long hall.

The dining room was empty. "Please have a seat, Monsieur. I will be right back with the coffee. How would you like yours?"

"Black would be fine, Father. Thank you."

Alphonse returned with two steaming cups of coffee and sat across from Andre where he could watch the young man's face. Where he could hide his own in the shadows if need be.

"You said your name was Andre Proust?"

"Yes."

"And you say you have come for your brother? What was his name?"

Alphonse quietly studied the young man over the rim of his coffee cup. He disliked deception, but it was necessary to protect the reputations of the men who came here—even from their families.

"David."

"David Proust? You have information David Proust is, or was here in some capacity in 1939?"

Andre felt a familiar sinking feeling. Was this to be yet another wild goose chase? Another lie? The frustration, the curses that rose in his throat were swallowed like a first love's rebuff. He showed no emotion when he answered the abbot's question. "That's correct."

Alphonse pretended not to understand. "You say your brother was a priest?"

Andre sipped his coffee, trying to control his temper. When at last he believed he could sound civil, he put the cup down. "Yes, David was a priest. I was told he had been transferred here."

"And on whose recommendation have you traveled so far, Monsieur Proust?"

"Bishop Meric of LaRochelle, France."

Andre pulled out the letters that had begun this bizarre chase and handed them to the abbot. "Maybe these will help."

In a completely unnecessary gesture, Alphonse read both notices.

"According to these two letters, Monsieur Proust, two members of your family were priests."

"Yes, and I would like to take them both back to France with me to be laid to rest beside my mother and father. It was my father's last request in life."

Handing back the letters, Alphonse shook his head with great sorrow. "I do not know why Bishop Meric would send you here. I cannot even fathom how he came to be under the delusion your brother, and possibly your uncle, had come to the Institut. The priests who come here are, for the most part, old and sick with no other place to go. Or they are like myself, a poor priest who has come to serve the needs of the sufferers. I cannot recall ever having a David Proust here. He was not old?"

"No, David was . . . he was thirty-five when he died."

"I am so sorry, Monsieur. Both for the death of your brother and that you have traveled all this way for nothing. There is no David Proust here. You have been misinformed."

Andre slumped, defeated. "Why would Bishop Meric tell me my brother was here if he were not?"

"I'm afraid I cannot answer such a question. Obviously, the Bishop must have been misinformed."

"I've traveled a long way. I've buried my father and been led to believe my brother has vanished from the face of the earth by the very people he served. By his church. I know I have been deceived by a Cardinal in the Vatican. Am I to believe Bishop Meric also lied to me?"

Alphonse's eyes widened.

"Why? I only wanted to fulfill my father's dying wish." Andre stared at the priest across from him. "Why? Why is the church hiding my brother and my uncle?"

Alphonse shrugged and spread his hands in a gesture symbolic of support, of assistance. If Andre Proust only knew how much he really was trying to help.

"Again, I am sorry, Monsieur. I wish I had an answer for you, but unfortunately . . ."

"I'm sorry, too, Father. I didn't mean to burden you with my problems." Andre rose to leave. "I won't take any more of your time."

"I am afraid you must," Alphonse began. "It will be necessary for you to stay overnight. Greatcoat will not be returning to Sanok until tomorrow morning and there is no other place to stay in the vicinity. I hope this will not inconvenience you too much."

Andre smiled, and gratefully sat back down. "No. As a matter of fact, it doesn't. I'm really too tried to travel any more today. I'll be more than happy to pay for my board."

"That will not be necessary, Monsieur Proust. We are happy to be of service. I know that our meeting has not brought you the results for which you had hoped. It is easy to see your disappointment, but you will feel better in the morning.

"I have taken the liberty of having a room prepared for you. If you would just follow me, I'll show you where you will sleep tonight." Alphonse hesitated. "You mentioned a Cardinal? Do you remember his name?" He tried not to sound too interested.

"Cardinal Gaston," Andre said absently. He was looking at a woman, an apparition of femininity in the middle of an insane asylum for priests! It was hard to determine her age, but she was young—of that he was sure. The dress she wore was long and plain, of coarse material, and she had swathed her head in the same fabric. Immediately, he found himself wondering about the color of her hair.

She glanced at him, and smiled for a moment before disappearing back into the kitchen.

Alphonse led Andre to a small room nearest the vestibule. "You can stay here tonight. I must ask you to confine yourself here or to the dining room."

Andre looked at him quizzically.

"It is not a sinister request, Monsieur Proust. It is only meant to spare you the agony of our brothers, and them, the embarrassment of being seen by strangers."

"No, I don't mind at all. I appreciate your hospitality."

Alphonse closed the door as he left the room.

***

"Cardinal Gaston." Alphonse had now heard the name from three different people. Bronski, Defont who, having heard it from Yorick was unaware that the man his prisoner condemned was a Cardinal, and now Andre Proust. He had said nothing of Bronski's note or preparations for suicide to the others. For the moment, he was the only one who knew Gaston's true identity. The others would know soon enough. He had written the pontiff requesting an Inquisition into the deaths of Abbot Bronski and Sabina and into the stature of the young man called Adam. His request had been carried to Rome by Father Michalowski with instructions that it was to be personally delivered to His Eminence. Greatcoat had brought His Holiness' reply.

In a matter of weeks now, the Inquisitors were scheduled to arrive and begin their investigation. Andre Proust's arrival had thrown the wheel out of sync. Alphonse had hated to deceive the young man, but could think of no other way to spare him from the blackness his family possessed. He sought out Dr. Martine for advice on the matter and found him making a cursory examination of their new arrival, Father Dubich.

"As Father Curvise stated, he is without any resemblance to David."

For a brief moment, Alphonse's words solidified Martine's claims about Adam. Like most of the other priests in the Institut, Alphonse had tried to stay away from the controversy surrounding Adam. He had been more than willing to add his opinion to the many discussions that had occurred over the years, but never with any true conviction. Adam was an exceptional youngster, but whether his genius came from genetics as Dr. Martine claimed, or from the environment surrounding him as Bronski had argued, was still anyone's guess.

Alphonse's main concern now, was to keep his attitude neutral. He could not, and would not, allow himself to fall into the same trap as his friend Zigman. His letter to the pontiff had come after much deliberation. Like Defont and Martine, he could not envision keeping Adam and Urbana at the Institut forever, but the rules here were firm and ancient. He could not defy them without proper authority. Even though he did not agree with Dr. Martine's way, he had been able to find no alternative. His only wish was that Adam would be found to be a genius of nature and allowed to go on his way.

Martine was incredulous. "How did he find out David was here?"

"Does the name Bishop Meric mean anything to you, François?"

"Yes. It was Meric who told Defont and I where Antoine had been sent." Martine shook his head. "He believed he had a reason to send us here. But why would he sentence David's brother to this place?"

"He hasn't yet. Andre Proust will leave in the morning with Greatcoat." Alphonse explained what he had told Andre earlier. "I did what was best for him, François. He is searching for his brother and his uncle. He has not found them. Tomorrow he will leave."

"Yes," Martine agreed. "Have you told the others?"

"Father Emil is passing the word as we speak. No mention of David or Michael will come from anyone here."

A far away look entered Martine's eyes. He longed to hear of France. Of his homeland. Alphonse noticed the melancholy expression of his companion.

"You may speak to Andre about France if you wish, Doctor. We don't wish to make him feel unwanted. You and I both know it is for the best that nothing of our activities or our . . ." Alphonse hesitated while he searched for the proper word ". . . problem is discussed."

Martine was suddenly excited. "I will say nothing, Alphonse." He closed his medical bag, his examination of Father Dubich complete. He was anxious to meet David's brother.

"At supper you and Edmund will have an opportunity to converse with Monsieur Proust."

***

Alphonse escorted Andre into the dining room. Martine and Defont stared in surprise at the newcomer, both of their thoughts singularly on Antoine Curvise and his description of David and Andre's father. *"There is absolutely no similarity."*

"Monsieur Proust, I would like you to meet our physician, Dr. François Martine and Brother Edmund Defont. They are countrymen of yours." Alphonse then introduced Father Ehrick.

"Please join us, Monsieur Proust," Martine invited.

"Andre, please," Proust said as he joined the men, shaking hands all around.

"I will leave you gentlemen to discuss France," Alphonse said courteously. "Come Father Ehrick. This is no place for us." The two priests departed, glad to be away from the expatriated trio.

"Father Alphonse tells us you have come from France." Martine hoped he did not sound too eager.

"I was born in France, although I no longer claim it as my country." Andre's comment was without disdain.

"But you are French, are you not?" Edmund watched Andre's confirming nod. "Then what you say is impossible."

Andre smiled, but Martine would not allow him time for a defense.

"You do not just say you are not French! A Frenchman is a Frenchman forever." Instantly, he decided he had little regard for David's brother.

"I'm sorry if I offended you, Doctor, but I now live in America. In the United States. I consider myself an American."

"You've given up your French citizenship?" It was Defont's turn to be aghast.

Andre laughed. It was something he had not done in quite some time. "Obviously you gentlemen have retained your loyalty to France. I am sorry. I certainly did not mean to insult you, but I left France in 1939 and returned only this year to bury my father."

"Hmm," Martine grunted. "So you are an American."

"Yes. It's not as bad as you make it sound."

"Could you not have kept both citizenships?"

335

"I suppose so, but I don't intend to serve two masters, Doctor. When I left for the United States and found out what a great country America really was . . ." Andre shrugged. "I have no fond memories of France."

Martine sighed heavily.

"You like living in America?" Defont asked.

"Very much. It's a great place to live and raise a family. It's young and growing and proud of its accomplishments."

"Raise a family? Are you married?" Defont was doing his best to keep François from the conversation.

"I was. My family was killed in an automobile accident." The conversation dragged as painful memories swept over Andre.

"I am sorry, Monsieur." Defont was the first to break the silence. Knowing what it was like to lose a wife, he could only imagine what it might be like to also lose one's children.

Martine's sadness was felt on an entirely different level. Andre's revelation had not been lost on the doctor. The chain was broken. The Proust family no longer carried the mark of the messenger. The angel was dead.

Suddenly, it became even more important for Adam to be recognized by the church. For Adam to remain alive. Realizing an expression of sympathy was expected, Martine chimed, "You have my condolences also, Monsieur Proust."

"Thank you, Doctor."

The need to talk of something else caused Andre to change the subject. "Did either of you know my brother, David Proust?" He had not intended to spring this question on Defont and Martine, but it was now the only thing that occupied his mind.

Martine had already cautioned Defont about remaining silent on this subject.

"No," he replied, answering calmly and without hesitation for himself and Defont. It was Edmund who blinked.

"Where did you live in France, Doctor? And you, Brother Defont?"

Once again Martine rose to the challenge. It was obvious to him Edmund was not holding up well under the lies.

"We lived in Paris."

"The one redeeming feature of France," Andre said almost with affection. "Paris."

"You are very hard on France," Martine snapped. His temper was beginning to rise. "Has she been that cruel to you?"

"Yes, Doctor. Suffice it to say she has been very cruel."

Interrupting the display of derisive tempers, Urbana came out of the kitchen carrying a tureen. Once again, Andre was surprised by her appearance. He watched as she served the stew.

She avoided his eyes, but her face carried a gentle smile. No one made a move to introduce the two strangers.

Father Ehrick entered the room with a large tray of freshly baked bread which he set before Andre in a grand gesture. "I hope you enjoy our simple fare, Monsieur Proust."

"Thank you. I am sure I will."

But Father Ehrick did not go away. As always, with strangers, he waited for Andre to taste his cooking.

Always hungry, Defont began to eat immediately. When he noticed the others had not started their meal, he motioned to Andre with his empty spoon. "Please Monsieur Proust. Taste Father Ehrick's stew and tell him what you think of it. He has so few outside connoisseurs."

Andre looked up at the smiling priest—the angelic, eager face. Were they trying to poison him? Of course not! All the bowls had been filled from the same tureen. He would have to stop these frightful fantasies.

Dipping his spoon into the hot savory stew he tasted it gingerly. "This is very good." He took another spoonful and repeated his praise.

Ehrick's smile magnified tenfold as he enjoyed the compliment. They came so infrequently. "Thank you, Monsieur," he said before hurrying back to the kitchen.

Martine picked at his stew.

"You aren't enjoying your meal, Doctor. I hope our conversation hasn't upset your appetite."

"It was adequate ten years ago. Now it is just something to fill my stomach." The significance of Martine's words were lost on Andre.

Singly and in pairs, the priests filtered into the dining room and sat down to their supper. The three men ate in silence until each was full. Defont wiped his bowl with the last of the bread.

Reveling in Andre's compliment, Ehrick poured his guest a cup of coffee and brought it to the table. "Would you care for more?"

"I would, but I'm afraid I have no room."

Ehrick sighed and glanced at Martine who had left more than half his dinner uneaten. He had yet to please the doctor with his cooking skills.

Andre picked up his coffee and was about to take a sip when his eyes suddenly widened. He sat mesmerized, the cup frozen halfway between the saucer and his lips. Their backs to the kitchen, Martine and Defont glanced around to see what had captured their visitor's attention.

"Robert," Andre murmured. It could not be! He was in a hospital, an asylum in the middle of nowhere seeing an exact replica of his dead son.

Ehrick invited the boy over. "Adam, please join us. I have someone I would like you to meet."

Andre became frightened. His son, his son at age ten was walking towards him. His dead son was smiling, his bright blue eyes friendly and inquisitive. It could not be!

The cup fell from his hand and clattered on the wooden table.

Ehrick was quick to wipe up the spill with his apron. "Are you all right, Monsieur Proust?" he asked solicitously.

Andre did not hear him.

Martine reached across the table and grabbed the American's hand. "Monsieur Proust. Andre."

Their eyes met. Andre's were filled with anger—Martine's with pity.

"You lied to me! All of you lied to me. My brother is here." Andre reached out and touched the boy who now stood beside him. Tears ran down his cheeks. He was not looking at his dead son, he realized at last, but at his brother's son. David's son!

The commotion drew Urbana from the kitchen to the trio's table. Instinctively, she knew the cause of the disturbance. "Adam, I need you to help me with the dishes, please." She held out her hand and led him back into the kitchen. Father Ehrick brought up the rear of their miniature exodus.

"You lied to me. Why?" Andre wiped the tears from his face. "Is that," he nodded towards the kitchen, "why my brother was sent here? Is that boy the reason you are ashamed of David? Is that my brother's sin?"

Martine and Defont exchanged a quick glance.

"Adam is not David's son," Martine said.

"You take me for a fool now. You don't think I see my brother at that age? My son at that age? Why do you insist on this charade? I've been lied to ever since I inquired into David's whereabouts. Lied to by priests and Cardinals, and now by you. What did David do that is so awful, so terrible that you can't tell me the truth? I have a right to know."

"Yes, you do," Martine said quietly. "Your brother is here."

"Alive!" Andre exclaimed.

"No. He died in 1940."

"1940?" Andre reached into his pocket and pulled out the letters that had traveled across countries with him. "This letter says he died in 1939. Another lie, Doctor? Or have the lies become so twisted no one remembers what the truth is?"

Andre felt nauseous. Angrily he stood, gaining a height advantage from which to glare at Dr. Martine. Then his stomach twisted. Sharp pains caused him to lean forward for relief. "I have a right to know the truth," he demanded grimacing from the pain.

"There is no truth, Andre. Your brother was here. He passed away in his sleep in 1940. That is all there is to this truth you seek."

"Are you so ashamed of David that you continue this farce even when a fool could see that woman is the child's mother and David is the boy's father?" Andre slumped down on the bench. Before him swam the gnarled and whiskered face of Greatcoat, laughing. *"They are all insane," he kept repeating. "You will be insane also if you stay."*

"Adam's mother is dead," Martine said softly, momentarily at a loss for words. "Father David, your brother did not violate his oath of celibacy, Monsieur Proust. He is not Adam's father." Martine needed an explanation. They all needed an explanation. "David was ill, Andre. His mind was sick. He came here of his own volition. He rests with the others who have come here and passed away. The dates may be confusing to you as to when your brother actually died, but they are simply a means to spare the families further grief. As far as David was concerned, he died the moment he stepped into this place. It is a place from which he knew he would never leave. If the truth is all you seek, that is the extent of it."

"Then why the deception?" Andre refused to believe Martine. "Why did Cardinal Gaston lie to me?"

Martine looked at Defont. "Gaston is a Cardinal?" He tried to keep calm. It was a shock to find out the name Yorick had screamed from the wall belonged to a Cardinal. "When did you speak to Cardinal Gaston?"

"I don't know. About three months ago, I would guess. What has Cardinal Gaston got to do with this other than the fact, like everyone else, he lied to me?" A sharp pain ricocheted through Andre's stomach. His eyes closed for a moment as he tried to ride out the gripping pain.

"You have an ulcer?" Martine asked. The symptoms were fairly obvious. "You will feel better if you lie down for a while."

"Yes, I will, but I'm not going to. Not until I find out what happened to my brother." Even over the pain, Andre was adamant.

"Would you care to see him?" Defont asked. He had stayed silent through this ordeal, but inside an anger was building. Gaston. *Cardinal* Gaston had sent Yorick.

"See him! I thought you said he was dead."

Defont clarified his offer. "He is, Andre. He rests below us in the catacombs. Your Uncle Michael is there, too."

Hesitantly, Andre straightened. The pain eased. He was feeling calmer until his thoughts came crashing back down. Maybe this was a trap. Maybe this hulk of a man will try to kill me also. Fear rose to the surface. "No, thank you. I think I'll stay here." He could not disguise the quiver in his voice.

"You have no reason to be frightened, Andre." Defont tried to ease the tension. "You are in no danger. We are not monsters here." The big man shrugged. "But if you don't wish to see your brother, that is fine with me."

"Please excuse me. I have some business to discuss with Father Alphonse." François shot a meaningful glance in Edmund's direction.

Defont nodded. It was best the abbot learn as quickly as possible who Gaston was.

Martine put his hand on Andre's shoulder. "Go and visit your brother. If you are a religious man, say a prayer for his soul."

***

"The doctor would not tell me, but will you? What happened to David, Brother Edmund? Why all of the deception? I'm entitled to know."

"Deception? That's a harsh word, Andre. You have to understand what this place is." Defont leaned closer. "It's more than an asylum or a hospital. It's an embarrassment to the church. The old, senile priests, the ones unable to take care of themselves are brought here to die. Priests, yes, priests who have committed horrible acts against their will, who have gone insane, are confined to live their entire lives here in torment. The priests who labor here have given up their lives to serve their brothers. Dr. Martine and I came here to find our friends—David and Antoine Curvise. We wanted to help them. That was over ten years ago.

"Deception? If there is, it is done only to spare the bereaved loved ones."

"You knew David before he came here?" Andre was not exactly sure what Defont was telling him.

"Yes. Dr. Martine and I knew David when he served at St. Margaret in LaRochelle. We knew him before he fell ill. But you must know that even his illness did not stop us from being his friends. If it had, we would not be here.

"But let me ask you this, Andre. Would you and your father have been better served knowing David had gone crazy? His death was to ease the effects of a lingering sickness. Your brother was not murdered in this place. He was not harmed. Whether you want to believe it or not, David Proust was loved and cared for by the brothers of this institute as all the wards are."

"Then why won't the church give me his remains? And those of my uncle?" Andre was still not sure he believed Defont, but for the first time, the words and actions moved in the same direction. Was it too much to hope that it moved towards truth? "My request was simple and harmless. It was my father's last wish."

"I know. But David and Michael belong here."

Having made a decision, Andre stood slowly. "Let me see my brother. Let me see what you have done to my family."

* * *

The candle flickered. Alphonse's room was cold and dark. He sat behind his desk watching Martine pace the small room.

"You knew Gaston was a Cardinal! How? When?" The doctor had brought his revelation to the abbot only to find it was already a known fact.

"The day Zigman died," Alphonse said softly, debating whether to continue covering his old friend's actions. He could see no benefit for the truth to be known, and yet, it had to be spoken. "Bronski knew why Yorick was here, François. He knew who had sent him and, in a brief moment of weakness and doubt, he was prepared to carry off the assassination. At the last moment, he saw the truth and attempted to stop the madness."

Tired and weary of the whole mess, Martine sat down. "So now we wait for Gaston to send another monster to consummate what he believes is a religious necessity? After we are dead and no one is left to protect Adam, they'll come again. You know that, Alphonse, as well as I do."

"I've written the pontiff personally as you have requested so many times in the past, François. I have written and told him what has transpired behind these walls. I have hidden nothing. He has promised to send the Inquisitors to hear Adam's defense."

Faced with the granting of his desires, Martine was unsure if he was happy or frightened.

"We are not all monsters, Doctor. No one here wishes to harm Adam, but we have to put our trust in our faith. Adam's future is now in the hands of the Inquisition. Whatever they decide will be carried out, regardless of our own personal feelings. You understand that as well as I. There will be no recourse from their judgment."

Until Yorick's assassination attempt, Martine had never believed the church capable of murder. Of fearing a child. François' spirit and beliefs that Adam was the true inheritor of the throne of Christ wavered for a brief second or two, but it would not, *could not* be disputed in his mind. All the facts, all the testimony he had accumulated over the years, cried out for Adam to be recognized. His facts were indisputable. The church could not find Adam to be anyone other than the Son of God, if not God Himself. He would not back down.

341

"What of Andre Proust?"

Alphonse ran his hands across his balding pate. "I had hoped he would leave in the morning. Now, I'm not sure what to do."

"Give him what he wants, Alphonse. David and Michael. That is all he truly desires."

"How easy that would be, but I am bound by the rules of my Order, François. I cannot make that decision. The door is still open for him, but he has to leave in the morning. If he refuses, his fate will be sealed."

"You cannot possibly mean that! He is an American. They will search for him." Martine tried desperately to negotiate a stay for Andre. "Let him stay a few more days, Alphonse. I am sure we can convince him it is best for David and Michael to remain here."

"As much as I would like to, I am afraid I simply can't." Alphonse hung his head.

"The Americans will not just let him disappear."

"Accidents still occur, François. Is this such a bad place to spend one's life?"

CHAPTER THIRTY-FOUR

Lying in bed, Andre tried to force himself to believe the things Edmund Defont had told him. It would have been easy had he not been lied to so many times earlier. He still could not get over the striking resemblance between David and Michael. They were identical twins in death. And the resemblance, no, the actual look of Adam. How could he not be related to David, or Michael, or himself? Yes, himself. At age ten, his son Robert had looked exactly as Adam did now. Andre had never really paid any attention to the extreme differences between himself and Robert just as he was sure his father had ignored the fairness of David. A trait from some distant relative. A son was a son and accepted as such. But the difference!

Yes, David had fathered Adam. There was no doubt in Andre's mind. Brother Defont and Dr. Martine could deny it forever, but the facts, so visible, were undeniable. Irrefutable! And yet, Defont insisted David was not the boy's father. Why?

For a priest to have fathered a child was not that great a sin. Everyone knew priests were human—that they had weaknesses. In fact, Andre was sure this situation had occurred many times before. That was the problem. If it had happened before, then why—why could they not forgive his brother?

The church had refused to allow David the weakness of man. Their zealous regard for him and his reputation would not allow them to envision him with a woman. Or perhaps the problem was not *a* woman, but which woman. Andre had seen Sabina in the catacombs—Adam's mother; David's lover. If his brother had seduced any woman other than a Jew, would his church have forgiven him?

Andre tossed against his pillow. How foolish of the church! Did they really think it mattered his brother had fathered a child? It did not matter to him. It should no longer distress the church. David was dead. What he had done during his priesthood was between him and his church. Now, if only Andre could convince the priests at the Institut that David *(and Michael?)* would carry no stigma of shame away from this place. That they deserved to be in France, buried beside their family.

343

Michael. What had Michael done? Had he, too, fallen prey to the same sin? Had a Jewess twisted his thoughts and driven him to insanity? My stars! These people were living in the dark ages!

A knock on the door startled him from his twisted thoughts. "Come in," he called, sitting up on the bed. His stomach wrenched in protest, but the pain was not quite as bad as it had been in the dining room.

Urbana opened the door and stuck her head into the room.

"Come in," Andre said getting off the bed. "Please."

Shy with outsiders, Urbana cautiously entered the room. "Dr. Martine told me to give you this." She extended a glass filled with pink liquid.

He looked at it suspiciously. "What is it?"

"Medicine for your stomach."

"I don't want it."

She shrugged her shoulders and started to leave.

"Wait. Don't go," he called after her. "Please, I'm sorry if I sounded rude."

Urbana extended the glass again. "Dr. Martine says it will help your stomach."

"Will you stay and talk to me for a while if I drink this?" He took the medicine.

Urbana blushed. "I can't stay long," she said, but it was with a smile.

The taste was chalky, but not unbearable. Urbana took the empty glass and waited as Andre pushed the wooden chair over for her. He waited for her to be seated before sitting down on the edge of his bed.

He was sure she knew who he was, but he had no idea who she was. The quickest way he could think of to obtain an introduction was to introduce himself. He stood, extending his hand. "I'm Andre Proust."

She took his hand and shook it vigorously as though she had never shaken hands with anyone before. "I'm Sister Urbana."

"You're a nun?" He was at once both startled and disappointed.

"No, but that is how the priests address me. Urbana is fine if you like."

Andre sat back down. "Have you been here long, Urbana?" He smiled at the way the word sounded coming from his lips. It had a nice feel.

"Since before Adam was born. Sabina and I came here together."

"How old is Adam now?"

"Ten."

"You've been here ten years! How? Why?" It did not seem possible, but nothing made sense in this place.

"I have no other place to go," she said. Almost as an afterthought she added, "I don't believe, even if I did, I would be allowed to leave." Smiling, she changed the subject. "Have you been to Israel?"

Now it was Andre's turn to be confused. "No," he said slowly.

"I've read of it in the papers Greatcoat and the gypsies bring for me. It sounds like a wonderful place to live."

"Yes, I'm sure it is. But why would you want . . ." Slowly the realization overcame him. "You're Jewish." He was embarrassed.

"Yes, that's where all the Jews have gone. At least, that is what Greatcoat tells me." She laughed. "To the land of milk and honey."

"Why did you say you can't leave?"

"Someone has to look after Adam," she replied matter-of-factly.

"But he's not your child! You know, none of this really makes sense. Why are you here in the first place?"

"I don't really know, but Dr. Martine says if I were not here I would be ashes floating in the wind. *Sometimes, sometimes I wish it were so. To see all the places the wind would take me. But right now, right this minute, I don't mind being me so much.*

It took Andre a minute to figure out Urbana's strange comment. Then he remembered the stories of the German camps. "Yes, Dr. Martine is probably correct."

"Are you from France like Dr. Martine and Monsieur Defont?"

"I was born in France, but now I live in America."

Urbana's face lit up. "I have heard of America," she said excitedly. "It is a grand place to live, yes?"

"Yes, it is." Andre wanted to laugh. Her face had become a child's, full of excitement and imagination. It made her very . . . well, pretty.

"I'd like to live there someday."

"I thought you wanted to live in Israel," he chided. She was so young.

"Oh yes, there, too. But America is exciting. Where in America do you live, Monsieur Proust? New York? Los Angeles?"

Andre laughed. "No, I live in a city in Tennessee."

"Ten-a-see." She tried the word hesitantly.

"It's a beautifully green place in the foothills just outside of the Great Smoky Mountain National Park."

Urbana shuddered. "It's cold in the mountains. I want to live where it is warm and the sun shines all year."

"Well, it does get a little cold in Tennessee, but not like here. Besides, without a little rain, you can't have flowers." Suddenly, Andre found he wanted to impress Urbana with the beauty of his adopted home.

"Do you work?"

"Yes, I do. I'm a physicist."

"I like physics," Urbana said happily.

Andre looked skeptical. "You are familiar with physics?"

Urbana nodded eagerly. "Father Simon taught me about matter and energy and how they interact. The sciences of physics are like rules for the world. If you can understand enough, the world is no longer such a mystery."

"I'd like to meet your teacher."

"He died last year," Urbana said. "He was very old."

"I'm sorry."

"Why are you sorry? Did you know him?"

"No," Andre shook his head slowly. He had to stay on his toes to follow this conversation. Urbana's view of the world was certainly different and perhaps a bit more interesting than his. "When I said I was sorry, it was just a form of condolence. I meant I was sorry for the world's loss, for *your* loss. When someone dies, we all die a little ourselves, don't you think?"

Urbana nodded vigorously. "That's how I felt when Sabina died, but I did not think anyone else felt that way." She smiled when she looked into his eyes.

She had a quality, Andre thought. She was not a ravishing beauty—not a glamorous femme fatale—but she had . . . possibilities. If her hair were fixed up and she had some decent clothes instead of those awful heavy skirts in depressing browns and blacks . . . He smiled back at her. She was easy to talk to and that was a surprise. He had never been very comfortable when it came to talking to women.

Urbana's rise from the chair interrupted his gentle musings. "I have to go now. I enjoyed talking to you, Andre." She extended her hand. It was obvious she liked shaking hands just as Andre savored her touch.

"Maybe we can talk later." He found he did not want her to leave.

"Yes, I'd like that." She started to leave, then stopped and fixed him with a concerned look. "How is your stomach feeling now?"

"Huh? Oh, fine." And it was. Andre was surprised to find the pain had gone. He rubbed his belly, testing it for aches. Perhaps if he could find even a twinge of pain, she would stay. "It feels fine. Thank Dr. Martine for me, will you?" Disappointment and relief fought to color his voice.

Urbana laughed and nodded before she hurried away.

***

"No, I will not leave here without David and Michael, Doctor."

"I'm afraid that is not your decision, Andre. Father Alphonse has kindly consented to your staying overnight, but you must leave in the morning.

346

Please." Martine did not want to see this young man trapped behind the walls of the Institut. "Your brother and uncle are resting peacefully here. This is where they belong."

"No, it is not. They were brought here because of some false accusations made against them. You tell me they came of their own volition. Hah! I won't believe it! Why should I when I've been fed nothing but lies since I left my father's bedside? No, Doctor, no." Andre was adamant. "I will not leave without them."

That may be truer than you think, Martine thought, but he said, "Please Monsieur Proust, Andre, you simply do not understand the situation here. You refuse to listen to good advice. I've tried to keep you from making a mistake. If you don't leave in the morning, you will never be able to leave. Ever." Martine regretted the words as soon as he said them. He was well aware that the last thing anyone should do was threaten a Frenchman.

"You'll keep me here forever," Andre said sarcastically. "You must take me for a complete fool, Doctor." Andre walked to the window. "I'll leave in the morning, but I will be back with the authorities. You can be sure of that."

Martine stood, his stance now equal to Andre's. "Well, I tried, Andre. Remember that. You are too stubborn. You remind me a lot of myself at your age. Bullheaded and determined. I just hope as the years pass, you come to accept your punishment gracefully."

Andre spun around. "Now you're telling me I can't leave in the morning? I'm to be held prisoner here like David and Michael? I'm not afraid of you, Doctor. Nor will I stand being threatened."

"You are a fool, Andre, as once I was." Martine walked out the door.

"Wait!" Andre's plea brought the doctor back to his room. "I'm sorry, Dr. Martine. I'm, well, I guess you could say I'm quite confused over this. I don't know what to believe anymore. I just can't see how you could think so badly of my brother. His sin was not that terrible."

Martine moved to put a comforting arm around the younger man. "Your brother committed no sin of which I am aware, Andre. By any standards, he was an exceptional and very brave man. If you were to ask anyone in the Institut, I believe you'd find they would all express that same opinion. Let him stay here. You have only to promise Abbot Alphonse you will forget this place and you can leave knowing your brother and uncle will be taken care of for eternity. Is that too much to ask?"

Andre hung his head. His mouth grew sullen. "I promised my father I would return his family. In order to do what you want, I have to break my vow to him. Would you trust me to keep my word?" Andre shook his head. "I have nothing but my honor, Dr. Martine. You are asking me to give up even that. You might as well take my life."

"But we do not want your life, Andre. We want your understanding. Not your honor," Martine explained, "but your compassion."

"Then you have only to tell me why David was here. Why Michael was brought here. You have to trust me, Doctor."

"If it were in my power, I would be more than happy to tell you, but to speak of these things only dooms you to a life behind these walls. I will not be the person who sentences you to such confinement. I suggest you think about what I have said, Andre. Very hard. The decision you make will affect the rest of your life, literally."

***

"The Inquisition is coming, Edmund." Martine sat across from Defont in the dining room. "I don't know if I should be happy or sad."

"It is what you wanted, François."

"Yes, but I'm not sure now if it is the right thing to do."

Defont took no pity. "It's a little late now, is it not?"

"You know what I mean. What other choice is there? To be still and watch Adam waste his life here? And Urbana? Have pity man, they deserve a chance at life."

"I'm not disputing that, François. It's just . . ."

"Just what? What other solution is there?" Martine huffed. He was angry, his conversation with Andre still occupying his mind.

"I don't know, François. But hear this. Whatever they decide, I will not let them harm Adam. He's done nothing to deserve their punishment."

Martine looked into Defont's face and met his gaze. "Whatever possessed you to say that? You don't believe they would harm Adam, do you?"

Defont's reply was a shout. "Where have you been, François? Have you already forgotten Yorick and Gaston? *Cardinal* Gaston? Adam is a threat to them. To their precious religion. Do you honestly believe they would come here and proclaim him their king or honor him by naming him their next pope?"

"Yes, I do," Martine declared emphatically. "The evidence I have accumulated is indisputable."

"The evidence you have means nothing. You are the only one still alive who witnessed Adam's birth. Everything else is just words written on paper. Why should they believe you or your notes?"

"And why shouldn't they?"

"Because if they believe you, the Catholic religion is dead. How can it survive when its foundation, the Immaculate Conception, is shattered? The entire concept of Catholicism will be proven a falsehood. An untruth."

Martine grinned with satisfaction. "That is the very point I want to make, Edmund! If you weren't so wrapped up in your own thoughts you would understand what I am trying to do." Martine leaned closer. "If I can convince them Adam's birth was an immaculate conception, then it does not destroy — it fortifies the church's beliefs. It proves Christ was born in the same manner. To deny that it has happened again, is to deny that it ever happened. Do you understand?"

Against his will, Defont nodded. As much as he hated to admit it, Martine was right. Still, he could not let it go without a fight. "But . . .," he began.

"There are no buts, Edmund. To deny Adam, is to deny Christ. As we know, they are one and the same." Martine leaned back, content in the knowledge he had won his argument.

"They killed Christ," Defont challenged.

"Yes, but the Jews killed Christ. Not the Christians. Not His followers. The Jews killed Him because He was a threat to their . . ." Martine stopped and looked at Defont.

"Exactly my point, François. Jesus was a threat to their religion. Jews, Christians, Protestants—whatever religion you want to choose—take your pick. Do you really think any one of them would allow someone to come along and expose them for what they are? They're charlatans and so, have reason to fear. You forget François, we know who God is and what He is." Defont caught his breath. "He is not what we were taught to believe as children."

"Ah, Edmund. You and your simple logic. I am right and I know it. I can feel it in my heart." Martine looked up. "Are you deserting me, Edmund?" he asked softly.

"No. If I am asked, I will tell them what I know. What I saw. What I believe."

Martine nodded. "I just want you to tell them the truth." He got up from the table. "I have to find Father Alphonse and tell him what Andre has said. I wish there were something we could do to make that young man leave in the morning."

"Let him have what he wants," Defont said. "That would take care of the problem, would it not? I tell you François, I can't understand why Father Alphonse won't let Andre take David and Michael back to France. They certainly won't tell anyone of their ordeal."

Martine shot Defont a glance filled with disgust and respect. He would not say it aloud, but Edmund had hit upon something he had not considered.

Why not just let the bodies go? It was true. What could they say?

***

Alphonse sat at the desk rubbing his eyes. For the first time in ages, the smoke from the candle stung and irritated his vision. Laying on the desk in front of him, was the Institut's Book of Records. He had been thumbing back, writing down dates that might or might not be relevant in the course of history. His finger shook as he found the entry of Adam's birth. It rested above the entry that announced Father David Proust's death. Born December 21, 1940, a male child. Father, David Proust. Mother, Sabina Lavitch. Baptized Adam Proust.

The grin on his face spread slowly. Zigman Bronski had saved the boy. Again. The same boy Bronski had at one time sought to have assassinated as the anti-Christ he had saved twice. Alphonse sighed and leaned back in his chair trying to envision a conversation with Dr. Martine with regards to what he had just discovered. To show François no matter what Bronski had written in his journal, he considered Adam the illegitimate son of Father David Proust. It would carry immense weight with the Inquisitors who, Alphonse was sure, would readily understand the desires of the flesh.

He would plead with the doctor to drop this matter. To let Adam's birth become just another false sighting of the Messiah. But it would have to be done carefully. François Martine was not a man given to changing direction at another's suggestion. If Alphonse could only think of a way to convince the doctor that it was his idea to let Adam remain mortal.

***

Martine barged into Alphonse's office. One had only to think of the doctor and, like a prophecy, he appeared.

"Andre Proust refuses to leave without his family. He is adamant," Martine said in a voice that left Alphonse regretting his earlier desire to see the doctor.

"I did not really think he would." Alphonse sighed. "I have decided to extend his grace period here." He waved down Martine's look of surprise. "In a short time, I believe he will see it is better for David and Michael to remain with us."

"Why won't you allow the bodies to be disinterred?" Martine's question was blunt.

"They are relics, François. Part of our history."

"Then that means you believe what happened, Alphonse! You can't deny it now." Martine was both surprised and pleased. He had another ally.

"It is as you say, Doctor. I cannot deny what has happened here." Alphonse was still on the edge of the circle. "A thousand years from now, who will be able to say this was not the beginning of a new era? If that happens, then we have in our possession the creators of our miracle. We have the mother—*the Chosen One*—and the father—*the Messenger, the Angel of God*. They are holy relics of our past."

It made sense to Martine insofar as the theology of the church went. This place would be a shrine some day. "They won't be relics if Adam is kept here and not allowed to exercise his stature. It will be just another ancient catacomb filled with decaying corpses."

He suspected Alphonse had worked out some sort of plan. Otherwise, why would the abbot allow Andre Proust to stay in the Institut? But try as he might, Martine could not figure out exactly what it was. One thing he knew for sure. It involved him.

The thought came to Alphonse in an instant. It was too late to stop the Inquisition and, he realized, too late to stop Dr. Martine's holy quest. Yet, somehow he knew, he felt, divine intervention was circling high above the Institut, waiting to be invited in. He would keep Father Zigman's records of Adam's birth a secret a little while longer.

***

With winter at hand, the night was still. Too soon, the mountains would be covered with snow. The Inquisition would have to begin quickly, and finish before the roads became impassable. It would do no good to be isolated inside the fortress walls until spring. By then, all would be lost for those who innocently suffered in the Institut d'Infantiles.

CHAPTER THIRTY-FIVE

Andre Proust slept soundly. How could he not? The turmoil of the day had taken its toll on him both physically and mentally. What surprised him was the lack of anxiety he felt before falling asleep. He had lain down anticipating a restless venture into slumber. Instead, almost immediately he had slipped into contented imaginations of Urbana and her smiling face. Almost more than anything else, that bothered him—that, in this depraved place, this institution with its morbid attitude and deranged thoughts had brought to him a moment of peace and serenity.

Early the next morning, the faint odor of coffee lured him from his room even before the sun had risen. A good night's rest, his survival of his first night in an asylum for the insane, made him more determined than ever to stay in this place—not only until he was permitted to take his family away, but also to discover what had brought them here in the first place.

Hoping to find Adam, Andre meandered his way into the kitchen where he found Father Ehrick busy cutting vegetables for the day's fare.

"Hello, Monsieur Proust. Come in. Sit down." Ehrick was always a friendly and gracious host in his domain. He pushed a chair towards his guest.

"You're Father Ehrick?" Andre glanced around, surprised to find the large kitchen spotless. He had expected something less. "Did you know my brother?"

"Yes, I knew Father David." Ehrick wiped his hands on his white apron. "May I pour you a cup of coffee?"

"No. No, thank you."

"A pączki or some bread?" the priest asked, reaching for a fresh loaf.

"No, thank you. Really, I'm not hungry," Andre lied. He was starving, and the odors of the kitchen did nothing but aggravate his desire to eat.

Father Ehrick returned to his chores and the conversation. "Yes, Father David was a fine young man taken from us much too early."

Andre plucked a carrot from the pile Ehrick had sliced. "How did he die?"

"Peacefully, in his sleep." Ehrick had to suppress the automatic urge to wish God have mercy on David's soul, but he was no longer sure it was appropriate.

"And my uncle, Monsignor Michael?" This time Andre's pilfering brought him a handful of carrots. "Did you know him?"

"Yes, Monsignor Michael was here for a long time," Ehrick said sadly.

"As a patient?"

"A patient?" Ehrick thought it over for a few seconds. "It is difficult to define a patient here. We are all here as patients. Some come voluntarily. Some in chains. We don't differentiate between ourselves." Ehrick was not trying to be vague. It was an attempt to spare his guest any pain. He found he could not. "Monsignor Michael came in chains," he finally said.

"What was wrong with him?" Andre asked, putting the uneaten carrots back on the cutting table.

"He believed, as did his church, that he was possessed."

"Possessed!"

"Yes, I'm afraid so. He suffered greatly for many years. But, I hasten to add, he never lost his faith. He never succumbed to temptations."

"And David. Did he come here believing he was possessed?"

"Yes. Of course, we found out later that he wasn't. Or, depending on whom you choose to believe, perhaps he was. There is still some disagreement about Father David's illness."

"What do you believe was wrong with him?" Andre could feel a knot growing in his stomach. How could he have two relatives who believed they were possessed?

"If I could honestly say, I would. At this point in time, I'm just as confused as everyone else. I simply don't know, Monsieur Proust."

"Andre. Please, call me Andre." Proust looked around. He had not heard the door open or any noise, but somehow he knew the boy was present.

So did Ehrick. "Adam, you've met Monsieur Proust."

"How are you today, Monsieur Proust?" Adam hopped up on the table.

"Andre, please."

"Andre. That has a nice sound." Adam reached for a slice of carrot.

"Your chores are finished young man?" Ehrick asked already knowing the answer.

"Yes, Father."

Andre could not take his eyes off Adam. The resemblance between his departed son, Robert, and this boy, Adam, was uncanny. The more he looked, the more he saw David. A chill ran up his spine. Frightened, he turned away.

"Are you leaving today, Monsieur Proust?"

"No, Adam."

"When you do leave, where will you go?"

"Back to America."

"Is it nice there?"

"Very much, yes." Andre smiled. His fear suddenly gone.

"Are you a priest?

"No, I'm a physicist."

Adam looked deeply into Andre's eyes, almost as though he were reaching into his thoughts and extracting bits and pieces of his knowledge. "Nuclear physicist?" It was a disconcerting question and, at the same time, an undeniable statement.

Andre was dumbfounded. How could this child know of nuclear physics? How could he know of anything living here in virtual isolation?

"Yes," he replied.

"Have you tested a thermonuclear device yet, Monsieur Proust?" Adam picked up another slice of carrot and stuffed it in his mouth.

Andre heard the crunch, as loud as the first testing of the very device about which Adam had just questioned him. His jaw grew slack. It was all he could do to compose himself.

"You can't possibly know of this?" His question was for Adam, but it was directed at Ehrick.

Ehrick shrugged and continued to slice vegetables. He had no idea what they were talking about.

Adam suddenly stopped and looked at Father Ehrick, then at Andre. "Destruction is not the only benefit that will be derived from nuclear energy, Monsieur Proust," he said. Hopping off the table, he waved goodbye. "I must go now. I have a lesson with Father Manuel. He's teaching me Portuguese." He smiled and was gone like a child late for fun.

Stunned, Andre could only sit and stare at the spot where the boy had been.

"He has a gift, Andre. One we can only envy," Ehrick explained simply.

"Someone told him of the atomic bomb," Andre finally said. "Someone here knows about nuclear energy."

"Atomic bomb?" Ehrick shrugged. "Adam mentioned destruction. I assume this bomb is for killing?"

"Yes, yes, of course. But that's not all we hope to use this new discovery for," Andre argued unnecessarily. "Are you familiar with the atom bomb?"

"No, I'm afraid not."

"Well, someone here knows of it. The boy was just repeating what he overheard." Andre searched for some plausible explanation as to how Adam

354

had known of the bomb.

Ehrick hid his grin. "I am sure he was."

As quickly as he had gone, Adam reappeared, his head stuck through the partially open kitchen door. "If you stay Monsieur Proust, will you teach me to speak English?"

Surprised to find himself thrilled at the child's return, Andre was happy to consent. "Yes, of course I will." He started towards the door, but Adam was already gone. "Wait," he called.

"You won't catch him, Andre," Ehrick said. "He's like the wind. Never still."

Andre returned to the table. "That offer for some coffee and sweet roll, Father Ehrick. Is that still open?"

Ehrick smiled.

***

"An atomic bomb, you say?" Defont shook his head in amazement. "And it killed hundreds of thousands of Japanese?" He sipped his coffee, trying to imagine so powerful a device.

"Yes." Andre was frustrated. He had spoken to almost every priest capable of thought, searching for whom had told Adam of the bomb. It was hopeless. "It was developed in the United States during the war."

"And Adam is familiar with this?" Defont asked.

"Yes, and I'd like to know how he became aware of it."

Defont smiled. "I'd like to know how Adam became aware of many things, Andre. I've never heard of this bomb, but it doesn't surprise me Adam has. Have you spoken to him?"

"I wanted to, but he was off and running to learn Portuguese from Father Manuel."

Innocently, unthinkingly, Defont extended a dangerous invitation. "Why don't you ask him now? He's in the garrison with Father Manuel."

"The garrison? Where's that located?"

"Across the courtyard. It's where we keep the children."

Andre took a deep breath and blew it out with a sigh. "What children? Adam's the only youngster I've seen." Every question he tried to get answered, just created another. As much as he wanted to speak to Adam, he was reluctant to leave the safety he had found in the dining room.

Defont searched for a tactful means of describing the children of the Institut. He could find none.

"Perhaps it is better if you wait. Adam will be back this afternoon to help

Father Ehrick in the kitchen. Maybe you could speak to him then."

Martine entered the dining room and joined the two men, at once taking control of the conversation. "I've spoken to Father Alphonse and he agrees to allow you a week, Andre. But I might as well tell you now that you're wasting your time. He will not release David and Michael to you."

His thoughts preoccupied with Adam, Andre nodded. "That's all right with me. I've made my position clear. I do not intend to leave without them."

"François, are you familiar with this new bomb Andre has mentioned?" Defont asked.

"Bomb? What bomb?"

"Atomic, I believe. Andre was just telling me about it. He says the United States used it to end their war with the Japanese. It killed thousands of people at one time."

Martine's look of astonishment was almost funny. "Is this true?"

"Yes, it is." The amusement Andre had found in the doctor's expression just a moment ago turned sour. Martine's bewilderment was evident. It was obvious the doctor knew nothing of this new form of destructive energy. "It is, as Monsieur Defont said, an atomic bomb. Nuclear fission."

Martine's look turned cross. He disliked being lectured. "How would we know of this?"

"Because Adam is aware of it." Andre had expected Martine to be shocked. Of course, he had expected all of the priests he had spoken with to express at least some surprise. Like the others in the Institut, Martine let him down.

"Nothing Adam knows surprises me, Andre."

"Why? Will you at least tell me why?" Andre asked helplessly.

"In time, you may find out, my friend, but do not be in such a hurry. If you do, you will end your days here with us. Your best hope is to leave now and forget this place." Once again, Martine tried to be diplomatic; but Andre Proust's stubborn ignorance made it hard.

Andre tried to be civil, but the doctor's arrogance made it difficult to control his temper. "If you're trying to frighten me, it won't work, Doctor. I'll leave only when what I've come for leaves with me."

"He's not trying to frighten you, Andre," Defont interjected. "He's only trying to spare you. David and Michael are resting in peace. You saw them. Why can't you leave them here and be content to know they are safe and where they belong?"

"You know why. My father wanted his brother and his son to lie with him in the soil of France." Andre tried to sound determined. It was the only way he knew to hide his fright.

356

Martine's patience finally reached its end. "You're a stubborn and bull-headed man, Andre Proust. You've been given the opportunity to leave and let the dead rest, but you insist on making demands that can only harm you. All right! All right. If you're quite sure you like me enough to spend the rest of your days here, I'll satisfy your petty curiosity. I'll tell you why David and Michael Proust were brought to this Institut. Why Inspector Defont and a skilled physician like myself are confined to this place where our talents are of little use. Why you are going to live the rest of your life within these walls."

"François, no." Defont tried to stop Martine's head-long charge. "You'll only be hurting, Andre. He had nothing to do with this."

"No, Brother Edmund. Let the doctor speak. I want to know what insanity has gripped your minds. I'm not frightened," Andre said.

"You should be," Defont shot back. "What he's saying is the truth."

Martine stood in righteous defiance. "Come with me, Monsieur Proust. We will start in the catacombs. That is the beginning of the tale."

Again, Defont tried desperately to halt the disaster. "Don't go, Andre. You don't really want to know."

For a brief instant, Andre hesitated, but not long enough. Ignoring Defont's plea, he swiftly walked after the departing doctor.

Waiting at the cellar door, Martine found he regretted his impatience and tried to find a way out. He did not want Andre to be hurt by the revelations he was going to tell him. To *show* him. If only . . .

Andre's steady stride and bold voice interrupted François' search for excuses.

"I'm ready, Doctor. Lead the way if you will."

For a brief moment, Martine fumbled, stalling for time. *Was there no end to this man's recklessness?*

"Monsieur Proust," Adam called from the vestibule.

Martine hesitated, his fingers gripping the handle of the cellar door. Andre waited for Adam to join them.

"I understand you've been wanting to talk to me, Monsieur Proust. I have time now."

"Thank you, Adam, but can it wait? Right now I . . ."

"Excuse me, Monsieur, I do not mean to be impertinent, but I am quite sure you will find talking with me more enlightening than listening to Dr. Martine." Adam smiled at Martine. "No offense meant, Dr. Martine."

Martine bowed slightly, grateful and relieved. "We can always talk later, Andre."

"You have succeeded in splitting the atom. I would be very interested in hearing how it was accomplished Monsieur Proust," Adam began.

Martine watched as Andre and Adam walked away, already deep in conversation. Gratefully, he returned to the dining room.

"You had a change of heart?" Defont asked his friend.

"No. Adam arrived and saved me from my own stupidity."

Defont nodded. "Somebody has to," he mumbled under his breath.

CHAPTER THIRTY-SIX

Gaston was fuming. He did not understand the pontiff's decision to send him to St. Sophie to head the Czechoslovakia Diocese. Like confetti, his arguments had fallen to the polished floor, whisked away by a single wave of Pius' hand more cleanly than a janitor's broom. He had no recourse. His power inside the Vatican had been reduced to nothing. Why? How? Had he not served faithfully?

It was true he had become involved with the Nazis, but who had not? At one time, it had seemed imminent the Germans would become the new Caesars of Europe, but now he had divested himself of his ties to that failed venture. Yes, he had served faithfully and this was his reward? Banishment to a pig sty in Czechoslovakia?

Well, he was still young as men go in his rank. Time would cure his problems with Pius, whatever they might be.

As he shut his office door in the Vatican for the last time, he thought of Yorick. At least he had freed himself of the last vestiges of his Nazi advocacy. At the same time, if there was even an infinitesimal possibility that Vasai had failed to properly take care of the problem in Poland, Gaston was secure in the knowledge that he had put in motion an irrefutable means of ridding his church of the anti-Christ. When it came time to reestablish himself in the pontiff's good graces, it was an act for which he would certainly be willing to take credit.

***

By lot, three Cardinals had been chosen to travel to the Institut d'Infantiles. Their instructions had been brief and to the point. *Weigh the matter of a child born through immaculate conception. Decide if the boy should be brought to Rome for an Ecumenical Council to judge his fate.* In the past, too many frauds had appeared on the surface of the Catholic religion. Too many times, the alarm had been raised only to find yet another false prophet had been discovered. *Do not create a martyr by your hands, but judge carefully and make your decision quickly. Do not linger within the walls of the Institut.*

As the Cardinals knew, the Institut was subject to Rome's influence, but its laws were not subject to the whims of any man on earth. Pius was their master, but only in a titular sense. Even he could not usurp such laws as were written at the time of Christ's death.

Take this letter to the Abbot of the Institut. It is to be given to him only if you find the reason for this Inquisition to be yet another hoax.

New enemies stood at the gates of Rome. Communists who saw no heaven or hell, but envisioned the power of Christianity as a wall to be trampled under their feet. The last thing the pontiff needed was for Christ to return and denounce the church's beliefs as false. Pius' words were direct. *Discredit or destroy and, if at all possible, disregard.*

The entourage left the Vatican minus their trappings of rank. Dressed in plain black suits, they were just men, their earnest devotion hidden under their layman's clothes. The three kings traveled incognito, lightly, and with a pronounced quickness in their steps through the communistic country of Poland, hoping not only to keep their religion, but their lives.

***

"Have you seen Sister Urbana?" Father Ehrick stuck his head out of the kitchen searching for his assistant.

Martine glanced at Alphonse, a glint in his eyes. "She's helping Andre in the wards," he answered.

A week had passed. Then two. Andre stubbornly refused to leave. At first, Martine was sure this devotion to his father's last wish would eventually break down Alphonse's determination to keep David and Michael in the Institut. He was wrong. It was no longer David and Michael that kept Andre here. It was Urbana and Adam. A bond had begun to form between this unlikely trio. But was it so unexpected? They were, after all, related—Urbana, surrogate mother of Adam, and Andre, the surrogate uncle. Adam, distant in form and substance from them both, needed the guidance only they could provide.

Martine saw the spark in Urbana's eyes as she worked beside Andre in the wards. He saw the intense conversations between Andre and Adam. Conversations that the others avoided. He saw the laughter and smiles when the three of them walked the Institut's long corridors together. And, he saw the despair reflected in his own eyes at their future. A future locked behind these walls.

"And where is Adam?" Ehrick came out of the dining room. All of his helpers had deserted him.

"He's helping Edmund in the garrison," Martine said.

With a sigh of resignation, Ehrick sat down next to Alphonse. "Andre is a very nice man," he said to no one in particular. "Very intelligent."

"Is something on your mind, Father Ehrick?"

"Yes, Father Alphonse, but they are just my thoughts."

"Your thoughts are ours, Ehrick," Alphonse acknowledged. "But there is nothing we can do about the matter."

Ehrick nodded in silent agreement with the abbot's statement.

"Why?" Martine asked suddenly. "Why can't something be done?"

"What would you suggest we do?" Already Alphonse knew what Martine's reply would be.

"Let them go. Let Andre take Urbana and Adam and flee this place."

Again, Ehrick nodded in silent agreement—this time with Martine's words, but he would not give his thoughts voice.

"If it were in my power I would, Doctor," Alphonse said sadly. "This is no place for them. I derive no enjoyment from their confinement, but we have our obligations. Obligations that, in this case, are most distasteful, yet they must be maintained. Andre Proust is still able to leave, but he must leave alone."

"You are as stubborn as . . ." Martine hesitated searching for the proper word.

"You, Doctor?"

"Yes, damn it. You're as stubborn as I am."

"Greatcoat has gone to pick up the Inquisitors. They will be here soon. The matter will be out of our hands."

Alphonse's words were not as exciting as once he had thought they would be. In fact, they crushed Martine with their weight. The doctor's thin shoulders slumped. His graying head fell forward, supported only by his hands. The thought frightened him. No one said it anymore, but Martine knew they all blamed him for Adam's coming ordeal. It was not as if they had turned their backs on him in animosity, but just the same, they blamed him for his stubbornness and determination.

As much as he wanted Adam to have the acclaim and recognition of the church, the thought of the boy leaving for Rome made him feel old and useless. He had to keep reminding himself it was in Adam's best interest. The boy simply could not stay here and wilt away like the aged Cardinals. He had to be given his place. It was ordained.

Urbana worked tirelessly and, it seemed to Andre, without effort. He enjoyed watching her, working with her, just being next to her. She had a charm that was impossible to buy from a scented bottle or a fancy package. She smiled or frowned as her emotions dictated. He wondered if she ever cried.

He had accepted Abbot Alphonse's dictate: *"If you refuse to leave, you will work as everyone else."* Andre knew it was the old abbot's plan to be rid of his intrusion. *"You must confine yourself to this building, and this building alone. If you venture into the garrison, your fate will no longer be in your hands."* Another of the abbot's schemes to frighten him away. Well, he was not buying any of it. He would outlast Alphonse. He was not afraid of work. Of the long dark nights. Only once had he been frightened *(badly)* when the screams from the garrison made him sit up and cover his ears. The howling had continued through the night. It had been impossible to sleep.

But that was yesterday. Or the day before. Today, he worked with Urbana and thought of how wonderful she was.

The sheets were changed. He had only to mop the floor now.

Her arms filled with soiled bed covers, Urbana stopped by his side. "I have to go now. Father Ehrick is expecting me to help him prepare supper."

Impulsively, Andre bent down and kissed her forehead wishing it had been her lips. Urbana blushed and ran from the room—before he could tell her he loved her. But it was all right. He had seen her smile.

***

"Dr. Martine, I'm glad I found you." Andre joined the doctor for a cup of coffee.

Martine looked into Andre's eyes, envious of the man's youth. Sorry it would be spent within these walls. François was tired and confused. Still, he managed a slight smile. "What can I do for you, Andre?"

"You have to let Urbana and Adam leave this place," Andre said. "They don't belong here."

"You are speaking to the wrong person. I have no control over what happens here." Suddenly his voice was grated and sour. "Speak to the abbot."

"I have, and he refuses to listen. What dark secret is so terrible that it confines them to this place?" Andre looked at Martine closely. For the first time he saw the doctor's age—a weariness that had been absent only a short time ago.

"Dr. Martine, you were going to take me into the catacombs and show me whatever it is that binds you and the others to this place. Are you ready to show me now?" Andre was determined to expose whatever secret Martine presented to him. Everything could be explained. The laws of physics were as solid as the rules of the church. More so. "I'm not leaving here without them, Doctor."

"Without whom?" Martine asked.

The question surprised Andre. Thoughts of visiting the catacombs vanished. "You know very well who I mean," he retorted quickly to hide his confusion. He was not sure now exactly who he wanted to take away from this prison.

"No, I don't. Tell me, Andre. Who do you wish to take away now?"

Silently, Andre walked away, leaving Martine alone in the dining room. He could not answer the doctor's question. At least not at the moment.

***

It had taken all of Martine's strength to push himself up from the table and return to his room. Resting in the chair next to his bed, Martine glanced at the books he had gathered—the journals of Monsignor DeValier, Antoine Curvise, Zigman Bronski, and his own. Proof recorded by men of honor who dared not lie. Men who had stood and watched this miracle occur. The written words that proclaimed Adam to be, at the very least, the Son of God. The reincarnation of Christ. He closed his eyes and fell asleep dreaming of his passionate speech in front of the Inquisition.

***

The day of the Inquisition was a most unusual day in the Carpathian Mountains. The sun was shining brightly.

Defont and Father Alphonse watched as Father Michalowski climbed the ladder to the top of the bell tower. Sitting in Greatcoat's car outside the gates, the three Inquisitors waited. They had refused to enter the grounds of the Institut without the symbols of freedom in their hands.

Father Michalowski removed the bell's clapper. The ancient signal to the villagers to hunt down an escapee would be silent while the Inquisitors conducted their business.

Balancing precariously, Father Michalowski then removed the bell rope before climbing down. The chain that locked the gate was removed and one item was given to each of the three Cardinals. Now, they were safe.

In the foyer of the main building, Father Ehrick hurried to set up the Court of Inquiry. This room would be the limit of what the Cardinals would see during their visit. From here, they would listen to the arguments and make their decision concerning Adam's future.

Walking quickly, heads down, the Inquisitors entered the grounds. There were no introductions. They would remain nameless. They pulled out long black caps and slid them over their heads covering most of their faces. It was not to hide them, but to hide what they might see.

Defont and Alphonse followed them inside. Several chairs and a table had been carried from the dining room into the foyer. In front of the Inquisitor who, by age, was deemed the wisest, a crucifix stood to protect him from the spirits of evil that had been purported to reside inside the Institut. The proceedings were to begin immediately.

Urbana, Adam, and Andre had been asked to stay in their rooms until called to testify.

"Why are they so frightened of this place?" Defont asked Father Alphonse.

"Because they created the Institut," he said softly. "Men always fear the rules they have imposed on others." He sighed. "If you would be so kind Edmund, as to wait in the garrison until you are summoned."

"What's going to come of this? What can they do to Adam?" Defont was worried. He had not liked this idea of Martine's from the start. Now, watching the three priests, *three kings,* he disliked it even more.

"They have no power to condemn. They are only here to decide if this matter should be brought before an Ecumenical Council. If they decide Adam warrants further investigation, all the princes of the church will be ordered to sit in judgment. That Council will have the power to denounce Adam." Alphonse glanced around searching for Martine. "Where is the doctor?"

"He went to the catacombs," Defont said. "He wanted to speak with Antoine."

Alphonse nodded. He understood the need to converse with the dead.

The doors to the main building had been left open so the Inquisitors had a clear view of the world outside the Institut. Uneasily, he looked towards the open gate.

Fathers Emil and Ehrick and Greatcoat stood guard. Defont, with his strength, would be alone in the garrison.

***

Defont walked slowly towards the garrison. For the last week he had been discreetly coaching Adam as to just what might be asked of him. It had been difficult in light of Adam's superior intelligence. The boy's understanding of the basics and the complicated problems that faced him did not allow him to

364

make excuses or alibis. He would not, *he could not* lie, so Defont had not asked him to. What words or statements Adam uttered in front of these men would be the truth. Defont had only asked the boy to consider each question carefully and, when possible, shy away from any reference to religion and its traps.

Adam had shrugged with indifference. "Why do you concern yourself, Monsieur Defont?"

It had taken Edmund several minutes to gather his thoughts and give Adam what he believed was a more than correct answer.

"Because you are special, Adam. Your reason for being here is more than just to live and die as we are all destined to do. You realize that as well as I, but some men have vastly different notions as to why you are here. It is they who will try to discredit you and possibly even end your existence."

The implications were clear, but they did not deter Adam. This life was not special. He had been born before, and he would be born again regardless of what happened to him now. Deep inside, he realized his time was coming to an end in this place. He was destined to leave the Institut, but how or in what manner he had no idea.

Defont had put his arm around the boy. "You are destined to accomplish great feats for humanity, Adam. I don't know what, or how, but it is important you live and do the things your father has placed inside of you. Take your knowledge and make our lives better."

Now, the infant he had held by his fingers was scheduled to appear in front of three men who had no understanding of the greatness that would stand before them. They would learn of Adam's birth and the circumstances surrounding his conception from men they could not or would not dare dismiss as charlatans. The records and journals accumulated by François Martine held a complete history of Adam's birth and the birth of Jesus Christ. Defont could see no way the Inquisitors could not sentence Adam to a lifetime of confinement. If not here, then, as Alphonse said, behind the walls of the Vatican. Adam's life would be wasted with the mundane ideas of religious fools. Try as he might, Defont could not see them allowing Adam to live. They would murder him, either physically or intellectually. How could they not? How could they live with the very person who had spoken the words that founded their religion?

***

"The accused will come forth."

Alphonse bowed and walked slowly to Adam's room. He took him by the hand and walked back to the foyer. He wanted to give the boy a hug, to whisper to him not to worry. Instead, he found his emotions locked in superstitious dogma that, for a brief moment, seemed silly and childish.

"Your name?"

"Adam."

"Your family name?"

"My name is Adam. My family name? I am sorry, but I am unaware of what it is."

"Do you find it strange to have but one name?"

"One name is all that is needed to summon me."

"Summon you for what reason?"

"To help in the kitchen. To mop a floor in the wards. To eat. To sleep."

"Do you know why you stand before us?"

"You are curious as to why I am here."

"Why are you here?"

"I think I am here so that I might ascend to the kingdom of my father."

"You think? Are you not positive?"

"At this point in my life, I can only say I believe that is why I am here."

"Where is this kingdom of your father?"

"My kingdom is not of this earth, but exactly where it is, I cannot say."

"Do you believe in God? Do you believe in our religion?"

"I believe there is a God. As for your religion, I have read of it and found it most interesting. It vaguely parallels my belief that I will ascend to my kingdom. I have also read of other religions and find that they also teach much of what I believe."

"Such as?"

"That there is a God. That man was created in His image."

"And?"

"That is really all I can think of when it comes to religion. I don't find it overly stimulating. However, I don't find it totally boring. Religion seems to be something man has created to allow himself to sleep peacefully through the night."

"You say you believe in God, but not His teachings?"

"I believe in God, but not as He is interpreted by men's words. The teachings of your particular religion are words of men. Men who have, over the years, interpreted the words of God to suit their own needs and fears. The God I speak of is not of this world. The God I believe in is our father."

Alphonse listened closely from his position at the door. He wanted to smile. Adam was not a threat to Catholicism or any other religion practiced throughout the world. If this hearing were to end now he thought, there would be no way these Inquisitors could condemn the child.

And he would have been right. The Inquisitors were finished with Adam. The boy claimed no throne, no kingdom on earth. He expressed no desire for gold or profit. He was just a child, albeit an exceptional one. At least for the moment. Dr. Martine's words and records might prove otherwise, but for a brief period, Adam was mortal.

"Abbot, you may take the child. Please bring Dr. François Martine before this Inquisition."

Alphonse did not hurry to do as he was told. He walked slowly towards the dining room. Towards Martine. Towards the end of peace.

CHAPTER THIRTY-SEVEN

"Antoine, my dear friend. I've come to seek your advice. Your counsel."
Martine sat down in front of the crypt and stared at his old friend. The
journals were tightly pressed against his chest. The pain had not let up.
Nightmares had crept through his room last night and into his thoughts. In his
hands, he held the greatest discovery in history. The originator of mankind.
The father. The creator. All the deities man's ignorance had created to solve
life's greatest mysteries. *Who are we and why are we here?* Adam had the
answer. Adam was the answer.

All those fools upstairs had to do was allow the boy his freedom.

Freedom. That was what Martine had attempted to achieve with his
constant bickering about what Adam was—who Adam was. He only wanted
the boy to have his place. What safer and more ingenious station could be
found than that of pontiff to the world's Catholics? They deserved to see their
creator. Their leader. *They deserved nothing but scorn.*

"Antoine, we know who he is. You know why I must pursue this matter.
Why I must testify on his behalf. Why he must be proclaimed the king. The
Christ. You know as well as I do he is our Lord."

How strange, Martine thought, that he, a man who had nothing but
disdain for religion was now ready and willing to proclaim a child, a young
man, his Lord. His God.

"I was there, Antoine. I excised Sabina's virginity to allow the child to be
born. He is the Christ come back to forgive us all our sins."

A sharp pain shot through Francois' chest. He had to hang on to the edge
of Curvise's crypt to fight the steady stream of tears that were forced from his
eyes. His breath came in short labored gasps. He was dying! Dying, when for
once in his life he had a reason to live!

"I am right, Antoine. I am right. I must prove to those fools who our son
is. Yes Antoine, he is our son. Without us he could not have been born. I
can't be wrong! I am not wrong! Adam is God, and I must speak out to save
him. To save him for the rest of the world to adore and worship."

Martine struggled up the stairs, pausing at the landing. Briefly, he felt a wave of despair as if Curvise disapproved of what he was doing. Then it was gone. "I'm right, Antoine. I know it in my heart."

After that, he could say nothing. It took all of his strength to climb the remaining stairs—to stagger and stumble through the cellar towards the dining room above. He was cold and shivering. Clutched tightly in his arms, the books were weights pulling him down, trying desperately to make him sink back into the catacombs.

François Martine refused to be stopped. The righteous doctor refused to listen to his old friend's cries for mercy—cries for the child's life.

"But I'm saving his life," he whispered. "They would not dare kill their master. Their God. He is, you know." Martine was laughing—laughing and dying all in the same breath.

He staggered across the dining room, seeking out the warmth of the fire. He needed it to rid himself of the chills that threatened his flow of blood. "I'm right, Antoine. Damn it, I'm right." He paused and cocked his head as if listening to an unspoken voice. "If I'm not . . . ." Gasping, he slumped down on the bench across from the hearth. "If I'm not Antoine, then show me what to do."

A draft of cool air blew through the hallway. The fire sparked, and an ember danced and landed on the journals Martine held tightly in his hands.

"Antoine!" he exclaimed. "Oh, Antoine."

The effort would kill him Martine knew, but he had to carry out his friend's wishes. Agonizingly, François tossed all of the written accounts into the hungry blaze of a fire straight from Hell. The records concerning Adam's birth disappeared.

Martine watched sadly as they began to burn, crackling and crying out— joining his destruction in their demise. He waited until they had become ashes before making his way to the table. Tears of pain rolled down his cheeks. He would sit and wait until Defont came for coffee. Then he would tell Edmund what he had done.

His last thought before laying his head on the table was why—why did today have to be such a sunny and pleasant day? After all the rain and storms he had endured over the past ten years, it was a shame to die on one of the few nice days nature had granted the Carpathian Mountains.

***

Alphonse did not hurry to the dining room, but he did not dally. A few more minutes would not save Adam any more than they would save them from themselves.

The fire was hot as if freshly fed. From across the room, Martine's familiar person was slumped in an unfamiliar state. "Dr. Martine," Alphonse said quietly, wishing to gently wake the Inquisition's next witness. When the abbot did not receive an answer, his footsteps hurried towards the doctor's prone body. His eyes searched for the journals, but the crackling of the fire told him what he searched for was no more. The ordeal was over. He had only to get the Institut's Book of Records and show the Inquisitors what Zigman Bronski had recorded on the date of Adam's birth.

It was over. The Cardinals, the kings, the Inquisitors would beat a hasty retreat. To linger here was insanity. After they were gone, Alphonse would take Martine down to the catacombs and lay him to rest beside his friend, Antoine Curvise. Then he would open the letter given to him by the Inquisitors as they retreated from the mountains of Poland.

***

François Martine's death struck Defont very hard. For all of their arguments and open animosity, the two men had grown close over the years of confinement. A grudging respect for one another had slowly matured.

Martine's insistence on an Inquisition for Adam had proved to be correct. What the outcome might have been had he not taken his last breath and burned his records, no one wanted to consider. It was impudent to question miracles and not to accept them.

"He looks so peaceful," Defont told Alphonse. They sat in the dining room waiting for Andre. "You did an excellent job on him." He tried to sound anything but remorseful. After all, death in the Institut was nothing out of the ordinary. "I hope you will do as well on me."

"Father Michalowski did most of the work," Alphonse said. "My hands are growing weak. When the time comes, I am sure our young priest will do us both justice."

Defont acknowledged Alphonse's comments with a nod. What he really had on his mind was what the abbot would do with Adam now. And Urbana. And Andre. Had François been here, he would have pestered Alphonse constantly until he had been given an answer. Once again, Defont found himself missing the craggy old doctor.

Defont had been patient, as had Fathers Ehrick and Emil and the others. Their only concern was for Adam and Urbana to have justice administered in their favor. Had a vote been taken, the trio would have walked out two days ago—free. But God and the Abbot of the Institut did not adhere to such procedures. They waited to find out what Alphonse had decided to do.

Father Alphonse had made a decision. It had not been easy. After putting Martine to rest, he had struggled with the problem he faced and continued to do so until he had visited Martine early just that morning. Then the answer had come—so easily. Alphonse knew it was not his idea alone, but even if it was, he was sure it would do Martine justice.

"You wanted to see me, Father?" Andre came into the dining room and sat down. His emotions ran the gauntlet—discouraged and angry, anxious and frightened. The man before him held his life in his hands.

"Yes, Andre. I have a proposition for you."

"My attitude has not changed, Abbot. My position remains the same."

"I understand that, but please, hear me out before you refuse."

Andre glanced at Defont. The big man's face was a blank. "I'm listening."

"Adam and Urbana are leaving here tomorrow."

Defont's face broke into a huge grin. It was all he could do to refrain from hugging the old priest. Even Andre found himself smiling.

Father Alphonse pretended not to notice. "But I am fearful for them," he continued. "They have been here many years. Urbana was only thirteen when she came. Of course, Adam was born here. Neither is familiar with the world, and neither is Edmund or myself."

Alphonse directed his attention towards Defont. "Yes Edmund, you are to leave also. You have served us well and have kept your part of the bargain you made with Father Bronski."

Andre reached across the table and grabbed Defont's hand. "I'm happy for you, Monsieur Defont."

"What I'm proposing to you, Andre, is that you act as the Institut's guardian to Adam and," Alphonse smiled, "a friend to Urbana. I want you to take them out into the world and educate them in its diverse ways. When you have finished your obligations to them, come back and resume your obligations to your father. At this time, or in any future that I can envision, I cannot see letting our brothers leave. I am sorry."

It took only a second for Andre to grasp what had been offered to him. Live souls for dead ones. He could leave with his honor intact. And, if after the years had passed he still needed to retrieve his family, he was welcome to try. "I accept your offer, Abbot." Then he added, "Thank you, Alphonse."

Alphonse stood. "Tomorrow morning Greatcoat will be at the gate with his automobile. He will take you on the first leg of your journey."

About to burst with excitement, Andre could only nod. He wanted to run to Urbana and Adam and tell them the news.

"May God be with you, Monsieur Proust," Alphonse said with a smile.

God would be with him.

"You look sad, Monsieur Defont. I would have imagined after all these years you would be singing at your good fortune!"

"I am happy, Andre, but also very sad. My friends are all here. David. Antoine. François. And the others who, over the years I came to know. I'll be leaving a great part of me behind."

"I understand, but think of it. You will be home. Home in France."

"Home in France." Defont laughed. Home where everyone I once knew will have aged or died, he thought. They will have read my death notice, and now I am to be resurrected? These feelings he kept to himself. His home had been France. Now he was not sure where he belonged.

He could see Andre fidgeting nervously on the bench. "Go," he said. "Tell them the news." Defont smiled as Andre hurried from the room.

Life and death were but momentary interruptions in the daily routine of the Institut. Defont walked out of the room. He was on duty in the garrison today.

***

That evening after he had been relieved, Defont wandered down to the catacombs and was surprised to find Adam standing in front of Martine's crypt.

"Good evening, Monsieur Defont," the boy said. "I was hoping you would come. Please, sit down." Adam pointed to a stool.

Defont did as requested.

"I need to take a lock of your hair." Adam clipped a portion of Defont's thinning gray and black hair. "Now I have everyone." Adam placed the hair in an envelope. Defont noticed his name printed on the outside.

"Everyone?"

"Yes. Dr. Martine. Dr. Curvise. My mother. Fathers Alphonse, Bronski, Ehrick, Emil, and now, you."

Defont looked at Adam's face, bright here even in the dark catacombs where a single lantern cast a faint glow. "May I ask? Why?"

"I am not quite sure, Monsieur Defont, but I will in time. I only know that this will be the only opportunity I have to repay those who believed in me. If I succeed, I believe one day we will all be together again."

Defont wanted to ask—When? Where? How? But he said nothing. He was content, he found, to believe in Adam. If the boy succeeded, they would be reunited. He would have the answer to his questions then.

***

Defont walked with Adam's hand grasped in his as he had so many times before. Only this time they did not circle the courtyard, but walked straight towards the gate. Ahead of them, he could see Urbana's hand locked inside of Andre's. It was a joyous day. It was a sad day.

Father Alphonse stood on the steps of the main building. He would miss them. He would miss them all.

He watched as Urbana turned and waved to him before she climbed into the back of Greatcoat's car. Adam waved and then also disappeared. Andre, he hoped would never find it necessary to return. Perhaps Monsieur Proust would make Urbana's and Adam's care his lifetime mission. Only time would tell, Alphonse thought as he watched David's brother vanish into the back of the waiting automobile.

Defont bent over and pushed his shoulders deep inside the car. For a moment, it looked as though he, too, would disappear. Then he straightened and slammed the door closed. The car sped off. Defont stood in the middle of the road waving goodbye.

Alphonse walked towards him, Pius' letter tucked inside his sleeve. It was a simple request to bring a priest to the Institut. The kind of request Bronski had received and responded to many times before. Alphonse decided to send Defont and Father Emil to St. Sophie to bring Emanuel Gaston back to the Institut d'Infantiles.

CHAPTER THIRTY-EIGHT

August 28, 1993

Professor Adam Proust glanced uneasily at his watch. He still had twenty minutes before the news conference was scheduled to begin. Twenty minutes to try and find answers to satisfy the hunger and curiosity of the news media. The questions would come hot and heavy, and deservedly so. After all, this was his project. His child, so to speak. His failure.

It was a world where success was measured in yesterday's news, forgotten almost immediately. "Yes," the reporters would say, "you did succeed with Apollo. And with the Venus probe. But what have you done lately?" Yes, successes were forgotten immediately, but failures . . . Failures lingered. Forever, it seemed. One could never escape their shadow.

Head of the National Space Agency, the catalyst for the United States' space accomplishments over the last twenty-five years, Adam Proust's achievements read like a *Who's Who* of success, although he had never taken the full credit he deserved. He was more than willing to share the laurels of success with his peers. And share, he had. It was not an unselfish act. The men and women he had sought out and enticed into the space agency were the articulators of his thoughts and knowledge. A knowledge so vast, the circumstances it could have put into play would have caused an upheaval in the scientific world no reasonable mind could comprehend.

His knowledge. It had come in intervals, designed to spare him many embarrassments. Or crucifixions. He had thought many times of Jesus Christ. How strange it must have been for Him to stand among the uninformed and preach of words and thoughts beyond that particular time. Many more had followed—some of them burned at the stake. Others cast out as Sayers of doom. Heretics and monsters. Had Christ lived to see his forty-fifth year Adam now knew, the thoughts so alien to Him would have become clear. Doubt had been a strain of matter that refused to be eliminated from the savages who had been born to His kind. But in time, it all returned as it had been originally planned.

It had been on his forty-fifth year that the entire spectrum of what and

374

where he had come from became clear. The Father, the Son, and the Holy Ghost. The Trinity. The mystical enigma Christ had spoken of, but the one which had never achieved His full understanding.

He was the Father.

And the Son.

And the spirit of knowledge that was destined to arrive.

It had happened. How a religion had grown around these words still amused Adam. It came from followers anxious and hungry to be led. The wonderment and mysticism that had spawned the many religious organizations that now flourished throughout the world were indeed a necessary force. A force that, for a time at least, had held the savage instincts of the uncivilized in check. Spiritual relief had not been planned. It had come to the creatures as an afterthought—as a means to rise above the beast that existed in all of them. It was new—unknown where Adam had been conceived. He would take back this phenomenon and leave it to the scholars of his world to dissect.

His world. It was not far in the universe. A mere 400 years of travel so many ages ago. Even now that amount of time was incomprehensible to the creatures of this earth, but it would not be for long. At the moment, travel in space at the speed of light was still impossible. In the scientific world, it still was a dream. Only he knew it could be a reality.

The voyage between the two worlds was now possible. When Adam had first come to this planet, the expertise had not been formulated. If it had, how easy it would have been to move about the galaxies. Eden had been a spaceship—a laboratory designed to traverse the blackness of outer space with living embryos awaiting birth. The vast distances of the universe would not allow sufficient quantities of oxygen and nutrients to be transported over the vast expanse of time, and so a means had been devised to move through the cosmos without exhausting the normal means of life.

He was the Father.

His sperm had fertilized the ova, and the blastocyst had been placed in a mechanical womb that would allow, at a predestined point in time, the prescribed rules of reproduction to be followed.

Eden had been twenty years away from Earth when Adam was born and nourished inside a weightless atmosphere with only the barest of necessities needed to sustain life. He and the hundreds of others who had volunteered for this mission had been born in space and brought to life, maturing as genetically prearranged, as they traveled so that at the precise time they stepped onto this new planet, they were capable of both thoughts and actions.

The Father became the Son.

Eden sat down on the surface of this wild and hospitable outpost. Released from their confinement, grown men and women stepped out on to the planet to be greeted by awe-inspired savages. Not yet humans, the primitive creatures had evolved as far as evolution alone could take them. But they were, in fact, a form of human being, unintelligent and wild. Truly a race that would survive in its infancy for as long as time and circumstances allowed.

Adam had read the Bible at age seven and found it fascinating, but it was only recently he had taken the time to discover the truths it contained. The Bible had indeed chronologized the story of his coming to this planet. His creation of the images in his likeness. If only it had been so simple.

The aborigines had been docile, friendly, and confused. Not the savages most thought of when cave or prehistoric creatures were mentioned. Brought into Eden, they were artificially inseminated with the fertilized ovum of his people. It was a shock at first when children began to be born without either of the two races' skin pigmentation. The subtle changes that the aborigines had genetically infused into the travelers' offspring caused concern at first. But in time, such changes in skin, hair, and eye color were practically eliminated so that it came to pass that the majority of the children were born in the image of God.

Time had no significance for the visitors. They had come prepared to live for centuries. The first batch of children had succumbed early as had been expected. The changes in atmosphere and climate brought a wave of death from unknown diseases. A program to duplicate themselves was initiated. It was from this group that vital organs necessary to sustain life were grown and transplanted into the original travelers.

Once the longevity problem had been solved, expeditions began to reach out further and further into this vast world. Continents were found, always inhabited by some form of aboriginal creatures. From these separate gene pools, the diversity of the earth took shape and form.

It had taken many decades to establish Eden as the base of their operations. They found minerals and wealth in abundance on this planet, but not enough to transport themselves back home. It was, in fact, impossible to return to Heaven at that early stage of the project. There would be a way in the future, though. They had genetically planned a solution for such a contention.

Within Eden, a race was engineered to carry on with the reproduction of specific travelers who would retain the knowledge of their people and the history of the newly colonized planets. The Chosen Ones—the Jews were created. And the Messengers—*the angels*, as David Proust had rightly come to believe of himself.

It had been a long time in coming. Over ten thousand years, and still it did not seem possible. In the beginning, he had lived almost a thousand years. Long enough to see the results of his work. The only thing he regretted was his absence of memories. It had been a safeguard, of course. No man was immune to the recollections of those he met in life—his loved ones.

Now, in a relatively short span of time, seventy years by his calculations, traveling at almost three-quarters of the speed of light, he would be home.

Home.

From the locks of hair he had carefully gathered, Urbana had broken down the DNA structure from his friends and recorded the vast gene chains of the double helix on microchips. Other than himself, he had taken only a few. Dr. François Martine. Inspector Edmund Defont. Dr. Antoine Curvise. Fathers Alphonse, Emil and Ehrick. Sabina and Zigman Bronski. And his immediate family, Andre and Urbana. They would all reawaken one day, reproduced from their genetic codes into exact replicas of themselves complete with their earthly memories. It would be a joyous day.

Adam's emotions had ceased at age ten. From that day on, he had found no one he could relate to with any feeling. Even the hug he had given Defont on their last meeting while the burly Inspector had still been alive, had been something he had sensed his friend required. It had been instinctual to provide aid, not an emotional act. His disciples had been his saviors, and would be rewarded with answers to the questions that had perplexed them here on earth.

The expedition that had set out for this planet called Earth had completed their mission. Adam was sure there were others out there accomplishing the same things he had. Finding worlds that fit the criteria for a civilized population. By the standards of what he had found on earth when he and his fellow travelers had first arrived, he was not sure if civilization had been necessary. When he allowed himself to ponder the advances it had made, the earth might have been better left alone. It had been a paradise where the creatures who had existed upon its surface had lived in a state of harmony, wanting nothing. Having all they desired.

The anchorman's voice interrupted his thoughts.

"Good evening, ladies and gentlemen of the press. As you know, two days ago, the National Space Agency announced they lost contact with the Mars Observer. After an eight month journey, at the cost of billions of dollars, we are determined this evening to try and find some answers as to why the satellite's computers have grown silent. We can only presume this first nuclear powered satellite designed to map, in detail, the surface of Mars has crashed into the Red Planet.

"We will now hear a statement from the Director of the Mars Observer program, Professor Adam Proust."

It would not be easy for Adam to stand in front of this inquiring group of reporters and lie, but he had no choice. He knew the Mars Observer had not been destroyed. He knew it was now traveling through the dark recesses of the galaxy at half the speed of light, propelled by a combination of Mars' slingshot gravitational push and the ignition of its nuclear powered rockets. It was on its way to Heaven.

Before it had completed a quarter of its journey, astronomers on Earth would discover a planet orbiting a star estimated to be thirty-five light years away. Speculation would run high that this newly discovered planet could possibly hold life.

**

Taking the podium, Adam Proust looked up at the bright blue sky.